AC.

MW01491832

They say it takes a village to raise a child–which is true–but I also say it takes a village to write and publish a book. Therefore, it is with deepest gratitude that I thank the following people for their contributions to this work:

My GoodReads friend, Blackbook, for giving me the writing prompt that sparked my imagination and started me on this crazy writing journey five and a half years ago.

Laura Stamps for her advice to this novice writer on how to begin writing a book.

Nina Benneton for encouraging me to write every day.

Tami Vinson for encouraging me to join Romance Writers of America (RWA) much sooner than I would have otherwise, because without this wonderful organization, I wouldn't have made it this far.

The members of the Valley of the Sun RWA for all your advice, support, and encouragement that has kept me going through many frustrations, and for your invaluable educational resources that have helped make me a better, more informed writer.

My critique partners, Tali Cruz, Karen Fulbright, and Kelly Garcia for all your suggestions that helped make this a much better story than it was in its first incarnation.

My beta readers, Danielle Hill, Bryan Lane, and Kathy Miles for your feedback on my finished manuscript. Special thanks to Bryan as well for helping me rewrite my first chapter when I was hopelessly lost on how to fix it.

Jimmy Thomas for being the best cover model a romance writer could ever ask for. Your photos are always stunning, and you're a beautiful person inside and out.

Jaycee DeLorenzo for the gorgeous book cover and marketing material designs. I'm in awe of your artistic talents.

My editor, Jillian Leigh, for your gentle guidance in cleaning up my manuscript. Your professionalism and attention to detail is phenomenal. I couldn't have asked for a better person to help me through this phase of publication.

My family for putting up with me spending an inordinate amount of time inside my own head, playing with my imaginary friends.

Most of all, I thank God for blessing me with a wild imagination, without which creating stories like this would not be possible, for giving me strength to keep going when I've felt like giving up, and for opening new doors when old ones close. With Your help I can do anything, and nothing is impossible.

DEDICATION

This book is dedicated to my wonderful husband of twenty years. You're my lover, my best friend, my webmaster and all-around technical guru, and my biggest writing cheerleader. No matter what hat you're wearing, you're the best. Our road together hasn't always been smooth, but somehow we've managed to navigate the bumps and come out stronger in the end. Thank you for believing in me when I've doubted myself. I love you!

"What is a friend? A single soul dwelling in two bodies."

– Aristotle

Chapter 1

It was the worst day of Rebecca Anderson's life.

She sat in the dry shelter of her little Honda Civic, weeping uncontrollably. She doubled over to rest her head on the steering wheel as the painful memories of what had happened that day sliced through her like a knife. Her arms were crossed tightly over her chest, as though protecting that most vulnerable part of herself, while violent sobs wracked her body. Having descended into the depths of despair over an hour ago, she couldn't seem to turn off the anguished voices in her head.

What was she going to do without her mom? Why did she leave Ethan this afternoon? How could she ever have thought that a guy like Jay would make a good boyfriend? She shouldn't have trusted him for a minute, much less months. She'd been a fool!

Now she was faced with the harsh truth. Her mother was gone. Her virginity was gone. And her boyfriend had been nothing but an illusion.

All she had left was her friendship with Ethan, though her stupid choice would probably make her look foolish even to him. She wanted nothing more than to seek the comfort of his arms. But wasn't it the desire for human contact that had gotten her into this mess in the first place? The logical part of her brain reasoned that Ethan could never be as cruel as Jay had been tonight. The mere thought of Jay's betrayal sent her into another round of gut-wrenching sobs, making it impossible for her to contemplate it further.

Finally, the sorrow subsided enough for her to lift her head. She stared sightlessly into the bleak night. Around midnight, the gray clouds that had blanketed Phoenix all day finally released their burden in a rare torrential downpour. Between the rain cascading over Becca's windshield and the tears obscuring her vision, Ethan's house was nothing more than an indistinct blur despite being only a few yards away. A war of indecision raged in her mind over whether to go to Ethan or go home. As she reached for the ignition, a memory of the last conversation they'd had before parting ways late this afternoon came roaring back to her with vivid clarity.

Ethan started toward the front door of her apartment, grabbing his suit jacket from the back of the sofa on the way. He reached for the doorknob, but instead of opening it, he turned and covered the distance between them in a two long strides. He grabbed her hands, squeezing them tightly, his green eyes holding hers with a startling intensity. "Promise me something, Becca."

She stared back, puzzled by his bizarre behavior. "What, Ethan?"

He loosened his grip on her hands, but still held her gaze with compelling force. "Promise me that you'll either come to me or call me anytime, day or night, if you need anything. Anything at all."

She nodded, feeling moisture in her eyes. "I promise," she replied softly.

Ethan leaned over and gave her a quick kiss on her forehead. He then released her hands, opened the door, and stepped out into early evening air thick with the scent of rain.

Becca couldn't believe she'd forgotten his words. It was almost like he'd had a bad premonition. If only she'd had the same gut feeling, she wouldn't be in this predicament now.

As she continued to contemplate her situation, the irrational, negative voices in her head warned that she might lose Ethan's friendship for being such an idiot, but she pushed them away. Instead, she replayed their conversation again and again until she finally convinced herself that he was indeed the one person she could trust. Eventually, the need to share her pain won out over her feelings of embarrassment and despondency, compelling Becca to leave the dry confines of her car.

Since she had no umbrella and no jacket, the huge drops of rain pelted her skin, sending an instant chill through her body. Even with the deluge pouring over her, instantly soaking her clothes and hair, she couldn't seem to make her feet move quickly. They felt like massive weights, which had to be dragged along one plodding step at a time.

After what seemed like an eternity, she finally reached Ethan's front porch. Her legs, weak from exhaustion, were no longer able to bear the heaviness of her heart. She leaned against the front door and then promptly slumped to the porch floor in a sodden heap.

* * * * *

Ethan Montgomery sat at his desk and grabbed a manila file folder from the stack in the corner filing tray. As he began to peruse the reports, a booming crack of thunder rattled the windows of the house, giving him a start. The thunder was followed by a massive gust of wind that sounded like it might rip the dwelling from its foundation. Minutes later, huge raindrops beat a cacophony on the roof and spattered against the windows so loudly he couldn't concentrate on his work.

Ethan's gaze was drawn to the inky blackness framed by the office window. The palm trees in his yard bent against the force of the wind while their fronds fluttered wildly. Raindrops slithered down the glass pane. Maybe it was the storm making him uneasy, but the sinking feeling he'd had earlier at Becca's apartment returned in full force.

His dog seemed out of sorts too. Rather than settling into his usual place on the rug at his master's feet, Buddy stood at the open door of the room, his ears pricked in concentration.

"Hey, Bud, what's up?" Ethan asked.

Buddy glanced back over his shoulder briefly, then nervously paced out of the room.

Ethan listened intently but heard nothing unusual over the din of the rain. Deciding that both he and the dog were simply rattled by the unusual ferocity of the storm, he returned to his paperwork. No sooner had he picked up the folder again than a dull thud came from the front porch, and Buddy began to bark.

Ethan rushed to the front door and flipped on the porch light. Buddy growled.

"Buddy, hush!" Ethan commanded.

The dog finally quieted but remained by his master's side, still alert.

Ethan peered though one of the small windows framing the door and was shocked to see a woman huddled against it. Mere seconds passed before full recognition dawned on him. With shaking fingers and pounding heart, Ethan worked to turn the locks and quickly flung the door open.

"Becca!" he exclaimed as he dropped to his knees beside the drenched form of his best friend.

With the noise of the rain pounding all around them, it took a moment for him to realize that Becca was sobbing uncontrollably. She didn't even seem to be registering his presence.

Ethan's heart rose in his throat, and his breathing quickened with fear. He grabbed Becca's shoulders and shook her gently. "Becca!" he yelled above the furor of the storm.

It seemed like hours passed before she finally raised her bowed head and looked at him with overwhelming sorrow.

His hands immediately framed her oval face as he looked deeply into her blue eyes, trying to fathom what was happening. "What's wrong, Becca?"

When she simply stared at him without immediately answering, Ethan rephrased the question. "Are you hurt?" By now, his voice was shaking with dread.

Her arms had been crossed over her middle, but now they came up, wrapping tightly around his neck. Becca buried her face in his shoulder as Ethan cradled her protectively in his arms.

One of her hands slipped down to rest over her chest. "It hurts in here..." she replied so softly he could barely hear her. "...so bad," she added in a mere whisper.

The state his friend was in terrified Ethan. Emotionally, she was a hundred times worse than when he'd left her earlier that afternoon. Physically, she was soaked to the skin, her clothes clinging to her slight frame and her wavy honey-brown hair hanging over her shoulders in sodden strands. Ethan's own shirt and pants had begun to absorb the moisture as he held her. Beginning to feel the chill himself, he knew that Becca had to be freezing.

"Let's get you inside, by the fire," he said, his voice gruff with worry.

Not even waiting for Becca to gain her feet, Ethan swiftly scooped her up in his arms. He kicked the door shut against the cold night air and carried her to a love seat next to the fire crackling in the living room hearth. Buddy followed and lay down on a rug by the fireplace, still watching over the pair with concern. Ethan attempted to lay Becca on the sofa, but she still clung to his neck like a frightened child. Instead, he sat down first and drew her snugly into his lap. Her body curled into him, but in spite of the warmth of the fire, she shivered. Ethan slipped a decorative fleece blanket from the back of the love seat and wrapped it tightly around her shoulders.

With her safely cocooned in his arms, Ethan rocked her for long minutes until her sobs subsided into hiccups. She didn't seem to be seriously injured as he had initially feared, but he wasn't absolutely certain. Still unsure what to do, Ethan raised his hand to push a strand of wet hair away from her face. His fingertips gently raised her chin so that he could look into her eyes. "Becca, sweetheart, you need to tell me what's wrong. You have me scared to death here. I want to help you, but I don't know what to do if I don't know what's going on."

Becca's face scrunched up as though she was about to start crying again. "I'm so stupid," she said in a pained voice.

"Shh," he soothed, his thumb caressing her damp cheek. "Whatever it is, we'll deal with it together, OK?"

She nodded almost imperceptibly.

Sighing deeply as he gathered his thoughts, Ethan tried again. "I thought you were going to spend the evening with Jay. Did he say or do something to upset you?"

Once again, Becca nodded weakly. Her gaze dropped to her lap and she shifted, burying her face in his chest. "Oh God, this is so embarrassing," she mumbled into his shirt.

Becca's movement sent her full peasant skirt cascading over Ethan's knees. As he reached to tuck it back into place, his gaze was drawn to a watery pink stain that had previously been concealed within the folds of ivory fabric. After taking a closer look, his heart began to race again.

"Becca, this looks like blood," he said shakily, then asked her again, "Are you hurt?"

Becca shook her head. "Not exactly," she murmured.

What was that supposed to mean? "Did Jay or someone else get hurt?"

She weakly rubbed her head back and forth over his chest.

Well, if she wasn't hurt and no one else was either, where had the blood come from? Ethan pondered for a moment. *Oh, you idiot! No wonder she's so embarrassed*, he thought as realization dawned on him. "Ah, is it...ah, that time?" He cleared his throat uncomfortably before adding in a rush, "I don't have any feminine...things...around here, but I could go get some if you need me to."

By now Becca's hands had come up to completely cover her face and she was sniffling into his shirt again. She shook her head. "It's not that," she wailed in frustration. Her voice muffled by her hands, she continued, "It's gone. I just made the biggest mistake of my life."

Ethan still had no idea what Becca was talking about, but her cryptic clues and vexed tone made it clear to him that this wasn't easy for her to talk about. He knew enough about the female mind to understand that she was probably hoping he would figure it out so she wouldn't have to say it. Ethan sent up a quick prayer for patience and wisdom.

Then almost in an instant, all the pieces of the puzzle came together in his mind. He found himself scowling fiercely at the picture they presented.

Once again, the pace of his heart quickened. Gripping her shoulders, he pulled Becca away from his chest firmly and made her meet his intense gaze. "Did Jay rape you?" he ground out through clenched teeth, "because I swear to God, if he did, I'll–"

"Ethan, stop!" Becca interrupted. Then, more reluctantly, she continued, "He didn't force me, but..."

"But what?"

"Oh God," she wailed. "He betrayed me. He broke my heart. I know you didn't really like him from the start, and you were right. I never should have trusted him. I know I shouldn't have slept with him, but I was so lonely. It felt good to be close to someone. But then he hurt me. I miss my mom so much, Ethan. I wish she was here, so I could talk to her. Oh, what am I saying? If she was here, this probably wouldn't have happened. I just don't know what to do..." Her voice trailed off.

Tears begin to well in Ethan's eyes at the exhausted, defeated look on Becca's face. He gathered her back into his comforting embrace and murmured against her temple, "I know I'm not your mom, but you can talk to me, Becca. Why don't you start at the beginning and tell me everything that happened?"

The beginning. It had all started that morning with her mother's funeral. It was a rare overcast day in Phoenix. The ominous dark clouds overhead portended the possibility of rain and cast a gray gloom over the grave site. The weather mirrored Becca's emotions that day. She sat on a chair in the front row next to her mother's casket, flanked by Ethan and her next-door neighbor, Edna Moffat. It was a small service, with only a few other friends of her mother in attendance. No family.

Becca had asked her boyfriend, Jay, to attend her mom's funeral, but he never showed. She thought they had a close enough relationship that he would want to support her, but she now knew that nothing could have been further from the truth. Instead, it was Ethan who sat by her side, holding her hand, comforting her, while the tears streamed silently down her cheeks. It was Ethan who escorted her home following the service. It was Ethan who kept her company and patiently listened to her troubles.

Feeling exhausted, Becca laid her head back down on Ethan's shoulder before she spoke. "Thank you again for coming to the funeral this morning."

Ethan's cheek pressed against the top of her head and his arms tightened around her. "I told you there was no place else I wanted to be."

"It meant a lot to me, having your support," she replied. "And Edna's too."

"Of course. We wanted to be there to support you. We both know how hard it's been on you, losing your mom like that."

Becca knew he didn't mean for them to, but Ethan's words brought a fresh wave of sadness as she was reminded again of her wonderful, loving mother. Caroline Anderson was the only family Becca had ever known. Caroline was an only child, and her father had died when she was young. When Caroline discovered she was pregnant out of wedlock at the tender age of nineteen, she was all but disowned by her conservative mother. Then the man she loved walked out on her, unable to handle the prospect of a child. Caroline had never even considered abortion, and so, without the love and support of family to sustain her, she struck out bravely on her own to have her baby.

That had been twenty-four years ago, and throughout all that time, Becca thought her mom was the most amazing woman in the world. Caroline worked hard to provide a roof over their heads and food to eat. Even when she returned home exhausted from long days on her feet as a hairdresser, she always found time to read Becca a bedtime story before tucking her in for the night. As Becca grew older, her mom became her best friend. Together, they were an inseparable team until the breast cancer robbed her mom of life far too young. It was a particularly aggressive form of the disease, and by the time Caroline had been diagnosed, it was already too late.

Becca had just completed her pre-vet degree and had been

accepted to vet school, but when the doctors told Caroline she had mere months to live, Becca didn't hesitate to set her dream of becoming a veterinarian aside. She wanted to be with her mom as much as possible. She still worked her job as a waitress to pay the bills, but spent her evenings and days off with Caroline, trying to make her final days as bright as she had made Becca's life.

Tears welled up again. "I miss her so much, Ethan."

Ethan stroked her arm through the thick blanket and rocked her gently. "Shh... I know."

"I don't know what I'm going to do without her. She always seemed to have the right advice when I needed it."

"Like I said before, I know I'm not your mom, but I want to help. I can't do that, though, unless you tell me what's going on."

She sniffled into the front of Ethan's shirt. "I know. It's just so hard."

His hand smoothed the damp strands of hair away from her face and continued stroking tenderly. "Jay hurt you pretty badly. That much is obvious."

She responded with only a nod.

Jay Cavanaugh. Becca never wanted to hear that name again as long as she lived. How she'd ever allowed herself to get sucked in by his act, she would never know. She'd met the guy a few months back when a college friend invited her to a party. Not being much of a social butterfly and wanting to spend all her free time with her mom, Becca politely declined, but when Caroline found out, she insisted that Becca get away from all the stress and have a little fun for a change.

Jay was a handsome athlete, and all the ladies in attendance seemed to be vying for his attentions. Becca also found him attractive, but never thought that a guy like him would ever take an interest in an ordinary, shy girl like her. Consequently, she was baffled and wary when Jay approached her. Before the night was through, his charming personality had won her over, and he had convinced her to start dating him. Becca would go to his place for a movie occasionally when her busy schedule would allow. From all appearances, Jay seemed like a nice guy. His only flaw had been his penchant for pressuring her to have sex with him right from the start.

Becca knew it was a rather antiquated, romantic notion, but she really wanted to be in love before making love. The few guys she had gone out with from time to time had never tempted her to give up her virginity, and when Jay had first started trying to seduce her, she had patiently explained her feelings on the subject to him. He backed off briefly, but before long, he was at it again. Becca couldn't deny that his kisses always made her feel good. It had become harder and harder to resist his advances, especially when she was feeling depressed over her mom's illness. Unfortunately, today, that one weakness had been her undoing.

Becca shook her head at her own foolishness. "I can't believe I trusted him. That crazy story about a broken-down car and a dead cell phone making him miss the funeral. God! How could I have been so stupid?"

"Hey, don't be so hard on yourself," Ethan gently admonished.

"No...no, I know you never liked him. I should have paid more attention to your suspicions. If I had, maybe I wouldn't be in this mess now."

A sense of guilt assailed Ethan. At the time, he'd thought that Jay would probably tire of Becca in pretty short order when he realized she wasn't going to put out for him. Now he wished he had done more to dissuade her from seeing the guy. She was right about one thing: he had never been able to warm up to Jay Cavanaugh. Call it a gut feeling, but he'd known something was off about the guy. He had always thought Jay was a little too slick for his own good–or more likely, the good of the women around him.

Earlier that afternoon, while Becca was on the phone with Jay, Ethan had been overcome with mindless jealousy and a fervent protective instinct. When Becca had related Jay's sob-story to him, his instincts told him the guy couldn't be trusted. A prickle ran up his spine, making the hairs on the back of his neck stand up. That was what had made him elicit a promise from Becca to come to him if she needed help.

Becca had always been soft-hearted, and her care and concern for others was one of the things he loved about her. The thought that she could show such kindness toward Jay in the midst of her grief, when it should have been the other way around, made Ethan's blood boil. In his mind, the death of a beloved mother trumped car trouble any day. Ethan didn't care what kind of difficulties Jay was experiencing, he should have called sooner. And what was the deal with Jay expecting Becca to drive over to his place after everything she'd been through? The whole scenario demonstrated to Ethan that the guy didn't have a clue, and it made him want to go plant his fist in Jay's face.

Now that he had the proof Jay was no good, Ethan somehow felt responsible for Becca's state. With her mom gone, she was incredibly vulnerable. He had tried to take care of her the best he could all day, but with the woman he loved curled up in his lap, her heart broken in pieces, he couldn't help feeling like he should have done more.

Ethan hugged Becca tightly to his chest and murmured against her hair, "I never should have left you this afternoon."

Becca immediately pulled back and lifted her head, looking him in the eye with a confused expression. "What are you talking about? None of this is your fault."

"Becca, I knew that guy was bad news. I should have tried harder to convince you of that."

Becca bowed her head to stare at her lap. "There's no guarantee I would have listened to you." Her shoulders lifted in a small shrug. "Although now I wish I had."

Ethan lifted her chin with the crook of his forefinger. "So are you going to tell me what happened between you and Jay that has you so upset?"

Becca found herself unable to hold Ethan's gaze. She toyed nervously with the fringe of the blanket as earlier doubts overtook her again. What if, after hearing the whole story, Ethan thought she was as stupid as she felt? After all, it hadn't been her brightest moment. The entire incident had been so unpleasant she didn't really even want to think about it.

"Take your time," Ethan calmly reassured her. "Why don't you start by telling me what happened when you got to Jay's place?"

After taking a few minutes to bring her emotions under control and gather her thoughts, she tentatively began. "When I got to Jay's apartment, he offered me a drink. He said it might help me to relax.

Since it had been a rough day already, I figured he was right, so I had a couple glasses of wine. He tried to give me more, but I said no. You know me." She smiled ruefully. "I'm a major lightweight when it comes to alcohol, and I was already feeling a little fuzzy."

Becca paused to take a deep shuddering breath, and Ethan gently squeezed her shoulder, encouraging her to continue.

"He put his arm around me and started kissing me like he's done lots of times. Except before, if things got a little too heated, I would tell him to stop. This time, when he kept trying to go further, I couldn't seem to say no. Maybe it was the wine, maybe it was the grief and loneliness, but having someone hold me and touch me like that was what I thought I needed. Before I knew what was happening, I was lying on the couch and we were going way further than we ever had in the past."

As she spoke, Ethan tenderly rubbed circles on Becca's back, and she was starting to relax a little.

"It was probably a combination of both," he mused softly. "The wine relaxed you enough to make you let your guard down a little, and it's only normal for a person who's lost someone close to seek comfort."

"You're so understanding, Ethan."

"I'm not really doing anything special, just trying to listen." He paused for a moment then continued, "I have a feeling you haven't told me everything, though."

Ethan was right. She hadn't even begun to scratch the surface. Without warning, the memory of what happened after that began to replay in her mind.

When Jay realized she wasn't going to stop him, any semblance of a seduction flew out the window. He seemed to turn into an animal right before her eyes. He pressed her back into the couch cushions and crushed his mouth to hers until his teeth clashed painfully against her own. He raised himself long enough to strip off his t-shirt, then frantically tugged at the buttons on her blouse until a couple of them popped loose, pinging on the coffee table before falling to the carpet. He made quick work of the front clasp of her bra. Then his hands groped and squeezed her breasts while he brought his mouth down to hers again, plunging his tongue inside and biting at her lips until she was sure she tasted blood.

"Jay, please, can't we slow down a little?" she asked when he briefly released her lips. "You're kind of hurting me."

"Oh, baby, I can't slow down. You made me wait too long. Now I'm wild for you," he answered unsympathetically.

"But–"

Her protest was cut short when he unceremoniously flipped up her skirt and pulled her panties down to her ankles. He reached between their bodies to unfasten his pants and shoved them down his hips. Everything moved so fast, she didn't have time to think before he pushed her thighs apart and entered her in one violent thrust. She cried out in pain at the invasion, but he seemed oblivious to her discomfort. He mindlessly pumped in and out while tears rolled down her cheeks. Finally, he came with a shout and collapsed on top of her, making it difficult for Becca to breathe. Moments later he abruptly withdrew, leaving her whimpering in pain again.

"What are you crying for?" he asked as he sat up and reached for his shirt.

"You hurt me," she replied.

"You were a virgin, weren't you? It's supposed to hurt the first time."

She lay there in utter disbelief at his callousness as he got up and headed for the bathroom without a backward glance. She knew what he said was true on some level, but she didn't think it was supposed to hurt like that. Many times Becca had imagined what making love to a man would be like, and it certainly wasn't what she'd just experienced. She'd always fantasized that her first time would be with someone who would handle her body with loving care and make it as good for her as possible. Jay hadn't even pretended to care. He'd taken his own pleasure and left her on the sofa half naked, feeling a vague sense of violation, and wondering what to do next.

She sat up, wincing at the soreness, and tried to set her clothes to rights while tears filled her eyes again. Becca had foolishly thought that being with Jay would alleviate her grief and loneliness, but if anything, she felt more desolate and empty than before. And as if that degradation wasn't enough, the real humiliation started when Jay's cell phone, which he'd carelessly left on the coffee table, beeped moments later, indicating an incoming text message.

Becca was drawn back to the present when Ethan cupped her face and softly brushed the tears from her cheeks. Until that moment, she hadn't realized she was crying again.

"Hey, you know you can trust me, right?"

In that moment, Becca instinctively knew that she could, that he wouldn't judge her for her moment of weakness. Still, the whole situation was rather embarrassing, and the idea of talking to a guy about it, even if that guy was her best friend, felt pretty daunting.

She nodded and swallowed hard, trying to calm the butterflies that fluttered in her stomach. She pulled the blanket tighter and snuggled into Ethan's shoulder, taking a few minutes to bring her emotions under control and gather her thoughts. She stared into the fire, allowing herself to be transported momentarily back to a time when she had hopes and dreams–hopes that were now a thing of the past after one innocent mistake.

"You know, I always wondered what my first time would be like, but I never in a million years thought it would be like it was tonight. I always dreamed it would be gentle and sweet, full of love and passion. I mean, I knew it was supposed to hurt and all, but I guess I thought the guy would take his time and try to make it hurt less, like in the romance novels." Tears stung her eyes again. "Really stupid, huh?"

"No, Becca. There's nothing wrong with wanting your first time to be magical," Ethan replied as he continued stroking her back. "So making love wasn't all it was cracked up to be," he stated more than asked.

"I wouldn't call it making love. Jay didn't act loving at all. When I say it hurt, I mean it *really* hurt. I started crying, and Jay didn't even seem to notice. He acted really impatient. I know he said some things to me, but I can't even remember what now. I couldn't even think because of the pain." Becca sighed. "I guess I expected too much."

A single tear rolled down Becca's cheek. Ethan brushed it away with his thumb. His other hand, which had been caressing her back, fisted in anger, and the muscles in his jaw began to twitch. If he had been the one introducing Becca to the joys of sex, he would have made damn sure she found her pleasure first, and he would have done everything in his power to minimize her discomfort. Trying to tamp down his fury to steady his voice, Ethan said, "I don't think you were expecting too much. It sounds to me like Jay was being a jerk."

"Yeah, well, that wasn't even the worst of it."

There was more? Ethan wasn't even sure he wanted to know what else the bastard had done to his sweet Becca, but he ignored the sick feeling in his gut and pressed on. "What else happened?"

"Um, after he finished, he got up and went to take a shower. That was it. He just left the room like nothing ever happened, without another word."

"Any guy who doesn't at least show a little appreciation to the girl who's given him the gift of her virginity is the biggest idiot on the planet," Ethan bit out. "Then again, I think we've already established his lack of brain cells," he added.

"I still haven't gotten to the worst part yet."

By now, Ethan was scowling so hard, he could feel the blood beginning to pound behind his temples. He was glad that Becca was still tucked under his chin and couldn't see the fierce expression on his face. "Go on," he said tightly.

"While he was in the shower, I didn't really know what to do. I didn't know if he wanted me to stay or go or what. I was trying to figure out what one does in that sort of situation when his phone beeped. I thought maybe it was something important, so I picked it up. It was a text message from a woman saying how she'd had a good time this afternoon, and wanting to know when Jay was coming back to join her in bed again."

Ethan had sensed all along that the jerk was not a one-woman kind of guy. "What did you do?" he asked.

"I know I probably shouldn't have, but I looked through his

texts. He'd been sexting with her for weeks, and she'd even sent him naked pictures of herself. God, I can't believe I got taken in by that slimeball!"

"I'm sure a lot of women have been, Becca." Ethan sighed deeply as he pinched the bridge of his nose.

"That still isn't everything. You know how I always wondered why Jay would date me when he could have lots of prettier, more experienced women?"

"Yeah?"

"Well, I found out why. When I was looking through that woman's messages, the phone beeped again. This time it was a text message from one of Jay's friends, asking if Jay had..." Becca choked on the words almost as though she was unable to repeat them. She took a deep breath and finally finished in an embarrassed whisper, "...if he had fucked me yet." Becca's bottom lip quivered and she worried it between her teeth as though trying to keep herself from crying again. "This guy was bragging that he'd bagged his third virgin and was going to win the bet. I went through their messages and found out they had some kind of wager going as to who could seduce the most virgins into giving it up by the end of the year. So I lost my virginity because of some stupid frat-boy bet that Jay's probably going to win now," she ground out through clenched teeth.

Ethan had a sudden urge to beat the bastard to a pulp. If only he were there right now.

Becca continued her story, interrupting his moment of fury. "After I found out all those things, I was going to leave quietly, but right then, Jay came out of the bathroom. I don't know where I got the courage to do it, but I confronted him about the other woman and the bet."

"What did he say?" Ethan inquired.

"Surprisingly, he didn't try to deny it. In fact, he admitted everything, including the fact that he never really cared about me or my mom. He just thought it would be easier to get me into bed because of the stuff I was going through. And, sadly, he was right."

Ethan pulled Becca to a sitting position, took her face firmly in his hands, and gazed into her eyes intensely. "Don't you dare blame yourself for this, Becca. What I'm thinking about that guy right now, I can't even say in front of a lady. He took advantage of you in the worst possible way, and if there were a way to put him in jail for it, I'd have the police on his doorstep in a heartbeat. As it is, I want to pound the crap out of him for what he did to you–and probably a dozen other women." Ethan's hands slid down to rub her shoulders. His head dropped down as he tried to calm himself with slow deep breaths.

"If it makes you feel any better, I hit him," Becca said timidly.

Ethan's head jerked back up. "You what?" he asked.

"When he admitted what he did, I slapped him really hard in the face and told him he was a bastard and a lousy excuse for a lover."

Ethan was so stunned by what his petite and ever-so-polite little Becca had said and done that he couldn't help but shake his head in wonder and laugh. He hugged her tightly and smiled against her hair. "Good for you, Becca." Ethan couldn't have been more proud of her, but at the same time, he knew that Jay deserved a hundred times worse than what he'd gotten.

"Obviously, my bravado didn't last very long, though," Becca said as she pulled back, her face mere inches from Ethan's. "After that, I ran from his apartment as fast I could and drove around aimlessly until I finally ended up here. I even sat outside in my car for a long time before coming to the door, because I was so upset. The whole time I kept getting more and more depressed, wondering how I could possibly have so much bad luck all in one day. That's why I was such a mess when you found me."

Ethan noted the deep sadness in her eyes that deadened their usual sparkle. "You did the right thing coming to me, Becca," he reassured her while chafing her shoulders. "You just need some rest and TLC, and eventually you'll start to feel better again. I promise. I'm going to be here for you as long as you need me and take care of you until you do." He mustered up a sympathetic smile and touched his finger to the tip of her nose affectionately. A little shiver ran though Becca, reminding Ethan that she was still sitting there soaking wet. "Let's start with getting you out of these wet clothes and warmed up."

Chapter 2

With Ethan's help, Becca slid off his lap and stood. She didn't feel quite as weak and wobbly as she had earlier, but he still led her down the hallway with a protective arm around her waist. He steered her though the doorway of a large bedroom that she immediately knew must be his. The sturdy, dark cherrywood furniture and the deep burgundy linens and pillows adorning the bed gave the room a masculine feel. A cheery fire crackled in a fireplace like the one in the living room.

In spite of her indiscretion tonight, Becca had never been in a man's bedroom before, and the intimacy of it suddenly made her feel shy. She cast her eyes downward toward the thick carpeting and pulled the blanket more tightly around her shoulders.

Ethan left her side for a moment. No sooner had he disappeared through another doorway to the right of the bed than a light illuminated the previously dark portal. Becca heard water running and assumed it must be the bathroom.

"Come on in here, Becca," Ethan called.

Becca slowly made her way to the threshold and peeked around the corner. Her eyes widened at the sight of the biggest bathroom she had ever seen. The sound of rushing water came from a huge whirlpool tub big enough for two people, which was situated in one corner of the room.

Taking her hand, Ethan drew her inside and seated her on a wicker chair. "It shouldn't take long to fill the tub. Then you can get warmed up with a nice soak."

Becca sat there, still rather awed at being surrounded by such luxury, while Ethan pulled thick, fluffy towels out of a cabinet and placed them on the wide ledge of the bathtub. Finally, she found her voice. "You don't have to go to all this trouble, Ethan."

"It's no trouble. Besides, you got drenched to the skin. You need to warm up before you take a chill. I don't want you getting sick." He raised a finger as though he'd just remembered something. "I'll be right back," he said as he headed back toward the bedroom.

A moment later he returned with three bottles, which he placed next to the towels. Opening one, he poured a generous amount of its contents into the water, immediately transforming the bath into a frothy cloud of bubbles and filling the air with the scent of lilac.

Becca couldn't help but smile at the notion of Ethan owning bubble bath, and him having thought to bring out that little comfort just for her. It lifted her spirits a little, and she couldn't help teasing him. "I thought you didn't have any *feminine things*. What are you doing with bubble bath?"

While Ethan replaced the cap on the bottle, he turned to look at her. His mouth dropped open, then his brows drew down in a puzzled expression. Becca could tell that she had taken him by surprise. The moment her meaning took hold, his face relaxed and a wide smile graced his handsome features, though she thought she detected a bit of color rising in his cheeks.

As he set the bottle back on the tub with the others and twisted the knobs to turn off the water, he glanced at her and answered, "Well, I still don't have any of *those* feminine things. I bought the bubble bath and matching body wash and shampoo as a birthday present for my mom. Now you can rest easy, knowing I'm not a pansy." He turned back to her with a mischievous grin.

Becca giggled shyly at his last comment.

"It's really good to hear you laugh, Becca," he said hoarsely.

"You always seem to know how to make me feel better," she replied. Her eyes traced the pattern in the tiles at her feet. "I feel really bad using your mom's birthday gift, though."

"Becca." Ethan drew out her name with a bit of exasperation. "Her birthday isn't for another two weeks. I can easily get her some more by then. Besides, I don't think you want to smell all manly from using my stuff, right? I'm glad I remembered I had it. You deserve a little pampering tonight," he finished in a slightly husky tone.

Becca's eyes rose to meet his in a meaningful gaze. For a moment, she thought she saw a flicker of something more than friendship in his regard, which left her wondering if her grief-stricken mind was playing tricks on her.

Ethan cleared his throat. "Well, you better get in the bath before the water turns cold," he said, his light, matter-of-fact manner returning, "or this exercise in warming you up will have been for nothing." He smiled. "You can leave your wet clothes on the floor, and I'll come back to take care of them after you're in the tub."

"You don't have to..." Becca began softly as she watched Ethan's retreating back. Before she could finish, he exited the room and quietly closed the door behind him.

After pondering what had just occurred between them–if anything–Becca finally rose from her perch on the wicker chair and draped the blanket over it. A small shiver went through her. She wasn't sure if it was caused by the cool air hitting her damp clothes or the recollection of how Ethan had looked at her a moment ago. Still, she knew that she wanted to warm up, and the bath looked incredibly inviting.

Slowly, Becca peeled out of her damp clothes and climbed into the steaming tub. She lowered herself into the fragrant bubbles, moaning as her aching muscles protested the movement. The warmth of the water immediately set to work relaxing and thawing her chilled body. Even the soreness between her thighs that she wanted so desperately to forget was beginning to calm from a sharp pain to a dull ache.

Becca folded one of the fluffy forest-green towels behind her head and leaned back, letting the bath work out all the discomforts. If only it could do the same for her battered heart, she thought wistfully. At least she still had Ethan, and in the past twenty-four hours, he had proven to be the best friend anyone could ever hope for. He had offered her more tender care than any man ever had before.

After leaving the bathroom, Ethan traversed his bedroom and lowered himself into a chair next to the fireplace. He leaned forward, propped his forearms on his knees, and stared into the flames.

He wasn't sure when he had first fallen in love with Becca.

Looking back, he'd been attracted to her since the day they met. What he did know was that, over the past several months, he'd started to feel things for her that were decidedly more than friendly.

But he never would have disrespected her relationship with Jay, although now he wished that he had. Even if Jay hadn't been in the picture, he knew Becca didn't need any further complications in her life. Like her best friend suddenly declaring himself madly in love with her. Somewhere along the line, though, he'd lost any interest in dating, much less sleeping with other women. Now, the adoring look Becca had given him over a simple bubble bath was seared into his mind, and the memory of her soft, slight body wrapped in his arms stirred his desires.

As he leaned back, his gaze wandered to the closed bathroom door. He couldn't stop himself from imagining what she was doing behind it: stripping off her clothes, climbing into the tub, sliding down into the steamy water as the bubbles cradled her body in a foamy embrace. He wanted nothing more than to be in there with her right now. He would take a soft washcloth and run it over her entire body, bathing her in the sudsy foam. Then he would wash her hair with the lilac-scented shampoo, rinse her off, and lift her from the tub to dry the beads of water from her skin with a big, thick towel before wrapping her up in it and carrying her to...

A rough tongue licking his hand jolted Ethan out of his sensuous fantasy. He glared at Buddy, then moaned at the realization that his lustful thoughts had gone straight to a certain part of his anatomy, which was now pressing painfully against the front of his jeans.

It only took a moment for him to recall the events of the day, which instantly brought his desire into check. He let out a disgusted sound as the thought occurred to him that he was no better than Jay. Well, perhaps he was marginally better, because he had no intentions of acting out the images that his brain had produced.

Ethan firmly reminded himself that, in spite of losing her virginity tonight, Becca was still very innocent and her tender heart had been broken in multiple ways. Right now she needed a friend and protector. That was exactly what he was going to be, even if that meant protecting her from himself as well. He was only going to think of what was best for Becca. If that meant putting his own feelings on hold, so be it.

"Thanks for bringing me back down to earth, Buddy," Ethan said as he reached over to scratch his dog's head. Back in control of his faculties and his formerly errant body, Ethan began to focus on what else he could do for Becca that would make her feel safe and loved, and keep that sweet look of adoration on her face.

The first thing that came to mind was dealing with her wet clothes as he had promised. Before doing that, Ethan realized she would need something to wear while they were washing and drying. He went to his walk-in closet and rummaged through the drawers, settling on one of his t-shirts. He couldn't help thinking that, as tiny as Becca was, she'd probably be swimming in it. At least it would keep her warm and covered.

As he was leaving the closet, he grabbed his terry-cloth robe from the back of the door before heading to the bathroom. He gently rapped his knuckles on the door, waiting for a reply before entering. When none was forthcoming, he knocked a little louder. Still no answer. Beginning to get worried, Ethan turned the knob and was relieved to discover Becca hadn't locked it. He slowly eased the door open a few inches, not wanting to give her a fright, and called, "Becca?"

When his inquiry was still met with silence, Ethan threw caution to the wind. Opening the door wide and stepping inside, the sight that met him made his heart clench. Becca was asleep, her head resting on a makeshift pillow made from a towel, her honey-colored hair fanned out over it. The bubbles gently lapped at her chest, barely covering her breasts as she breathed in and out. In her sweet repose, she looked like an angel newly fallen from heaven. She couldn't possibly be any more beautiful. All coherent thoughts flew out of his head, and he couldn't seem to stop staring at her.

Drawn by an unseen magnetic force, he took a step forward, only to clumsily trip over the leg of the chair and go crashing into the cabinets next to it with a loud thud.

Becca awoke with a startled gasp. She sat straight up in the tub, giving Ethan a brief but tantalizing glimpse of her almost bare breasts covered in nothing but a few soap bubbles. Automatically, her arms came up to cross over her chest.

Ethan quickly averted his gaze as heat crept into his face. Although he hadn't taken the time to check her cheeks for a telltale blush, he imagined that Becca was probably equally as, if not more embarrassed, than he was.

Ethan cleared his throat uncomfortably. "I'm sorry for waking you."

"Oh...um...it's OK." Becca's soft voice still sounded a bit sleepy. "W–what were you doing?"

Oh God, Ethan inwardly moaned. If she actually knew what he'd been doing in the moments before he'd so rudely awakened her, she'd think he was a pervert and run the other way, never looking back. And after what she'd been through tonight, she would have every right.

Still with his back to her and staring at the open doorway, Ethan decided to simply tell her the truth. "I, uh...I came to bring you something to put on after your bath, and to take your wet clothes to wash like I promised," he said hurriedly. "I-I, uh, knocked first, but you didn't answer. I got worried and came in to make sure you were all right."

"I'm sorry. I guess I was more exhausted than I thought," she replied. "It was really sweet of you to check on me."

Ethan mentally berated himself for not being entirely "sweet," as she had put it. To his credit, his intentions had been pure–until he'd seen her looking so completely innocent, beguiling, and thoroughly naked in his bathtub.

"What was that crashing noise, anyway?" Becca said, breaking into his thoughts with her inquiry. "You didn't hurt yourself, did you?"

"Oh, I caught my foot on the chair and fell into the cabinets. Really klutzy of me. Anyway, uh, here are the things I brought you," he said in a rush. He laid the robe and t-shirt on the chair that had managed to be a tool for bringing him back to his senses for the second time in the last half hour. "I'll just get your clothes and leave you alone."

As Ethan gathered up the soggy pile, a muffled growling noise emanated from the area of the tub. He realized almost immediately what it was, having heard the same disgruntled sound coming from his own stomach not more than an hour ago. "Have you had anything to eat tonight, Becca?" he asked.

"No," she answered rather sheepishly.

"After I get your clothes in the wash, I'll fix you something." Ethan smiled. "When you finish up in here, come out to the kitchen," he threw back over his shoulder as he walked out the door. With the tasks at hand giving him a renewed sense of purpose, he was finally back in control of his senses and determined to stay that way.

After Ethan left the room, Becca set herself to the task of bathing. As she lathered her body in the sweet-smelling suds, she thought of how strangely intimate it had been to have Ethan there while she was naked in his tub. It made her feel vulnerable, but at the same time, there had been an odd tingling sensation in her stomach that had instantly departed once he did. It was almost as though her body had wanted him to stay. For what purpose, she didn't know. A fleeting thought of him cradling her in his arms like he'd done earlier passed through her mind, except this time she was still in her current state of undress.

Becca shuddered. What on earth was she thinking?

She had already allowed her desperate desire for human contact to get out of control once tonight, and it had served no purpose but to completely shatter her already-broken heart. Not to mention Ethan was her best friend, and she'd never thought of him as anything else before. It must be the grief making her crazy. Or maybe it was hunger. Or lack of sleep. Or all three. When she really thought about it, the idea of sleeping with any guy right now didn't appeal.

Becca finished squeezing the water from her hair and released the drain plug before climbing out of the tub. She grabbed one of the thick bath towels from the pile Ethan had left for her and wrapped it around her head. As she took another towel and started drying her body, she was reminded of how painfully sore she was. That alone was enough to turn off any momentary sexual desire she might have been experiencing. That, and being completely spent on an emotional level. How could she have been so blind to the truth of what Jay had really wanted from her? Maybe it was because she had met him during a difficult time in her life, when she needed to believe that a handsome jock could be attracted to, and care for, an ordinary girl like her.

Whatever the reasons, they had been her downfall, and she definitely didn't need to make things worse by having even a momentary fantasy about Ethan. Anything she might be feeling for him right now was probably a result of him being nice to her. That was the kind of person he was, a guy who would never let a friend down. She had to make sure it stayed that way–just friendship–and she'd have to do it by somehow keeping her wildly fluctuating emotions in check and not allowing herself to be driven to do something stupid ever again.

Becca dropped her towel in a heap on the floor and reached for the shirt Ethan had left for her. As she drew it over her head, she was surrounded by an almost intoxicating redolence. The smell of cotton and laundry soap blended with another masculine scent that belonged distinctly to Ethan. That tingling sensation returned to her tummy, but this time an odd sense of comfort swept over her as well.

Feeling a slight chill, she wrapped herself in his robe as well and was instantly aware of the same pleasant odor. It made her feel that if she cocooned herself in the soothing aroma long enough, it might heal her aching body and soul.

Becca pulled the lapels up to her nose and took one last deep breath before snuggling them around her neck and cinching the belt at her waist. She walked over to the sink and smiled briefly, realizing Ethan hadn't forgotten a single thing. He'd even laid out a brand-new toothbrush for her. After putting a dab of toothpaste on the bristles, she vigorously scrubbed her mouth, needing to rid herself of the bitter taste of Jay's betrayal.

A quick spit-and-rinse later, she still didn't feel any better about it. Instead, she decided to apply herself to the tangled mass of wet hair. Dropping the towel in a pile with the other one and picking up the comb, she lifted her arm to perform the task, only to stop dead at the sight of her reflection in the mirror.

Becca had never thought of herself as pretty, but at the moment, she looked like nothing more than a pathetic ugly duckling. How could anyone ever love the unattractive woman who gazed back at her? Jay certainly hadn't. Even her own father and grandmother didn't want her. Only her mother had ever loved her and called her pretty, and now she was gone too, leaving Becca all alone.

After staring at her image for a few seconds more, she turned away in disgust. Her self-esteem had never been great, but tonight she was painfully aware that it was in utter shambles. Tears welled up again. God, she had to get off this wild emotional roller coaster ride before she truly lost her mind.

Just then, a new aroma filled her nostrils. Ethan had left the bathroom door open a crack, and the smell of food wafted in. Her stomach let out another unhappy rumble, reminding her of how weak she was from hunger. Still feeling irrationally angry with herself, Becca acknowledged her body's need for sustenance and headed toward the kitchen with the comb clutched in her hand.

She stopped at the doorway to the breakfast nook, where she watched Ethan place a bowl of something and a spoon on the table.

As he turned back toward the stove, he looked up and saw her standing there. "Hey, Becca," he said, greeting her with a smile. He took a step toward her, holding out his hand. "Come sit down. I made you a bite to eat. It's not much, but I think you'll like it."

As Becca started to move, her toe caught on the hem of the too-long robe, and she pitched forward.

Quicker than lightening, Ethan was at her side, his strong arm wrapped around her waist to steady her. "Easy there," he said softly. When she looked up, he still had that charming lopsided grin on his face. "I guess that robe is a little too big for you, huh?"

Becca looked back down at the floor, barely registering what he had said. "Yeah," she replied without mirth. In fact, her voice sounded depressing even to her.

With his hand still protectively placed at the small of her back, Ethan led her the few steps to the table, pulled out a chair, and seated her like a waiter in a fancy restaurant.

"I really hoped that hot bath might make you feel a little better," he said over his shoulder as he went to retrieve a plate and glass from the counter.

He placed them on the table next to the bowl, and for the first time she realized what he had made for her: tomato soup, a grilled-cheese sandwich and a glass of chocolate milk. They were the three things her mother always made for her when she'd had a particularly rough day, and they had always warmed her heart and soul as well as her body. This time the sight and smell of the food made her break into tears again.

Immediately, Ethan sat down in the chair next to her and pulled her to his chest. One arm wrapped around her shoulders while his free hand cupped the side of her face gently drawing it down to his shoulder. He lowered his cheek to rest on the top of her head. "Oh, Becca," he whispered into her hair. "I didn't mean to make you feel worse. I remembered your mom fixing this for us that one day after we worked at the shelter all night, hoping that we could help the vet save that poor abused dog that didn't make it."

A small sob escaped her.

He sighed deeply. "Oh, great. Now I'm really mucking things up by reminding you of more sad memories. I recalled that it seemed to make you feel a little better then, and I thought it might help now. I'm so sorry. I'll take it away and make you something else if it–"

"No, Ethan," Becca said as she placed her hand over his and looked up at him through the blurry veil of her tears. "It's OK. It's just me. I can't seem to stop going back and forth between being angry with myself and bursting into tears over the slightest thing."

Ethan turned his hand to entwine his long fingers with hers. He brought her hand to his chest as he caressed the back of it with his thumb. "Being on an emotional roller coaster is completely understandable. It's going to take some time to work things out."

"I suppose." She smiled ruefully. "Ethan, you've been so wonderful to me tonight. I don't how I can ever thank you. The food, the bath, it's *all* wonderful. Truly. I don't want you to think for a minute that I don't appreciate it or that you haven't helped me, because you have. I just can't seem to stop feeling sad...but it has nothing to do with you."

Ethan lifted the lapel of the oversized robe to dry the tears from Becca's face. "Don't be too hard on yourself. It hasn't even been a day. And remember, I said I was going to be here for you every step of the way."

"Thank you for everything, Ethan."

He smiled at her and inclined his head toward the table. "You can thank me by eating your food before it gets cold."

She nodded. "OK."

Ethan released her. She turned back to the table and sighed before picking up the spoon and tucking into the simple meal he had so lovingly prepared for her.

Becca was nearly finished with her soup when Ethan reached around her to pick up something from the table. He studied her for a moment with a hint of smile on his face. "Looks like you forgot something," he teased.

Becca looked at the big blue comb he held, and instantly, her hands flew to her tangled, still-damp hair. Remembrance of the image in the bathroom mirror of a bird's nest atop a haggard-looking face made her snatch the comb from his hand in embarrassment. "I was just about to do that before I came out here, but the smell of food must have distracted me," she mumbled into her lap before applying the comb to her hair with violent yanks of frustration.

"Easy there, Becca." Ethan's hand stilled hers in mid-pull and took the comb from her. His fingers under her chin gently raised her face to meet his eyes. "I was only kidding, OK? But if you keep that up, you're going to be bald inside of ten minutes. I, for one, think your hair is quite lovely, and I would hate to see it go."

"Ethan, how can you say that? It's a mess."

"Nothing a little patience and TLC won't cure," he replied with a gentle tone and one of those charming smiles that never failed to make Becca feel better. "Let me worry about your hair. You finish eating." He nodded at her nearly empty bowl. "You downed that soup pretty fast."

"I haven't eaten anything all day." She shrugged sheepishly.

"Would you like some more?"

"Yeah, I guess I am still a little hungry."

Ethan grinned. "Well, we can't have that."

After returning from the stove with her soup bowl refilled, he set himself to the task of removing the snarls from her thick tresses. His tender hands working slowly through each knot had a near-magical, calming effect on her, lulling her into a state of near bliss. Again she was reminded of the great comfort it had been to have her mother brush her hair. But instead of feeling sad this time, Becca realized that there was another person who could provide solace. For the first time since her mother had passed three days ago, she felt blessed and sent up a silent prayer of thanks for her wonderful friend.

Ethan had removed all the tangles from Becca's hair several minutes ago, but he continued to pull the comb through it with gentle strokes. Her closed eyes and peaceful expression seemed to indicate she was enjoying it very much. If he was honest with himself, he'd have to admit that he was enjoying it too. Perhaps a little too much. The silky sensation of her honey-brown locks cascading over his fingertips with each stroke was teasing a path straight to his groin. With a small sigh of reluctance, he allowed himself one last touch before finally pulling away from her tempting tresses.

"Mmm." Becca's throaty murmur only added fuel to his growing desire. "That felt so good."

The predictably male part of his brain suddenly decided to translate those words into a different context. In an attempt to distract himself, Ethan put aside the comb and set about clearing the table.

Becca turned in her chair to follow him with her gaze to the kitchen sink. "Thank you, Ethan. Brushing my hair was another thing my mom used to do when I was feeling down."

"You're welcome," Ethan replied as he rinsed the dishes and loaded them into the dishwasher. "I hope it didn't make you feel sad, like the soup did."

"No, oddly enough, it didn't. I think I finally realized that I still have you in my life, and you always seem to know how to make me feel better, just like she did."

Ethan closed the dishwasher and dried his hands on a kitchen towel as he thought of how he wanted to be there for her, making her feel better, for a long time to come. "I'm glad I could help."

Becca glanced at the clock on the wall which now read two a.m. "Wow, it's really late. I should probably get dressed and head home. Where are my clothes?"

"Hold on there a minute. You're not going anywhere, Becca," Ethan said sternly, ignoring her question.

"But—"

"No buts. You are not going out there in this weather. The rain may have let up, but that was one hell of a spring storm. It's bound to have caused some street flooding. I'd be the worst kind of friend if I allowed you to leave in the middle of the night when there are dangerous road conditions. Not to mention I really don't think you should be alone right now," he added a bit more gently. "You're spending the night here, and that's final."

"I thought you weren't finished painting your guest room yet. I don't want to put you out."

"It's not a big deal. You can have my bedroom, and I'll sleep out here on the couch."

"But you've already done so much for me already. I don't want you to give up your bed too," Becca insisted. "Let me sleep on the–"

Ethan covered the distance between them in two steps and placed a finger to Becca's lips. "I am not going to let you sleep on the couch after everything you've been through today. You need a good night's rest, and I'm going to make sure you get it. Now would you please let me take care of you like I promised?"

"OK," she mumbled against his fingertip, a slight smile playing at the corners of her delicate mouth. The light vibration and silky softness of her lips against the sensitive nerves of Ethan's finger sent a frisson of sensation through his entire body.

"Let's get you to bed then."

The moment the words fell from his tongue, he became uncomfortably aware of the double entendre he'd uttered. Once again, finding himself in need of a quick distraction, Ethan reached for Becca's hand and helped her up from her chair. Just as she was about to trip over the robe again, he halted her movement and, with a gallant bow, reached down to scoop up the portion of the garment that was dragging on the floor. "Your train, m'lady," he said with a mischievous grin as he draped the fabric over her outstretched arm.

Becca rewarded him with the biggest smile he'd seen from her in days, and it utterly warmed his heart. "Ethan, you are so goofy sometimes."

"Yeah, but it's one of the reasons you like me so much. Admit it." He grinned from ear to ear.

Becca nodded. "But of course, m'lord." She made a mock curtsy of her own.

They both shared a playful laugh as Ethan placed his hand on the small of Becca's back and guided her down the hallway to his bedroom, with Buddy eagerly trailing along behind them. Once there, Ethan helped Becca out of his robe and tossed it across the foot of the bed. Pulling the covers back, he lifted them, motioning with his hand for her to climb in.

Placing one knee on the mattress, then the other, she proceeded to crawl on all fours to the center of the big bed. Ethan knew that his sweet, innocent Becca was unaware of the seductive pose she presented to him. Having taken all her clothes to be washed earlier, he was also painfully aware that she wore no panties beneath the t-shirt he'd loaned her. Hell, the mere thought of her shapely little body ensconced in nothing but his shirt was almost more than he could bear.

"Ethan?" Becca's voice broke though his reverie. Somewhere in the midst of his naughty daydream, she had lain down on her side and was now looking at him with a puzzled expression as if he'd lost his mind.

Actually, he thought, she wasn't too far off the mark. He was still standing there holding the duvet like an idiot. Quickly, he pulled it up to her chin and tucked it around her in an attempt to conceal all the tempting parts he shouldn't be thinking about.

He cleared his throat uncomfortably and turned away from the bed. "I'll, ah, put another log on the fire, um, get a pillow and blanket from the closet, and then leave you to get some sleep." He could barely articulate the words.

Becca lay so quietly while he tended the fire, Ethan thought she had already fallen asleep. Knowing that would probably be the best thing for both of them, he slowly rose from his crouched position by the hearth and was about to head for the closet when her small voice reached him from the bed. "Thanks for insisting that I stay, Ethan. I'm a little scared to be alone right now."

"That's understandable," he replied softly.

"I hate to ask for anything else...but would you sit beside me until I go to sleep?" Becca asked.

Ethan knew that wouldn't be a good idea, but it only took one look at all the emotions playing across her face to realize that he couldn't deny her anything right now. "Sure."

He walked tentatively to the bed and sat down on the edge as far away from her as possible. After propping a couple of pillows against the headboard, he leaned back and stretched out his long legs, crossing his bare feet at the ankles.

Even without looking at Becca, Ethan could sense her reaching across the expanse. He almost flinched from the heat of the contact with her hand as she hesitantly pulled his from his lap.

"Could you talk to me for a while?" she asked sadly.

Ethan closed his eyes for a minute and felt a well of emotion bubbling up within him. It was no longer the flaming lust that he'd experienced moments before, but a gentler, deeper sensation. Love. He wasn't quite sure how he knew, but in that moment, he was certain beyond a shadow of a doubt that he was never going to let this woman beside him go. Someway, somehow, he was going to help her heal and make her his forever. A certain peace washed over him, born of the knowledge that his love for her would sustain him and keep his errant body in check while he waited for Becca to be ready for something more.

He threaded his fingers with hers, finally welcoming her touch. "What do you want to talk about?" he asked as he turned to look into her beautiful blue eyes.

"Tell me what you were thinking about when you were helping me into bed. You looked like you were a million miles away," she suggested with a yawn.

Ethan chuckled. "Um, it was nothing. Just a business deal I'm working on for the company."

He hated lying to her, but telling her the truth about what he had really been thinking was not going to happen.

"Tell me about that then."

"OK," Ethan drawled out with skepticism. "It might put you to sleep," he added with a grin.

"Isn't that the point?"

"Yeah." He laughed again and proceeded to tell her all about his latest project at work.

Ten minutes later, a soft snore made him smile. When he glanced over at Becca's sleeping form, he was stunned once again by how angelic she looked. Hers was a face he would never grow tired of seeing. He was surprised by the thought that her face was the last thing he wanted to see every night before falling asleep and the only thing he wanted to wake up to every morning.

He had no idea how he was going to maintain a friends-only relationship with this beautiful woman he had grown to love more than anything in the world, when all he wanted to do was draw her into his arms and make sweet, passionate love to her all night long.

With that thought, Ethan knew he needed to put some distance between himself and Becca before he woke her up and did exactly that. He carefully released Becca's hand and slid off the bed slowly, so as not to wake her. He padded to the bay window and sat on the window seat. Placing his feet on the cushion, knees bent, he rested his back against the wall with a heavy sigh. His warm breath momentarily fogged the cool panes of glass. His forearm draped over his knee, he leaned forward to stare up at the vastness of the heavens and watch the clouds lazily traversing the expanse.

The pounding rain had stopped nearly an hour ago, and an almost full moon could be seen as a nebulous glow behind its foggy shroud. Every once in a while, a bright star would peek through the haze. Ethan wished that he could see more of the tiny dots of light in the sky. Their cheerful twinkling never failed to lift his spirits. Even though they were almost entirely obscured tonight, their occasional sightings in between the clouds still helped to soothe his troubled mind. When contemplating the enormity of the universe, somehow his problems always seemed smaller.

For a long time he sat there, taking it all in, until his attention was drawn across the room by Buddy, who made a few restless circles before settling down on his bed near the fireplace. Resting his head on his front paws, Buddy promptly fell asleep.

A slight rustling from the bed brought Ethan's watchful eye back to Becca. She had rolled onto her back, but the steady rise and fall of her chest indicated she was still sound asleep. Ethan's heart warmed as he glanced back and forth between her and Buddy. Finally his gaze settled on the crackling flames of the fire as he remembered his introduction to his two best friends–one of the furry variety and the other, thankfully, not.

It had happened more than two years ago. At the time, Becca was only twenty-two and still in college working toward her pre-vet degree. At twenty-eight, upon his father's retirement from the family-owned company, Ethan had taken over as the CEO of Pet Emporium, a very successful chain of pet-supply stores. Giving back to the community had been extremely important to him since his teen years, so he always made time in his busy schedule to work at the local animal shelter a couple of weekends each month. He'd met Becca while both of them were volunteering there.

A smile curved Ethan's lips at the memory of their first encounter.

He'd walked in on Becca wrestling with a enormous scruffy dog that looked like a cross between a golden retriever and a St. Bernard. The silly creature obviously wanted to do anything but take a bath. He ran in circles around the big metal tub full of soapy water before coming to a screeching halt in front of Becca. Without warning, he jumped up, placing his huge paws on Becca's chest. Unprepared for the extra weight of the giant beast, Becca lost her balance, toppling backward right into the tub. The dog, seemingly pleased that he was no longer the one in the tub, sat back on his haunches and quirked his head to one side as if perusing his handiwork.

The sight made Ethan burst out laughing. Finally aware of his presence, Becca glared at him.

He crossed the enclosure to the tub. "You look like you could use a hand," he said, stating the obvious.

She extended her bottom lip to blow a piece of hair out of her face. "I think I could use about five," she quipped.

He held his hands up in front of him. "Sorry. How about two?"

"I'll take them." When she finally smiled, it lit up her entire face.

He extended a hand to help her up. "I'm Ethan, by the way."

Once she was upright again, she returned the introduction. "Rebecca."

It was then he allowed his gaze to roam over her body. A crown of soap bubbles sat atop her head. A smudge of dirt slashed across one cheek. Her soaked t-shirt and shorts were tantalizingly plastered to her petite curves. She looked like something the dog had dragged in. And yet she was still utterly adorable.

Becca scowled at the cause of her state of dishabille. "You're on my hit list today, buddy."

The dog merely continued to look at her with wide, innocent eyes, his tongue comically lolling out one side of his mouth.

Ethan and Becca instantly hit it off as they tamed the unruly beast into submission. By the time they were done with him, the dog's coat gleamed, and Ethan was a goner for those big brown eyes. He adopted "Buddy" on the spot and took him home.

As for Becca and him, they'd occasionally gone out together on platonic "dates" and continued to spend their weekends together, playing with the homeless animals and participating in pet rescue operations. She loved the animals and found the volunteer work every bit as rewarding as he did. She had even told him about her amazing idea for a free animal clinic and no-kill shelter that she wanted to start after graduating from vet school. Unfortunately, she'd had to give up all those dreams when her mom had fallen ill.

Ethan wasn't sure how long he sat there, quietly staring into the fire, but the patter of a few raindrops against the glass brought him out of his daydream. Glancing out the window, he saw that the moon and stars were now completely obscured by heavy clouds that looked as if they might unleash another torrent of rain any moment.

A soft moan drew his gaze back to the bed. Becca's eyes were still closed, but her face no longer held that sweet, angelic look. Instead, it was knitted with tension. Her body twitched, and her legs moved restlessly, as though she were trying to run away from whatever monster had invaded her dreams.

Unable to bear watching her discomfort, Ethan left his cozy seat and returned to the bed. Sliding in beside Becca, he gently gathered her into his arms. She continued to whimper and shudder but didn't awaken.

"Shh... It's all right," he whispered against her hair while rubbing circles on her back. "I'm here now. I won't let anything hurt you."

Almost instantly, she curled into his chest, and her body relaxed. He placed a tender kiss on her forehead. For a long while, he continued caressing her back, her arm, her hair. Until he lay down, Ethan hadn't realized how exhausted he was. Soon he was drifting off himself. The thought that he should move to the sofa surfaced briefly, moments before sleep claimed him and he was lost in dreams...of everything he wanted to do for, and with, the best friend who had somehow stolen his heart.

Chapter 3

Becca awakened slowly. Ethan's familiar scent filled her nostrils, bringing a feeling of safety...and something else she couldn't quite identify. She raised her hand to rub the sleep from her eyes and bumped it into something warm and firm. Her hand began to touch and stroke whatever it was as her sleep-addled brain tried to make sense of it.

A sharp intake of breath startled her eyes wide open. Taking in her surroundings, Becca remembered that she was in Ethan's bed, not her own, and apparently he had never left last night. The vivid dream she'd had of a strong man rescuing her from a flooded wash and wrapping her safely in his arms must not have been entirely a dream. She was cocooned in Ethan's arms, her head pillowed against his firm shoulder and her nose only inches from his chest. And it felt magnificent.

Now fully conscious of what she had been doing, Becca stilled the hand that had been caressing Ethan's chest and tentatively peeked up at his face through her lashes. He gazed back with dark, heavy-lidded eyes that seemed to speak of things she was too afraid to think about. They remained like that, staring at each other for what seemed like hours. Then, as quickly as it had begun, the moment was over, and whatever Becca thought she had seen in Ethan's eyes disappeared, replaced by a mischievous sparkle and a wide grin that lit up his face.

"Morning, gorgeous."

Becca was momentarily taken aback by his greeting. Her brows drew down into a frown. "Are you making fun of how I look in the morning?"

Ethan looked surprised by her question and his smile faded a little. "Not in the least. You ought to know I'd never make fun of you, Becca. I think you look very pretty this morning–even with a little bed head," he teased, his big smile returning.

Becca smacked his shoulder, but with him holding her so snugly it didn't make much of an impact. Ethan merely laughed at her puny efforts before reaching out to smooth down a few hairs. For a second, Becca thought she caught that special something in his gaze again, but it was gone before she could be certain.

"I thought you were going to sleep on the couch last night," she said.

Ethan suddenly looked uncomfortable. He loosened his hold on her and nervously cleared his throat before answering. "I'm sorry about that. I didn't mean to fall asleep here."

"Oh. No," Becca was quick to reassure him. "It's all right. I was just wondering, that's all. For the record, I'm glad you stayed. I think I slept better with you here."

Ethan appeared relieved. "I was hoping that was the case. I stayed for a while to make sure you were sound asleep, but you started tossing and turning and making distressed noises in your sleep. I think you were having a nightmare. I didn't want to wake you, and tried holding you instead. It seemed to work. You calmed down pretty quickly. I guess I was so tired I dozed off too."

"Yeah, I did have a nightmare."

Now that there was some space between her and Ethan, Becca played anxiously with the folds of the bedcovers as she remembered her frightening dream.

"Do you want to talk about it?" Ethan inquired with concern.

"No, not really. I only remember bits and pieces anyway. It felt pretty scary, but I think it was just the stress of yesterday coming out in my subconscious. I do recall hearing my mother's voice, though." For a moment, her thoughts turned inward as she wistfully remembered how hearing that gentle voice had given her such a sense of peace.

Ethan raised up on his elbow and looked down at her, drawing her attention back to him. "Are you OK with that?"

Becca gave him a wan smile as she nodded her head against the pillow. "I think it was the turning point in the dream. I felt peaceful after she spoke, not sad."

"That's good." Ethan smiled back. "I'm glad."

They looked at each other awkwardly for another moment before Becca sat up in bed.

Ethan's eyes suddenly glinted brightly as he seemed to have a brainstorm. He placed a hand on her leg to still her movement. "You stay right where you are. Don't move a muscle. I'm going to treat you to breakfast in bed."

"Ethan, you don't have to do that. You're spoiling me."

"And what's wrong with that?"

"Well..." She searched her brain for a good comeback. When nothing came to her, she flopped back against the pillows again. "Aargh!" she exclaimed.

"That's a pretty weak argument, if you ask me." Ethan grinned as he climbed out of bed and padded toward the kitchen in his bare feet. "Oh, and by the way, Talk Like a Pirate Day was six months ago," he said over his shoulder with a laugh as Becca growled and flung a pillow at his retreating back.

She shook her head but couldn't help but laugh with him. She'd always liked the way Ethan teased her, and if she was completely honest with herself, she actually liked all the wonderful things he was doing for her too.

Ethan hummed a happy tune as he turned bacon in one skillet and stirred scrambled eggs in another. Buddy watched with rapt attention, hoping for a tidbit to fall on the floor. Ethan couldn't think of a better way to spend the morning than having breakfast in bed with the woman he loved. Waking up with her snuggled in his arms was a dream come true. Only one thing could have made it better, but that would have to wait.

He was glad that he'd slept on top of the covers, because he'd awakened partially aroused. Holding Becca close, breathing her scent, and watching her sleep with her silky hair fanned out over his shoulder only added fuel to the fire. When she'd sleepily stroked his chest, he'd almost come undone. Thank goodness the comforter was bunched up between them, concealing the evidence of his desire. Still, he wasn't sure how well he had masked it on his face. He was grateful that their banter and more serious talk of her dream had distracted his male parts. Otherwise, it would have been impossible for him to get out of bed without giving himself away.

Setting aside those thoughts, Ethan served up the bacon and eggs on two plates. He added slices of buttered toast and poured glasses of orange juice, then placed everything on a lap tray. He broke off a small morsel of bacon and tossed it to Buddy, who deftly caught the treat in midair.

Ethan carried the tray to the bedroom with Buddy hot on his heels. He found Becca propped against the pillows with her reading glasses perched on her pert little nose. She looked absolutely adorable sitting in his bed perusing the latest mystery novel he'd been reading. He felt like his heart might leap out of his chest at the sight of her. She was so engrossed, she didn't notice him standing in the doorway.

Buddy ran ahead of him into the room and placed his front paws on the bed to get her attention.

"Hi, Buddy," she crooned at the dog as she scratched his ears.

"Breakfast is served, m'lady." Ethan smiled as he crossed to the bed. He placed the tray over her legs and ordered Buddy to lie down on the rug.

"Mmm, that smells so good," Becca said as she breathed in the delicious aroma. "My stomach has been growling ever since you started cooking."

"We can't have you starving. Better eat up before it gets cold."

Ethan sat cross-legged at the foot of the bed. Facing her over their makeshift table, he was intensely aware of the intimacy of the setting.

Becca set the book and her glasses on the bedside table before taking up a fork and eagerly digging in. After the first bite, she smiled blissfully. "Oh, Ethan, it tastes as good as it looks."

"It's only scrambled eggs. No biggie."

"Well, my taste buds are in heaven right now," she said with a giggle. "You know, my mom said that if you cook the simplest dishes with love, they always taste better." Her laughter faded to a rueful smile. "You have the same knack she did for making tomato soup and scrambled eggs taste like a gourmet meal."

"I'm glad you like my cooking," he answered, feeling a bit embarrassed by Becca's praise.

"I really appreciate everything you've done for me. The weird thing is you've been acting more like my boyfriend than Jay ever did. I always thought that he didn't really consider me his girlfriend, because we never...you know." Her eyes dropped to her lap, and her cheeks pinkened.

"Becca, you don't have to have sex with a guy to be his girlfriend," Ethan replied gently.

She nervously wrapped the belt of his robe around her finger. "Sometimes you seem like the only guy on the planet who thinks that way. I know I haven't dated all that much, but most of the guys I've been out with act like it's all part of the deal. You know...dinner, movie, sex. A lot of my friends from college said the same thing, although some of them didn't get why I wouldn't put out either."

"Well, you know me. I have respect for the women I date. There's no point in pushing them to do something they're not ready for, because it won't be enjoyable for either one of us. Besides, I'm not really into meaningless sex either. I'm more of a relationship kind of guy. A rare breed, I know, but I'm definitely not the only one out there."

"Rich, handsome, and a relationship guy? Ethan Montgomery, I'm amazed that no woman has snatched you up yet. I might have to ask you out myself," Becca said, chuckling as she teased him.

Her flirtatious words hit a little too close to home, leaving him wishing she'd do just that. Needing a distraction, he decided to change the subject. "You seemed pretty absorbed in my new novel when I walked in."

"You know me. I love books. I was curious what you were reading. I don't usually read mysteries, but this one sounds good."

"My brother, Nathan, recommended it. He and I have similar tastes. So far, I'm enjoying it. So what have you been reading lately?"

"Lately? Not much. I haven't had the heart for it," she replied sadly. "Maybe I should try again to help take my mind off everything."

"You should. Reading a good book always helps me to relax. It lets me escape for a while." Ethan paused to take a bite of bacon. "Since you aren't reading anything right now, tell me about the last book you read."

Becca's eyes dropped to her plate. "It was just a romance," she mumbled while pushing her remaining eggs around the plate with her fork.

Ethan's brows drew down. He reached across the space between them, gently lifting her face with a finger crooked under her chin. "Hey, you aren't embarrassed about reading romance novels, are you?"

"Not exactly," she said, shrugging, "but most people I know think they're silly. Mom always loved them and so does Edna, but other than them, I don't really know anybody who reads them. Even my old college girlfriends thought they were...well, I believe the word they used was 'trash.' Either that, or they made fun of me. I never know how people will react to my reading preferences."

"I already knew you read romances, Becca. After all, I've been to your apartment lots of times. I've seen what's on your bookshelves."

"Being a guy, I didn't think you'd notice or care enough to look."

"It has nothing to do with being a guy. Hello, I'm a fellow book lover. Of course I'd be interested in what's on your shelves. Besides, even if I didn't already know what you read, I'd never make fun of you. Not for your book choices or anything else. As to your girlfriends' opinion, I say they don't know what they're missing." He grinned at her.

The look on Becca's face was one of pure skepticism. "I bet you've never read a romance novel in your life. How would you know?"

"I know, because if you're reading them, they have to be good," Ethan replied in a serious tone. "Not to mention I think it's good for women to have a healthy fantasy life. After all, men do too, but in a different way."

Suddenly looking shy, Becca's gaze dropped back to her plate. Knowing that he'd embarrassed her, Ethan sought to lighten the mood again. "Come on. Tell me about your last book. Did a knight in shining armor ride in on his trusty steed to rescue the damsel in distress?" He brandished his knife in the air like a sword.

His theatrical flair had the desired effect, bringing a smile back to

Becca's face. "On the contrary, it was a kilted Highlander carrying the fair maiden off to his castle on the loch."

"Oh, do tell. Was Nessie there?" he inquired with wide eyes. Then he added with a waggle of his brows and a mock Scottish accent, "And what was the bonny lad wearing beneath his kilt?"

Ethan's heart swelled as Becca's laughter pealed throughout the room, even as a lovely shade of pink rose in her cheeks. He then became her rapt audience of one as she proceeded to regale him with highlights from the story while they finished their breakfast.

After enjoying a leisurely morning meal accompanied by an entertaining discussion of books, Becca insisted on helping Ethan clean up this time. For once, he relented. While Becca loaded the dirty dishes into the dishwasher and tidied the kitchen, Ethan gathered her clothes from the laundry room and went to change into some respectable-looking garments of his own, ones that weren't rumpled from sleeping in them.

Becca returned to the bedroom as Ethan was tying his athletic shoes. Indicating the clean clothes lying in a neatly folded pile on the bed, he gave her a quick smile before leaving her to dress in private.

Fifteen minutes later, Becca approached the doorway to Ethan's office. He was sitting in the leather chair behind his desk, his head bent over a manila file folder. Becca leaned against the doorjamb, covertly watching him. His expression indicated he was lost in deep thought as he pored over the documents in the folder. A lock of hair the color of dark chocolate had fallen down over his forehead. She longed to go smooth it back into place, and wondered what it might feel like to run her fingers through his thick locks. His hair looked soft and silky to the touch. Ethan wasn't an athlete like Jay, but Becca knew he worked out at the gym a couple of times a week. Her eyes were drawn to his broad shoulders and muscular biceps, which filled out his navy t-shirt. How good it would feel to have those strong arms wrapped around her again. The memory of his rugged chest beneath her fingertips brought a shiver to her body despite the pleasant warmth of the room.

Why hadn't she ever noticed how incredibly handsome Ethan was before? Inwardly, Becca sighed. She had been too caught up in the illusion of what she thought Jay was to realize the true man of her dreams might be right in front of her face. A rueful smile curved her lips as she thought of the mistake she'd made. She knew that Ethan was right about Jay being a pig who'd taken cruel advantage of her in a weak moment, but she still couldn't help feeling that she bore some responsibility too.

She decided to stop thinking about it before she went too far down the road of regrets, knowing it would only serve to upset her again. What was done was done, and all she could do from here was pick up the pieces and move forward.

She had no idea if the amazing man sitting before her would ever want her as anything more than a friend. She did know that she would never pursue anything more between them until she put her life back in order. That very moment, she mentally made a vow to herself to do exactly that.

Just then, Ethan looked up from his work and gave her a gorgeous smile. "Hey, how long have you been standing there?"

Becca cleared her throat as she felt a bit of heat rising in her cheeks. "Not long," she lied, hoping the embarrassment she felt at her perusal of his masculinity didn't show on her face. She took a couple of steps inside the office. "Um...I was thinking I should probably be heading home."

In all honesty, she didn't really want to leave, but Ethan had done more than enough for her already. If she was going to put the pieces of her life back together, she needed to start standing on her own two feet. And what better time to begin than now?

"I'll come with you. Let me get a jacket, and I'll follow you in my car." He pushed his chair back from the desk and started to get up. "Maybe we can hang out together this afternoon."

Becca put a hand up to stop him. "You don't have to do that, Ethan."

He looked at her with that care and concern in his eyes that never failed to make her heart melt. "No, I don't *have* to. I *want* to," he countered, his tone serious. "Unless, of course, you'd rather be alone."

"It's not that I don't want to spend time with you," she reassured him. "I just have a lot of thinking to do about my life."

"Sounds pretty intense."

Becca sighed. "Yeah, I guess it is. While I was getting dressed, I was thinking that maybe I should call for an appointment with the counselor at the women's clinic." She shrugged. "Maybe it's time I get a little professional help to put things back on track."

"I think that's a great idea." He cleared his throat. "Um, you mentioning the women's clinic reminded me of something that's been bothering me since last night. It just didn't quite seem like the right time to bring it up."

"What's that?"

Ethan sighed deeply. "I guess I should just spit it out." His Adam's apple bobbed as he swallowed hard before his intense green eyes bored straight into hers. "Did Jay use protection?"

The question hit her like a ton of bricks. It was something she knew she'd have to face at some point, but she had been trying not to think about it. Her gaze dropped to the floor as she shook her head. "I know I should have insisted, but everything happened so fast."

Ethan got up and rounded his desk. He took Becca's hand and pulled her into a gentle embrace.

Her arms automatically wrapped around his waist, and she rested her head on his shoulder. "What am I going to do if...?" She was unable to finish the thought.

"Shh..." he said soothingly while caressing her back. "Let's not borrow trouble by thinking about *what ifs*. Make an appointment at the clinic and get tested first."

She nodded in agreement. "All right."

"And remember, I meant what I said about being here for you no matter what," Ethan added softly. His mouth was so close that his warm breath tickled her ear, sending a shiver through her body.

Ethan must have felt the tremor, because he wrapped her more tightly in his arms and rubbed her shoulders. "Are you cold?" he asked.

"A little." She seemed to be making a habit out of lying.

"Well, if you're going outside, you should wear a sweater. The air is a little nippy this morning after all that rain we had last night." He pulled back to give her a questioning look. "You weren't wearing one last night. Did you leave it in your car? I can go out and get it for you."

"No, it's not in my car." Her eyes, filled with regret, dropped to

Ethan's chest. "I left it at Jay's apartment. It was my mom's favorite too, that pretty white cashmere one with the little embroidered flowers that you gave her for Christmas. Wearing it made me feel closer to her."

Ethan seemed taken aback, but his lips curved into a pleased smile. "That was her favorite?"

Becca nodded, as a smaller answering smile touched her own mouth and faded again quickly. The fingers of her right hand circled her left wrist, and she sighed before continuing. "If leaving the sweater behind wasn't bad enough, I think I may have lost the charm bracelet you gave me at his apartment too. I guess that was yet another stupid thing I did last night."

Ethan lifted her chin to look her in the eye again. "I know I'm starting to sound like a broken record, but don't be so hard on yourself."

"I'm sorry. I just can't believe I lost two things that meant so much to me. On second thought, make that three." She bit her bottom lip and blinked furiously, willing herself not to cry again. "I know the one is gone forever, but God only knows what he's done with my other things. I'll probably never get them back either."

Ethan gave her a little squeeze with the arm that still circled her waist. "Don't worry. We'll figure something out. I promise. In the meantime, you need to go home and get some more rest. You can borrow one of my jackets to keep you warm."

As he released her and walked to the hall closet outside his office, Becca missed his touch already. He returned only seconds later with a brown leather bomber jacket, which he held out while she placed her arms in the sleeves. She was practically swimming in it, but she didn't care one bit. Ethan's masculine scent clung to the garment, making her feel nearly as comforted as being wrapped in his arms.

He turned her around and zipped the jacket for her, his hand pausing as the zipper reached the top. His eyes seemed to lock onto her mouth, and for a brief moment, Becca thought he might kiss her.

Then his hand dropped to his side, and he let out a long breath as though he had been holding it. "Call me when you get home to let me know you're safe," he admonished in a husky tone.

"I will." Her feet didn't seem to want to move, but she forced herself toward the front door, one leaden step at a time. As she opened it, she turned to look over her shoulder at him one more time. "Thank you again for everything, Ethan. You really are the best friend I've ever had."

With that, she strode out onto the porch, quickly closing the door behind her, not giving him a chance to respond. She couldn't trust herself not to run back into his arms and plant on his lips the kiss that she had foolishly thought he was about to give her minutes before. She simply could not allow that to happen unless she was sure he felt the same way.

Ethan walked to the window. "You're welcome," he said softly, his breath fogging the glass as he watched Becca's retreating form traverse the sidewalk to her car and drive away. He closed his eyes and leaned his forehead against the cool pane as his unruly brain conjured thoughts of Becca's full mouth looming mere inches away. He'd wanted so badly to close that distance and press his lips to hers. It was only the vow he'd made to himself the night before to give her time to heal that kept him from doing exactly that.

Buddy's soft, fuzzy head nudged the hand that hung at Ethan's side. Ethan looked down at the playful pooch as he rubbed the dog's head and scratched his ears. "One of these days, Buddy, she's going to be mine. I just need to keep telling myself to be patient for now, right?"

"Woof." Buddy answered the rhetorical question, breaking some of Ethan's tension and making him smile.

"Come on, boy. I need to get back to work so I don't go running after her and make a fool of myself."

Ethan headed back to his office with Buddy trotting happily behind him.

Twenty minutes later, Becca called to say she was home. Although he would have loved to talk with her for hours, Ethan purposely kept the conversation brief so as to not stir up too many lingering feelings. He hung up the phone and returned to perusing the documents in the folder.

His pen beat a rapid staccato beat on the desk blotter. Nothing he was reading seemed to make sense. With a huge sigh, he scrubbed a hand down his face and finally gave up on figuring it out. He glanced at the small clock on the corner of his desk. Nearly an hour had gone by since Becca had left, and he hadn't accomplished a thing.

Ethan swiveled his chair to gaze out the window overlooking the front yard. Everything was still damp, and some of the plants were drooping from last night's storm. His eyes were fixed on the scene outside, through he didn't really see it as he idly twirled a pencil between his fingers. Unable to take his own advice, he couldn't stop thinking about the possibility of Becca being pregnant. For her sake, he prayed she wasn't. He knew what he would do, though, if worst came to worst and she decided to go through with it. He'd offer to marry her and raise the child as his own. Becca deserved all the love and security her mother never had.

With that issue settled in his mind, his thoughts turned to a more immediate concern–the forgotten sweater and bracelet. It was obvious from the look on Becca's face when she'd told him about them that both meant a great deal to her. Mental images of the lost sweater and bracelet merged with images of Becca last night, broken and distraught. Her words as she recounted Jay's awful betrayal reverberated through his mind. The lying, cheating, manipulative bastard.

Anger surged through Ethan's body. The pencil in his hand suddenly snapped, bringing him out of his reverie.

Tossing the broken pieces on his desk, Ethan grabbed the phone and dialed the one person he knew who might be able to give him what he wanted–justice.

A pleasant female voice answered his call. "Davis Security."

"Hi, Anna. This is Ethan Montgomery. May I speak with Todd, please?"

"Certainly, Mr. Montgomery. Just one moment."

Within seconds the jovial voice of his friend came on the line. "Hey, Ethan. How're you doing? You have some more employee background checks for me to run?"

"Actually, Todd, this isn't a business call."

Ethan hesitated a moment before revealing his reason for contacting the investigator. Todd Davis had been Ethan's closest male friend since college, where they'd met at the gym. They hit it off almost immediately, and had been workout buddies ever since. When

Todd started his firm, Ethan contracted with him to handle all the security and employee background checks for Pet Emporium. He knew that he could trust Todd to keep his request confidential.

"Or maybe I should clarify that. This is *personal* business," he added.

"Sounds serious. What's up?" Todd asked in a concerned tone.

"I want you to see if you can dig up any dirt on a guy named Jay Cavanaugh."

"So what'd this guy do to get on your bad side?"

"Let's just say he hurt a good friend of mine, and I think it's about time someone taught him a lesson."

"You hardly ever ask me for anything personal, and never something like this. A little dark for you, isn't it, Ethan?"

"You don't understand, Todd. This guy really pissed me off," Ethan ground out through gritted teeth. "I've had a bad feeling about him for months. If I'd had any sense, I would have had you check him out a long time ago."

"So you're feeling guilty, and you think what this Jay guy did is somehow your fault." It was more a statement than a question.

Todd's astute observation momentarily took Ethan aback. If he was completely honest, he was almost as angry with himself as he was with Jay. He heaved a sigh before answering. "All I know is that if I'd had you check him out before, she might not be in this mess."

"She? Hmm... So this is about a woman, huh?"

"I'm not jealous, if that's what you're thinking," Ethan replied sharply. "Hell, you ought to know me better than that, Todd."

"Hey, easy, man. I was just yanking your chain. This girl, though. Wouldn't happen to be Becca Anderson, would it?"

"What makes you think that?" Ethan replied hesitantly.

"C'mon, Ethan. I'm an investigator. Logical, deductive reasoning is my business. I don't think this is about protecting your sister, or you'd have told me up front. And you said *friend* anyway. Bottom line...you don't have any other female friends you'd go to this much trouble for." Todd paused to take a breath, then added in an undertone, "Not to mention you've been making pathetic puppy dog eyes at that girl since you met her."

"I do not make puppy dog eyes at her!" Ethan shot back.

"Uh-huh." Todd grunted skeptically. "You keep telling yourself that. You've barely even dated another woman since Becca came along."

"I've been out with other women."

Todd scoffed at that comment. "Yeah, maybe dinner or a movie, but when's the last time you slept with one?"

"I don't know," Ethan answered irritably. "A year, maybe? You know I don't sleep around anyway, so what's your point?"

"A year?" Todd's voice went up an octave, and Ethan could imagine his eyes nearly popping out of his head. Todd had always been popular with the ladies, and temperance–at least as far as they were concerned–had never been one of his better virtues. "What are you, some kind of saint?" Now Ethan was sure his friend's eyes were rolling. "You just made my point for me. It's obvious you want Becca in a *bad* way, so what are you waiting for? Get that girl in your bed and show her what she's been missing."

When Ethan didn't answer right away, Todd must have realized his mistake. "Hey, I'm sorry, man. You not putting the moves on her has something to do with this guy you want me to check out, doesn't it?"

"Yeah," Ethan answered soberly. He rubbed his temple, feeling a headache coming on. "Believe it or not, I had the woman of my dreams in my bed last night, but after what she'd been through, there's no way I could have seduced her. I wouldn't have been able to live with myself."

"What happened? He didn't-?"

"No, but it was nearly as bad." Leaving out the more personal details of Becca's ordeal, Ethan filled his friend in on how Jay had taken cruel advantage of her vulnerable state to seduce her just so he could win an idiotic bet, and how he had another woman–probably multiple women–on the side.

Todd whistled through his teeth. "Now that's just cold, man. I'm no Prince Charming like you, Ethan, but I don't hold with guys pulling that kind of shit with a lady. This Jay sounds like a real piece of work."

"That he is, my friend. That he is."

"Well, I'm behind you one hundred percent. Anything you need, just let me know. Give me a few hours, and I'll see if I can pull up anything on the bastard."

"Thanks. I owe you one, buddy."

"You don't owe me anything except a promise. If I find something, you can't use it to do anything illegal."

"Like I said before, you should know me better than that."

Todd chuckled. "OK then, I'll get on this right away. Oh, and Ethan, for what it's worth, I think Becca's a great girl. If I were the settling down type, I might even ask her out myself. But since I'm not," he was quick to add, "I'll be expecting a wedding invitation."

"Yeah, well, I'd like to oblige you there, pal, but it might be a long wait." Ethan laughed without mirth. "Right now, I think Becca needs me as her friend."

"Eeh... I'm a patient man. If I were to lay odds, I'd say something is gonna go down between you two within the next year. Tops. And for Little Ethan's sake, it better be sooner rather than later." Todd chuckled loudly.

This time Ethan was the one shaking his head at his friend's joke, but he couldn't help but laugh right along with him.

Chapter 4

Three hours later, Ethan sped through the streets of Phoenix in his Corvette, itching for a confrontation with Jay. Less than half an hour ago, Todd had arrived at Ethan's door bearing the information he'd been looking for, leaving him stunned, appalled, and more than ready to have it out with the low-life. When Todd saw how incensed the news had made his friend, he insisted upon accompanying him to Jay's apartment to keep Ethan out of trouble.

"Ah, Ethan, could you slow down a little?" In the passenger seat, Todd gripped the dashboard, eyes wide open with a terrorized look on his rich mocha-skinned face. "I'm really not diggin' this whole race-car driver impersonation."

Ethan took a deep breath and eased up on the gas pedal. He glanced at Todd out of the corner of his eye in time to see his friend visibly relax.

"Sorry, man." Ethan sent an icy glance toward the manila folder laying on the console between them. "That information you found really has my blood boiling."

"I get it, Ethan. You feel like tearing this guy apart. But your anger won't do anybody any good if we don't get there in one piece. Not to mention you promised me earlier you wouldn't do anything stupid if I found something on the bastard."

"Fine. I'll drive at the speed limit," Ethan replied with reluctance.

"We also don't need Jay claiming that we're the bad guys, so swear to me that when we get there, no matter how much you feel like bashing his face in for what he did, you'll stick to our plan."

"Todd, you know I'm not a violent man. I've never been in a fight in my life. Unless you count me pushing Tommy Jenkins in kindergarten. But he had it coming for stealing my Twinkie at lunch." The corner of Ethan's mouth quirked up at the memory.

"Yeah, well, a Twinkie is one thing, but you've never had a woman who's got you tied up in knots involved before."

"I know the plan, Todd. I keep him busy talking while you search the place for Becca's stuff. If that doesn't work, we try a little light blackmail." Ethan shook his head. "Only you could come up with a term like that, my friend."

"Hey, he doesn't know we already fried his ass with what's in that folder, so it's not real blackmail."

"Uh-huh," Ethan replied skeptically.

"Well, he played head games with your girl, Becca, all along. The way I see it, we're playing a different game to help her out and then giving the creep what he deserves."

"Works for me," Ethan said with a lopsided grin.

The two friends drove the rest of the way in silence until Ethan turned into an apartment complex near the college campus. He pulled over to the directory, looking for the location of Apartment #160.

After spotting it, he wound around the parking lot and came to a stop in front of a two-story cream stucco building that was identical to all the others around it.

The pair got out and walked to the door. Ethan carried the folder, nervously tapping it against his leg as he knocked. While they waited for a response, Ethan looked at Todd. An unspoken agreement passed between them. Ethan nodded almost imperceptibly to acknowledge that he was still on board with Todd's plan.

Just then, the door opened and the man they were looking for appeared in the portal. "Hey, Montgomery." Jay's slightly slurred speech, and an open bottle of beer in his hand, evidenced the fact that he was already drunk in the middle of the afternoon. "What do you want?" he asked, his lip curling with disdain.

"I think you have a pretty good idea why I'm here." Ethan looked over his shoulder with a meaningful glance. "But I'd rather not air our grievance in public. Can we come in?"

Jay motioned toward Todd with his beer bottle as he lazily leaned against the doorway with his free hand. "Who's he?"

Ethan's jaw began to tighten. "Todd Davis. He's a friend of mine."

Jay looked at Todd with a sneer and then took a swallow from the bottle in his hand. "Lemme guess. Little Miss Sunshine came crying to her bestie about how the Big Bad Wolf popped her cherry, and now you're bringing your bestie to help beat the shit out of me for it." Jay laughed like he'd made some great joke. "I didn't think you had it in you, Montgomery."

Obviously, Jay was no longer interested in playing the devastating charmer who could get anything he wanted. The real guy behind the facade had come out to play hardball.

Ethan was already losing patience and was about ready to throttle the idiot when Todd spoke up. "Look Cavanaugh, we're not here to beat you up." Todd sighed and then continued in his best professional tone. "Ms. Anderson left some of her things here last night, and we've come to collect them. That's all. We don't want any trouble. Now could we please come in and discuss this like civilized adults?"

"Ms. Anderson?" Jay snickered. "What are you, a lawyer or something?"

Todd rolled his eyes heavenward. "No, I'm not a lawyer."

But you're going to need one when we're done with you, Ethan added silently.

Todd's eyes opened wide in question as he motioned a hand toward the apartment. "So can we talk about this?"

Jay looked them over again and, apparently deciding they weren't a threat after all, finally stepped aside. "Whatever," he muttered, taking another swig of beer and backing into the apartment.

Ethan and Todd entered the living room, closing the door behind them. Ethan took a quick look around to see if he could spot Becca's sweater or bracelet, but all he saw was a worn brown sofa and a scarred coffee table strewn with empty beer bottles and pizza boxes. The muted television in front of them was tuned to a football game.

Jay interrupted Ethan's perusal of the room. "So what exactly are you two lookin' for?" he slurred.

"Becca left her favorite sweater and her charm bracelet here last night." Ethan tried to keep his voice civil, even though his body tensed. "All we want to do is get them back."

Jay seemed to consider Ethan's request for a moment, then replied, "Give me one good reason why I should help you guys. I never liked you, Montgomery."

At that remark, Ethan's temper snapped. "Trust me, pal, the feeling is mutual. The only reason you never liked me is because I was a threat to your little scheme. I always knew there was something off about you." He gestured toward Jay with the folder that was still in his hand. "Becca was supposed to be to your girlfriend, but you treated her like shit. How can you even live with yourself after taking advantage of a woman in such a vulnerable state?"

Out of the corner of his eye, Ethan saw Todd edging past Jay toward the bedroom. He knew he had to keep Jay distracted. He also knew that if the idiot kept saying moronic things, in Ethan's current state, he would have no trouble at all *distracting* the guy.

"If Little Miss Perfect hadn't been so wrapped up in saving herself for Mr. Right, I would have fucked her a long time ago," Jay said.

Yup, looked like he was going to continue his boneheaded streak.

"What is up with you, man?" Ethan asked. "Do you have some virgin fetish that compels you to go around having sex with every innocent woman you meet?" His lip twisted in disgust, not sure he really wanted an answer to that question.

"Yeah, well," Jay drawled, "I gotta admit there is something about being the first to stake a claim. Kinda makes me feel powerful, you know." Jay flexed his biceps for emphasis before continuing, "Not to mention they never forget their first. Believe it or not, Montgomery, some virgins can be real sex kittens. But then there're the ones who are too scared and uptight to be a really fun lay. The only reason I do them is for the dough. No one ever seems to believe that I can charm any girl into spreadin' her legs for me even if she's never done it for anyone else before, and I love taking my friends' money. I've won thousands off them because I always win the bet," Jay finished with an evil chuckle.

Ethan's stomach was beginning to roil, and he felt a headache coming on. He pinched the bridge of his nose and took a deep breath in an attempt to calm himself, then glanced down at the folder. Based on the evidence Todd had found, he was sure he already knew the answer, but he was going to ask the question anyway. "How the hell do you prove that you actually did it, that it's not just talk? Surely your friends wouldn't pay up on your word alone."

"How do you think?" Jay asked, then added in an almost conspiratorial whisper, "I videotape it."

"Becca would never have consented to being recorded," Ethan ground out vehemently through clenched teeth.

"Who said I asked?" Jay replied with a wicked smile.

This brief exchange confirmed Ethan's worst suspicions, leaving his control rapidly slipping away. His free hand balled into a tight fist as he struggled against a burning need to beat the crap out of this guy. When he was about to lose it, Ethan spotted Todd over Jay's left shoulder, making subtle hand motions while mouthing the words, "Calm down. I'm on it. Keep him talking."

Jay looked around. "By the way, what happened to your friend?"

"Just lookin' for the bathroom," Todd piped up with a bright smile. "Oh, it's right there." He let out a self-deprecating laugh as though he'd just now noticed it. "Do you mind?"

"Whatever."

Ethan watched Todd pretend to head for the bathroom, but as Jay turned back around, Todd darted across the hallway into what Ethan assumed was the bedroom instead.

Having been momentarily distracted, Ethan's anger had calmed a little, but it still bubbled just beneath the surface. He was pretty sure that what Jay had confessed to was illegal, which certainly added an interesting new dimension to the whole situation. Ethan desperately wanted to call Jay on the mat for what he'd done, but now his first priority had to be getting the recording back to prevent Becca any further embarrassment.

Ethan swallowed the lump that was rising in his throat before asking, "So, uh, what do you do with these tapes after your buddies pay up?"

Jay's evil grin returned. With his tongue apparently loosened by the large amount of alcohol he'd consumed, he appeared eager to boast some more. "See now, that's the beauty of it all. I get paid twice."

"You're peddling amateur porn," Ethan stated in a hard tone. He didn't have to ask, because Todd had already discovered the website registered in Jay's name.

"Maybe," Jay said, drawing out the word. "You know, I'm starting to sense an opportunity here. See, you wouldn't be here if you didn't care about the little bitch, so my guess is you don't want her sex tape going up on my website. I hear you're loaded. Soooo, how about you fork over–oh, say a hundred grand–and maybe I'll consider keeping your girlfriend's *indiscretion* under wraps."

Ethan really thought he was going to be sick now. He had more than enough money to cover what Jay was asking for, and a part of him would have paid any amount to ensure Becca's protection. The other more rational part knew it would be like letting Jay get away with murder.

As Ethan considered his options, Jay continued to goad him. "Yeah, that Becky of yours is a wild one. If I were you, I wouldn't want this to get out to the whole world. Everyone and their dog would come sniffing around that little firecracker. I had her screaming inside of two minutes."

Ethan dropped the folder and closed the distance between them in two long strides. He grabbed a fistful of Jay's shirt, slamming him into the wall and pinning him there with his left forearm. His right fist pulled back poised to strike. He bared his teeth in a feral snarl as he ground out through clenched teeth, "She was screaming in pain, you son of a bitch."

Before Ethan could take his first punch, Todd's voice penetrated his anger. "Ethan! Let him go, man! That piece of trash isn't worth an assault charge."

"You sure about that?" Ethan asked. His fierce gaze bored into Jay, and every muscle in his body was still tensed for a fight.

Todd appeared in his peripheral vision. "Yeah, I'm sure. I got everything we came here for, and then some."

Without letting Jay go, Ethan glanced toward his friend. A white ladies' sweater was draped over his shoulder. A charm bracelet dangled from the fingertips of his left hand, while he held up a video camera in his right.

"Even the video?"

Todd opened a small compartment in the camera and removed the tiny memory card, holding it up with two fingers. "Got it right here, man. Let's get out of here." Leaving the camera on the end table, Todd headed for the door.

Ethan finally released a shocked Jay with a final shove for emphasis. He picked up the manila folder from the floor where it had fallen during the fray.

"Hey, you can't take my video card!" Jay had the audacity to shout at Todd's back. "That's stealing!"

Todd spun around with his hands flung out to his sides, a look of utter disbelief on his face. "Are you a complete idiot, man? Who do you think you are, talking about unlawful acts?" Todd grabbed the folder from Ethan and waved it in Jay's face. "You asked me earlier what I am. Well, I'm a private investigator, and it didn't take but a couple hours of work for me to find out you're wanted in Alabama for having sex with an underage girl two years ago."

"She said she was eighteen."

"Tell it to the cops, man. Although I doubt they'll listen, seeing that we uncovered an illegal porn ring on top of it, and you just tried to blackmail my friend here. I called a friend of mine in the DA's office and informed him of your *activities*, so you are in some deep shit. If I were you, I'd be thanking me for taking your memory card, because that might be one less charge against you. Not that it'll matter much," Todd added with a shake of his head as he turned toward the door.

With a growl, Jay lunged at Todd's back. Ethan stepped between them just in time to block the empty beer bottle Jay was swinging at Todd's head. Then he landed a right to Jay's stomach, followed by a left to his face.

Still half drunk, Jay toppled backwards into the bar, rubbing his jaw while eyeing Ethan with a menacing look. "You've ruined my life, you bastard," he snarled before launching himself at Ethan again.

Ethan ducked Jay's punch and drove him back into the wall with a shoulder to the chest before landing a couple more well-placed blows.

Grabbing Jay by the collar of his shirt, Ethan got within inches of his face before grinding out his reply. "You've done a good job of that all on your own, and it's exactly what you deserve for messing with Becca's life and the lives of all those other girls."

With that, Ethan released Jay, who promptly slumped to the floor. Still breathing hard from anger and exertion, Ethan turned on his heel and followed Todd to his vehicle.

Once outside, Ethan leaned against the car. What he'd told Todd about never having been in a real fight was true, but now his body was buzzing like a live wire. He could almost sense the adrenaline coursing through his veins from both the physical altercation and having to listen to Jay spout off about Becca the way he had. He also felt some measure of relief at the thought of having been able to get a little justice for Becca, though he knew it would be a while before he was able to calm down.

A couple of unmarked police cars pulled into the apartment complex. Undoubtedly, they had been sent by Todd's friend. Todd patted Ethan on the shoulder as he handed over the sweater, bracelet and memory card. "I better go talk to these guys. You wait here."

Ethan pocketed the bracelet and memory card. He opened the car door and tossed the sweater in the back before sitting down in the driver's seat. It seemed like an eternity passed while Todd conversed with the officers and then spent some time on his cell phone. The entire time, Ethan prayed that he wouldn't have to turn over the memory card. He knew it would kill Becca to be exposed like that.

Finally, Todd returned.

Ethan rose and pulled his keys out of his pocket. As he handed them to Todd, they jangled in a pretty good imitation of his frayed nerves. "I think you'd better drive."

"No problem, man." As Ethan circled the car to the other side, Todd spoke over the top of the vehicle. "I talked with Blake, my assistant DA friend. I had no choice but to tell him about what went down here. He thinks he has more than enough to put the son of a bitch away without involving Becca, but no guarantees. He might still need to take a look at the memory card we snagged."

Ethan nodded morosely as he climbed into the passenger seat.

After Todd was seated behind the wheel, he turned to Ethan with a mischievous glint in his eyes. "I thought I told you to stay out of trouble."

"As I recall, you told me not to do anything stupid. I acted in self-defense, so I didn't break my promise."

Todd turned the key in the ignition, revving the engine of the sports car to life. "Yeah, well, you have a point. Blake assured me you won't have any trouble from the cops." Todd paused for a moment before his mouth widened into a grin that showed his white teeth. "But I bet you can't say you didn't enjoy it."

Ethan glanced at Todd from the corner of his eye and gave him a weak smile. "Nope. Because that would be lying, which is something I don't do."

The teasing over, Ethan once again felt the gravity of the situation weighing on his shoulders. He allowed his head to fall back onto the headrest and stared out the windshield with unseeing eyes. He thought of the tiny chip in his pocket. He knew he had to break the news to Becca in case the DA needed her testimony to prosecute Jay for filming her without consent, but it was not something he was looking forward to. He could hardly bear the thought of bringing her more pain.

"You're positive the memory card is the one with Becca on it?" he asked Todd.

Todd's deep sigh spoke volumes. "Yeah...and before you ask, I didn't watch the whole thing, just enough to be certain it was the right one."

Ethan glanced over at Todd with a mirthless smile. "I didn't think you would, buddy."

"So what are you going to do?"

Ethan shook his head uncertainly. "I'll have to tell Becca the truth. She's bound to hear it from someone, and I'd rather it be me." He swallowed hard and blinked back the sting in his eyes caused by the thought of having to hurt her more. Fortunately, for the moment at least, he possessed the only evidence of what had happened. "I hope she doesn't have to testify. I hate to think of what it might do to her."

"I think that girl is stronger than you're giving her credit for," Todd replied.

"I hope you're right, but you didn't see her last night."

As Todd backed out of the parking space, Ethan watched as a handcuffed Jay was led to a police cruiser. At least the bastard was going to get what he deserved.

* * * * *

Ethan stood at the door of Becca's apartment, desperately wishing he was somewhere else.

No. That wasn't entirely true. He loved being with Becca. He just didn't like being the bearer of bad news. He knew that it would be far better coming from him than from a total stranger though, so he'd been psyching himself up for the revelation all the way over.

Still, he'd been there for nearly ten minutes and had raised his hand to knock more than once, only to allow it to drop to his side again.

"So are you going to stand on Rebecca's doorstep all night, or are you going to knock?"

Ethan jumped at the sound of the voice and turned around to find Becca's little white-haired neighbor standing in the doorway of her own apartment across the sidewalk.

"Sorry, dear. I didn't mean to startle you," she said.

"That's all right, Mrs. Moffat."

"Oh, please, call me Edna."

"All right. How are you this evening?" he politely inquired.

"I'm perfectly fine, but you don't look so good. It seems to me you're having a really difficult time making up your mind about something."

Ethan sighed with resignation. "Yeah, well, I guess I am."

"Care to talk about it? Sometimes sharing your problems can help you find the right answer."

"No!"

Edna raised her brow at his terse answer.

He crossed the sidewalk to Edna's porch to keep their conversation more private. "I'm sorry. It's something really personal, and I'm not at liberty to talk about it. Let's just say I have some bad news to deliver, and I'm not looking forward to it."

"Oh dear!" Edna exclaimed. "I do hope it's not too terrible. Rebecca certainly has had more than her share of that this week."

"More than you know, I think. That's what makes this so hard."

"Does it have anything to do with that no-account ex-boyfriend of hers? I knew that weasel was trouble the minute I laid eyes on him."

Ethan's eyes widened in surprise. "It's nice to know I wasn't the only one who thought that."

Edna's face darkened. "Ooh, when I think of what he did to that sweet girl, it makes me furious. His actions are completely unforgivable. I'd love to go over there and give him a piece of my mind. And maybe a good swift kick you-know-where too," she added with an emphatic nod of her graying head.

Ethan tried to fight back a smile at the feisty old lady's words, but it wasn't long before the seriousness of the situation gripped him once more. "So she told you about last night?"

Edna nodded gravely. "I'm so glad she trusted me enough to share her burden. With her mother gone, she needs all the support she can get. And I think you and I are it for now."

"Becca knows that I'll always be there when she needs me. And I'm glad that she's found a friend in you too." He paused a few seconds, debating how much to tell her. "If it makes you feel any better, I took care of that son of a—um, sorry," he finished sheepishly.

Edna waved her hand dismissively. "Don't apologize, young man. I've heard far worse than that in my lifetime. It's not like I haven't thought it too. So did you kick him where it counts?" she asked enthusiastically with a wicked gleam in her eyes.

This time Ethan couldn't hold back a grin. "Not exactly. But he's in a lot of trouble with the police right now. Oh, and I did get in a couple of good punches."

"Oh, good." The little woman's face lit up like a Christmas tree. "I'm so glad that somebody taught him a lesson on how to treat a lady." Even though her height barely reached Ethan's chest, she grabbed him around the neck and pulled him down to place a peck on his cheek. "You're my hero. Well, actually, you're Rebecca's hero, but you're a hero nonetheless," she declared while tapping his chest with her finger.

Barely recovered from nearly being pulled off balance by Edna's exuberance, Ethan now felt his face heating at her compliment. He cleared his throat. "I don't know about that."

"Well, I do. You're so much like my Freddie. Always looking out for a girl and being a perfect gentleman," she said wistfully. She leaned toward him, adding in a playful whisper, "If I wasn't old enough to be your grandmother, I'd snap you up myself."

Ethan hadn't thought his cheeks could get any redder, and he had no idea how to respond to that comment. Thankfully, he didn't have to.

"Ethan?" A sweet voice from behind him filled the silence and his senses. "I thought I heard your voice. What are you doing here?"

Ethan turned to see Becca silhouetted in her own doorway. The light behind her gleamed like a halo against her honey-colored hair, which spilled in waves over her shoulders, bringing back memories of what it had felt like to have his hands in it last night. If he hadn't already been struck mute by Edna's comment, the angelic sight before him most certainly would have done the trick.

Ethan weakly raised his hand in a pathetic little wave, and finally found his voice. "Hey. I'll be over in a minute."

His heart clenched at the sweet smile she gave him, making him scream inside at the unfairness of having to bring more pain to this beautiful woman's life. He only wanted to see joy and happiness mirrored in her lovely blue eyes. But that wasn't meant to be. At least not tonight.

Edna must have sensed the disquiet within him, because he felt her hand come to rest lightly on his forearm. "You're a good man, Ethan. Whatever it is you came here to tell her, I know you'll find the words, and you'll do right by her. Go on," she finished softly, giving him a little nudge forward.

Ethan glanced back. He placed his hand over hers and gently squeezed. "Thanks, Edna," he said, using her given name for the first time.

It must have pleased her, because she smiled brightly at him. Then she shrugged. "For what?"

"For believing in me."

With that, he released her hand, and after giving her a small smile, he retraced his steps to the other side of walkway, praying that her faith in him was not ill-placed.

"Sorry about that." Ethan smiled contritely at Becca. He looked back over his shoulder, but the neighbor lady had already vanished. "I came to see you, but Edna kind of waylaid me," he explained, gesturing lamely in the direction of her apartment.

Becca's lips curved sweetly. "She has a way of doing that."

Ethan noticed that her hands had been clasping her bare arms against the nighttime chill since she came outside. "You look cold. Maybe we should go inside."

"Oh!" Becca startled. "Of course. Look at me daydreaming." She stepped aside to allow him to pass before closing the door behind them. As she turned back around to face him, her eyes caught on the white fabric draped over his left hand. She gasped in surprise. "Is that my...?"

The rest of her question dangled in the air between them as Ethan handed her the sweater. She held it up, looking at it for a moment, then hugged it to her chest as though her mother still wore it.

"Oh..." Ethan dipped his hand into his jeans pocket. When he pulled it out, he extended it toward her. "...And this too."

Becca looked up to see her charm bracelet resting in his palm and gathered it up as though it were the most precious jewel. She allowed it to slide over her fingers, the charms tinkling in the silence. The look on her face was one of awestruck wonder. "Ethan, how did you...? Never mind. It doesn't matter."

With that, she closed the distance between them, throwing her arms around his neck and placing a soft kiss on his cheek.

Ethan's arms automatically wrapped around her, drawing her into a snug embrace. His head dropped down close to hers, and he breathed deeply, drinking in the fruity aroma of her shampoo and that feminine scent that was uniquely Becca.

She slowly pulled away, and he reluctantly released her. Becca's eyes sparkled with unshed tears. "Thank you so much, Ethan."

Ethan swallowed hard around the lump that had formed in his throat. "You may not want to thank me yet."

Becca's brow drew down into a frown. "These things mean so much to me. I thought I'd never see them again, and yet somehow you brought them back. Why would I not be grateful?"

"Because...because I brought something else that... God, this is so hard."

"Ethan, what's wrong?"

"I...I found out something about Jay that affects you. We need to talk." He gestured toward the sofa. "Why don't we sit down?"

"OK." Her eyes filled with concern, Becca laid her things on the coffee table before seating herself on the couch next to Miss Kitty, her black-and-white long-haired cat. "Ethan, you're really worrying me."

"I'm sorry, Becca," Ethan apologized as he sat down beside her. "I don't want to cause you any more distress, but it seems there's no way not to. I guess I just need to man up and get it out in the open so we can deal with it."

Ethan gently took Becca's hand from where she had been absently stroking her pet's silky fur. He clasped it tightly in his own, rubbing comforting circles on the back with his thumb as he related the events of the afternoon to her.

When he finished, Becca pulled her hand out of his. Her arms crossed defensively over her middle, and she turned her face away. Even still, Ethan could see her cheeks were stained crimson and she was fighting back tears.

Ethan moved Miss Kitty to his other side and scooted closer to Becca, gathering her into his arms. He drew her around to face him and pulled her head down onto his shoulder.

With that, the floodgates opened. Deep sobs racked her body as Ethan held her close for what seemed like a lifetime. Gradually, she quieted, but Ethan continued to caress her back and her arm that rested on his chest, hoping that he was providing some measure of comfort.

"Did you...watch it?" She stumbled over her words that were barely above a whisper.

"The recording?"

Becca nodded against his chest.

Ethan pulled far enough away to see her, and lifted her face to his. She was having a hard time maintaining eye contact and seemed to be trying to look anywhere but right at him. He brushed a lock of tear-damp hair away from her face. With firm but gentle fingers, he held her chin in place as he locked his eyes with hers, challenging her not to look away this time.

"What kind of guy do you think I am?" he asked with a touch of anger in his voice. "Of course I didn't watch it."

"I'm sorry. I didn't mean to question your integrity. It's just... How do you know it's the right memory card?"

"Todd–"

"Todd watched it?" Becca virtually shrieked in horror at the thought.

"Shh..." Ethan placed his finger on her lips, imploring her with his eyes to hear him out. His patience was rewarded when she seemed to calm a little. "He only watched enough to know he had the right one. He wouldn't invade your privacy like that either."

Becca's shoulders slumped, perhaps with relief, although her face bore the same defeated look she'd had when she came to him the night before. "How could he do this to me?" She shook her head. "How could he do it to those other girls?"

"I don't know, Becca." Ethan shook his own head in a form of agreement. "I don't think I'll ever understand. I guess some people get their kicks out of screwing with other people's lives."

Becca's head dropped back down to Ethan's shoulder.

He continued to stroke her back and hair comfortingly for several long minutes. Knowing there was one more thing that needed to be settled, he finally broke the silence. "Becca, there's something else I need to discuss with you."

Her head jerked up, and she pinned him with a worried look. "What?"

More than anything, Ethan hated seeing the apprehension in her eyes, and tried once again to reassure her by squeezing the hand that rested against his chest before he spoke. "It's OK. I don't have any more terrible revelations. Just something you need to know."

"What's that?"

"Once I had the memory card in my possession, my first inclination was to destroy it. Since Todd's friend in the DA's office already knew about it, I might have been breaking the law. Still, I would have done it to protect you."

"Oh, Ethan. It's sweet of you to want to do that, but I couldn't bear the thought of you being in jail because of me."

"I thought of that, and I also realized to destroy it would be taking away a very personal decision from you. You've had enough taken away from you in the last few days, and I didn't want to add to the list. You have a choice, either to take the recording and your story to the DA and add your voice to the prosecution against Jay or, if you prefer, wait and see what happens. Todd's friend said that he probably had enough on Jay to keep you out of it, but no guarantees. If you talk to him up front, it might give him more ammunition against Jay. But it's completely up to you, Becca."

Becca's eyes darkened as her gaze dropped to their joined hands, and her body stiffened. It was abundantly clear to Ethan that she was struggling with herself over what to do. He wished with all his heart that he could fight that battle for her, but he knew the decision had to be hers and hers alone.

After what seemed like an eternity, Becca finally spoke, her gaze still directed downward. "You said there was plenty of other evidence against Jay. Other girls he taped without their permission. And the website. Plus the prior charges with the underage girl?"

Ethan nodded in reply. "Yeah."

Becca bit her lip as she contemplated that. "So he's probably going to jail with or without my testimony, right?"

"Most likely," Ethan answered softly.

The silence following his near-whispered response was deafening. Ethan listened to the ticking of his watch as it marked time. It seemed like hours before Becca responded, even though mere minutes had passed.

"I hate walking away from injustice when I know there's something I could do about it, and I feel like a coward for even saying this, but..." She hesitated, then finally lifted her eyes to his again. "I don't know if I have the strength to fight this battle," she finished in a choked whisper. Becca swallowed hard before continuing in a stronger voice. "I just want the nightmare of the last couple of days to be over so I can move on with my life. I'm not a horrible person for not standing up to him, am I?"

Ethan reached up to cup the side of her face. "Becca, you couldn't be a horrible person if you tried. And I don't think you're a coward either. You've been through more than anyone should be asked to deal with in a very short time. In all honesty, you're one of the strongest people I know. Not many young women would have given up their dream to take care of their mom the way you did. That took a lot out of you, both physically and emotionally. Now it's time for you to rest and take care of yourself. Let someone else fight the battle this time."

A rueful smile curled Becca's lips as her soft blue eyes locked with his. "You always seem to understand me and know how to make me feel better. And if the DA does need me, it'll be hard, but I'll do it."

"If it does come to that, I'll be right by your side, Becca. I'll always be here for you."

Becca wrapped her arms around him, squeezing tight, and buried her face in his neck. "I know."

Her warm breath whispered across his skin in a tingling embrace. Ethan closed his eyes and once again inhaled the fruity scent of her hair. His arm tightened around her waist. Becca may have decided not to fight the battle with Jay unless necessary, but his own battle with his feelings for her was far from over. Even though his bodily desires were trying to sabotage his plan, Ethan's commitment to allowing Becca the time she needed to heal from this betrayal and the grief of losing her mother was as strong as ever. But it was going to be a very long wait indeed.

Chapter 5

It had been more than a month since that horrible night, and during that time Ethan had done everything he could think of to support Becca. As part of his plan, he'd insisted on starting bi-weekly "dates" with her, lunch every Tuesday and Movie Night every Friday.

It was Friday evening, and even though they'd only been apart three days, he could barely contain his eagerness to see her again. He swiftly changed in the private bathroom in his office, out of his business attire and into jeans and a t-shirt. Then he snuck out the back way so that no overeager, workaholic employees could delay him with questions.

Before heading to Becca's, he made a special trip to the mall to pick up some of her favorite candies from Rocky Mountain Chocolate Factory. On the way to her apartment, he thought back over the past month. Thank God, there had been no more nasty surprises. Becca had been overcome with relief when the pregnancy test came back negative and even more grateful when further tests confirmed that Jay hadn't given her any dreaded diseases. She didn't need any reminders of her unplanned and unfortunate sexual encounter with that bastard. Receiving the test results had been the first step in Becca finally beginning to heal, even though there were still times when hints of melancholy dulled her beautiful green eyes.

As Ethan pulled into the parking lot of Becca's apartment complex, anticipation thrummed through his veins. When he reached Becca's doorstep, he hid the bag of chocolates behind his back with one hand and knocked with the other. He didn't wait long before the object of his affection swung the portal open and stood before him, looking like a vision. His mouth went dry as he took in the sight of her. She wore a flirty tank top with a low neckline that showed off a bit of cleavage, and denim short shorts that fit her pert little bottom like a glove. Her feet were bare and her toenails were painted a pretty shade of pink that matched her fingernails. Her honey-colored hair hung loose around her shoulders in waves. The innocently sexy look already had his groin tightening. At this rate, he wouldn't be able to look at her all evening without giving himself away.

"What? Do I have something on my face?" Becca asked as her hands went to her cheeks, feeling for something amiss.

Ethan cleared his throat and stepped inside. "Um, no." He could barely form a coherent thought and searched his mind for a cover story. "Did you do something different with your hair?" he asked, hoping she wouldn't notice his discomfiture.

Becca reached up to tuck a strand behind her ear, which only served to increase his desire. His fingers itched to bury themselves in her thick, wavy locks.

"I had it trimmed today. Why?"

"Oh, um, it just looked different, that's all."

"Good different or bad different?"

"Good. Definitely good."

"Whew," she exclaimed. "You had me worried there for a minute." Her hand went to her breast in a gesture of relief.

The last thing Ethan needed was his attention being drawn to that tempting bit of bare cleavage showing above her top. He longed to dip his tongue into that sweet valley. He searched desperately for a distraction before he embarrassed himself by drooling, or worse, tenting his pants.

Finally, remembering the bag of chocolates still dangling from the hand behind his back, he pulled them out and handed them to Becca.

She gasped in surprise. "What's this for?"

He shrugged. "For being you."

She gave him a shy smile and blushed prettily. "Thank you, Ethan. That's really sweet of you, especially since I know you had to go out of your way to get them. I'll go put them in a dish so we can share during the movie."

She headed for the kitchen, and he followed behind, watching the sway of her hips and feeling like a lovesick puppy.

"Mmm... These smell delicious!" she exclaimed while daintily laying the candies out on a pretty flowered dish.

Ethan reached into a cupboard for glasses and poured them each a soda. "So are you coming to the animal shelter tomorrow?"

"Oh, definitely," she replied enthusiastically. "It's been so great working with the animals again. I wouldn't miss it."

"You know, there's something I've been meaning to ask you."

"What's that?" Becca threw over her shoulder as she bent to retrieve the big popcorn bowl from a lower cabinet.

Ethan looked away, trying to ignore the way the movement molded her shorts to her cute little rear. "Since you started volunteering at the shelter again, you seem more alive than I've seen you in over a year. I'm wondering if you've considered going back to your veterinary studies in the fall."

Becca wrapped the huge bowl in her arms and leaned back against the counter, sighing heavily. "I want to, but I don't even know if could get in again. You know what happened last year. I was all set to accept my admission to vet school and move to Colorado. A month later, I did a one-eighty and turned my back on all of it. I don't know if the school board will look very kindly on that. Not to mention you and Edna are all I have right now. I don't think I could handle being that far away from you two."

"You know, you wouldn't have to move away. There's a new vet school opening right here in the Valley. I even know someone on the school board and could put in a good word for you. Why don't you apply there?"

Becca shook her head. "I don't know, Ethan. It's not that I don't appreciate your offer, but I'd rather get in on my own merits if I can. Besides, I really can't afford it. I maxed out three credit cards to pay the medical bills my mom's insurance didn't cover. Right now, I'm working full-time and taking overtime whenever I can get it, and I can still only manage a little more than the minimum payments. With interest rates as exorbitant as they are, I'm already feeling like I'll never get them paid off. If I went back to vet school, I'd have to cut my hours at work way back." She turned to sit the bowl on the counter and opened another cupboard for a packet of popcorn. "On part-time wages, I'd be lucky to manage rent, utilities, and groceries."

"You know there's an easy solution to all that."

"Oh, really?"

"Let me help you."

Still facing away from him, Becca's shoulders sagged. "That's really sweet of you, Ethan, but I refuse to take advantage of the fact that I have a rich friend."

"You wouldn't be taking advantage," he insisted. "I'm offering. This is your dream we're talking about, Becca. I want to help you achieve it."

"I know." She turned around and raised her chin up a notch. "And I will. It might take me a little longer to get there by doing it my way, but I'll figure out something. Please understand, it's really important for me to do this on my own."

"But why should you have to when you have someone who's willing to help?"

"Look, I appreciate the offer, but I've always tried to live my life by my mom's example. She raised me all on her own with no help from anybody. If she could do it, so can I."

"But, Becca–"

She held up a hand to stop his protest. "No!"

Ethan sighed and rolled his eyes at her. "You're being stubborn."

She shrugged. "Maybe..." A hint of a smile curved her sensuous lips as she slid the packet of popcorn into the microwave.

"Fine, I'll let it go...for now," he finished emphatically.

He picked up the glasses and carried them to the living room. On the way there, he passed by Becca's desk, where he spotted a stack of bills.

A plan instantly began forming in his mind. After placing the sodas on the coffee table, he returned to the desk and quickly flipped through the pile, looking for credit-card bills. When he finally found what he was looking for, he grabbed a notepad and pen and rapidly wrote down the names and account numbers of the creditors. Upon finishing the task, Ethan put everything back in its place, tore off the sheet of notepaper, and stuffed it in his jeans pocket just as Becca emerged from the kitchen carrying bowls of buttery popcorn and pretzels.

"Here, let me help you with those."

As he took the bowls from her, he gave her his most innocent smile, but inside, he was unrepentantly scheming. He'd be damned before he'd allow Becca to give up on her dream when there was something he could do about it.

* * * * *

A week and a half later, Becca sat at a corner table for two in a little bistro on the ground floor of Ethan's office building. It had become the usual meeting place for their Tuesday lunch dates. A glance at her reflection in the window revealed an unhappy expression on her face. It was the result of having a bone to pick with her best friend.

She didn't have to wait long before the man in question appeared at the door of the restaurant. Ethan gave her a little wave before making his way through a small crowd of people waiting to order at the counter. He looked incredibly handsome in his dark-gray pinstripe suit, crisp white shirt, and a blue silk tie imprinted with tiny geckos. The sight of him softened her anger and made her pulse flutter.

Becca couldn't deny that her heart did a little flip-flop every time she saw Ethan. She always missed him terribly when they were apart and excitedly anticipated their standing get-togethers. Ever since that horrible night when Ethan had cared for her so tenderly, Becca knew she was falling in love with him.

But after what happened with Jay, she didn't quite trust her own judgment where men were concerned. It wasn't that she thought Ethan was anything like Jay. When compared, the two men weren't even in the same universe. It was more about her not wanting to jump headfirst into another relationship until she had some time to heal.

Ethan seated himself across the table and spread a napkin over his lap. "Thanks for ordering for us. It saves me a lot of time, and it will allow me to spend more time with you before that meeting I have to go to in an hour." He pointed to the sandwiches and fruit salads that were already on the table. "The food looks delicious."

Becca gave him a small smile before answering. "You're welcome."

Ethan took a bite of his sandwich, while Becca glanced out the window again at the pedestrians milling about on the sidewalk.

"Is something wrong, Becca?" Ethan's voice startled her gaze back to him. He wore a look of concern on his face. "You're awfully quiet, and you're not eating anything."

She took a deep breath. "Something very odd happened yesterday."

His full attention was on her. "Oh? What's that?" he asked politely.

"I went online to make payments on my credit cards, only to discover that all three had zero balances."

"Really?"

She could tell he was trying to look surprised, but in her estimation, it wasn't working.

"Yeah. When I called customer service, they said it had been paid by a mysterious anonymous donor. All three of them gave me the same story."

"Well, that's a good thing. Isn't it? I mean, now that you don't have to worry about those extra bills, you can finally get back to school and follow your passion."

Becca's brows drew down into a frown. "Don't you think it's a little strange that a mere week after we had a conversation about this very topic, those bills magically disappeared?"

Ethan cleared his throat and took a sip of his drink. "Maybe it's just a weird coincidence. These kind of things happen, you know."

Becca gave him a gimlet stare. "Cut the crap, Ethan. We both know you're the one who did it."

Ethan sighed deeply and took a larger gulp before answering. "So what if I did?"

Becca thought she detected a note of hurt in his voice that immediately made her soften.

"Look, it's not that I don't appreciate the gesture. Truth be told, it's kind of sweet." She gave him a slight smile before sobering again. "What bothers me is that you went behind my back after I told you how important it was to me to do this on my own."

Ethan shook his head. "I know you might be upset with me, but if you want an apology, you're not going to get one. I was only trying to look out for you, and I'll never be sorry about helping you achieve your dream. I stand by what I said the other night. You're being stubborn. Why wait, when you can do it now?"

Becca could tell she wasn't going to win this fight, and in all honesty, she wasn't that upset with him. "Fine, I see your point. It is nice not having to worry if I'll have enough money to pay everything each month. But I still insist on paying you back."

"Becca, you don't owe me anything."

"I always pay my debts, and I won't take no for an answer."

Ethan gave her an exasperated look and threw his hands up in defeat. "Do whatever you think is right, Becca, but know that in my mind, there is no debt."

"Noted," she answered with a curt nod of her head.

"So now that that's settled, can we enjoy our meal, or is there something else you want to argue with me about?"

Even though he sounded disgruntled, she could tell he was joking.

"Nope, I'm good."

She grinned at him. He shook his head in return, telling her without words how vexing she'd been, but at the same time his own lips curved into a hint of a smile.

"So now are you going to apply to that vet school like I suggested?" he asked before taking another bite of his sandwich.

Becca chewed a juicy strawberry before answering. "I don't know. I'm still not sure if I can afford it. Like I told you before, it'll be really tough trying to support myself on a part-time income, and there are no traditional scholarships. For the full four years, I'd be racking up close to ten times the amount of debt you just paid off."

A look of pure frustration clouded Ethan's face. "Becca, I really wish you would let me help you. I could pay for your education and support you so you wouldn't even have to work."

"Stop right there, Ethan! Just stop." When the people at the tables near them looked her way, Becca added more softly, "You've already done more than enough."

"But, Becca–"

"No!"

Ethan sighed. "I don't understand why you won't let me do this for you."

Becca hung her head. The most amazing man she'd ever know was sitting in front of her, offering her the moon. She knew she should be grateful, but damn it, her pride was all she had left. "I know you mean well, but I already told you this is something I need to do on my own."

"Fine." The sad, defeated look Ethan gave her nearly made her waver in her decision not to accept his help. "But will you at least look into applying to the school? You never know. Maybe with them being a new school and all, they might be able to offer some kind of financial assistance you haven't heard of before."

She nodded. "I guess it can't hurt to ask."

Ethan reached across the table and took her hand in his. Even though they'd been arguing, his touch sent a tingle up her arm that suffused her entire body. "I may not agree with your methods, but I want you to know I'll stand by you. I'm proud of you for doing this, Becca. I know your mom would be too. It was what she always wanted for you."

Becca grasped his hand tighter as her eyes misted. "I know. I promised her I would finish my degree." With a rueful smile, she added, "Thanks for giving me the push I needed to try again."

"No thanks necessary. I made a promise to you too, and I'm just trying to keep it."

* * * * *

Two hours later, Ethan sat at his desk in his twentieth-story high-rise office. He gazed out the window at the other tall buildings nearby and the vivid blue canvas of the sky, dotted with a smattering of puffy white clouds.

Why was Becca being so damn stubborn about allowing him to help her? He may have talked her into applying to vet school again, but at what cost? He simply couldn't bear the thought of her working herself into exhaustion or going hundreds of thousands of dollars in debt when he had more than enough money to cover it all.

Ah, Becca! His mind conjured a picture of her beautiful face, her sparkling blue eyes, high cheekbones, pert little nose, and full lips, all framed with those luscious honeyed locks. God, how he wanted to bury his hands in that thick, wavy hair and draw her mouth to his for a kiss. It would start out tender and gentle, gradually growing more passionate until their tongues tangled in wild abandon.

Aargh! Ethan shook his head in frustration, trying to clear the sensuous image from his head. It wasn't soon enough to prevent his half-hard manhood from pressing uncomfortably against his zipper. After readjusting himself, he propped his elbows on the desk and ran his fingers impatiently through his hair, willing his body back into submission.

Maybe Todd was right about it being too long since he'd been with a woman. But the only woman he wanted was Becca, and it was still too soon. Maybe after the whole Jay debacle was resolved and she didn't have that memory hanging over her head, he'd try easing into a romantic relationship with her. For now, he needed to keep his body under control and his mind on other things. It wasn't easy.

Ethan's thoughts traveled back to the problem that had started his current line of thinking. No matter how hard he tried, he couldn't come up with a rational explanation for why Becca was refusing his help, except that she was being obstinate and prideful. Based on her reaction to him paying off her credit cards, he knew she wouldn't be happy with him if he tried anything else. But damn it! He refused to idly sit by and watch the woman he loved struggle when he could prevent it. He would gladly risk her wrath, taking comfort in the knowledge that he was providing for her well-being.

With that decision made, he picked up the phone and dialed his friend, Mac, from the vet school board. Mere minutes after Mac's secretary put him on hold, the man himself came on the line. Ethan greeted him warmly and pleasantly conversed with his friend for the next half hour, outlining his plan to sponsor one student each year, someone who was facing difficult circumstances or who had a pressing financial need. He would foot the entire bill for their four-year education, including textbooks.

Of course, the only catch was that he already had a student in mind for the first year, which was why he offered a generous donation to the school itself as well. Not surprisingly, Mac was more than happy to oblige.

When their conversation ended, Ethan leaned back in his chair, relieved that Becca wouldn't have the worry of massive debt hanging over her head for years to come. If only he could convince her to let him help with her monthly living expenses, everything would be perfect. It was unfortunate that he couldn't pay those bills without her finding out, but he'd definitely be looking for any way he could possibly assist her without drawing her ire.

* * * * *

After her lunch with Ethan, Becca went straight to the vet school to apply before she lost her nerve. The admissions counselor walked Becca through all the paperwork and promised to help her find every possible financial-aid opportunity available if she was accepted. The woman was very understanding of the plight that had caused Becca to turn down her acceptance to the other vet school the previous year and said she would do everything she could to get Becca's application fast-tracked. Unfortunately though, there were no guarantees, as the class was filling up quickly. Becca returned home with a sense of satisfaction for having taken the first step but worried about what might happen if she were to be accepted.

* * * * *

Three weeks later, Ethan arrived at Becca's apartment for their Friday movie "date." She met him at the door wearing a huge smile.

"What has you in such a good mood?" he asked as he followed her inside and closed the door.

She all but skipped to her desk, where she snatched up a folded letter. She returned to him, still beaming and bouncing on her toes. She opened the letter and turned it to face him. "I got in!" She was practically squealing in delight.

He returned her smile. "Oh, Becca, that's wonderful! I knew you could do it!" He grabbed her around the waist, lifted her up and spun her around while she giggled uncontrollably. "Congratulations!"

When he placed her feet back on the floor, she leaned back in his embrace to look up at him. "And that's not even the best part."

"What could possibly be better than you being accepted to vet school?"

"Remember how you said that, with them being a new school, they might have new financial aid programs?"

"Yeah," he said, trying to sound nonchalant.

"Well, they have this wealthy donor who wants to sponsor a new student every year for their full tuition." Her eyes became bright with unshed tears. "And they picked me."

He'd known what she was going to say, but that didn't lessen the impact. The pure joy on her face nearly moved him to tears himself.

He wrapped her tightly in his arms again. "Becca, that's amazing. I'm so happy for you."

Suddenly, Becca's mood clouded, and she pulled away from him. "You didn't have anything to do with this, did you?"

Her question surprised him, although it shouldn't have. Becca was a very intelligent woman. He should have known she'd start putting the pieces together.

But she simply couldn't find out the truth. Not when she was so close to finally realizing her dream. He tried to school his features into impassivity, but he couldn't stop himself from frowning a little when he answered. "Why would you think that?"

She laughed mirthlessly. "Because I know you. Because it would be just like you to do something like this. Because you *did* something like this barely a month ago."

Becca was obviously miffed. Ethan hated lying to her, but it was for her own good. Thinking of how she would sabotage herself if she knew what he'd done made it easy to muster enough anger to seem believable. "Yeah, and we already talked about that. You made it very clear how you felt, and I respect your feelings even if I don't agree with them. I would never do anything to hurt you, Becca."

At least he wasn't telling a complete falsehood. Every word he'd spoken was true.

Even though he hadn't answered her question directly, she visibly relaxed. "I know you wouldn't, Ethan. I trust you." She smiled and gave him another hug.

As he held her in his arms, relief washed over him. Thank God she hadn't questioned him further. If she had any lingering doubts, she was keeping them to herself. He'd been so sure he was doing the right thing. If that was the case, why did he feel so damn guilty about it?

Chapter 6

The summer passed by in a blur, and before Becca knew it, she'd been back in vet school for nearly three months. As she stood at the server station at Milano's, rubbing her aching back and wiggling her sore feet, she was beginning to wonder if this had been such a good idea after all.

She was attending classes the equivalent of full-time hours during the day, keeping up a rigorous study schedule at night, and working Friday, Saturday, and Sunday evenings at the restaurant. She was extremely grateful that her manager had allowed her to keep the prime slots on the schedule when tips were the best, but even still, she was barely making enough to pay the rent and utilities, with only a little left over for groceries.

Added to that was the stress of still not knowing what was going to happen with Jay. Todd's friend, Blake, had tried diligently to work out a plea agreement, but Jay adamantly refused to accept it, and his case had finally gone to trial last week. Although Blake was still planning to keep Becca out of it, he hadn't ruled out calling her as a surprise witness for the prosecution if things went south at the last minute. She shuddered at the thought that she might still have to give him that horrid sex tape.

Not to mention she still missed her mom terribly.

Everything put together had quite simply left her physically and emotionally spent. She had no idea how she was going to weather four years of this, although the thought of all the sacrifices her mom had made in her life gave Becca a little more strength to keep going. Then there was Ethan, her ever-present cheerleader on the sidelines. That thought brightened her mood a little, but she could barely manage to quirk one corner of her mouth. She was simply too tired for anything more.

As Becca massaged a knot in her shoulder, her co-worker, Rhonda, joined her in the servers' alcove. While entering her order into the computer, the other woman glanced at Becca. "You look beat, sweetie."

Becca picked up a pitcher and started filling water glasses. "Yeah, I am. I'm not used to working after school, except on Fridays, and at least then I don't have class the next morning. It's been a long day."

"Aw," Rhonda crooned in commiseration. "It was really sweet of you to fill in for Marcia while she's sick."

Becca shrugged. "I need the money."

Rhonda turned around and gave her a sympathetic look. "Well, I hate to be the bearer of bad news, but you've got customers at table Twelve."

"Why is that bad news?" Becca asked suspiciously.

"Because Candy, the hostess, told me the blond bimbo she seated there is the demanding type."

Becca's shoulders slumped. "Great!" She sighed. "That's all I need tonight."

"I'm sorry, sweetie." Rhonda elbowed her in the side and leaned in to whisper conspiratorially. "I got a look at the guy who's with her, and at least you'll have some nice eye candy to look at."

Becca finally managed a smile, but despite the prospect of a handsome man to ogle, it took everything she had in her to grab a couple of water glasses before heading to their table.

As Becca approached them, the man's face was blocked by his menu. So much for ogling. The woman wasn't unlike many of the socialites who frequented the upscale establishment. She was a stunning blonde dressed in a designer suit, with perfectly coiffed hair, beautifully manicured nails, and meticulously applied makeup. As Becca placed a water glass in front of the man, her eyes were inexplicably drawn to the woman. In her black-and-white uniform, with her hair coiled in a bun and wearing minimal makeup, Becca couldn't help feeling like a shrinking violet next to such beauty.

As she started to put down the second water glass, a familiar voice caught her attention. "Becca?"

Her eyes quickly turned to the man across the table. *Ethan!*

Becca was so shocked by the sight of him, she was no longer paying attention to what she was doing. She accidentally sat the glass on top of a spoon. It promptly toppled over, spilling onto the table. Some of the liquid dribbled into the woman's lap.

"You stupid idiot!" she practically shrieked as she jumped up from her seat, brushing at the wet spots on her skirt.

Becca's attention instantly returned to the angry woman. "Oh God! I'm so sorry!"

She ran to grab a couple of towels from the linen station around the corner, then rushed back. The woman was blotting a wet spot on her blouse with a napkin. "Here, let me help," Becca offered as she tossed one towel onto the table and tried to absorb the liquid from the woman's skirt with the other.

The woman snatched the towel from her hand and growled, "Give me that! I think you've done quite enough already."

"Lindsay, I think you're overreacting." Ethan used the second towel to sop up the water that had spilled on the table. "It was clearly an accident."

"Overreacting? This incompetent twit ruined my two-thousand-dollar custom-made suit."

"I–I'm really sorry, miss. I–it's only water. At least it shouldn't stain." Becca tried feebly to diffuse the situation, but her attempts backfired horribly.

Lindsay's mouth dropped open, and she gave Becca an incredulous look. "Only water?" she repeated in a deceptively placid tone. "For your information, you nitwit, water and silk do not mix, which is something you would know if you had half a brain in your head. I should have your manager take the cost of my suit out of your paycheck," she snarled, while pinning Becca with a malicious glare.

Becca swallowed hard. Her day had gone from bad to worse in two minutes flat. It would take more than two month's worth of paychecks to cover the cost of something so expensive.

Ethan's calm, firm voice broke through her cloud of dread. "Lindsay, that's enough. I'll pay for your suit myself. You're not going to Becca's manager over a spilled glass of water. Especially if you want to continue our negotiation."

Lindsay looked like she wanted to give him a sarcastic comeback, but she suddenly pasted on a smile instead. "Oh, Ethan, you don't have to do that. After all, it wasn't your fault."

"In a way it was." Ethan looked up at Becca with those gorgeous green eyes that she could so easily get lost in. "Becca was obviously surprised to see me here, and I distracted her by saying her name. Hence, it was my fault."

Becca looked away shyly, astounded by his generosity in taking responsibility for her mistake. Her white knight had ridden to the rescue again. She had a sudden desire for him to take her in his arms and shield her from this spiteful woman's venom.

"How very bourgeois of you to be on a first-name basis with the waitstaff, Ethan." Lindsay was trying to keep her voice sweet, but her features were marked with disdain.

"Lindsay, this is Becca. She's not just our waitress; she also happens to be my friend." Ethan looked back at her and continued, "Becca, this is Lindsay Harris, a business associate of mine."

"Nice to meet you," Becca said politely, although she certainly didn't mean it. How could she, after the way the horrible woman had been treating her?

Lindsay merely smiled tightly and nodded almost imperceptibly before looking back at Ethan. "Ethan, if you're done visiting with your little friend, do you think we could get back to our dinner?"

Becca sprang into action. "Again, I–I'm sorry for the mess. We're not very busy tonight. Could I move you to this table over here?" She indicated a clean, freshly-set table kitty-corner to the one where they were sitting.

"That would be great, Becca."

Ethan rose from his chair, and Lindsay followed him.

"While you're getting settled, I'll get you some new water glasses."

Becca returned with their water and was mindful of where she was placing the glasses this time. "Are you ready to order?"

She took their order and returned to the server station to enter it into the computer. When it was time to bring them their food, she used extra care in setting their plates on the table and was especially attentive to their needs throughout the meal.

Ethan was sweet and polite as always. Lindsay continued to treat her coolly, but thankfully, found no further reason to yell at her.

As Becca waited on other tables and attended to her duties, the couple ate their meal and conversed over folders laid open on the table. She couldn't help stealing glances their way. One time she caught Lindsay leaning across the table with her hand on Ethan's arm while she talked, as though sharing confidences with an old friend. Becca was pretty sure Lindsay was only doing it to show off her generous cleavage, in much the same way she showcased her long legs in the short shirt she was wearing. It all made Becca want to claw the woman's eyes out.

Another time, she saw Ethan perusing some paperwork intently. That unruly lock of hair she loved had fallen over his eye. Lindsay reached over and smoothed it back into place. The gesture sent a jolt of jealousy straight through Becca's heart. She ached to be the one touching him, and Lindsay looked like a woman who was staking a claim. What did she mean to Ethan that he would allow her to touch him so familiarly?

Could he actually like the horrible woman? Lindsay didn't seem like his type at all. Then again, Ethan never discussed his love life, so she really had no idea what his type was. Maybe women like Lindsay did turn him on. After all, men could be shallow. Usually, all it took was a pair of big boobs and a nice butt to get their motor humming. Lindsay had both, plus long shapely legs and the looks of a runway model to boot. Becca might be a lot nicer than Lindsay, but when it came to outward beauty, she couldn't even hope to compete.

After what seemed like forever, Ethan and Lindsay rose from the table, gathering their things in preparation to leave. Becca wanted to say good-bye to Ethan, but didn't dare with that witch around. Instead, she grabbed the tray of dirty dishes she'd collected from a nearby table and headed back to the server station.

She slid the dishes into a tub under the counter, then straightened. As she reached around to rub the knot in her neck again, a large pair of male hands descended on her shoulders and began to massage the area.

She started, but then that gentle, familiar voice murmured in her ear, "Easy, Becca. It's just me."

"Ethan, what are you doing?"

"You look dead on your feet. I thought you could use a little TLC."

"You were so engrossed in your dinner, I didn't think you'd notice."

"I'm never too busy to pay attention to my best friend. So what are you doing here tonight? I thought you only worked weekends."

"Covering for a sick friend–Oh!" Becca exclaimed when his thumbs hit a particularly sore spot. As his hands worked their magic, her initial moan softened into a hum. "So where's Lindsay?" she asked.

"We took separate cars. She already left."

"So what's going on with you two?" She tried to sound nonchalant, but the jealously was welling up inside her again.

"We're working on a business merger that's really important to the company. If we can make it happen, Pet Emporium will have its own pet food division, which could be very lucrative in the future. By the way, I'm sorry you had to take the brunt of her little temper tantrum. I know she's spoiled and can be a bit much to take sometimes, but I've never seen her act like that before. Truthfully, I think she's in over her head on this business deal, and was probably stressed out. Maybe that's why she lashed out at you."

Ethan's defense of Lindsay didn't make Becca feel any better about the woman. She was usually the type of person who gave everybody a chance, but Lindsay had rubbed her the wrong way from the moment she first laid eyes on her. Maybe it was jealousy clouding her judgment, but she truly hoped Ethan wasn't getting the wool pulled over his eyes where that woman was concerned.

She turned around and gave him a wan smile. "It's OK, Ethan."

"No, it's not. But thank you for being so gracious. It's one of things I love about you." He reached out and pulled her into an embrace. "I left a little something extra on your tip to help make up for Lindsay's behavior."

She pulled back and looked up at him. "Ethan, you didn't have to do that."

"Yes, I did," he replied firmly. "And it's still not enough to cover what you put up with, but I guess it'll do for now."

"Well, thank you. That's very sweet of you."

"You're welcome. I'd better get going. Go home and get some rest as soon as you can."

She smiled. "I will."

Ethan turned and headed toward the door right before Rhonda returned to the alcove. "Was that Mr. Eye Candy I just saw talking to you?"

Becca giggled. "Yes. He happens to be a friend of mine."

Rhonda gave her an incredulous look. "Are you serious, girl?"

Becca nodded.

"Whoo-wee!" Rhonda exclaimed while fanning herself with one of the leather folders used to hold meal checks. "I wish I had a hot stud like that for a friend, leaving me one hundred percent tips."

"What?" Becca asked, thinking she'd heard the other waitress wrong.

"That gorgeous man friend of yours left you a two hundred dollar tip."

Becca shook her head. "You must have read it wrong. Are you sure it isn't twenty?"

Rhonda held out the open folder. "See for yourself."

Becca took it from the other waitress's hands. Her jaw dropped. Right there in Ethan's neat hand-writing was the unmistakable figure of two hundred dollars on the tip line. Quickly regaining her composure, Becca rushed out onto the restaurant floor, looking for him, but the outrageous man was already long gone.

Chapter 7

On the Monday two days before Christmas, Becca curled up in her favorite overstuffed chair to read a new romance novel Edna had loaned her. Since starting vet school, she hadn't read a single book that wasn't for educational purposes. Friday had been the last day before winter break began. Earlier in the evening, when she realized there was no studying to do and she didn't have to go to work, a glorious sense of freedom assailed her. Now she relaxed while finally indulging her passion for reading again. It felt amazing!

Ethan always starred as the hero of every romance she read, and this one was no exception. She had reached a particularly steamy part, and imaginings of Ethan making love to her like that made her body tingle with an awareness that settled at the juncture of her thighs. She was thoroughly engrossed in the story until a knock sounded at the door. Confused, she glanced at the clock, which told her it was after eight p.m. She wasn't expecting anyone. Maybe it was Edna, needing a favor.

Becca reluctantly set her book aside and rose to answer the door.

Leaving the security chain in place, she cautiously opened it.

"Ethan!" She quickly closed the door to remove the lock, then swung it wide.

As he entered, the scent of his cologne, mixed with a masculine essence belonging only to him, wafted over to her. At the sight and smell of him her pulse raced, bringing back images of the naughty fantasies her brain had been conjuring a moment ago. Feeling a blush rising in her cheeks, she shyly glanced away, while busying herself closing and locking the door.

Finally, she turned and met his gaze. Instantly, she was lost in those gorgeous green eyes, and her body heated even more. She cleared her throat nervously. "So what you doing here?"

"I came to share some news with you."

"Oh! It must be pretty important for you to make a special trip, since we would have seen each other tomorrow at lunch."

He nodded. "It's very important, and I didn't think it could wait."

His grave tone effectively put a damper on her desire.

"Sounds serious. Come on in." She motioned toward the sofa. "Have a seat."

He hesitated. "Actually, would you mind if we sit out on the patio?"

"Um..." The mere thought of sitting on the patio in December made her shiver. "Don't you think it's a little chilly for that?"

Ethan laughed. "Trust me. I have a very good reason. Why don't you go get a sweater while I build a fire?"

She shrugged. "OK, if you say so," she replied skeptically, but headed for her bedroom to do as he'd asked.

By the time Becca joined him on the patio, Ethan had a cheerful, crackling fire burning in the free-standing fire pit.

He scooted to the other side of the love seat and patted the cushion where he'd been sitting. "Have a seat. I already warmed it up for you."

She gave him a gentle smile as she sat down next to him. "That's so sweet of you."

His heart clenched when he noticed she was wearing her mom's sweater, the same one he'd rescued from Jay's apartment.

"So what's this important news you have for me?" she asked.

He took a deep breath. "Todd's friend, Blake, called me today."

Instantly, her smile faded, and apprehension filled her eyes.

He reached out to take her hand, which was like grabbing an ice cube. "Don't worry. It's good news, not bad." He chafed her hand between his, trying to bring some warmth back into it.

Becca relaxed, and her face took on a hopeful expression.

Not wanting to keep her waiting any longer, Ethan dove into the reason for his visit. "The jury came back today with their verdict." He paused a moment for effect, then gave her a big grin as he added, "Guilty."

"Oh, thank God!" she breathed. She leaned back, a look of utter relief washing over her entire body.

"He said the sentence hasn't been passed yet, but it's looking like Jay is going to be in prison for several years, and that's just for taping his sexual encounters without the women's consent and using the recordings to make money on the illegal porn site. He's still going to be extradited to Alabama to face the statutory rape charges."

"Oh, Ethan, I've been worried about this for so long. I can't even begin to tell you how relieved I am that it's finally over."

Knowing that he'd been able to bring her a measure of peace made him happy. "I think I have a pretty good idea what it means to you. Now you see why it couldn't wait until tomorrow."

She nodded, her full, sensual lips turned up in a blissful smile. "Thank you." She squeezed his hand.

"Actually, there's one more thing I think you might want to do that will give you even more closure. It's why I insisted we talk out here."

Becca gave him a quizzical look. "What's that?"

Ethan slipped a hand into his jeans pocket and withdrew the tiny plastic card. After he had told her of its existence, she had asked him to keep it for her so it wouldn't become a constant reminder of the past, and of what she might have to do with it. He had readily agreed.

As she looked at the memory card, a host of emotions played over her face. "I'd almost forgotten about that."

Silently, he handed it to her, then glanced at the fire.

Her eyes glittering with unshed tears, she took a deep breath and tossed the memory card into the flames.

He wrapped his arm around her, drawing her into his side. She laid her head against his shoulder, and together, they watched it burn.

When the final physical reminder of that dreadful night had burned to a cinder, Becca said, "You know, it's like all the tension and anxiety I've felt for the last eight months has floated away with the smoke. I'm finally free." She laid a delicate hand on his thigh. "How is it that you always seem to know exactly what I need?"

Her touch fueled Ethan's desires. He knew she didn't mean it to be intimate, but it felt that way. In fact, he wished she'd move her hand a little higher.

If he wasn't careful, those kind of thoughts were going to cause him a huge embarrassment. He closed his eyes for a moment, willing his lust under control. It seemed to take forever, but eventually his brain formed a coherent response. "I think it's because we're a lot alike."

Becca turned her face up to his. "Well, it's the best Christmas present anyone could have given me."

Her tempting lips were mere inches away. From where she sat, nestled in the crook of his arm, it would have been a simple matter to close the distance between them. Instead, he swallowed hard and looked back at the fire. "I'm glad you liked it," he murmured.

She hummed in response and laid her head back on his shoulder. He rarely had the opportunity to hold her so close, and he relished the feel of her in his arms. He contemplated telling her that he loved her right then and there, but somehow the moment didn't seem quite right. She'd just closed the book on a very painful chapter in her life. He was happy that he'd been able to ease her heart, but he didn't want to cause her any further stress in the event she didn't return his feelings. So he simply held her in silence.

Ethan wasn't sure how much time passed, but he was roused from his sense of contentment when Becca shivered. The small fire he'd set was starting to burn low.

"Why don't we go back inside where it's warmer?" he suggested. He didn't really want the moment to end, but he didn't want her to catch cold either.

She hesitated, and for a moment he thought perhaps she was as reluctant to leave his arms as he was to let her go. Then, without a word, she slid from his embrace and slipped back inside.

Taking a small piece of wood from the pile, he spread out the ashes in the pit so that the fire would cool down.

A moment later, Becca returned with a cup of water.

He smiled. "Great minds think alike."

She handed him the water, which he poured into the fire pit. The embers hissed and sizzled in protest. He stirred the ashes around some more, and when he was satisfied the fire was out, he joined her in the living room.

"Make yourself comfortable. I'll be right back," Becca said before heading into her bedroom.

Ethan went to the kitchen to place the cup in the sink. He turned around to find Miss Kitty sitting next to her empty food bowl. She looked up at him hopefully and let out a piteous, "Meow!"

Ethan laughed. "So you're hungry, huh? Did Becca forget to feed you?"

Miss Kitty meowed again in response.

"OK, mooch, I'll get you something to eat. Now where does Becca keep the cat food?" he asked while opening cupboards.

The first few held only dishes. When he leaned down to check the lower cabinets, Miss Kitty came closer, winding her way around his legs while purring like a little motor. He scratched her head, and she pressed back against his hand affectionately. He picked up the cat and looked her in the eye. "So are you going to tell me where your food is?"

When no answer was forthcoming, Ethan chuckled again. "Well, you're no help."

Cradling the feline in one arm, he continued his search. Finally locating the food cupboard, he was shocked to find it nearly empty. It held only a few spices, cooking oil, a single packet of ramen noodles, a box of mac 'n' cheese, a can of tuna and a jar of peanut butter. A quick perusal of the other cabinets revealed nothing more. Suspicious, he opened the refrigerator to find it in a similar state.

His brows drew down into a frown. Did Becca always have so little to eat?

As he contemplated that question, Becca walked into the kitchen.

"Becca, why don't you have any food in the house?" he asked, beginning to suspect there was more to the situation than met the eye.

Becca appeared surprised by his inquiry but quickly masked it. "Why are you going through my cupboards?"

Her tone held a touch of annoyance, but he wasn't about to let the subject rest. "Miss Kitty said she was hungry, so I was looking for the cat food."

"Oh." Now she seemed nervous. "Um...I ran out yesterday, but I think I have a can of tuna."

"Yeah, you do, but that's about all you have. What on earth are you eating?"

She laughed uneasily. "It's not that big a deal, Ethan. I get meals at the restaurant on the weekends." She shrugged it off. "I just haven't had time to go shopping."

Somehow that didn't ring true to him. He knew she didn't have work or school today, so why hadn't she gone to the store? The only thing that made sense to him was that she didn't have enough money in her bank account to afford groceries.

That thought left him with a sick feeling in his stomach. He couldn't bear knowing the woman he loved was going hungry, but if her prideful response when he paid off her credit cards was any indication, she probably wasn't going to fess up about her financial difficulties. It was looking like he'd have to get sneaky again.

Ethan handed a happily purring Miss Kitty to Becca. "Why don't you get that tuna for her, and I'll go order us a pizza. My treat," he was quick to add.

Thankfully, she didn't argue with him. He ordered a larger pizza than usual to make sure there would be leftovers to hold her over until he could put his plan into action. When the food arrived, they sat it at the kitchen table, eating and sharing conversation like they always did at their Tuesday lunch dates.

A couple of hours later, finally satisfied that Becca was not going to starve, Ethan took off, but he was damn sure going to return tomorrow with enough groceries to keep her belly full for the next several months.

* * * * *

The next morning Becca stood in her kitchen having a slice of cold pizza for breakfast. It wasn't exactly her favorite meal to start the day, but at least she wouldn't be hungry. There was enough leftover pizza to get her through today, and she was having Christmas dinner with Edna and her family tomorrow. It was a good thing the other woman had invited her. Otherwise, Becca would probably be eating mac 'n' cheese.

She had been trying to stretch her budget as far as she could, but even still, there were some days she didn't eat much. At least she ate well on the weekends. Milano's gave their employees a free meal during their shift, which she always split into two. Despite that, she'd lost five pounds, and she could ill afford it on her slender frame.

When Ethan had asked her about the food shortage last night, she couldn't bring herself to tell him the truth. He would have run out and bought her an entire grocery store. It was bad enough he'd paid off her credit cards and given her that outrageous tip. The last thing she wanted was him buying her anything else.

After witnessing some of the things her mom had gone through when money was short, Becca couldn't stand the idea of being indebted to anyone, especially a man. The rational part of her brain tried to deny that Ethan would ever treat her the way that her mom's horrible "friend," Trent, had treated them all those years ago. Somewhere deep inside, she knew it was true, but it didn't stop the increasing anxiety she felt over owing a man money.

The phone rang, breaking into Becca's ruminations. She hurried to the living room to answer it. The caller ID revealed that it was the very man she'd been thinking about. After clicking the on button, she spoke. "Hi, Ethan."

"Hey, Becca." His voice was sunny and cheerful, but it didn't quite chase away her dark mood like it normally did.

"What's up?" she asked.

"I was thinking that rather than having our usual lunch date, since it's Christmas Eve, we could do something special."

"What did you have in mind?"

"Well..." he hedged. "It's a surprise."

"Ethan..." She drew his name out on an exasperated sigh. When it came to Ethan and surprises, she usually ended up uncomfortable, because it almost always involved large amounts of cash.

"Now, don't be like that, Becca," he gently reprimanded. "Trust me. It'll be fun. If you don't have any plans, I'll be over around four."

A small smile finally touched her lips. She couldn't deny how nice it would be to see him again. Even though he'd been over last night, she missed him already. "All right, I'll see you then."

Becca spent the next hour tidying her apartment. Then she wrapped the small Christmas gift she'd made for Ethan, placed it under her little tree, and had another slice of pizza for lunch. With those tasks finished, and with hours left before Ethan's arrival, she curled up to finish the romance novel she'd been reading. Miss Kitty lay sleeping, a warm, furry, comforting weight in Becca's lap.

Before long, she was caught up in her fantasy world where Ethan was her knight in shining armor. Three hours later, she turned the final page and closed the book on a contented sigh. The couple's happily-ever-after had been absolutely perfect, exactly what she wished for herself and Ethan.

As she contemplated a possible life with Ethan, Becca began to ask herself what was holding her back from revealing her feelings for him. When she had first realized she was falling in love, she'd been in a vulnerable state and didn't trust her emotions. Now, nine long months had gone by since her mom passed away, and her grief was beginning to subside. The uncertainties surrounding Jay had finally been resolved too, and although vet school was stressful, it was also fulfilling. Things were finally starting to look up for her, so maybe it was time she told Ethan the truth.

But what if he didn't reciprocate her feelings?

That thought weighed heavily upon her. In all the time she'd known him, he'd always been sweet and affectionate toward her, but from what she could tell, he was like that with everyone. He hadn't really given her any indication that his feelings went deeper than friendship. It would definitely make things awkward between them if he didn't feel the same way, and could eventually end their friendship. She couldn't let that happen. He meant too much to her.

Before Becca could reach a decision, there was a knock at the door. Jolted out of her musings, she realized it was already four o'clock. She hurried to answer.

Ethan greeted her warmly. "Merry Christmas, Becca!"

Becca's mouth dropped open at the sight that met her. She'd been expecting just Ethan. Instead, he was flanked by three other people. A woman in a white chef's uniform carried covered dishes, and two men held at least half a dozen large reusable grocery bags apiece.

"You can go put everything in the kitchen," Ethan instructed the trio.

Becca stepped back so they could enter, but a sinking feeling took up residence in the pit of her stomach. "What is all this?" she asked.

"It's your Christmas presents and Christmas dinner."

She shook her head in disbelief, then wandered back into her apartment in a daze and lowered herself into a chair.

Ethan trailed after her, holding a sizable box wrapped in brightly colored paper. After sitting it down next to the end table that held her Christmas tree, he knelt beside her and took her hand in his. "What's wrong, Becca? Are you feeling sad because it's your first Christmas without your mom?"

"No, it's not that, Ethan." She glanced toward the kitchen. "As soon as they leave, we need to talk."

"All right," he murmured, his brows drawn down in concern. He looked over his shoulder to check on the progress of his helpers.

As the two men headed for the door, one said, "We put all the perishable items in the refrigerator, Mr. Montgomery."

Ethan rose. "Thank you, guys. Have a Merry Christmas!"

The pair returned the sentiments, then left.

A few minutes later, the woman came back through the living room. "Everything is set up like you asked, Mr. Montgomery."

"Thank you, Susan." He followed her to the door and said, "Merry Christmas!" before closing it behind her.

Ethan returned to sit on the sofa across from Becca. "So what did you want to talk to me about?" he asked softly.

Becca closed her eyes for a minute, trying to gather her thoughts. When she opened them again, she began. "You're so down to earth, most of the time I forget how rich you are. Then you go and do something like this, and I can't ignore it anymore."

"It's only some groceries and a little Christmas dinner. I don't see the problem."

"It not just groceries and dinner." Tears welled up in her eyes, and she choked out, "First it was paying off my credit cards. Then it was that ridiculously huge tip you left at the restaurant. Now this. There were at least a dozen bags of groceries. That alone must have cost hundreds of dollars, and I can't even imagine what kind of premium you must have paid to get that caterer or chef or whatever she was to deliver food on Christmas Eve. Ethan, this has got to stop!" Throughout her tirade, Becca's voice had been increasing in volume, and she finished on nearly a shout.

When she risked a glance at Ethan, he looked genuinely hurt. A little stab of remorse hit her in the gut.

"Becca, I have to admit I don't really understand your issues with my money. Especially today. All this was a gift. Gifts are given freely, without strings attached."

Becca stared morosely at the carpet. "Not all gifts," she replied, barely above a whisper.

Ethan appeared confused. "What do you mean?"

She shook her head. "Nothing."

Ethan leaned forward and placed his hand on her arm. "I get the feeling this is coming from a deeper place than simply being uncomfortable with my financial status. If there's something bothering you, you can talk to me. You know that, right?"

For a moment, she considered telling Ethan the truth about what had happened to her mom all those years ago when she had relied on a man for money. He would probably understand. After all, he hadn't judged her for what had happened with Jay. But hot shame washed over her as she recalled the things Trent had said, the things he'd done, the threats he had made toward her and her mom. Christmas was already a shambles, and she didn't want to ruin it any further by going down that painful road. Instead, she locked her emotions down tight and refused to let them out.

Clearing her throat, she answered, "I told you before. It's important for me to be independent, to take care of myself. When you keep throwing money out every time you think I need something, it makes me uncomfortable." At least that wasn't a lie. "Promise me you won't do it anymore."

Ethan sighed. "It's hard for me to not step in when I see a need, but I don't want to upset you either." He seemed reluctant but finally finished, "I promise."

Once the agreement was reached, Ethan took Becca into the kitchen and seated her at the table like a proper gentleman. The caterer had decorated it with a green damask tablecloth and napkins and matching lit taper candles. Their Christmas Eve dinner was laid out on pretty china plates. While eating, they conversed pleasantly about Christmas traditions and what each of them would be doing the next day. Despite the delicious food and the lovely ambiance, a measure of tension still hung in the air, but Becca tried to ignore it and simply enjoy the moment.

When dinner was over, they cleaned up together and shared the task of putting away the mountain of groceries Ethan had brought. After those tasks were finished, they made hot chocolate and took it to the living room to drink while they opened their gifts. Ethan insisted that Becca go first.

"Ethan, you really didn't have to get me a present on top of everything else."

"I know," he answered patiently, "but I wanted you to have something fun and not just something functional."

The box was rather heavy, so Becca left it sitting on the floor as she broke the ribbon and ripped into the wrapping paper, which was bright red and sprinkled with festively decorated trees. She opened the flaps of the box, lifted the tissue paper, and promptly giggled at what she found inside.

"Aw, it's so cute," she crooned while pulling out an adorable black-and-white stuffed kitten wearing a Santa hat.

"When I saw it, it reminded me of Miss Kitty, and I couldn't resist."

Becca snuggled the soft, fuzzy kitten to her cheek before turning it around and taking another look at it. "I love it. Thank you, Ethan." She laid it on the sofa next to her cat. "Look, Miss Kitty, a playmate for you."

Becca and Ethan both laughed when the feline gave the fake cat nothing more than a bored stare.

"There's more," Ethan said as he nodded toward the box.

"I thought it was way too heavy for a stuffed animal," Becca answered while pulling out another layer of tissue paper. Underneath were a dozen of the latest romance novels, a couple by her favorite authors. "Oh, thank you, Ethan."

"I wasn't sure what genre you like best, so I picked up a variety."

"As long as it's romance, I'll read almost anything." She pulled out all the books, stacking them neatly on the coffee table so she could see the titles. "They're perfect. Although I have no idea when I'm going to read all of them."

Ethan chuckled. "Well, at least you have another week and a half off from school."

"True. I promise I'll read as many as I can before I have to go back."

Ethan reached under the tree for the gift she'd marked with his name.

Suddenly feeling self-conscious about her gift, Becca's gaze fell to the floor. "Since money's tight, I made something for you. I'm afraid it's not much."

Ethan closed the space between them and, with a gentle finger under her chin, turned her face toward him. "Knowing you made it with your own hands makes it all the more special to me."

Becca scoffed, "Maybe you shouldn't say that until you see what it is. You might not even like it."

Ethan gave her an exasperated look before tearing into the paper. He pulled out a sage-green knit scarf and fingered it almost reverently. "Wow, Becca! I didn't know you could knit. This is beautiful."

She smiled shyly. "Edna taught me a long time ago, but I don't usually have much time for it."

"This must have taken you hours to make. It means the world to me, knowing that you gave up your precious free time to make me a Christmas present."

Becca felt herself blushing at his praise. She'd gladly give up her free time to make him twenty scarves if it meant seeing that look of wonder and appreciation on his face each time. "There's more," she said, repeating his words from earlier.

"Oh!" Ethan looked surprised. "He lifted the scarf and found a plastic baggie. It contained a thin black cord, threaded with black and silver beads on each end, and a pewter dog charm dangling from one side.

"It's a book thong," Becca informed him. When he gave her a blank look, she continued, "A bookmark."

His eyes lit up with understanding. "OK, I see how it works. I promise I'll use it for marking all the books I read." He took a closer look at the charm. "Hey, this dog kind of looks like Buddy."

Becca chuckled. "That's why I picked it."

Ethan turned to her. "Thank you, Becca. I love my gifts. I'll cherish them forever."

The smile he gave her made her melt. She thought again of telling him how she felt, of leaning over and kissing those sensuous lips, of giving him her heart completely.

Before she could talk herself into it, he broke into her thoughts. "How about we get some of that delicious-looking chocolate pie and watch a movie?"

Disappointment washed over her as the moment was lost. "Sure."

Together, they shared pie and watched *It's a Wonderful Life*. When Ethan finally took his leave, he did so with her scarf wrapped around his neck and the book thong tucked safely in his pocket.

Becca took their dirty plates to the kitchen sink. She turned and leaned back against the counter, thinking about what he'd done for her. She couldn't deny that she'd had a good time with him tonight. Her brain warred between believing in the pure sweetness of his actions and feeling anxious as she remembered the past. When she couldn't seem to reconcile her emotions, she closed the door on them and headed for bed instead.

On the way there, she picked up the Christmas kitten and one of the romance novels. For the rest of the evening she would simply lose herself in the fantasy of being Ethan's woman.

Chapter 8

Ethan whistled a catchy tune as he rode the elevator up to his office. The new year had dawned without fanfare, and Becca had returned to school. Luckily, she still managed to carve out time in her busy schedule to keep up their Tuesday lunch dates. He had just walked her to her car, but before leaving her he'd drawn her into a tight hug. Becca's arms had automatically wrapped around his waist, returning the embrace. When she'd laid her cheek against his chest, the feel of her body pressed so tightly against his wreaked havoc on his senses. Now, as he headed back to work, it dawned on him that he was whistling a sappy love song he'd heard on the radio.

When the elevator reached his floor, he got out and started toward the hallway to his office. He didn't get ten steps before he was accosted by Lindsay. His whistling immediately stopped and an uncomfortable tension took the place of the relaxed, peaceful feeling that had filled him a moment ago.

"Lindsay, what are you doing here?" he asked. "I thought we weren't scheduled to work on the merger again until tomorrow."

"We aren't," she replied in an overly cheerful voice. "But I had a few new ideas I wanted to run past you. Cathy said you didn't have any appointments this afternoon."

It was true he didn't, but he'd been looking forward to a nice, leisurely afternoon of tying up loose ends on paperwork and hopefully taking off early. Since his secretary had unfortunately let that bit of information slip, he probably couldn't get out of this impromptu meeting now.

"Sure, come on into my office," he said reluctantly.

As they walked down the hallway, Lindsay took his arm and leaned into his side, brushing a bit of lint off his lapel. She was a little too close for comfort. "What has you in such a good mood?" she asked, smiling up at him in what appeared to be an attempt at seduction.

Maybe if she thought another woman was in the picture, she'd lay off the alluring act. "I had a really nice lunch with Becca."

At first Lindsay looked confused, then recognition of the name must have hit her. Her smile faded a little. "Oh. That little waitress from Milano's?"

"That's her," he replied as he ushered Lindsay into his office and closed the door behind them.

"So she really is a friend of yours," Lindsay said, looking appalled and astounded at the same time.

Her condescending attitude was beginning to annoy him. "Yes, she is. I already told you that. I have lunch with her every Tuesday."

He extended his hand, indicating the conference table on one side of the room. As they took their seats, Lindsay continued the conversation while removing folders from her attaché case. "Judging by that smile you were wearing when you came into the lobby, I'd say there's a lot more going on than lunch. I don't normally see a smile like that on a man unless he's...um..." She hesitated while placing the papers on the table. "How do I put this delicately–?"

"I get your meaning, Lindsay," Ethan said. "But my personal life is really none of your concern."

"All right, Ethan." Lindsay placed a hand on his arm placatingly. "You don't have to get testy about it. I was merely observing that you seem to like her as more than a friend."

The annoying woman was far too close to the truth, but feeling her comment didn't warrant a response, he opened the top folder and started perusing the paperwork.

Lindsay didn't seem inclined to let it rest, though. "I'm a bit surprised at you, getting involved with someone of the...um...lower classes."

His gaze shot up, pinning her with a fiery intensity. "Lindsay, I already told you I'm not discussing my love life with you, and I won't have you badmouthing Becca like that either. She's a very intelligent woman who works hard. She may not make much money, but she's never asked me for a dime, even when she didn't have enough to eat. Someday soon she'll be making plenty of money of her own. She's going to vet school, and I have no doubt that when she graduates, she'll be the best damn veterinarian in Arizona."

"My goodness, Ethan. I was merely making an observation, but I can see this is a sore subject with you."

Ethan turned his attention back to the papers before he gave into the temptation to strangle Lindsay. Sore didn't begin to cut it. He was livid at the woman's snobbery. They'd both been raised in the lap of luxury, but at least his parents had taught him to respect others no matter what their financial status was.

"Makes me wonder, though," Lindsay mused, "how she can afford a higher education like that on a waitress's salary?"

For a moment, Ethan's hands balled in a fists on top of the folder. He took a deep breath, willing himself under control before turning his gaze on Lindsay again. "She was awarded a private sponsorship," he replied tightly.

"Oh! Private sponsorship..." Lindsay pondered while tapping a perfectly manicured nail against her chin. "Wonder what she did to earn that."

Ethan rolled his eyes. The woman must be completely obtuse. "Like I said before. she's very smart, and with her financial need, I'm sure the sponsor thought she'd be a great candidate."

"Hmm...that reminds me. My father has been looking for new animal-related causes support. Have you made any donations to this vet school?"

The rapid shift in conversation made Ethan's head hurt. "Yeah, as a matter of fact I have."

"Then you would recommend them as a reputable organization?"

"Of course," he replied without hesitation.

"Oh, good! Do you happen to have a contact person there?"

"Sure."

Ethan got up and went to his desk. After rummaging around in a drawer, he found a business card for his friend, Mac, and gave it to Lindsay.

"Why, thank you, Ethan." Lindsay gave him a sunny smile. "I'll pass this on to my father."

After that, she finally shut up and let him get back to looking over the proposals she'd brought, though it was still hours before she left his office.

Once Lindsay was gone, Ethan allowed his head to drop onto the desk blotter. He banged his head against the desk a couple of times for good measure before flopping back into his leather executive chair with a moan. The negotiation of this business deal was already pure torture, and they probably had several more weeks yet to go. He didn't know how he was going to make it for that long without wanting to throttle the woman.

He recalled telling Becca that night at Milano's that Lindsay could be a bit much to handle, but even he hadn't known exactly how difficult she was going to be. Rumor had it that her father, finally tired of her running up his credit card bills and wanting her to put the business degree he'd paid for to good use, had put her to work for his company. Problem was he'd immediately thrown her in with the big fishes when she could barely swim. It wasn't that she didn't have the competence to handle the negotiations; she just always made things far more complicated than they needed to be.

That, combined with her earlier game of twenty-questions and the way the woman was hanging all over him, made him feel like jumping out his twentieth-story window. Since they'd started the negotiations, Lindsay couldn't seem to keep her hands off him. He had a feeling she wanted him back.

Well, if she thought he'd ever give her a second glance, she had another thing coming. He'd only gone out with her a few years back as a favor to her father. Ethan had known after only one date that it wasn't going to work out between them. Being the nice guy that he was though, he ended up dating her for a whole month before finally telling her so. At first, she'd been clingy, but eventually, she had seemed to get over it. He'd met Becca a few short weeks later. Even though he hadn't realized it for a while, she'd spoiled him for any other woman.

Sweet Becca! He sighed and smiled to himself as her lovely face floated into his imagination. He wished he could go back to their lunch and do it all over again. He loved their "dates" at the little bistro where they shared sandwiches and deep conversation at an intimate table for two. At the same time, they were torturous in a way. Every time he had to bid her farewell, he had the almost uncontrollable urge to scoop her up in his arms, carry her to the hotel two blocks away, get a room, and take her body to the heights of ecstasy all afternoon.

But who was he kidding? In nine long months, Becca hadn't given him the slightest inkling that she thought of him as anything more than a friend. He longed to tell her about his feelings, but he didn't want to ruin the beautiful friendship they had going. Maybe after this merger was finished and Lindsay wasn't stressing him out on a daily basis, he'd figure out the perfect way to tell Becca. But for now, he would simply have to stay close to her and show her his feelings through his actions.

* * * * *

Lindsay Harris was a woman who knew what she wanted and would do almost anything to get it. Right now the only thing she wanted more than signing a merger deal with Ethan Montgomery was the man himself–in her life, in her bed, and putting a ring on her finger. She may have let him get away once, but she had no intention of allowing him to slip through her fingers again. He was even richer than her daddy and could well afford to keep her in the manner to which she was accustomed. It didn't hurt that the man was hotter than sin either. The mere thought of touching and tasting every inch of that hard male body made her sweat, and she was determined to do just that.

To Lindsay's way of thinking, only one thing stood in the way of her getting what she wanted–Becky. During the dinner with Ethan at Milano's, Lindsay had noticed the way the girl gazed at Ethan when she thought he wasn't looking. Based on his dreamy faraway look and vehement defense, it appeared Ethan was taken with the little mouse too. It positively defied comprehension, and Lindsay was determined to put a stop to it, no matter what she had to do. Her lips twisted into a wicked smile as she thought of putting the waitress back in her place and having Ethan all to herself again.

Lindsay sat at her desk in the sitting room of her suite at her parent's mansion. She reached into her purse and pulled out her cell phone and the business card Ethan had given her yesterday. Even though Ethan hadn't said it in so many words, she had a sneaking suspicion that he had something to do with Becky getting that sponsorship. Of course he would never tell her the truth, but she had a pretty good idea how to get the information she wanted.

She dialed the number on the card, and the secretary put her through to Ethan's friend, Mac. Once the man was on the other end of the line, she poured on every ounce of charm she possessed. "Hello, Mac. My name is Lindsay Harris. You don't know me...yet, but we share a mutual friend. Ethan Montgomery?"

"Yes, of course. How can I help you, Miss Harris?"

"Well, Ethan told me that he gave a very generous donation to your vet school, and I'm calling on behalf of my father, who is considering making a donation as well. He's interested in doing something very similar to what Ethan is doing for you."

"That would be amazing! And very much appreciated, especially by the needy student who receives your sponsorship."

Bingo! Lindsay grinned from ear to ear. "Ethan told me he was offering a private sponsorship, but he didn't give me all the details on how that works. Could you fill me in?"

"Of course, Miss Harris. You see, Ethan chose a student based on their financial need, and he is providing a full sponsorship for their entire four-year education. He'll be repeating this at the beginning of each school year with a new incoming student."

"And does the student know who's sponsoring them?"

"Oh no! That's all kept private and confidential."

"Thank you, Mac. You've been very helpful." *You have no idea how helpful.* "I'll pass all this information on to my father, and we'll get back to you if he decides to go ahead with it."

"Well, thank you, Miss Harris. We would certainly love to have you on board. If you have any further questions, don't hesitate to call me."

"I'll be sure to do that, Mac."

After they signed off, Lindsay giggled with glee. Between her conversation with Ethan yesterday and what Mac had just told her, she now had strong evidence to suggest Ethan was the one footing the bill for Becky's sponsorship, and the girl probably didn't know about it. Ethan had also mentioned that Becky never asked him for money, even when she was going hungry, which seemed to indicate pride on her part too. Lindsay was banking on her intuition being correct, and if it was, she was going to have a delightful time stirring up a little trouble in paradise between these two.

Chapter 9

It was a busy Sunday night at Milano's. Becca stood at the server station, entering an order, when Rhonda joined her.

"Remember that bitchy blonde chick from a couple months ago? The one that came in with your friend?" the other waitress asked.

Becca rolled her eyes. "How could I forget."

"Well, don't look now, but she's back and sitting at one of your tables with a couple of equally snooty-looking friends. No Mr. Hot Pants, though." Rhonda sighed dramatically with disappointment.

Becca couldn't muster any enthusiasm for her co-worker's playful comment. All she could think about was the way that bitch had treated her the last time. And now Ethan wasn't here to act as a buffer. She slumped back against the counter. "Ugh!"

Rhonda chuckled. "I hear you. Good luck!"

"Thanks. I'm going to need it."

Becca gathered three water glasses and headed for their table. Before she got there, she took a deep breath and pasted on a smile. As she distributed the glasses, she said politely, "Hello, Miss Harris. It's nice to see you again."

Of course it was anything but nice, but Becca hoped that a little buttering up would go a long way toward better treatment this time around.

Lindsay looked up from her menu. "Well, if isn't...um..." She seemed to be searching her memory. "What was your name again?"

Becca opened her mouth, but before she could answer, Lindsay interrupted her. "Oh yes, I remember, Becky."

"It's Becca," Becca retorted tightly.

Lindsay raked Becca with an assessing gaze and a condescending curl of her over-bright lips.

Becca quickly regained control and asked, "Can I get you ladies something to drink besides water?"

Lindsay ordered one of the most expensive bottles of champagne on the menu. "We're celebrating my birthday," she commented while handing the wine menu back to Becca.

Becca gave the other woman birthday wishes before going to get their champagne. When she returned, the two women with Lindsay were fawning over her sapphire earrings. Becca couldn't help but listen as she poured each of them a glass of the sweet wine.

"Those earrings he gave you are gorgeous," the brunette said.

"Not nearly as gorgeous as the man himself," the redhead added with a saucy smile.

Lindsay touch her earlobes and preened. "Aren't they, though. A gift like this definitely means things are headed in the right direction. Ethan and I have been spending a lot of time together." She laughed conspiratorially. "A few more weeks, and he'll be putty in my hands."

The redhead tapped Lindsay's arm with her fake French

manicured nails. "If he gives earrings like that, I can't wait to see the engagement ring he buys you."

The champagne bottle nearly slipped from Becca's hand, but she managed to grip it tightly just in time to prevent it from falling to the floor, then placed it back in the ice bucket next to the table.

Ethan bought Lindsay those earrings? Why would he do that? Lindsay mentioned them spending a lot of time together. Maybe they'd been dating in addition to working on a business merger.

But if he was serious enough about Lindsay to be thinking of an engagement, why hadn't he told her? Questions whirled through her mind.

"We're ready to order," the brunette said impatiently.

"Oh y-yes," Becca stammered. "What can I get for you?"

When Becca returned a while later with their entrées, she took another look at Lindsay's sparkling earrings. She remembered the gifts Ethan had given her for Christmas, and a red-hot poker of jealousy stabbed her heart. It wasn't that she wanted the sapphire jewelry that must have cost a fortune. She wouldn't even know what to do with it. It was that her presents seemed drab in comparison. More than anything, it made her feel drab next to Lindsay's incomparable beauty. In that instant, she had to know exactly how close Lindsay and Ethan were.

As she placed Lindsay's plate in front of her, Becca casually asked, "So, Miss Harris, you and Ethan seem to know each other pretty well. How long have you been business associates?"

Lindsay seemed eager to answer. "Oh, Ethan and I have known each other for years. Our fathers have been doing business together since we were teenagers. We finally met a few years back at a company party. With our fathers being friends, I always knew it was inevitable that we would get together." She giggled. "We dated for a while, but what with Ethan taking over the company for his father and me finishing business school, we were too busy to nurture our relationship like we should have." Her eyes took on a sickeningly adoring gaze. "But I'm thrilled this merger we're working on has brought us back together again. With you and Ethan being such good friends, I'm surprised he never told you about me," she finished smugly.

Becca shrugged. "No, I'm afraid he didn't mention you before we met last year."

Becca wanted to think that Ethan's failure to tell her about Lindsay meant there was nothing to tell, but the smirk the awful woman gave her and the shining sapphires dangling from her ears seemed to suggest otherwise.

"Your earrings are really beautiful."

"Why, thank you."

"It was very generous of Ethan."

"Yes, it was." Lindsay fingered the sparkling jewels. "But you know all about Ethan's generosity, don't you?"

Becca's brows dropped into a frown. Certainly, Ethan had been generous with her, but how would Lindsay know about that? Unless he'd told her. Becca felt a pain in her chest at the thought of him sharing personal information like that with this woman.

Before Becca could form a question to dispel her confusion, Lindsay continued, "You must have really rocked Ethan's world to make him give you that much money."

A chill went down Becca's spine. She had a bad feeling about where this conversation was headed. "W–What are you talking about?"

Lindsay leaned closer. She spoke in a hushed tone behind her hand. "I mean why else would a gorgeous man like him give someone like you 150,000 dollars?"

A wave of shock passed through Becca. "I did not sleep with Ethan for money," she ground out through clenched teeth. "I would never do something like that."

"Well, that's a relief!" Lindsay breathed while pressing a hand to her breast. "I don't know if I'd want to be involved with a man who would pay for it. I must have completely misread the situation. I thought you and Ethan had some sort of *arrangement*, but it appears you didn't even know that he was the one paying for your sponsorship. I'm so sorry for spilling the beans. Please don't tell him that I'm the one who told you. I don't want him to be upset with me."

The woman was worried about saving her own neck when she'd just ruined Becca's life?

Her head buzzed with confusion. Drawing her last ounce of strength and willing herself not to cry in front of these women, Becca said, "Please excuse me. Enjoy your dinner."

It was all Becca could do to keep her pace to a placid walk when she wanted to run from the building screaming. As she passed Rhonda, she stopped briefly. "I'm going on break. Can you cover my tables for me?"

"Of course, sweetie."

Before the other server could say another word, Becca dashed through the kitchen and out the back door. The brisk January air outside nipped at her face and hands. She found a spot in the shadows away from the door and leaned back against the brick wall. Only then did she finally allow the tears to fall. They coursed down her cheeks in rivulets.

Ethan had told her he had nothing to do with the sponsorship. How could he lie to her like that? He had promised he wouldn't try to give her any more money or expensive gifts. Did a promise mean nothing to him? Lindsay's words as she'd intimated that Becca was sleeping with Ethan for the money echoed in Becca's head, followed by memories of Trent and what he'd done to her mom and nearly to her.

Maybe Ethan was planning to use the money as leverage for sex.

Suddenly, she felt dirty and sick to her stomach.

No! The rational part of her brain screamed back. *He's sweet and kind. He supported me all through Mom's death and the incident with Jay. He would never do something like that.*

Then again, she never thought he would lie to her either, but he had. Nothing made sense anymore.

Becca slid down the wall to her haunches, her arms crossed over her stomach, and sobbed.

She had no idea how long she'd been out there, but at the sound of the door being opened, she quickly came back to herself and dashed the tears from her cheeks with the back of her hand.

"There you are."

Becca rose from her crouched position as Rhonda approached.

"Oh, honey, you've been crying." The other woman placed a hand on Becca's shoulder and rubbed it in a motherly way. "Are those bitches treating you like dirt again?"

"Yeah," Becca answered hoarsely.

Rhonda was one of the nicest people she worked with, but they weren't exactly close friends. She didn't feel like explaining the whole sordid situation to her. Besides, *those bitches*, as Rhonda had put it, were partially responsible for Becca's tears, so it wasn't exactly a lie.

"I'm sorry." Rhonda glanced toward the door. "You've been gone for twenty minutes. I know it's hard, but you probably better get back in there before the manager comes looking for you. You can't allow those women to make you lose your job. They're not worth it."

Becca sniffled and gave her a nod.

"Tell you what, you come back in with me, then go to the restroom and wash your face. I'll finish up with the spoiled brats while you take care of the rest of your tables. OK?"

"All right. Thank you, Rhonda."

Becca allowed the other woman to lead her back inside, and she did as she'd been bid.

She finished her shift in a state of numbness. Since she was closing, she didn't get off work until 11 p.m. As she drove home, she considered the situation again. Maybe Lindsay only said those things to upset her. After all, the woman had been ready to call the manager over a spilled glass of water the first time they met. Perhaps it was all part of a horrible plot to get revenge on Becca for ruining her designer suit.

She had to talk to Ethan. It was probably all just a misunderstanding, or maybe Lindsay was a liar. She hoped so, anyway.

By the time Becca returned home, she'd calmed down some. She hated calling Ethan so late on a work night, but for her peace of mind, she had to try.

Unfortunately, there was no answer. He was probably already in bed.

She replaced the phone in the cradle and went to her room, completing her bedtime routine by rote. Exhausted, she slipped under the covers and fell into a fitful sleep.

* * * * *

After a restless night, Becca awakened feeling almost as worn out as when she'd gone to bed. Even after a shower and two cups of coffee, she could still barely keep her eyes open.

She yawned and checked the clock. She had half an hour before needing to be in class, so she picked up the phone to try Ethan again. It immediately rolled over to voice-mail. She left a brief message asking him to call, and then headed for school.

In between classes, she continued calling Ethan, but his voice-mail picked up every time. Where was he? Each time she was unable to reach him, Becca became increasingly frustrated, resulting in her messages becoming increasingly urgent. That afternoon, as she climbed in her car to leave school, she dialed Ethan's cell phone one more time.

When the recorded message came on again, the bombshell Lindsay had dropped on her, the lack of sleep, and Becca's own anxiety combined to make her lose it. "Ethan, where the hell are you? I need to talk to you about something really important. I've been trying to reach you since last night. You promised you'd be there for me." Her voice caught on a little sob. "Please call me. I need you."

Becca leaned back in her seat, closed her eyes, and took a few deep breaths, trying to calm herself. After wiping the tears from her eyes with her sleeve, she drove home.

Upon arriving, she dialed Ethan's office. It was only three in the afternoon, so he might still be there.

Ethan's secretary, Cathy, picked up and greeted her with a cheerful voice. "Pet Emporium. Ethan Montgomery's office."

"Hi, Cathy. This is Becca Anderson."

"Oh, hi, Becca. What can I do for you?"

"I've been trying to get in touch with Ethan since last night, but he's not answering his cell phone. It's really important. Do you know where he is?"

"Yes, I do. Some people are in from out-of-town, working on the big merger deal. He's staying with them at a resort out in Scottsdale so that they can get more work done. He said his cell phone would be off while they're in meetings. I think they've been at it all day, though. He probably hasn't had time to check messages."

"I see," Becca replied with disappointment. "Any idea when he might be finished?"

Cathy sighed. "Sorry, no clue. But I could give you the landline for the resort if you'd like. A long time ago, Ethan gave me instructions that if you ever called, I should put you straight through, no matter what he was doing. Since I can't connect you directly, this would be the next best thing. Maybe you'll get lucky and catch him in his room."

"Thank you, Cathy. I would appreciate it."

Cathy gave her the phone number for the resort and Ethan's room number. "As soon as he checks in with me, I'll be sure to let him know you called. I hope you can reach him."

"Me too," Becca replied hopefully. "Thanks again."

As soon as Becca hung up with Cathy, she immediately dialed the resort and asked for Ethan's room. It rang several times before being picked up. A sultry female voice answered, "Hello."

"I–I'm sorry, they must have connected me with the wrong room."

"What room are you looking for?"

Becca gave her the number.

"This is the correct room. Perhaps I should ask *who* you're looking for?"

"Ethan Montgomery," Becca replied hesitantly.

"Why, yes, this is Ethan's room."

Tension flooded her body as she realized with whom she was speaking. "Lindsay?" she asked softly, barely able to get the name out.

"Yes, who's this?"

"Becca Anderson," she answered tightly, feeling like all the air had left her lungs. *What the hell was this woman doing in Ethan's room?*

"Oh, hello, Becky. What a coincidence. I wondered what happened to you after our little chat last night."

Becca ignored the woman's comment and asked, "Would you please put Ethan on the phone?"

"Um..." Lindsay hesitated. "I'm afraid he's a bit indisposed right now, since he can't take a phone into the shower." She laughed.

The shower? Ethan was in the shower while Lindsay was in his room?

An image of the two of them entwined in a passionate embrace, rolling around in the sheets, came unbidden to Becca's mind. Her chest tightened until she could barely breathe. "I have to go," she said numbly.

She hung up before Lindsay could say another word, then lay down on her bed, buried her face in a pillow and sobbed. She might be angry and hurt about Ethan lying to her, but even that couldn't compare to the pain of him being with another woman, especially when she desperately needed him. How could he even like a bitch *like* Lindsay? That question haunted Becca as she slipped into a uneasy sleep.

Lindsay hung up the phone with a devilish grin on her lips. That couldn't have worked out better if she'd planned it. She couldn't believe her luck. She had no idea that waitress was going to call here, and it was purely by chance that she'd been the one to answer. Ethan was in the middle of explaining some very detailed sales numbers to the owners of the pet food company when his room phone rang. No one ever called his room. With his cell phone off during the business meeting, he thought it might be urgent, and asked her to answer it for him.

Lindsay had gone to pick up the extension in the bedroom for privacy, leaving the others in the sitting area of Ethan's spacious suite. Once she'd realized it was Becky on the other end, she'd decided to have some fun. The horrified expression on that girl's face last night at Milano's probably paled in comparison to what she must look like now. Lindsay wished she could be there to see it. Becky hanging up without even asking for Ethan again or leaving a message definitely indicated the little mouse was upset, a fact that made Lindsay positively gleeful.

Before returning to the meeting, she made sure to paste a placid look on her face, as if nothing had happened.

When she reentered the sitting room, it appeared that Ethan had finally finished his boring exposition. He looked up and asked, "Who was it?"

She gave him a serene smile. "Wrong number."

Chapter 10

By the time Becca awoke, darkness had descended. Her head ached, and every muscle in her body protested as she rolled over and sat up on the edge of the bed. A quick look at the clock told her it was a little past seven. She went into the bathroom, wet a cloth with cool water, and pressed it against her red, swollen eyes.

She had no idea what to do. She was in love with Ethan, but he'd lied to her. And now it seemed he was more interested in a roll in the hay with a blonde bitch than keeping his promise to always be there for her.

Becca lowered the cloth and took a look in the mirror at her haggard face and tangled hair. She could hardly blame the man. Lindsay might be mean, but she was undeniably beautiful. Unlike her. The plain, ordinary girl next door.

Running fingers through her hair, she padded to the kitchen in her bare feet. It had been hours since she'd last eaten. Becca opened the refrigerator, but as she gazed blankly at the contents she realized she had no appetite. After pouring herself a glass of water, she went back to the living room and pulled out her textbooks. She spread them on the coffee table with the intention of studying.

Half an hour later, she was still staring at the same page.

A knock sounded at the door, startling her. Not really in the mood for company, she reluctantly got up and went to answer it.

Ethan waited impatiently on Becca's doorstep. He hadn't been able to get away from the negotiations until well past six. As he'd listened to Becca's increasingly frantic messages, his heart had risen in his throat. Worried that something terrible had happened, he immediately left the resort and sped to her apartment. On the way, he dialed her cell phone multiple times but got no answer. When he arrived, her lights were on. He hoped that meant she was home.

Finally, the door opened. Becca stood there in rumpled clothes, her hair mussed. Her eyes were swollen, with dark streaks under them as if she hadn't slept in days. Something was terribly wrong.

"Becca, I didn't get your messages until about an hour ago. I got here as fast as I could. Why didn't you answer your phone?"

As she stepped back, allowing him to enter, she answered hoarsely, "I fell asleep for a while. I guess I didn't hear it."

After closing the door behind him, he reached out, intending to take her in his arms, but she shied away, walking toward the sofa.

He hadn't seen her this despondent since the night Jay used her, and even then, she'd allowed him to hold her. Fear gripped his heart. "Becca, what's wrong?"

She picked up an empty glass from the coffee table and rolled it nervously between her open palms. She didn't look at him when she spoke. "I received some very upsetting news last night, and I need to know if it's true."

He closed the distance between them, but once again she retreated, this time to the kitchen. "Tell me what it is," he prodded gently as he followed.

Becca turned and leaned against the counter, clutching the glass to her chest. Her beautiful blue eyes, marred by signs of misery, glittered with unshed tears. She swallowed hard, as though having difficulty forming the words. Finally, she spoke. "Are you the donor who paid for my sponsorship?"

Her question stunned him. *How had she found out?* Ethan briefly toyed with the idea of lying again but sensed it would do more harm than good. He sighed deeply and resignedly. "Yes."

Becca's face crumpled, and the tears she'd been holding back trickled down her cheeks. "How could you do this to me? I told you how important it was for me to do this on my own, and yet you've stepped in repeatedly. I told you accepting your money makes me uncomfortable, but you keep going behind my back, giving it to me anyway, in ways that I can't refuse."

Ethan ran fingers through his hair in frustration. "Becca, I only did it to help you."

"I thought I could trust you, Ethan," she said with a sob, "but you lied to me. Last fall, I asked you point-blank if you had anything to do with my sponsorship, and you said you didn't."

Ethan searched his memory for that conversation, recalling that he'd avoided an outright lie. "As I remember it, I said that I respected your feelings and would never do anything to hurt you."

Becca shook her head. "How can you say that you respect my

feelings when you keep doing what I asked you not to do? It was still a lie, Ethan, and that hurts me more than anything. You've destroyed my trust in you." Her hands shook with anger. The glass she was holding slipped from her grip and shattered on the floor. "Damn it!" She crouched down to pick up the pieces.

"Becca, be careful," he admonished.

As he bent over to help, she cried out in pain as one of the shards sliced through her finger. She slid the rest of the way to the floor, her back against the cabinet. Cradling the injured hand as blood dripped onto her jeans, she sobbed.

Ethan scooted some of the broken bits of glass aside with his shoe and reached for her. "Here, let me help you."

Becca flinched. "Get away from me," she ground out through clenched teeth, then screamed, "Get the hell out of my apartment! I don't ever want to see you again." She curled into a fetal position and wept inconsolably.

Seeing her like this brought tears to Ethan's eyes. He desperately wanted to hold her, explain everything to her, make it better, make her understand, but she obviously wanted nothing to do with him. Tightness took up residence within his chest. Time stood still as he felt his chances of giving Becca all his love and receiving hers in return slipping away, along with their friendship.

A few drops of bright-red blood falling to the white tile broke through his desolation and spurred him to action. Becca could need stitches, and if she wouldn't let him touch her, he had to find another way to help her.

Edna Moffat was watching one of her favorite television shows when someone began pounding on her door. The noise gave her a start. Then a male voice called her name. She recognized it as belonging to Rebecca's young man.

"Coming!" She paused the DVR, rose from her chair and went to answer the summons as quickly as her old bones would carry her.

The moment she opened the door, Ethan blurted out breathlessly, "Edna, I need your help." The young man looked scared to death.

"What is it, dear?"

"It's Becca. She cut her hand. I don't have time to explain, but she's really upset with me and won't let me near her. Can you please come see if she's all right?"

"Of course!" she exclaimed.

They rushed across the sidewalk to Rebecca's apartment.

"She's in the kitchen," Ethan said.

Before she'd even reached the kitchen, Edna heard the unmistakable sound of crying. She entered the room to find Rebecca curled up against the cabinet, surrounded by broken glass. "Oh my. Rebecca, don't move until I clear this broken glass."

She needn't have said it. The poor girl didn't even look up at her voice. Something awful must have happened to put her in such a state.

Edna grabbed a broom from the pantry closet and carefully swept the shards to one side of the floor, allowing enough room to pass safely. After propping the broom against the wall and pulling a clean dish towel from a drawer, she went to Rebecca's side and placed a comforting hand on her shoulder. "We need to stop that bleeding. Give me your hand, dear," she commanded in a soothing, motherly voice.

For the first time, Rebecca lifted her head. Her face was red and tear-streaked. She looked like she'd lost her best friend, and based on what Ethan had said, perhaps she had. Edna wondered what had happened between these two young people to cause such turmoil.

But first things first. When Rebecca raised her hand a little, Edna took it gently in her own and wrapped part of the towel tightly around the injured finger. "There we go. Now, can you stand up for me?"

Rebecca nodded morosely. Edna supported her beneath one elbow. Grasping the counter with her good hand, she rose from the floor.

"Good girl. Let's go sit at the table." With a hand at the young woman's waist, Edna directed her toward a kitchen chair. Once Rebecca was seated, she took a seat next to her.

Edna caught sight of Ethan still lingering near the kitchen doorway. Rebecca faced away from him, and Edna had a feeling it was probably for the best that she couldn't see him. The poor young man looked almost as hopeless as Rebecca did. The girl's hands lay on the table in front of her, and she had yet to speak a word since Edna had arrived.

Tenderly patting Rebecca's uninjured hand, Edna asked softly, "Do you want to tell me what happened here?"

The young woman's face scrunched up and a fat tear rolled down her cheek. "He lied to me, Edna."

Edna was pretty sure she knew the answer, but she asked the question anyway. "Who?"

"Ethan," Rebecca whispered.

"What did he lie about, dear?"

Rebecca sobbed quietly. "About being the donor for my

sponsorship. I asked him last year if he had anything to do with it, and he led me to believe he didn't."

Edna's brows rose in surprise. "Well, that certainly is a big thing to lie about."

She considered it for a moment, unable to believe that a nice young man like Ethan could have intentionally been devious. She had a feeling he was only trying to help, even if his methods were somewhat misguided. "Is it such a terrible thing that he sponsored you? After all, something good has come of it. You were able to return to school and pursue your dreams. You might not have been able to otherwise."

"I know, but he went behind my back when I specifically asked him not to. And it's not just this. He's been giving me money in sneaky ways for months. He secretly paid off the credit cards I took out to help pay Mom's medical bills. He left me an outrageous tip at Milano's. He bought me hundreds of dollars' worth of groceries."

Edna frowned with confusion. It sounded to her like Ethan was only looking out for Rebecca's best interests. Many times she'd wanted to help the girl herself, and if she'd had the kind of money Ethan did, she wouldn't have hesitated. "Rebecca, dear, I know that you're a very proud, independent woman like your mother, but it sounds to me like Ethan was only trying to help out where he saw a need."

"But I told him I didn't want his money." Rebecca's jaw tensed. "Him throwing money around like that, especially without asking, makes me uncomfortable."

The wheels in Edna's head started turning. True, Ethan probably shouldn't have tried to hide his involvement, but if he thought

Rebecca was going to refuse his help, she could see why he might. What she couldn't fathom was what had the young woman so upset. She was obviously deeply troubled about this when most people would probably be grateful. "Can you tell me why the idea of Ethan giving you these things makes you so uncomfortable?"

Rebecca bit her lip as though willing herself not to cry again and looked down at the table.

Edna tried again. "I'm trying to understand why this has you so upset. If it were me, and a generous man like Ethan was giving me gifts that were so helpful, I'd be very appreciative."

Rebecca pinned her with an angry glare as she replied hoarsely, "Expensive gifts come with a price."

Instantly, Edna recalled a story that Caroline had told her years ago. Caroline believed that she'd kept the real reason for her and her daughter moving to Arizona a secret. Had Rebecca somehow found out? There was no way to know except to ask. "Did someone give you money in the past, and then something bad happened because of it?"

All the fight went out of Rebecca. She blinked furiously, then nodded almost imperceptibly.

Edna reached over to rub the girl's shoulder and asked gently, "What happened, dear?"

Without looking at her, Rebecca answered in a small voice, "When Mom and I were still living in California, she had this client at her salon. A man named Trent. I don't know if he was as wealthy as Ethan, but he had plenty of money. He kept trying to get Mom to go out with him by giving her huge tips and expensive gifts. He charmed her into liking him, so she was kind of flattered by the gifts at first.

She went out to dinner with him a few times. Then he found out she was having trouble paying the rent on her storefront, so he bought the whole strip mall. After that, I overheard a few phone conversations, enough to put the pieces together that he was trying to leverage his *gifts* into getting her to sleep with him." Rebecca's voice had gone quiet and she cried softly.

Edna wrapped an arm around the girl's shoulders and squeezed comfortingly.

After taking a deep breath, the young woman finally continued her story. "Trent started coming to our apartment a few evenings a week. Mom always told me to watch TV in the living room, while they went in her bedroom to talk. I heard moaning. I was fifteen at the time, so I wasn't stupid. I knew what was going on." She shuddered. "The guy always made my skin crawl, but I guess Mom felt grateful enough to give him what he wanted. Maybe she even liked him. I don't know. But when Mom found out he was married, she decided to break it off. That night when he came by, she sent me to my room, but I was worried about her. I left my door open a crack so I could hear what they were saying. He threatened to evict her from the salon if she didn't keep having sex with him, but she still refused. Then he casually mentioned what a pretty daughter she had, and if she wouldn't give it to him, maybe he'd take payment from me."

Rebecca laid her head down on her arm, her deep sobs wracking her small body. "I was so scared. He gave her two days to make up her mind, but before he could come back, Mom had us packed up, and we moved here. She always let me believe that she just needed a change of scenery. I didn't want to worry her more, so I never told her that I knew Trent had threatened me. She probably should have gone to the police, but I think she was afraid he'd buy off the cops, not to mention he could take her to court to get her to pay the back-rent she owed him."

"Shh..." Edna soothed as she smoothed her hand over Rebecca's hair. "You're absolutely right. Your mother told me that story not long after you two moved here and we became friends. She wanted me to be on the lookout in case he showed up. Thankfully, he never did, and he can't hurt you now."

Edna looked up to see Ethan standing in the doorway, his cheeks wet with tears. He looked for all the world like he wished that dirt-bag was here so he could lay him flat, and she couldn't blame him. She would gladly do it herself. Then his face softened, and he took a step toward Rebecca. Edna held up her hand to stay him, and he reluctantly backed away.

"Rebecca, dear, I need to check that cut. I'm going to get the first aid kit. I'll be right back."

With one last rub over the young woman's back, Edna got up and went to the living room.

Ethan was pacing back and forth. When he stopped and opened his mouth to speak, Edna placed a finger to her lips and motioned him outside.

Once they were on Rebecca's front porch, the young man ran fingers through his hair in frustration. "Edna, you have to believe me, if I'd known about any of this I never would have done what I did. I would have found a way to convince Becca to accept my help instead of doing it secretly. I hope you don't think I would ever do to her what that bastard did to her mother."

Edna laid a calming hand on Ethan's arm. "The thought never crossed my mind. If it makes you feel any better, I don't think that Rebecca believes that either. She's just very confused right now."

Ethan made a move to return to the apartment. "I have to go to her. Apologize. Make her understand."

Edna grasped his arm tighter to stop him. "I don't think that's a good idea right now. She needs time to work through all of this, and at the moment, she sees you–or at least your money–as being part of the problem." She gave him a rueful smile. "It would probably be better if you went home. I'll talk to her. I'm sure this will all blow over soon."

She could tell that the thought of leaving Rebecca distressed him. He looked like he might cry again. "What if she needs to go to the hospital for stitches?"

Edna could tell he was looking for an excuse to stay. Patting his shoulder, she patiently replied, "I'll take care of her like she's my own granddaughter, I promise. And if she does need stitches, I'll get her to the hospital and I'll call you. Now go home and get some rest."

Ethan nodded morosely. "Thanks for looking after her, Edna. Good night."

"Good night, dear."

With one last soothing pat on his back, she sent him on his way, but there was a definite reluctance in his gait.

Edna went back inside. After retrieving a first-aid kit and a couple of washcloths from the bathroom, she returned to the kitchen. Rebecca still sat with her head on her arms. She had stopped crying, but her breathing was occasionally punctuated by the hiccuping of a person who had wept hard and deep.

Edna wet the cloths at the sink and sat down next to Rebecca, gently taking the injured hand in hers. "Let's take a look at that cut now."

The girl finally raised her head and leaned back in her chair.

Carefully, Edna unwrapped the dish towel and washed away the dried blood with one of the damp cloths. "It doesn't look to be very deep, and the bleeding has stopped. I think you'll be fine without stitches." As she continued her ministrations on Rebecca's finger, she spoke calmly. "Your mother never had any idea you knew about that pig's threats and manipulations. She only wanted to protect you."

"I know," Rebecca answered softly. "That's why I never said anything to her about it."

Edna knew she was going to have to tread cautiously to get the girl to see the error in her logic. Craftily, she said, "I've always thought Ethan was a very nice young man. Was I wrong about him? Has he asked you for sexual favors in exchange for the money he's been giving you?"

"No. Of course not," Rebecca replied with more animation than Edna had seen from her all night.

Inwardly, Edna smiled as she finished applying a bandage to the young woman's finger. "Are you afraid that he might?"

Rebecca pondered that question for a bit before dropping her eyes to the table and shaking her head.

"Then can you explain why you seem to be lumping him in with that horrible cretin who hurt your mother?"

The girl's face took on a perplexed expression, and she shook her head again. "I don't know, Edna. I'm so confused. I was fine with

Ethan being rich until he started paying my bills and giving me expensive gifts. I guess it brought back bad memories."

"Given what you overheard, then kept to yourself at such a young age, I suppose that's understandable. It must have been a heavy burden to bear. It probably felt like Ethan was doing the same thing, so it makes sense that his actions would make you uncomfortable. But since you clearly aren't afraid of him, don't you think perhaps you're being a little too hard on him?"

Rebecca shrugged. "He destroyed my faith in him. I trusted him from the moment we met, but now I find out he lied to me." She looked like she might start crying again.

"True. He wasn't entirely truthful with you." Edna finished bandaging Rebecca's finger, then used the clean, damp cloth to wipe the tear stains from her face. After finishing the task, she sat back in her chair with a sigh. "I'm going to tell you what I think. The impression I've gotten of Ethan is that he's an incredibly generous young man who can't stand to see someone in need and not help when he has the means, especially someone he cares about as much as you. I honestly don't think he had any devious motives for the things he did. In fact, I think he had your best interests at heart. Should he have been more forthcoming with you about what he was doing? Possibly. But it sounds to me like you were adamantly against him helping right from the start, mostly because of what that sleazy Trent did to you and your mother. Am I right?"

Rebecca nodded. "Mostly, but that's not the only reason."

"What else is bothering you?"

"There's this woman, Lindsay."

"That woman you told me about, who treated you so horribly that night at the restaurant?"

"Yeah. Ethan says they're only business associates, but she told me they used to date. I think they're back together, because she said as much when she came into Milano's on Sunday. Not to mention she answered the phone when I called his room at the resort where he was working on the merger today. Anyway, she's the one who told me that Ethan paid for my sponsorship, and she thought I was sleeping with him to get it." Rebecca's face crumpled. "She thinks I'm a whore."

Edna wrapped her arm around the girl's shoulders. "You poor thing. I can see how that only added insult to injury. What an awful woman to imply such a thing."

"What I don't understand is why Ethan would tell her about sponsoring me and lie to me about it."

"Assuming he's the one who did tell her. This Lindsay sounds like a horrible person. Perhaps she found out some other way, and only told you to hurt you."

"The thought had crossed my mind, but I don't know why she hates me so much. All I did was accidentally spill a glass of water on her. She would have to be the most spiteful person on the planet to hurt me like this over something so trivial."

Now that she knew Lindsay had dated Ethan before, Edna had a feeling that the woman's nastiness had more to to with jealousy than a spilled glass of water. She was probably pea-green with envy over Ethan's attentions toward Rebecca. In her present state though, the poor girl would never believe that.

"Well, I don't know about Lindsay's motives, but it seems to me that Ethan's heart was in the right place with the things that he did. You had very good reasons for the things you thought too. That being the case, maybe it would be a good idea for you two to talk it out before writing off a friendship that obviously means the world to both of you. Don't you think?"

The young woman gave her the barest of smiles and answered softly, "Yeah. I guess I did overreact. With school and work, I've been so tired and stressed out, and then the things Lindsay said and the things Trent did got all mixed up in my head and confused me. Not to mention I really care about Ethan, and I'm worried that Lindsay might be taking advantage of him."

Edna brushed a strand of Rebecca's hair away from her face and patted her hand. "That's all completely understandable."

"When I think about it the way you said, I realize that Ethan was just being Ethan. As long as I've known him, he's always been kind and generous. I know he lied to me, but I probably shouldn't have gotten so angry with him. I should have trusted him enough to let him explain." She worried her bottom lip. "Do you think he'll forgive me?"

Edna grinned broadly. "I'm sure he will, dear. Now, why don't you go change into something more comfortable and then sleep on it? I'm sure everything will look a lot better tomorrow, after you've had a good night's rest."

Rebecca nodded again and headed for her bedroom. After Edna cleaned up the first-aid mess and the broken glass, she went to the girl's room and knocked on the door.

"Come in."

Edna entered to find Rebecca sitting on the bed, clutching a stuffed Christmas kitten. She recalled the young woman telling her it was a gift from Ethan, which made Edna smile. It looked like their talk already had her thinking of her young man in a more favorable light.

Edna picked up Rebecca's clothes from the floor. "I'll take these clothes and the towels over to my place and put them to soak in cold water."

"You don't have to do that, Edna."

"It's no trouble. I'm sure you don't want them to stain, and you don't need anything else to worry about after the difficult evening you've had."

"Thank you. Not just for the clothes, but for taking care of my finger." She held up the bandaged appendage. "And most of all for talking to me. It really helped."

Edna came to stand in front of Rebecca, placing a hand on her cheek. "You're welcome, dear. Call me if you need anything."

"I will."

"I'll turn out the lights and lock the door on my way out."

When Edna reached Rebecca's front porch, she paused a moment to breathe deeply of the night air. She wrapped her arms around herself to ward off the chill while gazing off in the direction Ethan had taken earlier. Her lips curved, and she was certain her eyes sparkled. There was no doubt in her mind that boy was madly in love with Rebecca. No man would do the things for her that he had if he wasn't. The poor girl was simply too blinded by the trauma of the past and that awful Lindsay's comments to see it right now, but Edna was pretty certain that Rebecca returned his affection.

Those two were star-crossed lovers, just like she and her husband,

Freddie, had been. She knew it in her heart. Now, if she could only get them talking again and find a way to get them to admit it to themselves and to each other, life would be absolutely perfect.

Chapter 11

With his chin in hand and his elbow propped on the arm of the chair, Ethan sat staring into the crackling flames of his bedroom's fireplace. This evening had been a total nightmare. Was there no end to the terrible things Becca had endured in her life? More than anything, he wanted to go pound that Trent guy into a pulp for treating Caroline the way he had and for threatening Becca. The bastard deserved to be locked up.

Ethan's heart ached as he thought of Becca, broken, sobbing, and bleeding on her kitchen floor. All he'd wanted–all he wanted still–was to hold her in his arms and make it all better, like he had the night that son of a bitch, Jay, had used her. What hurt him more than anything was the knowledge that *he* was the one who'd caused her pain this time. If he'd had any idea what Becca had been through, he never would have pushed her to accept his money, never would have been so secretive about it. He would have tried harder to sweet-talk her into it instead.

Now he might have lost the most important person in his life because of money. He'd give away every dime he had and live the life of a pauper to see Becca happy again, and for things to go back to the way they were between them.

He'd never meant to hurt her. He'd only thought she was being stubborn and prideful. Even if that had been the case, he now realized he hadn't shown enough understanding of her situation. His parents may have taught him and his brother and sister to view everyone as equals, but he'd still been born with the proverbial silver spoon in his mouth. He'd never wanted for anything a day in his life. If he needed or wanted it, he simply bought it. That certainly hadn't been the case for Becca. Her mother had scraped to get by on her meager wages, and now Becca was doing the same.

Ethan couldn't live with the thought of someone he loved struggling when he had the means to help, but in doing so, he'd taken away Becca's dignity and self-respect. Making a disgusted sound, he slapped his hand down hard on the arm of the chair. There had to be something he could do to restore Becca's confidence in him and herself and reassure her of his honorable intentions.

With a deep sigh, he leaned forward. His elbows resting on his knees, he massaged his temples as he tried to think of a solution.

Buddy sat up from where he'd been laying at his master's feet. Placing his head in Ethan's lap, the dog looked up at him with doleful eyes.

"You look how I feel, Bud," Ethan told the canine while stroking the silky fur of his head. "What would you do if the woman you loved didn't want you around anymore?"

The dog's forehead rose and his ears quirked up, but his only response was a yawn.

Ethan laughed. "Am I boring you with my troubles?"

Still uncertain what to do, Ethan rose and prepared for bed. As he slipped beneath the covers, he vividly recalled sleeping here with Becca in his arms. He grabbed the extra pillow and hugged it tightly, but it was a poor substitute for the real thing.

Half an hour later, sleep still eluded him. Flopping onto his back, he stared up at the dark ceiling. After turning the problem over in his mind about a dozen times, he finally lit upon a solution, one that had been staring him in the face all along.

Becca was an independent woman who wanted to feel self-sufficient. Because of her past experience, being given money also made her uncomfortable. So what if he made it seem like he wasn't giving it to her after all?

First thing tomorrow, he'd have his attorney draw up a repayment contract for the sponsorship, making it more like a loan. However, unlike most loans, it would be interest free with very manageable monthly payments that wouldn't take effect until two years after her graduation. That should give her plenty of time to start practicing, although he'd make sure there were provisions made in the unlikely event she didn't.

Of course, he hoped to marry her long before that if she was able to return his love. As soon as this merger was finished, he'd finally reveal his feelings for her and pour on every ounce of charm he possessed in hopes of accomplishing that goal. With his mind finally at ease, Ethan smiled and drifted into a peaceful sleep, dreaming of a future with Becca as his wife.

* * * * *

The next evening, Becca was surprised once again by a knock at her door. She answered it to find Ethan on the other side.

"Hi, Becca," he greeted her solemnly.

"Hi," she answered back softly. Feeling embarrassed by her outburst the night before, she couldn't quite look him in the eye.

"Look, I know you're probably still upset with me, but I was wondering if I could talk to you. You don't have to talk to me if you don't want to. All I ask is that you hear me out."

She nodded. "Come in."

She stepped back to allow him to enter.

Once they were comfortably seated on her sofa, Ethan turned to her. Reaching out, he took her hand in his, then hesitated as though he wasn't certain she would welcome his touch. If she was honest with herself, it felt really good. After she'd calmed down last night, she'd worried he would never speak to her again after the terrible things she'd said, so this was a nice start toward repairing the damage to their friendship.

Finally, he spoke. "Becca, I did a lot of thinking after I got home last night. I realized that I went about all this the wrong way, and for that, I'm sorry. When you wouldn't accept my help, I thought you were just being stubborn, but now that I know the truth I understand why you were so uncomfortable with the idea." He'd been staring at their clasped hands, but now, he raised his eyes to hers.

A sense of dread assailed her at the implication in his words. "What do you mean?"

"I have a confession to make. I didn't leave last night when you told me to. I was too worried about you. After I got Edna to come help you, I stayed in here for a while, out of sight. I only did it because I had to know you were OK. I didn't mean to eavesdrop, but I overheard a conversation that I think you meant to be private."

"Oh God!" she gasped as hot shame washed over her. She turned her head away and tried to pull her hand from his grasp, but he held onto it tightly.

"Becca, none of that was your fault. You were only a girl at the time."

Ethan rubbed circles on the back of her hand with his thumb. His kind words and tender caress reminded her of the wonderful man he was and helped her to relax. Feeling guilty about ever thinking the worst of him, she bit her lip to keep herself from crying.

"I hope you don't truly think I could be like that bastard. I'd never take advantage of you like that."

Slowly, she turned her head back toward him, but she still couldn't meet his gaze. She answered in barely a whisper, "I know."

"Thank God," he breathed. "I don't think I could have stood it knowing you thought so little of me. Why didn't you tell me?" he added gently.

She shrugged. "I don't know. I had already been through so much, I guess I just didn't want to open another old wound. I probably should have, huh?"

Becca risked a peek at his face and found an empathetic expression there.

"I would have understood," he said. "I do understand. I should have listened to you, and I'm so very sorry I didn't. But I'm listening now, and that's why I brought something that I hope will ease any lingering doubts you might have."

He finally released her hand, withdrew an envelope from the inside pocket of his suit jacket, and handed it to her.

"What's this?" she asked.

"Look and see."

Her hands trembling slightly, she removed the documents from the envelope, opened them, and skimmed their contents. They contained a lot of legal jargon she didn't understand, but she comprehended enough to figure out what they were. "You're turning the sponsorship into a private loan?"

"Yes," he replied. "A lot of people in your life have taken away your choices, and that's undermined your sense of independence. I realize now that I was doing the same thing. This repayment contract is my way of giving that back to you. Feel free to have an attorney look it over for you. In fact, I recommend it, even though I can assure you that every part of it is in your favor. The payments won't start until two years after your graduation, and there are plenty of provisions in the event of financial hardship."

Becca's heart swelled, and tears misted her eyes. He really did understand. How could she have ever doubted him? "Thank you, Ethan. This means a lot to me."

"You're welcome. I want you to know that I truly had only the best of intentions for everything I did, but I understand that I still hurt you. Again, I'm sorry, and I hope you'll find it in your heart to forgive me."

Without hesitation, she answered, "I do. And I'm sorry too. I feel awful for how I treated you last night. I was really tired and upset and confused by what happened to my mom, but all that's no excuse for thinking so badly of you. You've just proven to me that you're nothing like that, and that I can still trust you. Forgive me?"

"Of course." Ethan grinned. "Does that mean I have my best friend back?"

She returned his smile. "Yes."

In a heartbeat, he clasped her face in his hands and planted a kiss on her lips. Her eyes went wide.

He pulled back quickly and looked away sheepishly, clearing his throat. "Sorry. When I left here last night, I thought I'd lost you forever. I guess I got a little carried away by the excitement of having things back to normal between us."

She smiled at him wistfully. "It's all right. I'm happy too."

Truth be told, her lips still burned from the intimate contact. Even if he'd only kissed her in a moment of elation, she'd remember it forever.

Chapter 12

Three months later, Becca was readying herself for a party. The spring temperatures had been unseasonably warm, and Ethan's parents had decided to throw an impromptu company pool party at their house one Friday night. He had asked her to be his plus-one, and she had gladly accepted. She'd eagerly made arrangements to trade shifts with a co-worker so she would have the night off.

Her heart soared at the knowledge that Ethan was taking her to the party and not that bitch, Lindsay. She still had no idea what was going on between them, if anything, other than business. Perhaps in her overwrought state, she'd only allowed her imagination to get the best of her. Ever since they'd made up over the sponsorship debacle, Ethan had been nothing but sweet and attentive toward her even though she knew he was still working on the merger negotiations. Thankfully, Lindsay hadn't returned to Milano's while she was waitressing there.

Becca dressed in a floral-print sundress and strappy white high-heeled sandals. She'd made a little extra in tips the weekend before, and even splurged on sexy new underclothes. Even if Ethan couldn't see them, they made her feel prettier. She could always fantasize that the evening would end with him getting a glimpse of them.

After carefully winding up her hair and securing it in a French knot, she sighed. Ever since the night they'd made up, that kiss he'd given her had been seared into her memory. She closed her eyes for a moment and recalled what it had felt like to have his lips on hers. She desperately wanted to feel that again, but the brevity of the kiss and Ethan's apparent embarrassment over his exuberance led her to believe that it was nothing more than a knee-jerk reaction from him. She opened her eyes and took a deep breath as she started styling the corkscrew curls at her temples.

The only reason Becca hadn't told him she loved him yet was the intense pain she'd felt when she thought she'd lost him forever. Having tasted that bitterness, she couldn't bring herself to do anything that might jeopardize their friendship again, even if it meant keeping her feelings to herself.

She smiled bravely at herself in the mirror before starting on her makeup. It wouldn't stop her from trying to make herself look as nice as possible in the hope that he'd take notice of her. After completing her makeup application, she added a small pair of gold filigree earrings as the finishing touch just as a knock sounded at her door. Becca took one last look at herself in the mirror, smoothed a stray hair back into place, and hurried to answer it.

Ethan stood on the other side, looking handsome, as always, in his khaki trousers and polo shirt. He seemed slightly taken aback at the sight of her, but quickly recovered. "Wow, you look great!"

"Thanks," she replied, shyly looking down at her toes and then glancing back up at him from beneath her lashes.

"So are you ready to go?"

She nodded. "Let me get my purse."

Becca grabbed her purse from the table near the door, locked up, and joined Ethan outside. As they were about to head down the sidewalk to the parking lot, they were startled by a voice from behind them.

"So where are you two going tonight looking so dapper? I thought you always stayed in on Fridays."

Becca swung around to greet her elderly neighbor with a smile. "Hi, Edna. I haven't seen you all week."

The old woman waved her hand dismissively. "I went down to Tucson for a few days to spend time with my son and his family. I barely got back this morning."

"Did you have a good time?"

"I had a wonderful time, dear. So where are you headed off to?"

"Ethan invited me to the company barbecue at his parents' house out in Scottsdale. I suppose we should probably be going. I wouldn't want to make us late."

"Oh, don't let me keep you. I'm just out for my evening stroll. You kids go on and enjoy yourselves," she urged while making motions with her hand to shoo them off.

Becca laughed at her friend. "We will," she said as she turned back to Ethan. "Bye, Edna," she called as they both waved over their shoulders.

When they got to the parking lot, Becca was stunned to see an elegant white limousine waiting by the curb. "Ethan, I thought you were driving!"

He shrugged. "I decided this would be more fun."

"Oh my gosh," she gasped with delight. "I've never been in a limo before."

"Really?" he asked with a surprised look. "Not even for prom?"

She shook her head ruefully.

"Well then, come, m'lady. Your chariot awaits," he replied with a smile and a flourish of his arm. With his hand lightly resting at the small of her back, he guided her to the car and opened the door.

Becca slid inside. Her mouth formed an O as she took in the richly appointed interior of the car. The tan leather seats felt buttery soft under her fingertips. A mahogany wet bar lined one wall of the vehicle, a television dropped down from the ceiling, and God only knew what other amenities were hiding behind all the panels. Through the sunroof, she could see the gray fingers of twilight fading from the evening sky as the last rays of the sun slipped below the horizon.

"Wow, I feel like Cinderella going to the ball," she enthused.

Ethan chuckled softly. "I thought you might like it."

Becca smiled shyly. "Seems you know me well."

"Of course I do," he answered with an air of certainty.

The seriousness of his expression drew her gaze fully toward him. For a moment she was lost in his eyes, and in that instant, Becca thought she saw something mirrored there that she hadn't seen before. She imagined him leaning forward and kissing her tenderly.

But the fantasy was broken when Ethan released her gaze and turned toward the bar instead. He slipped two flutes from the glassware rack. "How about a glass of champagne to celebrate your first limo ride?"

She nodded. "Sure."

He opened one of the panels and withdrew a bottle. After carefully removing the cork, he filled both flutes with the sparkling liquid and handed one to her. "To a fun-filled evening," he toasted.

She clinked her glass to his and took a sip. From the corner of her eye, she watched Ethan do the same. The way his full mouth curled around the lip of the wineglass made her involuntarily shiver.

"Are you cold?" he inquired.

She shook her head. "I'm fine." So as not to give her thoughts away she turned toward the window. The sights and sounds of the city passed by in a blur. The reflection of Ethan behind her shone clearly in the glass. Once again she imagined him leaning over to kiss her, this time on her bare shoulder and up the side of her neck.

For a moment, she closed her eyes and pretended that he was drawing her into his lap. He would gently turn her to face him, parting her legs to straddle his. Starting at her knees, his hands would graze lightly along her thighs, slowly lifting her dress until he found the pretty pink lace panties she was wearing.

Ethan's hand on her shoulder gave Becca a start, making her whirl around with a squeak.

"I'm sorry," he said. "I didn't mean to startle you. You looked like you were a million miles away."

"I–I, um..." she stuttered. "I guess I was lost in a daydream."

"Must have been a pretty good one," he teased.

She merely smiled in response. *You'll know how good*, she thought.

The remainder of the ride passed in amiable silence. She loved that about Ethan, how he didn't feel the need to fill the quietness with banal chatter. Sometimes it was nice just to be still.

Soon Becca noticed that the limousine was slowing. She looked out the window to see they were pulling into the wide circular drive of a palatial house. Her eyes went wide. She took a deep breath and swallowed hard against the butterflies that suddenly began fluttering in her stomach. She wasn't sure she would ever feel at home in this side of Ethan's world.

As soon as the limo stopped by the front door, Ethan hopped out and offered his hand to Becca. She grasped it tightly in an attempt to still the tremors in her own. He pulled her out of the car, then wrapped his strong arm around her waist, drawing her into his side. His free hand still clasped hers, and his thumb caressed the back of her fingers.

"You're trembling," he said softly into her ear. His warm breath feathering against her hair and the sensitive skin of her cheek made her shiver even more. His arm tightened around her. "Are you nervous?"

Becca glanced up at the huge sculpted hardwood door in front of her. Through the high windows above it, she could see a large crystal chandelier hanging from the vaulted ceiling inside. She took a deep breath. "A little," she finally answered. "When you said we were going to your parents' house, I imagined something more like yours, not something quite so...big."

Ethan chuckled and shrugged. "I've never been the type of guy who stands on ceremony. The simple life suits me fine, but my parents are a little more old-school, I guess you might say."

"Oh," Becca replied lamely, still trying to settle her nerves.

Ethan turned her to face him and took both her hands in his. He leaned down, searching out her gaze until her eyes met his. "They may live in a big house, but my parents are really nice. I promise they don't bite."

Becca finally smiled. "OK. I trust you."

"I'm glad to hear it. Shall we go inside now?"

She took a deep breath and nodded. Ethan led her through the portal that reminded her of a castle door. She could scarcely take in the opulence that surrounded her, and stopped trying to when a well-dressed older couple approached them.

Only then did Ethan release her hand to give them both a hug. He made the introductions, and they immediately put her at ease, leaving her feeling silly about being so nervous. Becca realized then he'd been true to his word–his parents were every bit as nice as he was.

At his mom's invitation, Ethan took Becca's hand and led her through a maze of hallways to the back door. Outside, many guests were already taking advantage of the gigantic swimming pool. Dozens more people gathered in small groups around the pool deck and in the side yards talking. At the other end of the pool stood a wet bar, and right next to it, two men dressed in chef uniforms were cooking a variety of meats on one the largest grills she had ever seen. Even though she was wearing a brand-new outfit and had tried to make herself look nice, Becca still couldn't help feeling out of place amidst such luxury.

She followed Ethan to the bar where a man sat, nursing a beer. Ethan greeted him warmly, and Becca knew immediately that this must be his brother, Nathan. He was about the same height and build as Ethan, but his hair was a couple of shades darker, almost jet-black. He did, however, share the same striking green eyes, framed by gorgeous dark lashes that would be the envy of many women. He was very handsome. Becca imagined that the ladies must clamor for his attention.

"Nate, this is my friend, Becca," Ethan said. "Becca, this is my little brother, Nathan."

She shyly extended her hand in greeting. "Pleased to meet you."

Nathan shook her hand before answering in a deep but quiet voice, "Likewise. It's nice to finally meet the girl I keep hearing so much about."

He smiled at her, but Becca noted it didn't quite reach his eyes. There was a sadness mirrored there that she suspected had something to do with the recent loss of his long-time girlfriend in a car accident. She wanted to offer her condolences, but the moment seemed rather awkward for it.

Ethan had started talking again anyway. "So where's Alex?"

Nathan shrugged. "You've got me. She was headed to her room about an hour ago, before the party started, but I haven't seen her since. Maybe she hasn't come down yet."

"I haven't had a chance to talk to her since she got into town. She went to L.A. first to sign her final divorce papers, didn't she?"

Nathan nodded with a rueful look.

"Is she doing OK?" Ethan asked.

"As far as I can tell, but who knows with a woman."

Ethan smiled at Nathan's attempt at a jest, then turned to Becca.

"I really wanted to introduce you to my sister, but it looks like she's missing in action."

"That's OK," Becca replied. "I'm sure she'll be down soon."

"You and she have a lot in common. She's a vet too, you know."

Becca smiled. "Well, I'm not exactly a vet yet."

"Close enough. And you will be," he asserted.

"Are you sure you want to get the two of us together? We might bore you talking shop."

"I wouldn't mind in the least. And I think you could use more friends."

Becca suddenly became engrossed in studying a crack in the cement. "You know I don't make friends very easily, Ethan."

"You made friends with me."

She glanced up at him. "You're different." She shrugged, not sure how to explain it. "You were...sweet," she finally finished.

Nathan choked back his laughter. "Ethan sweet?"

Ethan punched Nathan in the shoulder. "Hey, leave her alone, bro. She can call me sweet if she wants."

"OK, OK." Nathan held his hands up in surrender. "I wasn't making fun of you, Becca. I was teasing this dork."

"Watch who you're calling a dork, numskull."

Becca shook her head and chuckled at the two brothers, who quickly tired of trading insults. Leaving Nathan behind at the bar, Ethan escorted Becca around, introducing her to various friends and business associates. She was surprised when Ethan told a select few about her plans for the free animal clinic, and even more shocked when many of them offered generous donations to get it started when she was ready.

Soon, Ethan's dad made the announcement that dinner would be served. They rejoined Nathan and seated themselves at a small round table in a corner of the yard, along with a middle-aged couple.

While the waitstaff served the food, Becca turned to Ethan. "Don't you think it's a little premature to be telling people about the free clinic? I mean, I don't even have my degree yet."

Ethan shook his head. "It's never too early to plant a seed."

"What sort of free clinic?" a woman at their table asked.

Becca quickly found herself engrossed in conversation as she ate. The lady and her husband expressed a great deal of interest in her idea, and once again Becca was astounded by their generous offer to donate. Apparently, Ethan was right. She only hoped she could rally these people's support again after finishing her degree. If she could, then her dream could become a reality far more easily than she had originally thought.

As her chat with the couple wound down, Becca caught sight of a blonde woman in her peripheral vision. Her body went cold as Lindsay took the empty seat on Ethan's other side, grabbed his arm, and leaned into him flirtatiously.

"You didn't come over to talk to me earlier, Ethan," she pouted with her perfectly-painted red lips.

Becca's grilled chicken dinner turned to stone in her stomach at the sound of Lindsay's sickly-sweet voice.

Ethan smiled indulgently. "We've been talking nearly every day, Lindsay. I thought maybe you could use a break from me."

"Oh, silly!" She slapped his shoulder playfully with her elegantly manicured fingertips. "I could never get tired of you," she said, giggling like a schoolgirl. "Come join me in the swimming pool, and maybe I'll forgive you."

Ethan turned to her. "Becca, do you want to go swimming?"

"Oh...um...I didn't bring a suit."

"Alex might have something you could borrow," he offered, then added with a smile, "if we can find her."

Becca wasn't a very good swimmer and hated to be in the pool with a crowd of people. She shook her head. "That's OK, Ethan. I'm not really much of a swimmer. I think I'll pass. But don't let me stop you from swimming if you want to," she hastened to add.

"All right. If you're sure."

She didn't really want him swimming with Lindsay, but she didn't want to spoil his fun either. She nodded. "Go on. I'll be fine." She looked across the table at Nathan. "Are you going swimming?" she asked him.

"Nope."

"See, I'll stay here and keep Nathan company."

"I guess I can't argue with that," Ethan responded. He turned to Lindsay, who had a triumphant grin on her face. "I'll go up to the house and change and meet you in the pool in a few."

Lindsay started to follow him, but Ethan pointed to the cabanas set up on one side of the pool for the convenience of the guests who needed to change. Becca was sure she saw disappointment flicker across the woman's features, and she breathed a sigh of relief that Lindsay wouldn't be anywhere near Ethan while he was in a state of undress.

The older couple at their table left. Becca tried to talk to Nathan, only to find that he wasn't much of a conversationalist. Being rather shy herself, she had a difficult time keeping the dialog going and finally gave up. If her suspicions were right, Nathan was well on his way to being drunk too.

Nathan rose from the table. "I'm headed to the bar for another drink. Can I get you something, Becca?"

"No, I'm fine. Thanks."

Becca turned in her seat to peruse the gathering and saw Ethan returning from the house. Her heart fluttered at the sight of his well-toned body in a swimsuit. Her fingers itched to caress the hard, muscled planes of his chest. Her gaze followed the light dusting of hair where it trailed over his abdomen and disappeared into the waistband of his suit. Her mind filled with images of the secrets held there. Desire coursed through her body as she dreamed of skinny-dipping with Ethan in the moonlight.

"Hot, isn't he?"

Becca startled as the syrupy voice broke into her fantasy. "I–I don't know what you're talking about," she stammered.

Lindsay chuckled coldly before asserting, "Of course you do. You don't think I saw the way you looked at him during our little business dinner at Milano's last year, when you thought he wasn't watching? The way you were looking at him just now. Like you wanted to eat him up," she finished in an icy whisper right behind Becca's shoulder.

Becca swallowed hard and turned to face the woman. "He's my friend," she ground out through clenched teeth.

Lindsay smiled and clucked her tongue. "Poor Becky. It's all right," she began with false sympathy, "I know women are bound to stare. He is an incredibly sexy man." Lindsay's face grew hard. "But they'd do well to remember that he's *mine*."

Becca's brows drew into a puzzled frown. "What do you mean?"

"I mean," she continued stonily after raking an assessing gaze over Becca, "that a poor church mouse like you doesn't stand a chance with a rich, gorgeous man like him. Enjoy your fantasies, dear, because they're all you'll ever have to keep you warm at night. I'm the one who'll have the real thing in my bed, and he's damn good in it. Too bad you'll never know," she finished with a cheeky grin.

Becca's heart dropped into her stomach at the implication in Lindsay's words. Her entire body quivered with anger and embarrassment. She fought against the sting of tears behind her eyes but refused to cry in front of the vile woman.

"Well, well, well, look what the cat dragged in."

Becca looked up at the sound of a female voice to find a pretty, statuesque brunette glaring at Lindsay like she was a piece of gum she'd found stuck to the bottom of her shoe.

Lindsay's mouth curled into an expression of equal disdain. "I heard you were back from your little foray in the desert. Where was it you went again?"

"Someplace you probably couldn't find even if you had a map," the brunette jabbed back.

Lindsay smiled coldly. "Yes, well, wherever it was, I also heard you slunk over there with your tail between your legs after that handsome rock star husband of yours dumped you."

An inscrutable mask descended over the brunette's face before she answered. "I see you haven't changed a bit, Lindsay. Why don't you go find someone else to bother?"

"Fine," Lindsay replied in an icy tone as she rose from her seat. "I was leaving anyway. The air has become rank with the smell of commoners. Apparently, your parents allow anyone into their parties these days," she finished while throwing an insulting glance at Becca.

Lindsay then proceeded to promenade around the pool deck. Becca had no doubt the woman was fully aware of the fact that her skimpy bikini was drawing the stares of nearly every man she passed.

Becca looked away in disgust.

The brunette took the seat Lindsay had vacated. "Whatever she said, don't let it get to you. She may be rich, but she has absolutely no class."

"You seem to dislike her as much as I do," Becca commented.

"Yeah, well, I have every reason to. She's a gold digger, pure and simple."

"But I thought she was rich."

The woman shrugged. "Her family certainly is, but I heard that her father got tired of supporting her credit-card habit and put her to work. Personally, I think she's not happy that she can't go shopping every day and has set her sights on finding a wealthy husband so she doesn't have to work anymore."

So that's why she's trying to sink her claws into Ethan, Becca thought. She hoped that Ethan was smart enough not to fall for Lindsay's tricks, but having seen the way the woman hung all over him, she wasn't so sure. A man's head could be turned by far less than the perfect assets Lindsay had on display tonight in her barely-there bathing suit.

The woman broke into Becca's musing. "Another reason I can't stand Lindsay is that a bitch just like her stole my husband. Not that he was really worth taking. As far as I'm concerned, they deserved each other. Besides, we vets have to stick together, right?"

Instantly, the woman's identity dawned on her. "Oh my God, you must be–"

"Alexis Montgomery," the woman finished, while offering her hand along with a warm smile. "And I already know that you're Ethan's friend, Becca."

Becca's mouth dropped open in surprise as she shook Alexis's hand. "How did you–?"

"Ethan showed me a picture of you two a while back, so I recognized you right away."

"I'm sorry I didn't know who you were at first, Alexis."

Alexis waved her hand dismissively. "Don't worry about it. And call me Alex. Everyone does."

"OK." Becca grinned, immediately liking Ethan's sister. "Ethan was looking for you earlier."

Alex sighed. "Let's just say these social things aren't really my scene. I'm putting in an appearance to make my parents happy, but I decided to be fashionably late," she finished with a chuckle.

"Ethan said you barely got in from out of town. Where do you live?"

"Well, I used to live in L.A., but after my husband and I separated, I thought it would be a good thing to get as far away as possible. I ended up halfway around the world in Kabul."

Becca couldn't hide her surprise. "You mean..."

Alex nodded. "Yup, Afghanistan."

"Wow! Ethan mentioned that you were finding homes for stray dogs and cats from the Middle East, but I didn't put two and two together to realize you were actually living there. Isn't it scary?"

"It can be sometimes, but mostly, I've been able to keep a pretty low profile as an aid worker. Except I happen to be there to aid animals instead of people. We have a small shelter set up, but it's been an uphill battle to get locals interested in adopting companion animals. Some people are afraid of them, some abuse them, but most are simply indifferent to them."

"That's so sad. I guess the people over there have a lot of other things to worry about, though. Stray dogs and cats must seem pretty trivial when you're in a war zone."

"That's very true," Alex conceded.

"Is there anything I can do to help?" Becca asked.

"You can get the word out about the animals needing homes. Most of our adoptions are foreign, but many people don't even know about the work we're doing. We do the best we can, but there are still far too many dogs, cats, and other animals wandering the streets, sick and homeless. The faster we can get the ones in the shelter adopted, the more animals we can take in and help."

"That makes sense. Of course I'll let as many people as I can know about the work you're doing."

"You know, a lot of the animals are brought to us by U.S. and British military personnel. Some of the men and women have found a furry friend that they'd like to take home when their tour ends, but they can't afford the transportation fees or have trouble navigating the paperwork, so we're helping with that too."

"That's wonderful!" Becca exclaimed. "You're doing amazing work, Alex. I almost wish I could be there with you."

"Well, we sure could use the help."

For the next hour, Becca conversed enthusiastically with Alex about her work in Afghanistan and about Becca's own dreams to start a free animal clinic and no-kill shelter. It was incredibly fun to interact with someone who was as interested in animal welfare as she was.

They probably could have talked all evening and into the wee hours of the morning, except that Alex stopped the conversation short and nodded in the direction of the pool where Ethan was finishing up a water volleyball game with three other guys. "Did you want to go swimming?" she asked.

Becca shook her head. "I don't really like swimming with a crowd."

"Hey, a woman after my own heart."

"You don't like swimming with a crowd either?" Becca inquired.

Alex sighed. "Let's just say I have some flaws that don't look good in a swimsuit, and I don't want to scare the guests away."

Alex was such a beautiful woman, Becca couldn't imagine what she might mean. Before she had a chance to ask, Alex pointed toward the pool. "I think Ethan is trying to get your attention."

Becca turned around to see Ethan gliding gracefully through the water to the edge of the pool. "Hey, Becca, why don't you come over here?" he called.

Becca looked at Alex. "Go on and see what he wants. We can chat more another time." She rose from her seat and scanned the assembled guests. "I should probably go find Nathan and make sure he's not getting into any trouble." Alex headed off toward the other side of the pool, throwing back over her shoulder, "Have fun!"

Becca was sure she detected a hint of a limp in the other woman's gait, but before she had time to give it much thought, her attention was diverted again by Ethan.

She ambled over to where he was waiting.

"Are you sure you don't want to get in?' he asked. "The water's great."

Becca shook her head ruefully. "It's really sweet of you to ask, but no thanks."

He patted the edge of the pool. "Why don't you sit here for a while, take your shoes off, and soak your feet? I'm pretty tired after that water volleyball match. We could hang out here and talk."

Becca couldn't deny that the clear water lapping at the side of the pool did look inviting. She gave him a small smile. "All right."

She removed her sandals and carefully hiked her dress up to her knees so it wouldn't get wet before seating herself on the pool deck. The water was exactly the right temperature and felt heavenly on her aching feet.

Ethan floated next to her. "So I see you finally met Alex."

Becca grinned. "Yes, and she's great!"

"I told you the two of you would hit it off."

"And you were right. Oh, Ethan, the work she's doing is amazing!"

"Let me guess," he began while grasping her ankles and pressing her feet into his chest, "you wish you were helping her."

"Are you reading my mind?"

"No, I just know you."

Ethan pressed his thumbs into the soles of her feet, massaging exactly the right spots. Becca closed her eyes for a moment, savoring the feel of his hands. She knew it was only a friendly gesture, but his touch sent an electrifying charge straight up her legs to settle at the juncture of her thighs. Her earlier daydream of skinny-dipping with him returned full force, but before she had a chance to relish it, something collided against her back, sending her toppling into the pool.

Becca could barely swim, and the water where she'd been sitting was deep enough to top her petite height. Ethan's strong arms immediately lifted her above the surface, but the shock of being unexpectedly dunked into the pool left her coughing and gasping for air.

"Are you all right?" he asked.

After a couple of deep breaths to calm her nerves, Becca was finally able to speak. "Yeah, I'm fine."

Ethan drifted along beside her as she took a couple of strokes toward the shallow end of the pool. As soon as they could stand up, Ethan grasped her waist and lifted her back onto the deck.

He looked up at the figure behind her. "Why the hell did you shove Becca into the pool, Lindsay?"

Becca's teeth clenched and her heart pounded with anger and frustration. It figured that awful woman would be behind this, and Becca had no doubt it had been on purpose. Lindsay probably saw Ethan rubbing Becca's feet and decided she was too close to "her man." Becca turned and stood, water streaming from her sodden dress.

"Oops! Sorry, Becky," Lindsay said, giggling. A wine glass dangled precariously from her elegant fingers as she turned her back toward Ethan. "I guess I had a little too much and got a bit tipsy."

Becca knew this last part had been said only so Ethan wouldn't know the truth. The glint in Lindsay's eyes and the hint of a smirk on her lips told Becca that she wasn't that drunk and was anything but sorry. It made Becca want to shove the evil woman into the water to show her how it felt, except she refused to stoop to that level.

By then, Ethan had climbed out of the pool. He grabbed the wine glass from Lindsay and unceremoniously poured the contents into a nearby potted plant. "I'm going to tell the bartender you've had enough for tonight."

"What?" Lindsay exclaimed indignantly.

"You can't go around drowning my guests, Lindsay. I'll arrange a ride home for you."

"But I'm not ready to go home yet, Ethan," Lindsay whined, hanging onto Ethan's arm.

"Fine. Go find some coffee and sober up then."

"I don't see you telling your brother that," she muttered before finally slinking off.

"Are you sure you're OK, Becca?"

She nodded.

"There are towels over by the cabana. I'm going to find Alex and see if you can borrow some clothes."

"Thanks."

Ethan headed toward the house while Becca grabbed a towel and plodded back to their table. She lifted the hem of her soaked skirt and tried to wring some of the water out of it.

"I saw what that bitch did to you."

Becca started at the sound of a deep male voice and turned to find Nathan sitting in the shadows.

"Sorry, I didn't mean to scare you," he said with a slight slur.

"It's OK. I just didn't see you there." Her brows drew down in puzzlement. "Are you hiding?"

Nathan released a snort of laughter. "Let's just say I'm not really fit company right now. But at least I know when to stay away from people. That woman," he said, pointing vaguely toward Lindsay who was strutting back toward the pool, flirting with a couple of men along the way, "she never knows when to quit."

"So you don't like her either, huh?" Becca asked while pulling the pins out of her hair. The waterlogged mass dropped over her shoulder, and she began rubbing it dry with the towel.

"She's a spoiled little rich girl who always wants what she can't have." Nathan lifted a long-neck beer bottle to his lips and took a sip.

"That's what Alex said too."

"A few years back, Lindsay got it into her head that she wanted me. I told her I was already spoken for, but one night when I was out dancing at a club with my girlfriend, Jenna, we ran into Lindsay. When Jenna went to the restroom, Lindsay came over and started pressing up against me and trying to get me to dance with her. I politely told her no and tried to push her away. I could tell she was half drunk, and I didn't want to be rude. Jenna, she had no such reservations. When she came out and saw Lindsay hanging on me, she threw a drink in her face and told her to get away from her man before she tore her bleach-blonde hair out by the roots." Nathan stopped for a moment to laugh at the memory, but sobered quickly. "God, my Jenna was a little spitfire," he finished wistfully.

The dim light filtering into the corner through the leaves of a nearby hedge cast a lattice pattern over his face, revealing droopy, red-rimmed eyes filled with sorrow.

In that moment, Becca couldn't help feeling bad for Nathan. He'd obviously been drinking heavily, trying to mask all the grief and pain he must be feeling over Jenna's loss. Having lost her mom less than a year ago, Becca could relate. "I'm so sorry about what happened to Jenna."

"Thanks," Nathan murmured. He blinked furiously, as though trying to hold back tears, before taking another swallow of his beer.

Becca wasn't sure what else to say, so she was glad when Alex walked up. One look at Becca's disheveled state, and her expression filled with sympathy. "Oh, sweetie, I'm so sorry about what Lindsay did. That bitch!"

Becca felt a smile tugging at the corners of her lips at Alex's insult, but it wasn't enough to stave off the depressed feeling that assailed her. She'd tried so hard to look nice for Ethan tonight. Now he'd probably only remember her looking like something the cat dragged in, while Lindsay looked hot and sexy in her bikini. "I must look like a drowned rat," she said, pushing damp strands of hair out of her face.

"Aw, it's not that bad." Alex patted her shoulder comfortingly. "Here, I brought you some capri-length yoga pants and a t-shirt. Since I'm a good six inches taller than you, I figured they were the only things of mine that would fit."

"Thanks, Alex. I'll go change, and then I think I'll head home."

"You're welcome, sweetie. Hope to see you again soon." Then turning to Nathan, she said, "Nate, honey, why don't you let me drive you home? I think you've had a little too much to drink."

Nathan tipped up his beer bottle and drained the contents before answering. "In my estimation, Lexie, I haven't had nearly enough."

Despite his words, he went with Alex.

Becca changed in one of the cabanas and went in search of Ethan.

She found him at the bar with Lindsay, who was sipping on a cup of coffee.

"Hey, Becca. I see Alex found some clothes for you to wear."

"Yeah, thanks."

"I was going to come back and check on you, but I wanted to make sure Lindsay wasn't getting into any more trouble first."

"Don't worry about it. I'm going to call a cab and head home."

"You don't have to do that. Give me a minute to get changed, and I'll take you."

"No, Ethan. It's fine. You still have guests."

"Well, technically, they're my parents' guests," he protested weakly.

"Yeah, but this is a company party, and you are the CEO. You should stay. I can get home by myself."

"I guess you're right," he finally conceded. "But you're not taking a cab. The limo is still out front. The driver is waiting, and he knows your address."

"I don't–"

"No arguments," he said.

Becca didn't really want to take the limo. It was going to be a long, lonely ride filled with memories of the trip over with Ethan. Knowing she wouldn't win the argument, she finally nodded in acquiescence. While bidding Ethan good night, she saw Lindsay's smug face behind his shoulder. She could hardly bear the thought of the woman possibly trying to seduce Ethan after she was gone, yet she was feeling too emotionally drained to stay and fight. If Ethan hadn't fallen in love with her yet, he probably wasn't going to, and maybe it was time she gave up on her girlish fantasies.

Chapter 13

Edna sat on the wooden park bench that adorned her front porch, knitting a blue afghan. The small globe light above provided enough illumination to see, but she knew the pattern by heart anyway. She cheerfully hummed a 50s tune, something she and Freddie had slow-danced to at their senior prom. Her happy memories were interrupted by the sight of a slumped, bedraggled figure plodding up the walkway. When recognition dawned, she uncharacteristically dropped a stitch.

"Rebecca, dear, is that you?" she called into the dark night.

"Oh! Hi, Edna. I didn't see you there."

As the young woman who was like a granddaughter to her edged closer to the porch, she could see that Rebecca was dressed differently than when she'd left, and was carrying the pretty sundress and shoes in one hand.

"What on earth happened to you, dear?"

Rebecca sighed heavily. "A witch named Lindsay is what happened."

"That horrible woman Ethan used to date?"

"That's the one," she replied with a defeated look.

Edna patted the bench. "Come, sit."

Rebecca plopped down beside her and dropped her shoes and soggy dress onto the concrete.

"Want to talk about it?"

"She shoved me into the pool," she replied simply.

"Why in the world would she do a thing like that?"

"Because she hates me. Because she thinks I'm trying to steal Ethan away from her. Because she's a bi-" Rebecca stopped short. "Sorry."

Edna smiled. "That's all right," she said as her fingers continued to weave the yarn into perfect stitches. "You were only saying what I was thinking."

Silence fell between them for long minutes before the calm of the night was punctuated by a single sob. Edna's head jerked up from her work to see Rebecca's face crumpled in sorrow.

"What should I do, Edna?"

Edna laid her knitting aside and drew the young woman into her arms. "About what?"

"I love him so much," she sniffled.

"Ethan?"

Rebecca nodded. "But why would any man want this—" She pulled back to sweep a hand over her own body. "—when he could have her? She looks like a supermodel and I'm..." Her voice trailed off.

"There is absolutely nothing wrong with the way you look," Edna stated emphatically. She reached across the space to smooth Rebecca's damp hair away from her face, and gently lifted her chin to look her in the eye. "You're a beautiful young woman, and any man should be proud to have you on his arm."

Rebecca said, "No man has wanted me so far."

"What are you talking about, dear?"

"I've never even had a real relationship. The handful of guys I've gone out with only lasted for a few dates, and they were usually the one to break it off."

"They broke up with a pretty, kind, intelligent girl like you? If you ask me, they weren't using the sense God gave them."

Rebecca didn't look convinced. "I thought Jay might finally be the one, but he ended up being the most horrible man I've ever known in my life except for that snake, Trent."

"That jerk doesn't count. He was nothing but a sociopath, plain and simple."

Rebecca still looked skeptical. "Even my own dad didn't want me. Twenty-five years, Edna, and never once has he tried to contact me." The tears silently rolled down her cheeks as she continued. "And he was only the first in a long line of losers that Mom dated. She was a great mom. Until Trent, she never brought the men home, especially when I was little, but I could see it in her eyes every time she broke up with one of them."

In that moment, what had Rebecca so upset finally became clear to Edna. "Ah, now I see what this is all about. You think that because your father didn't love you, no man can."

Rebecca seemed to ponder what she'd said for a while before answering. "I hadn't really thought about it that way, but I guess maybe you're right."

"Well, let me tell you something," Edna began while patting

Rebecca's knee in a comforting gesture. "One time, your mother told me about your father. It sounded to me like he was too young and too afraid of responsibility to step up to the plate and do his duty."

"But if it was a matter of maturity, why didn't he come looking for me when he got older?" Rebecca asked sadly.

"I don't know, dear. Maybe he started another family and didn't know how to tell them about you. Maybe he didn't know how to apologize to you for not being there. Maybe he simply never grew up. You know, some men are like that. But I'll tell you this, if he ever did meet you, he couldn't help but love you. There's nothing not to love." She finished by giving Rebecca's knee a reassuring squeeze.

"But what about Mom. She never found Mr. Right. What if I'm doomed to be like her?"

Edna gave her a sympathetic smile. "You know what else I learned from those talks with your mother?"

Rebecca shook her head. "What?"

"You're father was the love of her life, and I don't think she ever got over the pain of losing him or the hurt he caused by abandoning her when she needed him the most. Even though she never said it in so many words, I think she was afraid to love again, so she subconsciously chose men who were emotionally unavailable to avoid the hurt of another broken relationship."

"Wow! That's so sad to think of Mom alone all those years with no one to love or to love her in return."

"Oh, I wouldn't say no one, dear. She had you, and she adored you more than any mother I've ever known."

Rebecca scrunched her face into a frown. "Still, I can't imagine living my entire life without a loving husband to share it with."

"And that, Rebecca, is why you are not your mother," Edna stated emphatically. "The way I see it, you're a hopeless romantic who would never give up on love. You have an open, giving heart, and you have a pretty good head on your shoulders too. You may have made one mistake with that slimy weasel, but that doesn't mean you don't know a good man when you see one. You told me a few minutes ago that you love Ethan."

"I do. More than I could ever begin to tell you. He's amazing and wonderful and everything I've ever dreamed of." Rebecca's gaze dropped to her hands, folded in her lap. "But I don't think he loves me."

"I don't know what would make you say that. After all, he's been coming over every Friday like clockwork for the past year, and even started coming late to accommodate your schedule when you began working the Friday evening shift."

Rebecca finally looked up and shrugged. "But it's not like it's a date or anything. We're two friends getting together to watch movies."

"Well, that's neither here nor there." Edna waved her hand dismissively. "What's important is that you have feelings for him, and I can certainly see why. He's handsome, rich, and has a great job. He loves his family and loves animals every bit as much as you do. And you know what I think is the best thing about him?" She paused momentarily until Rebecca met her eyes. "I haven't met a nicer, more gentlemanly young man since my Freddie," she added, answering her own question with a wistful smile. After allowing herself a moment to indulge in fond memories, Edna crossed her arms over her chest and exclaimed, "So what are you waiting for? Tell him how you feel."

"Oh, Edna," she sighed. "It's not that easy."

"Any relationship worth fighting for never is," Edna countered.

"It's more complicated than that. I may have fallen in love with Ethan, but that doesn't mean he feels the same way about me. If he doesn't, I'll lose him. It would be too awkward to try to continue our friendship after one of us dropped a bombshell like that. Besides, I'm still not convinced that Ethan isn't seeing Lindsay again."

"Why would you think that?"

"The few times I've seen them together, he's been pretty solicitous toward her."

"You told me he was working on a really important business merger with her. Maybe he's just being nice to make sure the deal goes through."

"I suppose it's possible. But that doesn't explain Lindsay answering the phone when I called Ethan's room at the resort where they were supposed to be working on the merger, or the things she said to me tonight. I'd rather be pushed into the pool a dozen times than to hear her tell me that Ethan belongs to her and all but say that she's sleeping with him."

Edna's eyes widened in surprise, but it didn't take long for the wheels to start turning in her head. She might be an old woman, but her mind was still sharp. "Tell me exactly what this Lindsay said."

"I don't remember precisely. Something like a poor church mouse like me didn't stand a chance with a rich, handsome man like Ethan. And then she said my fantasies were all I'd ever have to keep me warm at night, because she'd have the real thing in her bed, and he was damn good in it."

"And what did she say when you called the hotel?"

"That Ethan couldn't come to the phone because he was in the shower."

"Was that after she told you about Ethan funding your sponsorship?"

"Yeah, but what does that have to do with anything?"

"Hmm," Edna hummed while tugging her earlobe in contemplation. "You know what I think?" Before Rebecca had a chance to answer the rhetorical questions, she continued, "I think she's jealous and scared of you."

"What?"

Edna could tell that she'd completely shocked and bewildered the poor girl. "I said that she's scared of you," she repeated. "And all the things she's said and done to you were engineered to make it look like she had the upper hand."

"But why would she be scared of me?" Rebecca asked, still obviously puzzled.

"Because I've seen the way Ethan looks at you, and she probably has too."

"And how does he look at me?" Rebecca asked skeptically.

Edna rolled her eyes heavenward and threw up her hands dramatically. "Why, the same way you look at him, for goodness' sake. His eyes light up like a firefly whenever he's around you, and he looks like a man in love. Tonight, when you opened the door all dressed up in your cute little sundress and strappy sandals with your hair and makeup so pretty, I thought his eyes might pop right out of his head. And while you were chatting with me before you left, he couldn't take his eyes off you. In fact, he was practically devouring you from head to toe. Looked like he'd like nothing better than to scoop you up and carry you off to his bedroom."

"Edna!" Rebecca gasped before turning a bright shade of red.

Edna spread her hands in a placating gesture and glanced at Rebecca. "I'm just calling it like I see it."

"Maybe you should get your eyesight checked."

Edna gave her a look of indignation. "My glasses are perfectly fine, dear. And I'm telling you that boy is madly in love with you. You know, that night you were so upset and cut your finger, he looked utterly miserable, and I even saw him crying too."

"Really?"

"You better believe it!"

Rebecca's brows drew down in thought. "But if he's in love with me, why didn't I pick up on it?"

Edna gave her a motherly smile. "Rebecca, dear, you may be twenty-five, but in the ways of the heart, you're still very young. Maybe you don't have enough experience with men to pick up his signals. Tell me, has he ever found little ways to touch you that make you feel special?"

Rebecca's eyes came up to meet Edna's, and they glittered in the light from the porch lamp. "Tonight he massaged my feet while I was soaking them in the pool."

"Ooh, that's a good one!" Edna exclaimed while bumping shoulders with Rebecca conspiratorially. "How about gifts? Has he ever given you some little thing that might show he cares?"

Rebecca thought about this one a little longer. "One time, he went out of his way to buy me my favorite chocolates. Not to mention he went way overboard at Christmas," she answered as the beginnings of a smile played at the corners of her mouth.

Edna gasped. "See, what did I tell you? How about looks? Has he ever given you a longing look? You might have to think a little harder about that one, especially if you didn't know what it was at the time."

Rebecca ruminated on that one for a while, and finally responded with an affirmative nod. By now her face was practicality beaming. "I do remember him giving me some odd looks. It was usually only for a moment, so I thought I was imagining it."

"It's true that the eyes are the windows to the soul, my dear. They never lie."

Rebecca's gaze dropped as she added so softly Edna had to strain to hear, "He kissed me once too."

Edna's eyes flew wide. "What? When did this happen? Why didn't you tell me?"

"It was the night we made up after arguing about the sponsorship. I didn't mention it because he seemed embarrassed and kind of blew it off. He said he got caught up in the emotion of the moment."

That sealed it in Edna's mind. "Rebecca, sweetheart, that boy is crazy about you."

"But if he really does love me, why hasn't he said anything?"

Edna chuckled. "Why haven't you?"

"Because I'm..." Her voice trailed off as Edna saw the light going on in her head. "Oh!"

"From the look on your face, I'll guess you finally figured out that he's as afraid as you are."

"Oh, Edna!" One hand flew to her mouth, and she appeared

completely overwhelmed with joy. "What should I do?" She'd come full circle to the question that had started their whole conversation.

"Tell him that you love him, dear," Edna answered simply.

"Oh God!" Rebecca's hand now pressed against her chest, and she looked overwhelmed in a different way. "I'm so scared. I don't know if I can."

"Allowing yourself to be vulnerable to another person is always frightening, but you've done it with Ethan before. After all, it was him you went to first when you were hurting so much last year, not me. Even though you didn't know you loved him then, I think that's very telling. You can do this," Edna said with certainty, "and I don't think you'll be sorry."

"All right. OK," Rebecca stammered nervously. "Now I have to figure out how and when and where..."

"Don't overthink it, dear. Let it happen naturally."

Rebecca threw her arms around Edna. "Thank you so much." After expressing her appreciation, Rebecca pulled back. "It's really late. I should probably let you get some sleep. But *I* probably won't be able to," she finished with a laugh before getting to her feet and collecting her dress and shoes.

"Have a little faith in yourself, Rebecca, and you'll do fine."

"I'll try. Thank you again, Edna." The young woman threw a little wave back over her shoulder as she headed for her own apartment.

Edna sighed and chuckled to herself. *Oh, the wonder of young love,* she thought. *There's simply nothing like it.* She couldn't wait to receive an invitation to this couple's wedding, and as sure as the sky was blue, she knew it was going to happen. She could feel it in her bones.

* * * * *

Ever since her talk with Edna, Becca had been on cloud nine. The mere thought of Ethan loving her as much as she loved him made her feel like dancing on air. For three days, she worked on mustering up the courage to finally tell him the truth, and planning exactly how to do it. She decided on their usual Tuesday lunch date, but instead of going to their favorite little bistro, she packed a surprise picnic lunch for them to share at the Japanese Friendship Garden, only a few blocks from Ethan's office.

With the *when* and *where* settled, she now rummaged through her closet searching for something pretty to wear that Ethan might not have seen before. Her wardrobe was pathetic, leaving her with few choices. She finally picked a simple pair of black leggings and an emerald-green tunic top. The shirt had cute little cap sleeves, pretty embroidery on the shoulder, and best of all, a plunging neckline that showed a bit of cleavage. It had always been one of Becca's favorites, because it complimented her hair and skin tone perfectly.

Once dressed, she added comfy black sandals and a pair of faux diamond stud earrings in a silver flower-shaped setting. She brushed her hair and gathered it into a high ponytail before applying a little makeup. Taking one last look in mirror, she smiled at her reflection. Nothing could bring her down today.

Becca gathered her purse, the picnic basket and blanket. Locking the door of her apartment behind her, she headed for her car with a spring in her step. During the drive to Ethan's office building, she hummed along with the upbeat songs on the radio and imagined what her lunch with Ethan would be like. After sharing their meal in the beautiful garden, she would take Ethan's hand and tell him about her feelings. She hadn't rehearsed exactly what she would say, because she wanted the words to come straight from her heart. In all her dreams of how the scene would play out, Ethan was always surprised. He couldn't believe that she loved him too, and was ecstatic to find out. Then he gathered her into his arms for a deep, passionate kiss that left her breathless.

After replaying the fantasy in her mind several times, Becca arrived at the parking garage for Ethan's building. She pulled into an empty space and bounded from her car into the elevator. Excitement thrummed through her veins, making the ride up to the twentieth floor seem to take forever.

When Becca stepped off the elevator into the reception area, she nearly ran into Cathy on her way out to lunch. The secretary greeted her warmly, and Becca gave her a sunny smile in return.

"Mr. Montgomery is finishing up a business meeting, but he should be out shortly," Cathy told her as she took the elevator Becca had just vacated.

"Thanks," Becca replied before the doors closed.

She seated herself on the sofa, with the picnic paraphernalia at her feet, and stared out the window. Now that she was finally here, her nerves started to get the better of her. She rubbed her sweaty palms against her leggings and took a few deep breaths, trying to calm herself. When that didn't work, she got up and paced the length of the waiting area, making sure to avoid getting too close to the windows. The last thing she needed in her current agitated state was a case of vertigo.

After a while, she checked her watch. Fifteen minutes had passed since she'd arrived. Ethan was late. It was highly unusual for him, so he was bound to be out soon. Cathy had said he would. Instead of allowing her mind to conjure any further anxiety, Becca sat down again and picked up a magazine from the coffee table. She found an interesting article on animal welfare that engaged her attention. By the time she finished reading it, another fifteen minutes had passed.

Where on earth was Ethan? Had he forgotten their lunch date? It was becoming harder and harder to remain patient, but this was a really important day for Becca. She was determined to wait as long as necessary. When another ten minutes went by and Ethan still hadn't emerged from his office, her resolve began to waver along with her excitement.

Not knowing when Cathy would return from her lunch break, and not wanting to leave without seeing Ethan, Becca headed toward the hallway to his office. She hated to interrupt his business meeting, but maybe he wouldn't mind if she just said a quick, "Hello." If he was still too busy to go out, she would simply leave.

After taking a couple of steps down the hall, Becca could see Ethan's door stood ajar. Taking that as a sign that he was finally finished with the meeting, her steps quickened, the smile returned to her face, and her heart felt like it might leap out of her chest.

Lindsay was determined to get Ethan back, but Becky had become an ever-present obstacle to her reaching that goal. It was obvious that the girl was crazy for Ethan, and for some reason that was beyond Lindsay's comprehension, Ethan seemed taken with the little mouse too. So far, her efforts to separate the two hadn't worked, so now it was time to get down and dirty.

She had arranged everything perfectly, and now it was time to put her plan into action. After months of negotiations, which she had purposely drawn out to spend more time with Ethan, they had finally reached an agreement for the merger deal. She was supposed to be at Ethan's office at noon Tuesday to sign the contracts, but knowing that Ethan had his usual lunch date with Miss Goody Two Shoes that day, she had deliberately showed up a half hour late. Luckily for her, the normally punctual Ethan was so disconcerted by her tardy arrival that he had forgotten all about his "date."

He now sat at his desk, scanning the contracts before placing his signature on the bottom line. While waiting for him to finish, Lindsay excused herself to use the ladies' room, but instead, she crept down the hall far enough to see Becky pacing the reception area.

Lindsay smiled gleefully. The girl was obviously agitated, which played into Lindsay's plan perfectly. Hopefully, Becky would get impatient enough to come to Ethan's office, where she would soon get an eyeful.

Lindsay returned to the office quietly, carefully leaving the door ajar. She turned to see Ethan signing the last page before gathering up the papers and arranging them in a neat stack.

"Well, that's all of them." he said. "Looks like your father and I are now officially business partners."

She put on a wide smile and walked to his desk, swinging her hips enticingly. "We should celebrate."

"What did you have in mind?" he asked suspiciously.

She bent over to retrieve her tote bag from the floor, making sure that Ethan got a good view of her shapely rear and long legs in her short business skirt. With a flourish, she pulled out a bottle of champagne and two glasses. "I brought some bubbly for the occasion."

"All right," he agreed, "but only one glass. I still have a lot of work to do and need a clear head."

Lindsay placed the glasses on the corner of his desk and retrieved a corkscrew from her bag. She opened the bottle and filled both flutes, then rounded the desk, ostensibly to give one to Ethan. As soon as she was close enough, she pretended to catch her stiletto heel in the carpet. Pitching forward, she spilled both glasses down the front of Ethan's shirt just as she'd planned.

Ethan jumped as the cool liquid penetrated the garment, but being the gentleman he was, he grabbed her waist to steady her. "Easy there, Linds. Are you OK? Did you twist your ankle or anything?" he asked with concern.

She put on a show of testing her ankle while savoring his hands on her hips. "I'm fine. Oh, Ethan, your shirt and tie are ruined," she purred sympathetically.

He looked down at his soaked front with a rueful smile. "I thought I was going to be drinking champagne, not getting christened with it."

"I'm so sorry."

"Don't worry about it." He loosened his tie and began to unbutton the shirt. "I have a spare in the bathroom closet."

"I'll get it for you," she offered enthusiastically. "And here, let me take these too. I'll see if I can salvage them. I've heard cold water helps. It's the least I can do for being such a klutz."

By then, Ethan had the shirt unbuttoned, and he stood to tug it out of his pants. "All right," he acquiesced as he shrugged out of the shirt and tie and handed them to her.

The sight of his bare chest made her feel like drooling. She wanted to run her tongue all over it, lapping up every drop of champagne. Instead, she ruthlessly tamped down her desires, reminding herself that there would be plenty of time for that once she got rid of her nemesis.

Lindsay glanced out the slightly open door on her way to Ethan's private bathroom. No Becky yet. She continued on her mission, putting the shirt and tie to soak in a sink full of cold water and retrieving a crisp, clean white shirt from the closet.

She stopped a moment in the bathroom doorway, once again taking in the sight of a shirtless Ethan. He was turned away from her, which gave her the perfect opportunity to stare without him knowing. He reclined in his leather executive chair, looking relaxed as he perused a business magazine. He looked so powerful and masculine sitting behind his desk, the muscles of his upper body hard and well defined. As her eyes roamed his partially naked body, she slowly unbuttoned her blouse. The sight before her and the thought of what she was going to do next aroused her.

A quick glance through the cracked office door brought a smile to her lips. Excitement coursed through her veins as she saw Becky entering the hallway, headed this way. Tossing the shirt over a nearby chair, Lindsay opened her blouse wide, rounded Ethan's desk, and flung herself into his lap, straddling his thighs. Faster than lightening, she claimed his mouth in a searing kiss before he could even protest just as she saw the little mouse gasp in horror from the corner of her eye. Her revenge complete, Lindsay was sure Ethan would now be hers for the taking.

When Becca reached Ethan's office, she raised her hand to knock on the door, but she needn't have bothered. What she saw through the narrow opening made her knees nearly buckle and her heart plummet to the floor. Her hand flew to her mouth as a small gasp escaped her constricted throat. Instantly, she turned and all but ran back down the hallway.

In her haste to escape the sight of Ethan kissing Lindsay, she nearly plowed into Cathy as the other woman exited the elevator.

"Sorry."

"That's OK. Hasn't Mr. Montgomery come out yet?" the secretary asked.

Her emotions numb, her mind racing, Becca could barely form a coherent thought. "Um...no. P-please tell him I'm not feeling well and went home."

"All right. Are you sure you're OK?" Cathy inquired with concern.

"Yeah, I'll be fine. I think I feel a migraine coming on."

"Aw..." Cathy crooned with sympathy. "Well, you go home and get some rest. I hope you feel better soon."

By now, Becca was already on the elevator. "Thanks," she replied weakly as the doors slid shut.

Becca bit her lip and willed herself not to cry until she was away from the building. Once again, the ride seemed to take forever, but this time for a completely different reason. The moment the door opened on the parking garage, Becca bolted for her car. Tears slid down her cheeks as she fumbled with her key several times before finally fitting it in the lock. Inside the vehicle, she finally released all her anger, disappointment, and sorrow in a round of gut-wrenching sobs.

When Lindsay jumped into his lap and kissed him, Ethan was utterly blindsided. He'd had suspicions that she might want to hook up with him again, but he never expected her to do anything like this. For a moment he couldn't even think, but when his brain finally started processing what was happening, he immediately shoved Lindsay away, unceremoniously dumping her on the floor.

From her sitting position on the carpet, she looked up at him with a stunned expression.

He felt a bit guilty for pushing Lindsay. "Look, I'm sorry for being rough with you, but..." He shook his head still trying to make sense of the situation. "But what the hell!" he finally finished, still unable to articulate much else.

Now she was starting to look a little hurt. "I thought if I reminded you of how good things were between us, you might want to rekindle what we had a couple of years ago."

"What we had?" Ethan felt like he'd just walked into an episode of the *Twilight Zone*. "How good it was?" He pinched the bridge of his nose. "Lindsay, I have no idea what you're talking about. We went out to dinner a few times. We never *had* anything."

"Well, it meant something to me," she ground out, her mouth twisting into an unattractive moue. Now she was obviously pissed.

"Look, I don't think I did anything to lead you on, and if I did, I'm sorry, but let me make myself very clear. I have never had feelings for you, Lindsay, at least nothing beyond those of an acquaintance or a business associate. I don't think you can even call what we have a friendship. I'm sorry if that hurts you, but I can't have you going around thinking that we might start dating again, because it's not going to happen. Ever!"

Ethan extended his hand to help Lindsay up, but she brushed it away like a petulant child, rising to her feet on her own. "Fine!" she shouted. "Go to your precious little bitch. But when you get tired of her skinny little body, remember, you could have had a *real* woman!"

Lindsay flashed her generous breasts–which were practically spilling from her bra–at him before savagely closing her blouse. Then she snatched up her bag and flounced from his office, slamming the door emphatically behind her.

Feeling a headache coming on, Ethan propped his elbows on his desk and massaged his temples. *God!* What was that woman thinking, attacking him like that? He had kissed Lindsay a couple of times when they dated, but he hadn't felt an ounce of desire for her then. Now he felt less than nothing, if that was possible. He realized that most men would kill to be in his shoes, having a beautiful blond bombshell like her ready to jump his bones, but he wasn't most men. There was only one woman he wanted to be kissing, and it wasn't Lindsay.

Even though he never had feelings for her, he hadn't believed Lindsay was a bad person, yet he was beginning to think that Nathan and Alex were justified in their dislike of the woman. She'd just shown him a whole other side of herself that he hadn't seen before.

Ethan's thoughts were interrupted by Cathy entering his office. "Is everything all right, Mr. Mont..." She hesitated a moment upon seeing his shirtless state before faintly finishing his name. "...gomery."

With a deep sigh he replied, "Yeah. Nothing you need to worry about, Cathy. And by the way–this is not what it looks like."

Cathy smiled. "Wasn't thinking a thing, sir. My lips are sealed."

Cathy's trustworthiness and discretion were two of the reasons she had been his secretary for so long. "Good," he said, then indicated the garment that Lindsay had carelessly tossed over the back of a chair. "Could you hand me that shirt, please?"

While Cathy did as he'd asked, she commented, "Boy, the ladies sure can't get out of here fast enough today."

"Ladies?" Ethan asked, with emphasis on the plural, as he stood to don the shirt and began buttoning it.

"Yes, sir. Miss Harris nearly ran me over as I was coming down the hall to your office, and right before that, Miss Anderson did the same as I was getting off the elevator. Are you sure everything is OK?"

Instead of answering, he asked a question of his own. "Miss Anderson?" His brows drew down into a frown. "What was...? Oh God! Today's Tuesday, isn't it?"

"Yes, it is," Cathy answered.

Ethan sank weakly into his chair. "I forgot."

"Forgot what?"

"Nothing." He waved his hand dismissively. "Did Becca say anything before she left?"

"That she wasn't feeling well–something about a migraine–and that she was going home."

Ethan struggled to gather his thoughts so he could figure out how to deal with the situation. Right now, he was feeling like he needed a stiff drink, but that probably wouldn't do much for the muddled state of his brain.

After closing his eyes for a moment and taking a deep breath, a plan began to form. "Here, could you take care of these contracts for me, please?" He handed her the sheaf of papers. "I don't have any more appointments today, do I?"

"No, sir."

"Good. Hold all my calls. I'm taking the rest of the day off."

Cathy gave him a sunny smile. "Certainly."

Once he was alone, Ethan opened his laptop and went straight to FTD.com. While perusing the floral arrangements, he picked up his phone and speed-dialed Nathan.

Nate's voice came over the line. "Hello."

"Hey, you busy, bro?"

"Not really. Why?"

"Could you meet me at my office for lunch in half an hour?"

"Sure, what's up?"

"Sorry for the short notice." Ethan sighed. "Let's just say, I screwed up pretty badly and could use some advice."

Ethan thought he detected a huff of laughter from Nate before he answered, "All right, bro, I'll see you in thirty."

After ending the call, Ethan went back to his other mission. Once the contracts were signed and he was released from that pressure, he had hoped to find a way to tell Becca how much he loved her. He realized he certainly wouldn't be winning any points by missing their lunch date. Sparing no expense, he placed a huge order with the flower shop before heading downstairs to meet Nathan.

Chapter 14

Becca wasn't sure how she got home. She had traversed the route by rote and was barely able to see the road in front of her through the blur of tears filling her eyes. Shoulders slumped, she plodded up the sidewalk to her apartment. A sense of déjà vu washed over her. It was nearly a repeat of last Friday night, except the circumstances this time were far worse.

She stopped at a fork in the walkway and considered for a moment what to do. Rather than heading for her own door, she went in the opposite direction to Edna's.

At her knock, the petite white-haired lady almost immediately opened the door. One look at Becca's red-rimmed eyes and tear-stained face was all the older woman needed in order to know something was terribly wrong.

She took Becca's hand and gently pulled her inside and seated her on the comfortable sofa.

"Rebecca, dear, what's wrong?" she asked in a motherly tone.

"You were wrong." Becca's face crumpled and the tears began to flow again. "He's with her. I told you he didn't want me," she sobbed.

Edna enfolded Becca in her arms. "There, there," she soothed, while lightly patting Becca's back.

Becca had no idea how long they sat like that, but when no more tears would come, she finally lifted her head. Edna handed her a couple of tissues from a box on the end table.

While Becca mopped her face and blew her nose, Edna rubbed her knee and said, "Why don't you tell me what happened?"

In between hiccups and sniffles, Becca recounted her story. "I was going to take your advice. I planned a special picnic lunch and was going to tell Ethan how I feel about him. But he missed our lunch date."

"Well, you said he was working on an important business merger. Maybe he got tied up," Edna reasoned.

"That's what I thought at first too. But after forty-five minutes went by and he still hadn't come out, I decided to go to his office to say hello before leaving."

When Becca hesitated, Edna prompted, "And did you?"

"No," she answered, barely above a whisper. Her heart was breaking all over again, thinking about what happened next. "The office door was ajar, so I thought maybe his meeting was finished. I started to knock, but then I saw him with her."

"Her?"

"Lindsay." Becca could barely hold back the tears to finish. "Ethan wasn't wearing a shirt, and her blouse was open. She was straddling his lap, kissing him." She could hardly get out the last words before another sob escaped.

"What did you do then?"

"I ran. I couldn't get out of there fast enough."

"So you didn't see what happened next?"

"No! Why would I even want to, Edna? She was all but making love to him right there in his office."

"Well..." Edna bit her lower lip as she pondered the situation. "I don't know, dear. There's just something about this whole situation that seems fishy to me."

Becca shrugged. "She's a beautiful woman. He's a man. They have history. It makes perfect sense that they'd get back together."

Edna shook her head emphatically. "No. I know what I saw in that boy's eyes. He's crazy about you."

"Well, he has a strange way of showing it, missing our lunch date to hook up with his ex."

"See, that's just it," Edna began again while thoughtfully tugging on her earlobe. "From everything you've told me of Lindsay, she doesn't seem like the kind of girl Ethan would even like, much less want to...*hook up* with, you said? And with the door open, no less."

Becca lifted her shoulders again. "Maybe they forgot it was open."

"I don't know." The older woman tapped her lip as she thought some more. "You told me that Ethan's brother *and* sister didn't like this Lindsay woman at all. She said some terrible things to you at the party Friday. She's been working with Ethan long enough that she probably knows you have a standing lunch date with him on Tuesday. Ah-ha!" Her eyes went wide as though she just solved a great mystery. "That horrible woman set you up, and Ethan was blinded to her machinations by his kind, trusting nature."

"I don't know, Edna." Becca shook her head incredulously. "That's seems a bit far-fetched even for someone like her."

"Maybe, maybe not. But since you didn't stick around to see what happened next, how do you know he didn't push her away and read her the riot act?"

"He certainly didn't look upset by it," Becca answered, still feeling skeptical.

"Well, only time will tell. But even if he did kiss her in a moment of weakness–and he certainly doesn't seem like the kind of young man who would, mind you–I don't think it means anything to him. I know what I saw, and I still stand by my assessment that that boy is in love with *you*, not that little witch, no matter how attractive you say she is."

Becca's shoulders slumped in defeat as she stared at her hands folded in her lap. "I really don't want to get my hopes up. I don't think my heart can take this kind of pain again. Right now, I don't want to think about it anymore." She glanced at the clock on Edna's wall. "I'm filling in for someone, and I have to be at work in an hour anyway. I'd better go get changed." She rose from the couch and headed toward the door. "Thanks for listening to me, Edna."

"You're welcome, dear. Call me when you get home later. I want to know you're all right."

Becca nodded and left.

* * * * *

Ethan and Nathan sat in a quiet corner booth of their favorite bar and grill a couple of blocks from Ethan's office. The waitress had just delivered platters of hamburgers and fries along with two ice-cold beers.

Nathan started the conversation. "Since I met you at your office, all we've been doing is exchanging small talk. On the phone you said something about needing advice. So what's up?"

Ethan sighed. "Ah, man, it's Lindsay."

"What'd she do this time?"

"What didn't she do?" Ethan returned with chagrin.

As the two men ate their food, Ethan recounted the torturous contract negotiations and all the events that occurred in his office an hour before.

When he was through, Nathan shook his head. "I told you that woman was trouble."

"I know, bro. You and Alex never did like her. But other than being a little clingy when I broke up with her, she never did anything to make me think she was a bad person."

"She was probably being nice to you because she wanted you back."

Ethan nodded. "I get that now. I can't believe I didn't see it coming."

Nathan chuckled. "It's probably because it's your nature to always see the best in everyone. Sometimes you're just too nice, man."

Ethan shook his head in dismay. "Yeah, well, there's one person I wasn't very nice to."

"Who's that?"

"Becca. Thanks to Lindsay's antics, I missed my lunch date with her today."

"Yeah, I can see how that might be a problem." Nathan chewed his last bite of hamburger thoughtfully before wiping his mouth with his napkin and tossing it onto the table. "So...are you ever going to tell that girl how you feel about her?"

Ethan nearly choked on his beer at the sudden turn in their conversation. When his coughing fit finally ended, Ethan gave his little brother a pointed look. "Where did that come from?"

Nathan smiled and chuckled softly. "What? You think I don't know you're madly in love with her? You're with her at least twice a week. You brought her as your date to the barbeque. I may have been drunk that night, but not enough that I didn't notice how you were looking at her every time you thought she wasn't paying attention. If I'm not mistaken, she was giving you some longing looks too."

Ethan shook his head. "I don't know, bro. I haven't picked up on anything like that from her."

Nathan shrugged. "I suppose I could have misread her, but I know I'm not misreading you. So what gives? Why aren't you trying to make her your girlfriend instead of just your friend?"

Ethan sighed deeply. "Nate, you know how that creep used her right after her mother died. I've been giving her some space."

"I can understand that, Ethan, but a whole year? I'd think she'd be in a better place emotionally by now. She seemed to be in pretty good spirits at the party. At least until Lindsay knocked her in the pool."

"Yeah, I felt really terrible about that. I wish she'd let me take her home. That debacle aside, she has been doing really good."

"So...what are you waiting for?"

Ethan leaned his elbows on the table and steeped his fingers. "I don't know. It's just...I don't want to ruin things between us by moving too fast. If she doesn't feel the same way about me, it'll lead to all kinds of awkwardness, and eventually, it would probably end our friendship."

"Ah." Nathan leaned back in his seat and looked Ethan straight in the eye. "So you're scared." It was a statement, not a question.

"Hell, yeah, I'm scared," Ethan replied without hesitation. "I'd rather have her as my friend than not at all."

"But at what cost to your future happiness? How long can you go on like this? What if she finds someone else, and you never tell her how you feel? Sooner or later, keeping quiet might end your friendship anyway."

Ethan shook his head. "I've been thinking about it a lot lately, but I don't know, Nate..."

Nathan leaned forward again, pinning Ethan with an intense gaze. "You know I waited too long to ask Jenna to marry me. Now I'll never get the chance to propose."

"Are you ever going to stop beating yourself up about that?"

Nathan's eyes darkened. "Stop changing the subject, Ethan."

"Fine. But Becca and I are not you and Jenna. Our situations are totally different."

"How so?"

"Becca and I aren't even in a romantic relationship yet. We're friends. You and Jenna lived together for two years, and you were high-school sweethearts long before that. She knew you loved her, Nate."

"Yeah, she knew I loved her. But all she ever wanted was the ring, the big wedding, the kids, the whole nine yards. I could have given her all that. She could have been my wife for those two years. We maybe could have even had a baby. But I never made that commitment to her. I kept making the excuse that we were too young and it wasn't the right time. Now she's dead. None of us knows how long we have, Ethan. She was only twenty-three years old. I think you made my argument for me when you said Jenna knew I loved her. Doesn't Becca at least deserve to know that much?"

When he'd invited his brother to lunch, Ethan hadn't been looking for this kind of advice, but Nathan's words really hit home. That one question haunted Ethan long after he and Nathan parted company. Although he wasn't so morbid as to think that either he or Becca would be passing on anytime soon, he was realistic enough to realize that Jenna was certainly proof that it could happen.

And what had he been waiting for anyway? Nathan had hit the nail on the head when he declared that Ethan was scared.

An hour later, Ethan sat in his home office contemplating the fear of losing Becca altogether versus the relief of finally having his feelings out in the open and the possibility of her reciprocating them. That thought sent a shiver of a thrill through him. The more he considered the positive aspects of telling Becca he loved her, the more his anxiety began to dissipate. He now knew beyond a shadow of a doubt that it was time for him to put his fears aside and tell Becca the truth.

A smile lit up his face as a plan began to form in his mind. He knew exactly how he was going to do it. It was a gesture so grand, it would leave Becca with absolutely no doubt about his love.

* * * * *

Becca trudged up the sidewalk to her apartment with a heavy heart, her arms filled with grocery bags and the day's mail. After working the dinner shift, her feet ached badly. All she wanted to do was take a nice, long hot bath to soothe her sore muscles and curl up in bed for an hour or two with a romance novel before getting a good night's sleep.

At her door, she rummaged in her purse for the key. After what seemed like an eternity, she finally located it and fumbled several times while trying to fit it in the lock, nearly dropping her load in the process.

Once inside, she was greeted by a soft meow.

"Hello to you too, Miss Kitty. And how was your evening?" Becca crooned to the animal. "I bet you spent it curled up sleeping, huh?" she muttered wryly. "Boy, that sounds great right about now."

She sighed heavily as she kicked off her shoes, then tossed her keys and mail on the desk before flipping on the light switch. When she turned around, her mouth dropped open with a gasp and her hand flew to her throat.

Her entire apartment looked like it had been turned into a gift shop. The grocery bags slid to the floor, temporarily forgotten as she slowly ventured closer, taking it all in. Every flat surface was filled with gift baskets. There was a wine and cheese basket, a fruit basket, and a pretty pink spa basket. She also found a huge box of Godiva chocolates. A gorgeous arrangement of at least three dozen red roses in a cut-crystal vase graced the center of her dining room table. It was flanked by an adorable brown teddy bear holding a balloon that said, "I'm sorry."

One hand now covered her mouth as she stared at everything in amazement.

"Pretty impressive, huh?" At the sound of Edna's voice from the doorway, Becca jumped. "Sorry, dear. I didn't mean to startle you."

She spun around. "Who on earth...?"

"Who do you think?" the older woman asked with a look of indignation, as though it were a silly question.

"Ethan?" Becca replied weakly, still barely able to form a coherent thought.

"Of course." Edna chuckled softly as she closed the door behind her. Taking Becca's arm, she steered her toward the couch. "You look like you need to sit down."

"Yeah." Exhausted and shocked, Becca slumped onto the sofa. Miss Kitty leaped up next to her and began kneading her paws against Becca's leg. Finally, the cat settled down with a contented purr while Becca absently stroked her fur. "How did all this get in here?"

Edna smiled. "Well...since you weren't home, the deliveryman asked me if I'd accept a floral delivery for you." She laughed. "I thought he meant a vase of flowers, but when I saw how many gifts he had, I let him in with the spare key you gave me."

"How do you know it was Ethan?"

"Who else would go to all this trouble and expense?"

"I guess you're right," Becca replied lamely.

"But in case there's any doubt in your mind..." Edna reached into the basket on the end table closest to her and withdrew a card. "...read for yourself."

Becca took the card and carefully opened it. She read the message aloud. "I'm sorry for missing our lunch date. Please forgive me. Ethan."

"See, I told you that boy's madly in love with you."

Becca's shoulders slumped. "This doesn't prove anything except that Ethan has a big heart and feels bad about missing our date. It doesn't change the fact that I saw him kissing Lindsay today."

"Nonsense. I still think that woman engineered the whole thing to upset you."

"I don't know, Edna. I think because you had a happy marriage, you believe everything will work out for everyone else. I used to be a hopeless romantic like you, but I don't think I am anymore." Becca laid her head back against the cushions and stared up at the ceiling. "Sometimes it just isn't meant to be," she finished resignedly.

Before the older woman had a chance to reply, they were both startled by the chiming of her doorbell. "Who in the world could that be at this hour?"

She dragged herself from the sofa and headed for the door just as a loud impatient knock sounded.

"I'm coming," she called as amicably as she could in her still-depressed state.

When she reached the door, Becca peered through the peephole. She was surprised to find a young man wearing what appeared to be a deliveryman's uniform. Hadn't she already received enough gifts for one day?

Leaving the safety chain in place, she cautiously opened the door as far as it would allow. "May I help you?" she inquired.

The man, who had been scanning his clipboard while waiting, seemed startled to finally see someone in the now-open doorway. "I'm from the Executive Courier Service, ma'am," he said, "and I have a special delivery for..." He glanced down at the manila envelope in his hand. "Rebecca Anderson." He looked back up with a slight smile and a question in his eyes.

"I'm Rebecca Anderson," she replied warily.

The man extended the clipboard to her and pointed to a blank line on the delivery log. "Sign here, please, ma'am."

Becca took the clipboard and slipped it through the narrow

opening in her door to sign it. After handing it back to the deliveryman, he passed the envelope to her. "Have a nice evening, ma'am."

"Thank you. You too." She closed the door. It was strange enough to receive a delivery this late in the evening, but it coming via an exclusive private courier service made it all the more odd.

Becca inspected the package in her hands. Only her name and address graced the front of it. There was no return address or any other identifying marks to indicate who might have sent it. Taking a deep breath, she grabbed a letter opener from the desk and slit the top. She pulled out a blue folder embossed with the logo of Paradise Travel. OK. This was getting stranger by the minute.

"What is it, dear?" Edna asked.

"I don't know." Becca carried the folder back to the couch and sat down, drawing her feet up under her. Miss Kitty climbed back into the lap from which she had temporarily been dislodged as Becca perused the contents of the folder. "It looks like arrangements for first-class air travel to Las Vegas, limo service to and from the airport, and four nights' accommodation in an exclusive penthouse suite in a hotel just off the strip."

Wait a minute. Had she read that correctly? Becca shook her head in bemusement, and rubbed her tired eyes thinking that they might be playing tricks on her.

"How exciting," Edna enthused. "Who's it from?"

Becca reread the itinerary, but it added no new clues as to what this was all about. "I have no idea."

Edna was so excited she looked like she was about to burst. "I bet it's another gift from Ethan."

As if on cue, the phone on the end table at Becca's elbow rang. She picked it up and glanced at the caller ID. The name and number she saw instantly put a smile on her face. "It's Ethan," Becca told her friend.

Edna rose. "I'll go put away your groceries and give you some privacy."

Becca nodded before pressing the talk button and placing the phone to her ear. "Hello."

"Hey, gorgeous."

The endearment from the sexy male voice on the other end of the line secretly thrilled her. The last time she could remember him calling her that was when she had woken up in his arms a year ago. The memory brought a flush of heat to her cheeks.

"So did you get the gifts I sent you?"

"Yes," she said, drawing out the word. "Isn't all this a bit much?"

"No," he responded emphatically. "As far as I'm concerned, it's barely enough to make up for missing our lunch date. Lindsay showed up late to sign the contracts, and I got so caught up in getting this deal finished, I totally forgot. I'm so sorry."

A stab of jealousy shot through her at the mention of the other woman's name, but his apology sounded so sincere and contrite, she couldn't hold a grudge. "I forgive you, Ethan."

"I don't deserve it, but thank you. You're an amazing woman, Becca."

"I don't know about that." His compliment made her smile shyly even though he couldn't see her. "By the way, did you send a big manila envelope via a special courier service?"

"Of course it was me. Who did you think sent it?"

"Um, well, actually I was quite confused by it. I couldn't find a return address, and I was beginning to think that maybe it was one of those sales pitches for a time share."

"Oh no," Ethan groaned in frustration. "I forgot to put the card in the folder to explain everything. Sorry about that. I guess it's a good thing I called you when I did, or you might have thrown it out."

"I suppose so," she agreed, "but what's this all about? You know how I feel about you spoiling me, and if this another 'I'm sorry' gift, it's way too much."

"No, it's not an apology gift. I know how hard things have been for you this past year, and since we're coming up on the anniversary of your mom's passing, I wanted to do something special for you."

"Oh, Ethan!" Becca felt tears prick her eyes. "I don't know. You've already been incredibly generous, and you know I don't like taking your money."

"You're not taking my money, Becca," Ethan retorted with an edge in his voice. "I can easily afford a dozen trips anywhere in the world. It's just to Vegas, not the moon, and my uncle owns the hotel. My family leases the penthouse from him, so it's not like I have to pay extra for it. Think of it as a gift–an early birthday present."

"An incredibly extravagant gift!"

Ethan's exasperation hissed through the phone line as he expelled a long breath. "I know my spending money on you makes you uncomfortable, but I thought we were getting past that. I'm only trying to help you create some happy new memories to associate with this time of the year. At least think about it before turning me down cold... Please." He drawled out the last word.

Becca smiled and rolled her eyes at his pleading persistence. "All right, Ethan. I'll think about it. And for the record, you've been a great friend to me. You don't have to give me expensive things or pay my bills to keep me around. I like just spending time with you."

"That's one of the things I love about you, Becca. You like me for who I am, not what I can give you. I never have to worry that you're only hanging out with me for my money, because you won't even take it when I offer. Would it kill you to accept this time, so I don't have to be sneaky about it?"

"OK, I said I'd think about it, and I promise I'll give serious consideration to accepting your offer this time."

"I can live with that," Ethan consented. "Talk to you tomorrow?"

"Sure. Goodnight, Ethan."

"Goodnight."

Becca leaned back against the soft cushions of the sofa and shook her head at the phone as she turned it off. She felt on the verge of tears merely thinking about the kindheartedness of her best friend. It warmed her to the very core to think that Ethan had remembered all that had happened at this time last year and wanted to help her through what was sure to be a rough patch.

He hadn't said that he was going with her to Las Vegas. A part of her longed to go on this trip with him, but that desire was hampered by her nagging suspicions about Lindsay. The image of the two of them in their passionate clinch tore at her heart even more painfully than the thought of living with her unrequited love for Ethan.

Becca was deeply lost in thought when Edna's voice called from the kitchen startled her. "So was I right about the trip being from Ethan?"

Becca rose from the sofa and headed for the kitchen, where she found Edna bustling around. The counter was filled with mixing bowls and all the ingredients for some delectable treat. "What on earth are you doing?"

"Oh, I'm sorry, dear. It's just that all this excitement has me worked up, and when I get anxious I like to bake. I thought I'd whip up a batch of chocolate-chip cookies. Would you like to help?"

Becca thought longingly about the hot bubble bath and the romance novel that had been calling to her when she'd walked in the door, exhausted. But now she was surprised to find that she'd gotten a second wind. Not to mention she could hardly ever say no to Edna. "Sure, why not?" she answered. "After all, you are in my kitchen."

"Oh no. I wasn't even thinking. You must be tired. Should I put all this away and go home?"

"No, it's fine, Edna. I was tired when I got home, but now I'm wide awake. Tell me what to do."

"Oh, good!" Edna clapped her hands. "I love having company when I'm baking. With you to share the cookies, I won't have to worry so much about my waistline." The old lady giggled girlishly as she pulled out two cookie pans and turned on the oven.

Hands on her hips, Becca feigned a look of mock indignation. "Uh...what about my waistline?"

Edna *tsked* in Becca's direction and waved her hand in a dismissive motion. "You have a beautiful figure, dear. I don't think I've ever seen an ounce of extra weight on you." Edna cracked eggs and melted butter while Becca measured and sifted the flour. "I think Ethan *really* appreciates your shapeliness...among other things, of course. And speaking of Ethan, you didn't answer my question about the trip."

"Yes, Ethan was the culprit. I haven't told him whether I'll go yet."

"Well, why not?" Edna asked with a look of utter shock.

"You know I hate taking money from Ethan. Or expensive gifts for that matter," Becca added as an afterthought.

"Rebecca, dear, I know that horrible man taking advantage of your mother really hurt you, but I think it's time for you to move beyond this phobia of men who are richer than Croesus, and just let Ethan pamper you for once."

Becca considered Edna's words. Maybe the older woman was right. Because of that bastard, Trent, she'd been painting all wealthy men with the same brush. A part of her was still scared to accept such extravagances, but another part of her was thrilled that Ethan would do something like this for her.

"Besides," Edna said, interrupting Becca's reverie with a conspiratorial smile. "This might be the perfect opportunity for a little seduction."

"Edna," Becca drawled almost to the point of a whine as her cheeks heated. "Ethan didn't even say he was coming with me."

"Why wouldn't he?"

"I can think of one very big reason why. Lindsay." Becca opened the bag of chocolate chips and popped a few in her mouth. She wished that all her doubts could melt away as fast as the bittersweet candies melted on her tongue. "You didn't see them together today, Edna," she added morosely.

"And you saw them for all of what...five seconds...before you bolted out of there. You already know how I feel about that woman, and I still think she did it on purpose." Edna whipped the cookie batter vigorously, as though she was imagining Lindsay's face in the bowl. "I simply cannot imagine someone like Ethan liking someone like her."

"I know Ethan's wonderful and all as a friend, but when it comes to relationships, men can still be shallow, no matter how nice they are. Look at the few guys I dated. And Jay. And all the guys my mom dated. When it came right down to it, they all wanted only one thing. If any one of them had a bombshell like Lindsay sniffing around, they'd be all over her in two seconds flat."

Edna shook her head as she dropped spoonfuls of batter onto the baking pan. "Even if Lindsay did use her good looks to charm Ethan into kissing her, that doesn't mean he loves her, or that he's sleeping with her, for that matter. I bet if you set you mind to being seductive, you'd have that boy wrapped around *your* finger in two seconds flat."

"Edna," Becca said, sighing in exasperation. "We've been over this before. I don't have anything on Lindsay. She's absolutely drop-dead gorgeous, and if he's really into her, there's nothing I could possibly do to turn his head."

"That's where you are dead wrong!" Edna stated emphatically. She slid the first batch of cookies into the oven and came over to take Becca's hand. "You are a lovely young lady, and you need to have more faith in yourself. If Ethan has half a brain in his head–and, trust me, he does–then there is no way he could love that airheaded hussy more than he loves you. I have a lot more experience with men than you do, and you know what I think?"

"What?"

"I think Ethan has a little more in mind than just being the nice friend who's giving you a get-away-from-your-troubles trip, and you need to swallow your pride, tell your low self-esteem to take a hike, and get on the phone right now and accept his offer." Edna nodded with an air of finality.

Becca still felt uncertain, but she had been reduced to a state of speechlessness and couldn't think of another thing to say to counter her friend's forceful opinion.

Edna's face softened in empathy, and she patted Becca's cheek. "Take a chance, sweetie. Go on this trip and have fun, no matter what. But if that young man of yours shows up, you tell him once and for all that you're madly in love with him. I'm almost certain that what happens next will be the nicest surprise you've ever had."

"Or the biggest disaster," Becca muttered.

"Come on. Would a wise old lady like me, who enjoyed almost fifty years of happy marriage, steer you wrong?"

Becca's lips curled up at the corners of their own volition. "Fine, I'll go," she said with resignation. "And *if* Ethan comes with me, I'll try to muster up the courage to tell him how I feel."

"That's my girl! Now you get back in there, call that that poor man, and put him out of his misery by telling him, "Yes."

In the living room, Becca paced back and forth, wondering for the twentieth time if she was making the biggest mistake of her life. Miss Kitty perched on the arm of the sofa, watching her mistress with a bored stare before laying her head on her paws and drifting off to sleep.

Becca had picked up the phone twice, only to put it back down again. Letting out a noise of frustration at her own indecision, she finally grabbed the phone and hit the speed dial number for Ethan before she had a chance to change her mind again.

It rang only twice before Ethan answered. "Hey, gorgeous. I didn't expect to hear back from you until tomorrow."

Becca dispensed with their usual pleasantries so she could get right to the point before she lost her nerve. "OK, I'll go," she said tersely.

After a brief pause, Ethan replied, "You don't sound very thrilled about it. I was kind of hoping you'd be more excited. I really want to do this for you, Becca, but I don't want you to go unless you really want to. I hope you don't feel like I'm twisting your arm."

"No, no. It's not that."

"This isn't still about the money, is it?" Ethan asked.

"No, it's not that either," Becca reassured.

"Good, because I insist on spoiling you rotten on this trip, and I don't want to hear a single complaint about it."

"I think you already have, and the trip hasn't even started yet." Becca finally began to relax and seated herself on the couch.

"Babe, you ain't seen nothin' yet," Ethan replied with a smile in his voice.

"Does that mean you're going too?" Becca inquired with a hopeful note in her voice.

"Um...well...about that," Ethan said with resignation. "I might have a few loose ends to tie up on this business deal, but I'll see if I can get away and join you for a while."

"Oh, of course, you have business to take care of." Becca couldn't quite disguise the tinge of disappointment in her voice.

"Something like that." It wasn't like Ethan to be secretive, and his reticence made her feel suspicious again. "I promise I'll do everything I can to meet you there."

"OK then, I guess...maybe it's a date?" she said, laughing nervously.

"Are you all right, Becca?" Ethan's voice had returned to that of the tender friend. "You seem a little out of sorts. Are you already thinking about the anniversary of–"

"No, really, I'm fine," she said. "I just hope you can make it. I don't think I'll have much fun exploring Vegas by myself."

"Don't worry, Becca. I'll make sure you're taken care of, and that you won't be alone."

Becca's brow creased into a puzzled frown. "I'm not quite sure what that's supposed to mean, but please don't do anything weird on me, OK?"

"Like what?"

"Oh, I don't know. Like hiring one of those beefcake strippers to show me a good time."

"Becca Anderson, I thought I knew you. Do you have some secret fantasy involving male strippers that you haven't told me about?" Ethan inquired mischievously.

"God, no, Ethan!" Thank goodness he couldn't see that she was blushing to her toes. "I said *not* to do that. You know darn well I'd be mortified."

The sound of Ethan's chortling on the other end of the line made Becca realize that she'd neatly set herself up for that one, and now Ethan was just teasing her.

Once his laughter died down, Ethan continued with wonder in his voice. "You're so different from most women, Becca. I can't think of a girl I know who wouldn't be thrilled to be escorted around town by some hot guy, and here you are cutting off any possibility of that at the pass."

"Hey, I'm not immune to hot guys. I just can't help wondering what they're like on the inside. Like whether they have a brain, or if their personality is as beautiful as the wrapping it comes in. I've always dreamed of a special hot guy," she finished wistfully, thinking of the gorgeous man on the other end of the phone.

She closed her eyes for a moment and imagined Ethan as a stripper in a show meant only for her.

Ethan sighed deeply. "Trust me. I promise you'll have the time of your life in Vegas, and maybe all your dreams will come true too."

Something in the tone of Ethan's voice made a shiver of delight trail down Becca's spine, as though he'd just touched her in the most intimate way. "I believe you."

"So are we still on for Friday?" he asked, his playful mood back.

"Sure."

Chapter 15

Before he knew it, Friday night had arrived. While Becca made popcorn and poured sodas, Ethan scanned the titles on the huge bookshelves that covered an entire wall of her apartment. If all went as he hoped, one day he would build an entire library room for Becca, dedicated to her passion for books.

He covertly pulled a couple of particularly racy titles off the shelf. His eyebrows shot up at the sight of a nearly naked couple in a passionate embrace on both covers. As he carefully put them back in their places, he grinned at the thought of his sweet Becca reading something that looked so wild. He hoped that this meant she had an active fantasy life and that she would soon be playing out those fantasies with him...and *only* him.

Ethan continued to peruse the shelves. Yesterday, he had lit upon a brilliant idea. Her books could be his window to her hopes, dreams, and all her romantic and sexy fantasies. Things he couldn't ask her about without giving himself away.

"So, Becca," he called toward the kitchen. "Which one of these books is your favorite?"

Becca came sauntering through the doorway, nibbling on a handful of popcorn with a confused look on her face. "You're interested in romance novels?" she asked.

"Sure, why not?"

"I don't know... Maybe because you're a guy, and most guys think they're stupid."

"Didn't we have this conversation...ooh...about a year ago? Breakfast in bed," he spoke slowly, giving her time to recall. "Ringing any bells yet?"

Her eyes dropped to the floor, and Ethan thought he detected a slight blush in her cheeks. "Yeah, I remember."

"Well then, you'll also remember that I'm not 'most guys.' Second," he continued while ticking off the reasons on his fingers, "you're an intelligent woman and you read them, so they can't be stupid. Third, you've told me about some of the books you've read before, and I happen to think they sounded intriguing. And fourth, what's wrong with a guy reading a romance novel? Come on, I'm man enough," he finished while flexing his biceps in his best muscle-man impression.

Becca smiled shyly and began to giggle. "Nothing, I suppose." Her smile quickly faded, and her gaze fell again. "I guess I could make a recommendation, as long as you promise not to make fun if you don't like it."

Ethan placed a finger under her chin and raised her head until her eyes met his. "You know I wouldn't do that to you, right?"

After a mere second's hesitation, she nodded again, but now her cheeks definitely turned a very becoming shade of pink. "Yeah, but you might not let me live down some of the stuff that's in them."

"Ah, yes, the sexy stuff."

Ethan hadn't thought her face could turn any redder. He decided to try to lighten the mood to ease her embarrassment, and turned his attention back toward the shelves. "Well, the way I see it, reading a few of these books might give me some insights into the female mind. Help me figure out what kind of things a lady really wants. Maybe even fulfill a fantasy or two."

"Oh. OK."

When Ethan glanced back at Becca, she had a look on her face like someone had just slapped her. She quickly recovered her composure, leaving him to puzzle over her reaction. As she began pointing out titles and chatting about them, he temporarily set aside his confusion and refocused on her words, not wanting to miss out on a single thing she told him. They conversed pleasantly about her favorite books for several minutes, with him subtly asking questions about why she liked them so much. When they were through, Ethan had a few books to take home with him, and he made special note in his mind of the one she had specifically named as her all-time favorite.

Becca returned to the kitchen for the snacks. As she filled two glasses with ice and poured the soda, she thought about Ethan's request. She was more than happy to recommend books to him, and was actually impressed that he wanted to try a romance novel, but his comment about fulfilling a woman's fantasy had resurrected images of him and Lindsay in their passionate clinch. Becca knew she had to clear the air about this before the trip to Vegas, but the thought of doing so had her stomach tied up in knots. She wasn't sure she wanted to know the answer to her question.

She gathered up everything and headed back to the living room. Ethan had the movie in the DVD player, and they sat in their usual places, side by side on the sofa, with Miss Kitty curled up, napping, between them. Becca pulled her feet up beneath her, and he casually stretched his legs out, resting his feet on the coffee table. The remote lay next to her on the couch, but she didn't hit the play button. Instead, she stared at the coffee table and took a few deep breaths to prepare herself for what she needed to do.

"Are you going to start the movie?"

Ethan's query gave her a start.

She glanced at him out of the corner of her eye. "Um...no," she said, her voice wavering, "I wanted to talk to you first."

Ethan looked concerned. "Sure. What's up?"

"There's something I need to ask you about, and I don't want you to think I'm being nosy."

Ethan smiled and reached across Miss Kitty to place his hand over hers. His touch wreaked havoc on her brain. "We're best friends, Becca. You can ask me anything. I promise I won't think you're nosy."

Her gaze dropped to her lap, and her heart pounded as though it was trying to escape from her chest. She took a deep breath and blurted out, "Are you in love with Lindsay?"

A moment of deafening silence ensued, and Becca risked a peek at Ethan's reaction. His eyes had grown round and his lips parted in a stunned expression. Then he burst out laughing. For the life of her she couldn't figure out what was so funny.

As his mirth died down, he leaned his head against the back of the sofa and replied, "Becca, I have never been in love with Lindsay." His face took on a puzzled frown. "What would make you think that?"

"Well, you're really nice to her."

"As my brother so deftly pointed out to me a few days ago, I'm nice to everybody. Too nice sometimes."

True, she thought.

"Not to mention, I had a lot riding on this business deal with her, and I couldn't afford to screw it up by telling her what I really thought."

This sounds promising.

"She came into Milano's one night with some friends," Becca said. "I overheard some of their conversation. They mentioned you buying an expensive pair of earrings for her birthday, and it sounded like you two were dating again."

Ethan shook his head. "You must have misunderstood. I've never bought her earrings. In fact, I don't even know when her birthday is. And aside from sharing meals while discussing business, I haven't taken her out in years."

"She also told me at you parents' party that you two were...um..." Becca cleared her throat nervously, unable to finish the thought.

"That we were what?" No sooner had he asked the question than realization seemed to dawn on him. "Oh my God! She did not say we were sleeping together, did she?"

"Yeah," Becca answered sheepishly. "She sort of did. Not to mention that day when I was so upset and you were negotiating the merger at the resort, I called your room when I couldn't reach your cell. She said you were in the shower."

Ethan looked stunned. "I remember her answering the phone that day. In fact, I asked her to, because I was in the middle of explaining some very detailed sales projections, *not* because I was in the shower." He ran his hands through his hair in frustration. "God, I should have listened to Nathan a long time ago about that woman, but I never thought she would stoop so low. I hope you believe me when I tell you she was lying through her teeth on all counts. I have *never* slept with her, not even when we dated. We went out to dinner three or four times a few years back, and that was it. I knew right away it wouldn't work between us."

Things were definitely looking up. If Lindsay was underhanded enough to lie about all those things, maybe Edna was right, and she somehow engineered the kiss too. "There is one other thing. I probably should have said something sooner, but I was kind of embarrassed to admit it."

"What's that?" Ethan asked gently.

"You know the other day when you missed our lunch date?" She hesitated for a moment, and he nodded. She took another fortifying breath before continuing. "I saw the two of you kissing, and it looked pretty intense."

Ethan smiled. "And did you also see me push her off my lap onto the floor?"

Becca finally felt the burden she'd carried for days begin to lift, leaving her giddy. "You did?" she asked, barely above a whisper, before finally regaining her wits. "I—I mean, no, I didn't see that. I felt like I'd walked in on a private moment, and left immediately."

"Oh, Becca, had I known you saw that, I would have explained right away. Nothing happened between me and Lindsay. At least, not from my perspective. She wanted to celebrate signing the contracts with a glass of champagne, but she accidentally spilled it on my shirt and tie. She offered to put them to soak in the bathroom, and when she came back, she threw herself at me. I shoved her away and told her off. She was really pissed, but I think she finally got the message that we are *not* getting back together."

Becca shook her head in dismay. "Now that you've told me the whole story, I feel really silly for thinking what I did about you two."

Ethan lifted a finger to her chin and gently turned her to face him. "Hey, don't feel bad. If Lindsay had told me all those lies and I'd seen what you did, I would have thought the same thing. But know that I would never deliberately keep something that important a secret. Except for my one slip-up, we've always been completely honest with each other, and I swear that will never change. Promise me something, though."

Becca's gaze locked with his as she asked, "What?"

"If you ever have questions about something like this again, just ask, all right?"

Becca nodded and smiled as a complete sense of relief washed over her. Edna had been right about Lindsay after all, so maybe she was right about Ethan's reasons for inviting her on this trip. Excitement bubbled within her at the thought, along with a few butterflies, but if she had found the courage to ask about Lindsay, certainly she could find the courage to tell him she loved him.

Not far into the movie, Ethan found his mind wandering. He was so glad that he and Becca had cleared the air about Lindsay. Had he known about Lindsay's lies, and that Becca had witnessed the kiss, he would have explained right away. The last thing he wanted was another woman he didn't even have feelings for getting in the way of wooing Becca. The fact that it bothered her seemed to indicate jealousy on her part, which made him ecstatic. She probably had feelings for him too–he hoped.

A full year of loving her from afar had been utter torture, yet he had loved every minute of it. Nothing could have prepared him for how much deeper his love for her had grown as the days passed by. And his desire for her had seemed to grow proportionately.

He wouldn't have given up all their friend dates and movie nights for anything in the world, and yet every moment of being with Becca–but not really being with her–was sweet torment. Many times he'd watched a romantic chick-flick like this one with a throw pillow in his lap to hide the evidence of his inability to stop thinking of Becca and himself in the same scenario. When it was his turn to pick the movie, she thought he always favored intense action flicks because he was a guy. It really had more to do with not being able to stand another minute of watching passionate kisses and sexy bedroom encounters without feeling like he was going to go insane.

The night of the company barbecue had been particularly intense. The minute he'd seen Becca in that dress and shoes, with her hair and makeup done so prettily, he was floating on cloud nine. He'd wanted to sweep her into his arms and kiss her senseless...maybe more if she'd have let him. That night, and on many others, he'd gone home after being with Becca and gotten really friendly with his own hand while hoping against hope that maybe he was affecting her the same way.

And yet, despite his burning need to kiss her, to taste her, to touch her, to be inside her, lust wasn't the thing that kept him going.

It was the pure joy he felt when she walked into a room, the way she could make his heart do flip-flops by curling her sweet lips into a smile, the contentment he felt after talking to her for hours, the way she made him laugh with her good-natured teasing. Those were the things he couldn't live without. Now he was finally going to bring everything full-circle by telling her the truth. His heart swelled as his dreams for next weekend filled his mind.

As the male lead on screen swept his leading lady into his arms and planted a passionate kiss on her lips, Ethan imagined himself and Becca in the same scenario, except on the balcony of a Las Vegas penthouse. As the two lovers made their way to the bedroom, Ethan's body began to react in its predictable way. Unfortunately, the throw pillows were on at the other end of the couch, effectively preventing him from reaching one without rousing Becca's suspicion. Instead, he put his feet down and crossed one ankle over the opposite knee. He glanced at Becca from the corner of his eye to make sure she hadn't noticed. He needn't have worried. Her eyes were glued to the television, but her hands were rubbing her bare arms that were covered with goosebumps.

"Hey, are you cold?" Ethan leaned toward her, whispering as though they were in a movie theater. He couldn't imagine how she could possibly be chilled when the actors were practically setting the screen on fire.

"Huh?" Becca seemed confused by his question. "Oh." She glanced down at her arms, but only for a second. She couldn't seem to tear her gaze away from the love scene playing out in front of her. "Um...yeah, a little," she finally replied distractedly.

Ethan rose to grab a hand-knitted afghan from the back of an overstuffed chair, most likely one of Edna's creations. He was grateful for the momentary distraction from the sensual assault that the movie was wreaking on his desires. He glanced back over his shoulder to see Becca still enthralled by it all, and he grinned at the dreamy look on her face.

Had he imagined that Becca's breathing quickened when he'd leaned over to ask if she was cold? Could she possibly be having the same kinds of fantasies that he always had when they watched one of these shows? And if so, who was starring in these fantasies with her?

God, he hoped it was him.

When Ethan turned back to the sofa, he was thrilled to see that Miss Kitty had moved to the windowsill, leaving the space next to Becca open. He sat down closer than he had been before, but still not close enough to touch. She leaned forward as he wrapped the blanket around her shoulders, then he allowed his arm to rest on the back of the sofa behind her. He breathed in her womanly scent, the one that never failed to arouse him. His heart was bursting at the thought of making her his forever.

By the time the movie credits rolled, Ethan had no idea what else had happened on screen. His mind was far too wrapped up in the wonder of his love for Becca.

She followed him to the door and handed him the books she'd selected earlier. "Don't forget these," she said.

"Nope, wouldn't want to do that," he replied while tucking them under his arm. "I'll let you know what I think of them."

He was reluctant to leave, but he knew that if he stayed much longer, it might arouse her suspicions. Instead, he wrapped his free arm around her waist and pulled her into a warm embrace. His heart raced when her hands slipped around his back and her breasts pressed into his chest. He wanted nothing more than to lean down and claim her lips in a passionate kiss, but he also wanted the moment to be perfect, and this wasn't it. *Only one more week*, he reminded himself for the tenth time that night before grazing his lips softly against her cheek and bidding her goodnight.

As Ethan disappeared into the darkness of the night, Becca's hand rose involuntarily to the cheek he had kissed. She closed her eyes, remembering the feel of his lips on her skin. She caressed the spot with two fingers, which she then slid to her own lips, imagining him kissing her there again.

It wasn't unusual for Ethan to embrace her. He often gave her a quick hug at the end of their "dates," but this time he seemed to linger a little longer and draw her a little closer. He also rarely kissed her, and when he did, it was typically a chaste brotherly peck on the forehead. This one had felt more like a promise of something more. The thought sent a shiver through her body that had nothing to do with the cool night air.

Becca closed and locked the door, then crossed the room to straighten up. Placing their empty glasses in the popcorn bowl, she carried the dishes to the kitchen and returned. The discarded afghan lay in a heap on the sofa. As she neatly folded the blanket and draped it over the back of the chair, she recalled how thoughtful he had been.

She smiled. He always was. Of course those goosebumps had had nothing to do with being cold either. It was the intensity of the romantic scene playing out on her television screen and her wild imaginings of it being her and Ethan that had caused her shiver. When he sat so close to her, resting his arm on the cushion behind her, it only added fuel to the flames of her desire. He had never done that before either, and it made her wonder again if Edna might be right. Could Ethan possibly love her as much as she loved him? God, she hoped so.

Chapter 16

Becca didn't see Ethan again before the trip. He had canceled their Tuesday lunch date, saying he was tied up with some important business. He bade her safe travel and promised to call after she was scheduled to arrive in Las Vegas. Becca couldn't help but be disappointed, but it only made her anticipation that much sweeter. She truly hoped he would join her there.

The night before her flight, Becca pulled her suitcase from the closet in order to pack, carefully choosing the most flattering outfits she owned in hopes that Ethan would indeed come. Her spirits were dampened a bit at the realization that Ethan had probably already seen her in everything she owned with the exception of her underwear, but she refused to let it get her down. Maybe she could pick up a new outfit before he arrived. Or maybe if she got really lucky, modeling her pretty bras and panties for him would actually make it onto their agenda. That thought jangled her nerves, so she decided not to ponder it any further. After changing into her nightgown and brushing her teeth, Becca climbed into bed and finally fell into an exhausted sleep.

She awakened, shocked to discover it was her wedding day. She was dressed in an elegant white satin gown with a sweetheart neckline trimmed with lace and tiny beads. She was thrilled to see that the cut of the dress showed a hint of cleavage, something that she was rarely able to achieve with her small breasts. The skirt gathered at the waist in back and fell into a stylish train trimmed in the same manner as the neck opening. She carried a bouquet of white and pale pink roses, accented with greenery and baby's breath, tied with a wide satin ribbon. The sweet scent of the blooms wafted to her nostrils filling her with delight.

She stood at the back of a small chapel filled with fragrant flowers that matched her bridal bouquet. A minister and a man in a tuxedo waited for her at the front of the chapel. An organ began playing the wedding march, and she started her walk down the aisle. Butterflies fluttered in her stomach as the tuxedo-clad man turned to take her hand. Then relief spilled over her in a wave of ecstasy as she saw that he was none other than her beloved Ethan. He was wearing a brilliant smile that made his whole face light up. Tears of joy spilled down her cheeks as they both said, "I do," and then the minister told Ethan he could kiss his bride. He placed one hand on her waist, drawing her close, and the other cupped the side of her face tenderly. He had a look of complete adoration in his eyes as his head tilted to the side and his lips lowered toward hers, making Rebecca's heart skip a beat.

Suddenly an annoying beeping sound intruded on their moment of perfect bliss, and the entire scene faded away into darkness.

Becca's eyes fluttered open to the sound of her alarm clock. She moaned in disappointment and smacked the button to turn off the noise that had ended her exquisite dream. Not quite ready to leave behind her cozy bed and the feelings the dream had evoked, she allowed herself to snuggle back into the sheets, hugging her pillow for a few moments longer. Maybe the dream was an omen of good things to come. Sighing contentedly, she finally threw back the covers and headed for the bathroom. With a smile on her lips, and humming the wedding march, Becca hurriedly showered and dressed. She'd slept in this morning, hoping to feel refreshed and energized for her big day of travel, and now she had several last-minute things to do before the ride to the airport Ethan had arranged for her arrived.

Three hours later, Becca settled back into her airplane seat feeling happier than she had in a long time. She'd never flown first class before, and she was amazed at how much more comfortable it was than coach. The seats were larger, with lots more leg room, and the flight attendant had been very attentive, offering her refreshments even before the plane had taken off.

She had also been stunned earlier this afternoon when a uniformed chauffeur had knocked on her door and led her to a big black limousine. When Ethan had said he was sending a car, she'd expected nothing more than a taxi or an airport shuttle service. She was already feeling like a fairy princess, and the trip had barely begun. What other luxuries might be in store for her upon her arrival, she could scarcely imagine.

As the plane continued on its course for Las Vegas, Becca took a deep breath, leaned her head back and closed her eyes. Instantly, images from her dream of the night before filled her mind. She couldn't help herself from picking up the fantasy where it had left off. This time it didn't stop at the kiss.

Desire coursed though her body, the very thought of making love with Ethan heating her core. She could only dream of what that might be like, since she had never truly made love to anyone. Ethan was such a sweet guy, she was confident that he would be a gentle lover, and that thought made her sigh with contentment.

"Ladies and gentleman." The captain's voice over the intercom intruded on Becca's daydreaming. "Please fasten your seat belts. We are about to begin our decent into Las Vegas."

It wasn't long before the plane landed and Becca was met in the transportation area by a uniformed chauffeur. As she sank into the luxurious leather seats of the limousine, she made a promise to herself that if Ethan showed up, she would put all the uncertainties to rest once and for all and finally tell him how she felt.

* * * * *

Ethan sat on his balcony, sipping a margarita and watching the sun slip behind the western horizon. Shades of red, orange and pink streaked the dusky sky. He had traveled around quite a bit and seen his fair share of sunsets, but he would always be partial to desert sunsets. They could be some of the most beautiful in the world. As the sun continued its downward trek and the stars began to twinkle in the gray of the eastern sky, Ethan's mind wandered to his beautiful Becca and marveled as her form took shape in his mind's eye.

So much had happened in the last few days, he could scarcely believe that it had been less than two weeks ago that he'd finally made up his mind about his future with her. Since then, he had put into motion numerous detailed arrangements that he hoped would make this an unforgettable weekend for her. So far, everything was coming along very nicely. The construction workers had finished yesterday, and the decorator had left barely an hour ago. He'd paid them all a hefty bonus for getting the work done so quickly, but the results had been worth every penny. He couldn't wait to see the look on Becca's face when she saw what he'd created for her.

Ethan rose from his chair and walked to the edge of the balcony. He leaned his forearms on the railing, absently studying the myriad of sparkling city lights below, then glanced at his watch. Becca was due to arrive any minute. A jolt of excitement flowed through him.

The cell phone in his pocket chimed. He continued to take in the night lights of the city as he pulled it out and answered. "Hello?"

"Mr. Montgomery, this is Juan from the front desk," a slightly accented voice came through the phone.

"Has she arrived?"

"Yes, sir. Ms. Anderson is on her way up to the penthouse right now. She just got on the elevator."

"Thank you, Juan."

"My pleasure, Mr. Montgomery."

Ethan pressed the button to end the call, then immediately dialed Becca's cell number.

"Hello." Becca's voice sounded particularly cheery.

"So you arrived safely in Vegas, and you're on your way up to the penthouse." He said it more as a statement than a question.

For a moment there was silence. Ethan could imagine Becca looking for the hidden cameras. She finally replied, "Um...how do you know that?"

"I'm psychic." Becca's giggle on the other end of the line made him lose his own deadpan voice and break into a smile. "I have some people keeping an eye on you."

"Oh, so now you're spying on me?" she asked with mock indignation.

Ethan laughed. "Just watching out for you. Plus I wanted to know what you think of the penthouse. Hear your thoughts when you see it for the first time."

"Well, I guess your timing is perfect. We're at the door right now."

Ethan could hear the bellboy opening the door for her in the background, followed by a gasp. "Oh, Ethan. You have way outdone yourself. This place is beautiful."

"I take it you're happy with your accommodations, madame?"

"Are you crazy? Happy? I'm ecstatic. I never in a million years would have imagined this. There's a crystal chandelier. And a fireplace."

Ethan laughed at the enthusiasm in her voice. "Wait 'til you see the bedroom."

"Oh, hang on a sec." Ethan heard the jangling of Becca's purse as she tipped the bellboy. She thanked him for his help and then closed the door. "OK, I'm back. Now what's this about the bedroom?"

"Go take a look."

The clicking of her shoes on the tile floor indicated her compliance.

"Oh my God! Ethan, this bed is huge." She laughed. "I'm going to get lost in it."

"Don't worry, I'll come find you," he teased, wanting nothing more than to share it with her.

"Mmm, the carpet is so thick, I feel like I'm walking on a cloud."

"I bet you couldn't resist taking your shoes off."

"Of course not. Oh! What do we have here?" Another sharp intake of breath made him suspect she'd found the bathroom. "Oh, Ethan. The faucets are gold. That's not real gold, is it?"

Ethan laughed. "No, I don't believe it is."

"Well, it sure sparkles like it." Becca sighed as she moved back toward the bedroom. "And the bed is made up so pretty. And roses too!"

"I was wondering when you were going to notice those."

"They're gorgeous, Ethan. Everything is. You're going to spoil me."

"That's the idea."

Becca was so excited, she could hardly take it all in. When Ethan had given her this trip, she had known it was going to be nice, but she never expected such luxury. The bedroom was decorated in a romantic Victorian style, her favorite. As she ran her hand over the thick floral comforter gracing the huge four-poster bed, a picture of herself and Ethan lying in it came unbidden to her mind. Heat rose in her cheeks. She walked to the bedside table, wiggling her toes in the soft, thick rug beside the bed as she went. The heady scent of the dozen red roses in a crystal vase filled her senses as she turned around to take in the entire room. It all made her feel like a pampered fairy-tale princess.

"Becca, are you still there?"

The sound of Ethan's voice reminded her that he was still on the phone with her.

"Oh, yes, I'm still here. Sorry. I guess my mind is still trying to take everything in."

"If you like the inside, I bet you'll love the view from the balcony."

As Becca turned toward the sliding glass door, the sheer white curtains undulated like a gentle ocean wave. The soft breeze beckoned her to the open portal. When she crossed the threshold, she was met with a myriad of sparkling city lights as the last rays of the setting sun disappeared below the horizon.

She walked to the railing while feasting her eyes on the beauty before her.

"Oh, Ethan, you weren't kidding. The view is amazing," she said.

"I'm glad you like it," came his husky reply from behind her.

At the sound of his voice next to her ear, Becca whirled around. He was standing so close she nearly bumped into him, and she put out her free hand to steady herself. It connected with the solid muscle of his chest, sending a tingle up her arm and through her whole body, then settling low in her belly. She lowered her phone while her gaze locked with his, and she looked into deep-green eyes that reflected sparkles from the lights below. Her mouth dropped open and her jaw worked up and down as she tried to form words through her surprise.

Ethan slowly lowered his phone too, and a huge smile lit up his face. "Hey, gorgeous," he said softly.

Becca squealed with delight as she threw her arms around Ethan's neck. His arms circled her waist, hugging her tightly. He lifted her feet off the floor and twirled her around before setting her back down again.

It felt so good to be in his arms she didn't want to let him go. Becca gave him another squeeze and a peck on the cheek before reluctantly pulling back a little to look up into his smiling face.

"You little sneak," she said, reprimanding him playfully. "You made me think you weren't going to be here when I arrived, and that you might not come at all."

"I wanted to surprise you," he replied, not sounding the least bit contrite.

"Well, you certainly did that. I never in a million years expected all this." Becca slid out of Ethan's embrace to wave her arm around, indicating the suite and the view, then turned back to face him. "Much less the pleasure of your company."

"I'm delighted that you're pleased, m'lady." Ethan took her hand and made a courtly bow over it before placing a light kiss on the back.

The feel of his soft lips on her hand sent desire coursing through her entire being. Her breathing quickened. She wanted to know what it would feel like to have those lips elsewhere on her body...her face...her neck...her breasts...and even lower. She swallowed hard through the lump that was forming in her throat at the mere thought, and took a deep breath as she tried to gather her wits about her.

Ethan lifted his eyes to meet her gaze, and his thumb rubbed over the spot he had just kissed, sending another wave of sensation through her. His touch made her want to moan, and she bit her lip to hold the sound in.

When she thought she'd surely give herself away, he graced her with one of those mischievous lopsided grins that never failed to make her feel giddy. Then he released her hand to playfully tap her nose. "You think you're surprised now. Wait 'til you see what else I have in store for you."

"Oh, Ethan." Becca shook her head. "You don't have to give me anything else. Having you here to share all this with is more than enough."

Ethan's expression turned a bit skeptical. "I don't know. You might think that now, but you haven't seen what else I have planned. I'm almost certain you're going to love every bit of it."

"If it's even half as wonderful as all this is, I know I will."

"You ain't seen nothin' yet, babe. It's only going to get better from here."

"I can't imagine how that would even be possible." Then Becca thought of the greatest desire of her heart, and knew that what she'd said wasn't entirely true. "Well...there is one thing..." Becca gasped as she realized that she'd voiced her thoughts aloud.

"What's that?" Ethan inquired.

"Oh...I...um," she stammered. "Never mind me, I'm just thinking out loud." She waved her hand dismissively.

"If there's something I can do to make these next few days the most memorable you've ever had, I'm at your service."

Ethan's words brought all sorts of naughty thoughts flooding into her mind. Thank goodness for the darkness. She was sure from the heat rising in her cheeks that she was blushing. "Thanks. I'll let you know," she answered, hoping that her tone didn't sound as embarrassed to him as it did to her.

"So are you hungry?"

Oh, she was hungry all right, and not merely for food.

Becca forcibly roused herself from her distracting thoughts about the delicious man standing in front of her. "Yeah, I'm starved."

"Good," Ethan replied as he checked his watch. "Because I think that our dinner should be waiting for us by now."

Ethan offered Becca his arm. "Shall we?"

She gladly accepted, and was grateful when he escorted her back inside through a different door, one that didn't lead through the bedroom.

The beautiful glass-top dining table was laden with covered dishes. The lights in the chandelier overhead were turned down low, and candles flickered on the table. As Ethan seated Becca, she couldn't help but think that the ambiance spoke of intimacy and romance.

An ice bucket perched on a stand next to the table held a bottle of champagne.

"Madame?" Ethan inquired, offering her the bottle with all the finesse of a waiter in a five-star restaurant.

Becca nodded. "Yes, please."

Ethan filled both of their glasses before lifting the lids from the plates. "I took the liberty of ordering your favorite, Chicken Alfredo. I hope you like it."

"It looks delicious," Becca answered as she placed her napkin in her lap and lifted her fork to dig in.

Throughout the meal they chatted about topics both mundane and profound. When she was finished, Becca wiped up the last bit of sauce with a piece of bread and popped it into her mouth before licking her fingers. "Mmm," she moaned at the pleasure her taste buds were experiencing.

Ethan gave her an oddly dark expression as he watched her over the rim of his champagne glass.

"What? Do I have sauce on my face?" she asked.

"No." He shook his head. "It's nothing," he added dismissively. The mysterious look quickly disappeared, replaced by a smile.

"My compliments to the chef. I think that was the best meal I've ever tasted."

"I'll be sure to let him know."

Ethan rose from the table. He collected their empty plates and deposited them on a nearby serving cart. On the top shelf sat another covered dish. He lifted the lid and, with a flourish, placed the dish in front of her.

Becca's eyes went round at the scrumptious sight.

"I hope you saved a little room for dessert. I thought you might enjoy a piece of chocolate lava cake."

"Ugh! I swear you're trying to make me gain ten pounds, Ethan," she said with a laugh.

"Come on. It's only one night of indulgence," he cajoled.

"OK, you twisted my arm."

"Yeah, I can see how hard I had to twist."

"But...I'll only eat it if you share it with me."

"Deal."

Becca slid the plate to the center of the table where they could both reach it. They took turns savoring bites of the gooey chocolate confection until only one spoonful remained.

Ethan scooped it up and was about to put it in his mouth when he seemed to change his mind. Instead, he extended the spoon toward her. "You should have the last bite."

"No. You take it," Becca insisted. "It was your turn, fair and square."

"I want you to have it."

"But–"

"I insist. Besides, you know you want it," he teased while waving the spoon in front of her face.

Becca finally succumbed and leaned in to take the bite. As Ethan withdrew the spoon from her mouth, Becca closed her eyes. Another little moan of satisfaction rose from her throat as she swallowed the last bite. When she opened her eyes again, that strange look had returned to Ethan's face. Her gaze locked with his for a moment before he cleared his throat.

"Uh...you have a little chocolate on the corner of your mouth," he said as he pointed to his own.

Becca extended her tongue, searching for the right spot. "Did I get it?"

"Here, let me help you." Ethan took the napkin from his lap and leaned across the table to gently dab at the corner of her mouth. As he did so, he continued to stare at her lips intensely. She could have sworn that his breathing took on a ragged rhythm, and he swallowed hard. Then he broke the contact and leaned back into his seat. "All gone now."

"Thanks." Becca smiled at him shyly, wondering if he might be feeling the same emotions she was.

Before she had time to consider the matter further, Ethan broke into her thoughts. "It's still early," he observed as he glanced at his watch. "I picked up that new movie you were wanting to see, *Always a Bridesmaid*. Would you care to watch it with me?"

"Of course. I've been dying to see that. But I can't believe it's your turn and you picked a girlie movie," Becca teased.

"Well, this weekend is all about you, so this time I chose the movie with your tastes in mind."

"Would you mind if I go change into something more comfortable while you get it set up?"

"Not at all. Go right ahead."

Becca hurried off to the bedroom, where she found her suitcases neatly placed on luggage racks. As she rummaged around for her nightie and robe, she hummed a lighthearted tune. Becca took her clothes to the bathroom to change, and when she looked up, she caught her reflection in the mirror beaming back at her. In that moment, she realized the she'd never been happier. She had the man of her dreams waiting for her in the next room, and he was treating her like a fairy princess. Her life had never felt so perfect. It was all nearly too good to be true.

Yet it was, and she decided to savor every minute of it.

While he waited for Becca to return, Ethan placed the movie in the DVD player and laid a small fire in the hearth. It was crackling away merrily by the time she emerged from the bedroom wearing fuzzy slippers and a pink fleece robe open in front. Underneath, he glimpsed a night-shirt that barely covered the tops of her thighs. Her honey-colored hair cascaded over her shoulders in soft waves.

The whole look was utterly charming, and even though it wasn't exactly designed for sex appeal, he instantly grew hard at the sight before him. Her nightie said *Angel* on the front, and that's precisely what she looked like. Next thing he knew, pictures of Becca licking her fingers at dinner and that throaty moan of satisfaction she'd made began replaying in his mind. God, how he wanted to be the one eliciting those sounds from her.

Down, boy. Stick to the plan, he told himself. *Only one more day, and with any luck, you will be.*

Becca joined him in the sunken living room. She took off her slippers and curled up in the corner of the sofa with her feet pulled up underneath her like she often did at home.

Together, they enjoyed the movie in companionable silence. As the credits rolled, Ethan looked over to find Becca's head resting against the back of the couch and her eyes closed. As usual, he had little idea of what had happened in the film. Instead, he'd been covertly watching her from the corner of his eye. He knew exactly the moment she had dozed off. She would be disappointed that she'd missed the ending, but he couldn't bear to wake her. She was so ethereally beautiful, he wanted to watch her sleep.

Sighing deeply, Ethan reluctantly rose from the sofa. Becca needed her bed, or she would wind up with a crick in her neck. With all he had planned for her in the next couple of days, he certainly didn't want her to be in pain, so he decided to sacrifice his own desires for her comfort. Placing one arm around her shoulders and the other under her knees, he lifted her into his arms. Her head rolled against his shoulder, and she mumbled something unintelligible in her sleep.

Ethan carried Becca to the bedroom and gently laid her on the bed. The maid had turned down the covers earlier, so all he had to do was pull them back and tuck her feet underneath.

As he tried to slip the robe from her arms, her eyes flickered open. "Ethan? Wha...?"

"Shh," he soothed. "Help me get your robe off, and then you can go back to sleep."

"Um...K."

He chuckled softly when her arms started flopping around and her eyes drifted shut again. In her present state, she really wasn't being much help, but eventually he managed to get the garment removed. No sooner had he drawn the covers up to her chin than a cute little snore emanated from her slightly open mouth. Ethan silently laughed again as he turned off the bedside lamp. When he leaned forward and placed a soft kiss on her temple, she let out a sweet sigh. It took every ounce of self-control he possessed not to climb into bed with her and take her in his arms, but finally, he left her side.

As he reached the doorway, he paused for a moment to look back at her sleeping form. He could sacrifice one night of bliss for the hope that he would be able to share her bed for a lifetime and watch her sleep anytime he pleased.

Chapter 17

Becca woke to see bright rays of early morning sunshine streaming through the Arcadia door of her bedroom. She lifted her arms above her head and stretched lazily before snuggling under the sheets and hugging her extra pillow like she often did at home.

She smiled as foggy memories of Ethan carrying her to bed last night came to the forefront of her mind. If only he were still here this morning. She clasped her pillow tighter imagining it was him.

It was then that she made up her mind. Tonight, she would finally tell him how much she loved him. Then maybe she wouldn't be spending another night alone in this big bed. Happy with her plan, and eager to find out what other surprises Ethan had up his sleeve, she sprang from the bed and donned her robe.

After a quick morning ablution, she headed for the kitchen. Halfway there, she stopped dead in her tracks at the sight of Ethan sprawled on the sofa, still asleep. A lock of dark hair fell over his forehead, making her fingers itch to smooth it back into place. She had touched his hair a few times before, in a friendly way, and knew that it was as soft and silky as it looked. She imagined burying her fingers in it and pulling his mouth to hers for a deep, passionate kiss.

Becca allowed her eyes to rove over the rest of his body. The lower half was covered by a blanket, but one leg peeked out. She felt a pang of disappointment to find that he was wearing sleep pants, but thankfully, no shirt.

Her breath hitched at the sight of his gorgeous chest and muscular arms. She closed her eyes for a moment and thought of those arms encircling her while she trailed kisses all over that smooth chest. She opened her eyes again and bent over him, unable to resist running a finger over his hard planes.

When he stirred slightly, she snatched her finger back, afraid she might wake him. *Tonight*, she told herself, *if all goes as planned, I can touch him to my heart's content.*

Then she willed herself to go into the kitchen. After all, they did say that the way to a man's heart was through his stomach, so preparing a nice breakfast for Ethan certainly couldn't hurt her chances of making her dreams come true.

Twenty minutes later, Becca was having serious second thoughts about that. The meal she had managed to produce probably wouldn't even tempt Ethan's dog, Buddy, much less the man himself. As she surveyed the plate of charred bacon and scraped over-browned scrambled eggs from the bottom of a skillet, she felt like crying.

Just then, Ethan entered the kitchen still wearing only his sleep pants and a sunny smile. He yawned as he ran his fingers through sleep-tousled hair, making it stick out at odd angles. He looked absolutely adorable–and hotter than hell. For a moment, she stopped what she was doing and stared.

"Morning, gorgeous. You didn't have to fix breakfast."

She looked again at the carnage littering the stove and countertop, the mess effectively putting a damper on her desire. Her shoulders sagged. "I don't think it's fit to eat anyway," she replied morosely.

"Uh-oh." He grimaced. "I thought I smelled something burning."

"Try blackened."

She gave up on the skillet and tossed it into the sink, then leaned back against the counter. She crossed her arms over her chest and stared at the floor glumly.

Ethan's bare feet came into view, and his masculine aura filled her senses. He reached out a finger to lift her chin. His eyes locked with hers as he tenderly cupped her face in his hands.

"Hey. Why so upset?"

Becca could barely think with his hands touching her like that. She took a deep breath and somehow found her voice. "You've been so nice to me. I wanted to do something nice for you in return."

Ethan drew her into his arms, and then she was well and truly lost. Her cheek rested against his bare chest. She wrapped one arm around his waist and laid the other on the well-defined pectoral muscle right next to her face. She wanted to slide her thumb over his pebbled nipple–better yet, flick it with her tongue. She bit her bottom lip and tried to calm her erratic breathing.

He laid his cheek against the top of her head and gently rocked her as his response broke into her lustful thoughts. "That was really sweet of you, but I told you this weekend is all about you."

"But..." Becca was dismayed to find that her voice squeaked out the word.

"Uh-uh. No buts," he said mildly as he lifted her face again and gave her a smile that fairly lit up the room. "Besides," he continued while opening the cupboard behind her and pulling out a box of cereal, "occasions like this are why Frosted Flakes were invented."

Becca rolled her eyes at Ethan's jest, but nevertheless, the corners of her mouth turned up in response. She withdrew from his embrace and gathered bowls, spoons and milk while he poured tall glasses of orange juice.

She spotted the loaf of bread she'd laid out earlier. "How about I make some toast to go with the cereal?"

Ethan narrowed his eyes skeptically. "How about I make the toast? I think you've murdered enough food for one morning."

She snorted in indignation and playfully slapped him on the arm for good measure, earning her a hearty laugh in response.

"Hey, the weather is beautiful. Why don't we have breakfast out on the balcony?" he suggested while placing slices of bread into the slots of the toaster.

"I'd love that."

As they ate their breakfast, the cheerful sunshine warmed Becca all the way through to her bones. Not that she really needed any help with that. She continued her perusal of Ethan's body through the veil of her lashes. He was doing a fine job of heating her up without even trying.

Becca cleared her throat. "If I'd known you were going to sleep on the sofa, I would have let you share my bed." She tried to make her tone playful even though she was dead serious. "It's way too big for one person."

Ethan choked on his juice.

Becca reached over to pound him on the back. "Oh my gosh, are you OK?"

When his coughing fit ended, he managed to croak, "Yeah...yeah, I'm fine."

"I'm sorry. I didn't mean to make you choke. I–I was just joking," she lied.

Momentarily, she wondered if the thought of sleeping with her was undesirable to him. Maybe he did think of her as nothing more than a friend, and had never even considered it.

There was that time last year, she reminded herself. But Ethan was only comforting her that night, and neither of them had really intended to fall asleep together.

She quickly reigned in her racing thoughts, refusing to let her doubts get the best of her.

"Don't worry. It's not your fault." Ethan took her hand in his and squeezed it gently. He chuckled. "And for the record, the sofa was surprisingly comfortable."

Becca's hand tingled at his touch, and she smiled at him shyly. "I'm glad. But I thought you had another bedroom here. What's that door on the other side of the living room?"

"Oh! Um...yeah." Ethan released her hand and scratched his brow. He seemed rather flustered by her questions, making her wonder if he was hiding something.

"I-I'm having that bedroom remodeled. You don't want to go in there. It's really messy with all the...uh...sawdust and everything."

"OK." She shrugged, but still couldn't shake the feeling that he was acting strangely.

Ethan glanced at his watch. "We should get ready, or we're going to be late for my next surprise."

She grinned. "What do you have up your sleeve now?"

"Well, if I told you, it wouldn't be a surprise anymore, would it?"

Becca rolled her eyes at him and sighed. "Fine. Have it your way."

Ethan started gathering up their dirty dishes. "Since it takes ladies longer, why don't I clean up here while you get started. We can meet in the living room in say...forty-five minutes?"

"It's a date!" she replied enthusiastically as she got up from the table and headed to her room.

Becca showered quickly so that she could take a little extra time with her hair and makeup. By the time she had finished, there was only ten minutes left to dress, but she had already figured out what to wear while she was in the shower. The pretty sundress she'd donned for her "date" with Ethan to his parents' barbecue would be perfect. If Edna was right about him eyeing her that evening, maybe the outfit would turn him on today too.

She slipped on her strappy sandals and took one last look at herself in the mirror. Taking a deep breath, she opened the bedroom door to find Ethan sitting on the sofa, reading a magazine. He was dressed casually in khaki pants and a polo shirt. As always, he looked magnificent.

The soft click of her shoes on the tile floor brought his head up. He slowly rose from the couch, his eyes never leaving her. Maybe Edna was right. He seemed to be devouring her from head to toe, leaving her with the impression that he was undressing her with his eyes. His perusal of her ended as he turned to round the sofa.

Once by her side, he smiled. "You look beautiful."

Suddenly feeling self-conscious, Becca dropped her gaze to the floor. She nervously tucked a strand of hair behind her ear and gave him a shy smile. "Thanks."

"So are you ready for our adventure?"

She extended her arm in a flourish. "Lead the way, my good man," she replied, her jovial demeanor returning.

Before she knew it, they were traversing the streets of Las Vegas in the luxury of Ethan's limo. "So where are we going?" she asked.

"You'll see," he answered coyly.

A few minutes later the driver turned into the parking lot of a shopping mall. She turned to Ethan. "The mall?" she inquired incredulously.

"Yes, *the mall*. I'm taking you on your first shopping spree."

"Ethan! You know–"

"Ah." He held up a finger to interrupt her. "No protesting, remember? Not to mention you should be thanking me. I wanted to take you to the upscale place across town, but I knew you'd be uncomfortable there."

"Thank you, I guess." Becca adjusted the folds of her dress nervously, still feeling out of her element. "But I have no idea what to buy. I've told you a million times that you don't have to spend money on me."

"I know I don't have to. I'm doing it because I want to. Just buy something you need."

"What if I have everything I need?"

"Then buy something you want."

"What if I can't find anything I want?"

The driver pulled up to the curb next to the door. "Would you stop being contrary and get out of the car?" he replied firmly. "We're going shopping whether you like it or not."

Becca could tell from the tone of Ethan's voice that she wasn't going to win this argument. "Fine. I shall do my best to spend your money even though I don't want to," she replied reluctantly.

For the next couple of hours they wandered in and out of stores. Becca tried on several outfits while Ethan patiently waited outside the dressing room. Each time she came out, he gave her his opinion, and a couple of times he said they looked really nice on her. Becca pretended that the clothes didn't catch her fancy, because the price tags made her feel a little guilty about the idea of spending someone else's money so extravagantly.

As they were leaving the fifth store of the day, Ethan took Becca's hand, led her over to a bench and pulled her down beside him. "Becca, we need to talk," he began in a serious voice.

"What about?"

"You really don't know how to do this shopping spree thing, do you?"

She tried to defend herself by showing him the small shopping bag in her hand. "I bought something."

Ethan took the bag from her and dumped the contents onto the bench between them. "Uh, Becca, I hate to tell you this, but...as nice as it is, I don't think your new miniature glass angel figurine is going to break the bank," he said while waving the item in question in front of her face.

Becca grabbed the angel and stuffed it back into the bag. "Well, for your information, it's the only thing I found that I really wanted. I happen to love angels, and it's even in my birthstone color."

"I'm glad you found something you like, Becca, but you're missing my point."

"Which is?"

"Geez, Becca. Are you that dense?" he asked in an exasperated tone. "I think you must be the only woman on the planet who isn't interested in spending my money."

"I'm sorry, Ethan. You know it's difficult for me to accept money, because of...you know. Besides, I don't have much money of my own, and I never have. I've just learned to be frugal, and it's hard to break the habit," she finished dejectedly.

Ethan reached over to lift her chin so he could look her in the eye. "Hey, I'm the one who should be sorry. I never meant to make you feel bad. This is all supposed to make you feel good. We're supposed to be having fun."

"It's fun just being with you."

Ethan smiled at her. "I know, and I feel the same way. But you know what else would make this even more fun for me?"

She gave him an inquisitive look before he leaned in to whisper conspiratorially in her ear. "Loading up the car with so many boxes and bags that there's hardly enough room left for us."

She laughed.

"Come on, my shopping-challenged friend. I'm going to show you how this is done."

With that, he took her hand again and pulled her up.

Becca could barely keep up with Ethan's long stride. He took her the window of a ladies' dress shop that sold fancy gowns. "I like that green one," he said as he pointed it out. "I bet it would look beautiful on you."

"I don't know, Ethan. I wouldn't have any place to wear something that nice."

"But do you like it?"

"I love it. It's gorgeous."

Ethan dragged her into the store to the first salesperson he spotted. "The lady would like that green dress in the window in...what's your size?" he asked as he turned back to her.

"Um...a four."

"We have one right over here. Would you like to try it on?" the salesgirl inquired.

"Um...yeah." Becca was feeling oddly overwhelmed as the girl bustled her into a fitting room.

She changed into the dress and was surprised to find that it fit like it was made for her. She smoothed her hands over the satiny fabric, marveling at how silky it felt. It had a rather daring neckline. She'd never worn anything quite so low-cut, but she had to admit that it made her look rather sexy.

She shyly emerged to take a look in the full-length mirror, and found Ethan and the salesgirl waiting for her.

Ethan took one look at her and let out a low whistle. "What did I tell you? It looks way better on you than it did in the store window."

"He's right," the girl added. "It looks great on you. It compliments your hair and eye color perfectly."

"We'll take it," Ethan said without hesitation.

"Ethan, could I talk to you for a second?" When Ethan was close enough for her to whisper without the salesgirl hearing, Becca continued. "When I was putting it on, I got a look at the price tag."

"And...?"

Becca bit her lip. "And it's two hundred dollars."

Ethan glanced back over his shoulder toward the salesgirl. "Is there a problem, sir?" she asked.

He looked back at Becca. His gaze never left hers as he answered, "Nope. No problem at all. Like I said, 'We'll take it.'"

A few minutes later, they left the store with Ethan carrying a big box under one arm.

Next he took her to Bath & Body Works, where he insisted on buying her half a dozen different scents of body wash, bubble bath and lotion. From there, they went to Yankee Candles and bought at least a dozen candles of every conceivable shape, size and scent. Then he insisted on going back to the women's clothing store for the outfits that had looked good on her. By the time they exited that shop, Ethan was juggling so many boxes and shopping bags, he nearly dropped a couple.

"Oh, here, let me help you," Becca offered as she reached for the falling bags. "So have we spent enough money now that we can barely carry everything?"

"Not even close, sweetheart." Ethan laughed. "Here, can you get my cell phone out of my pocket?" He turned to the side and tried to rearrange the packages in his arms.

Becca pushed a couple of bags aside to find Ethan's pants pocket. She swallowed hard around the lump that was forming in her throat at the thought of putting her hand in there.

At her hesitance, Ethan tried to peer over the top of the boxes. "Can you reach it?"

"Um...yeah," she answered, sounding breathless to her own ears.

Time seemed to stand still. Her heart pounded as she slipped her hand inside his pocket and breathed in Ethan's masculine scent. The intimate contact infused her body with heat that pooled low in her belly and weakened her knees. She desperately wanted to touch more of him than the restricting material of the pocket would allow, but being in a public place, she held her desires in check. There would be plenty of time for that later if things went as planned.

She willed herself to grasp the phone and remove her hand. "Got it," she said raggedly as she held it up.

"Great! Just speed-dial seven. That will call Thomas. Tell him to meet us at the east entrance to pick up all these packages."

Becca nodded. Her fingers were still a little shaky. She had to dial twice to get it right.

No sooner had they left their loot in the care of Ethan's driver than Becca's stomach let out a loud growl.

Ethan grinned. "Hungry?"

"Shopping is hard work."

"Come on, I'll buy you lunch. After all, we're just getting started. I can't have you passing out on me, now can I?"

"Getting started? We've been here for hours."

"Yeah, but I saved the best stores for last."

"Really?" she asked skeptically.

"Yes, really," he answered. "I'm glad you're enjoying yourself now."

"Well, I don't know if I'll ever get used to spending so much money at once when it's not for rent or a car payment. But yeah, it's kinda nice. You make it fun, like everything we do together."

"Making you happy makes me happy."

Ethan stood there, staring into her eyes, until Becca began to feel self-conscious and lowered her gaze. He slipped his arm around her waist and pulled her into his side. Oh, how she loved the feel of being in his arms. *Tonight*, she told herself. When they were alone back in his suite, she would tell him how much he really meant to her, and hopefully be in his strong arms all night long.

After sharing a delicious meal with Becca at a Mexican restaurant, Ethan was ready to pull out all the stops. The shopping they'd done so far had been a warm-up for the "main event." He was probably taking a chance by steering her toward the stores he had in mind, and he hoped he didn't tip his hand too soon. He had big plans for this evening and didn't want to screw things up, so he'd have to tread very carefully.

"So where are you taking me now, Mr. Big Spender?" Becca teased as they exited the restaurant and ambled down the wide aisles of the mall.

"Ooh, someplace with pretty things that women like."

"Doesn't that describe all the stores we've been to today?"

"Touché." He chuckled. "But this one is...well, different," he finished lamely as he came to a halt in front of Victoria's Secret.

"Ethan...lingerie?" she whispered without even looking at him. A becoming blush infused her cheeks.

"Sure, why not?" he answered blithely. "I don't have to come with you this time if you'd be embarrassed. But I figured it would be good practice for me. Like with the romance novels. It'll help me figure out what a woman likes."

Becca gave him a questioning glance.

"I thought maybe you could give me some advice. I've never

bought lingerie for anyone before, and I was curious about what's available." He led the way into the store. "What kind of things do you like?"

Her brow furrowed. "I–I don't know." She shrugged. "It's not like I've ever had much money to spend on lingerie. And I've certainly never had a boyfriend buy any for me. Giving you book recommendations was easy, but this..." Becca's voice trailed off and her cheeks flamed. She couldn't even look him in the eye anymore.

Ethan decided to take pity on her and try to figure this out on his own. "Hey, I'm sorry. I didn't mean to make you uncomfortable. Why don't you go find yourself something pretty, and I'll just ask a salesgirl to help me."

"OK." She sounded relieved and headed for the back of the store.

Way to tread carefully, doofus, Ethan told himself while watching her retreating back. This was not going well. All he'd wanted to do was find out what she liked so he could buy her something sexy. But instead, he'd botched it up so badly, she probably thought he was either a perv or had another girlfriend.

With a sigh, he began wandering around the store.

It wasn't long before he was accosted by an employee. "Can I help you find something, sir?"

"Yes, I want to buy something for a special lady." He pointed at Becca, who was perusing a rack of frilly nighties. "Actually, it's that lady right over there," he said softly. "And I want it to be a surprise."

"No problem." She smiled at him. "I promise to be discreet. What did you have in mind? A chemise? A baby doll? A cami-tap set?"

"Um...to be completely honest, I have no idea what you just said. Are you sure you're speaking English?"

The salesgirl giggled at Ethan's joke. "How about we try it this way? Are you looking for something sweet and demure or hot and sexy?"

"Definitely hot and sexy," he answered, his eyes still lingering on Becca as she headed for the changing rooms.

"What color would you like?"

Once Becca disappeared behind the door, he turned his attention back to the girl. "Do you have anything in red?"

"Sure." She led him to a rack. "How about this?" she asked while holding up a very hot little concoction.

To Ethan, it looked like a bra with a sheer fabric draping down from it and a little scrap of a thong to match. He felt himself getting hard at the mere thought of Becca in that outfit. Or better yet, out of it.

"That would be perfect."

"Do you know the lady's size?" the salesgirl inquired.

"Yeah, she said she was a four."

"Well then, this one right here should fit her fine. But let me go check with her sales associate to see what size she's trying on."

"That sounds great. But remember–"

"I know," she said. "I'll be careful she doesn't find out."

A few minutes later, the girl returned. Ethan paid for his purchase and arranged for his driver to pick it up, so that Becca wouldn't suspect anything. He looked around the store and found her standing at a checkout on the other side. When she drew a credit card from her purse, Ethan rushed to her side.

His hand closed over her wrist as she was about to hand it to the cashier. Hoping not to embarrass her in front of the woman, he simply reached for his own wallet before saying, "Today's my treat, remember?"

Becca nodded a little uncomfortably as she tucked the card back into her purse and allowed him to pay.

He thanked the saleslady, picked up the shopping bag, and with his hand lightly resting at the small of her back, guided her toward the exit.

Once they were out of earshot of the employees, he asked, "What was that all about?"

"Nothing." She waved her hand dismissively. "I was just a little embarrassed to have you buying me...unmentionables."

"Sorry if I made you uncomfortable. I thought every lady could use some pretty *unmentionables*, but I promise I won't *mention* them again."

Becca's mouth quirked up at the corners. "Ethan, you are so goofy sometimes."

"I live to please, m'lady."

They ambled a little father down the main thoroughfare of the mall in silence. Ethan noticed that Becca wasn't as bubbly as she had been this morning after he'd loosened her up about the shopping excursion. He decided that she was probably getting tired, but he only had two more stops planned anyway. Then he'd take her home. He couldn't wait to unveil the rest of his surprise for the evening.

Ethan stopped in front of a jewelry store. "Ah," he said, drawing out the syllable with a flourish. "Here's something else that every lady needs...jewels."

"Ethan, you've already bought me so much already. I really don't need jewelry too."

"Well, it can't hurt to look. Let's go in."

Reluctantly, she allowed him to draw her inside. After Ethan made a show of perusing the cases, Becca's interest was finally piqued by a display of pendants. He requested assistance for her from a nearby salesclerk, then escaped to the other side of the store. Scanning the rings, his eyes settled on a delicate gold band with a modest diamond setting. He asked the salesman behind the counter to see it.

While the man retrieved the ring from its velvet box, Ethan glanced back over his shoulder at Becca. She fastened one of the pendants around her neck and then admired it in the mirror sitting atop the case.

Ethan turned back to the salesman and picked up the ring he had placed on a velvet cloth. It was pretty, but after taking a closer look, he wasn't quite satisfied with the quality of the diamond. He requested to see a few others, periodically checking to make sure Becca was still occupied. After looking at a half-dozen rings, he still didn't find anything that caught his fancy. Besides, he had a much better idea in mind. After thanking the man, he returned to Becca's side.

She wore a delicate emerald pendant. The stones were cut in a heart shape with a small one atop a slightly larger one. Both cascaded from the shiny white-gold setting at a jaunty angle, making them look like a pair of cherries still attached to their stems.

"It looks beautiful on you." He fervently wished he could get her alone wearing that pretty necklace and nothing else. After clearing his throat uncomfortably, he added, "And it matches the dress I bought for you earlier."

She unfastened the pendant and laid it back on the velvet mat. "And costs nearly twice as much," she muttered under her breath.

Turning to the salesclerk, he said, "We'll take it."

"Ethan!" she exclaimed.

Ignoring her, he smiled and added, "And the matching earrings too."

At Becca's gasp, he turned to see her eyes wide and mouth agape. "What do you think you're doing?"

He gave her mischievous grin. "Spoiling you."

She shook her head in exasperation. "You're impossible."

His only reply was a chuckle.

Five minutes later, they left the jewelry store and headed back down the main thoroughfare of the mall. "You seem kind of tired. Are you up for one more stop before I take you home?"

"Are you crazy, Ethan? I've been keeping track, and with the necklace and earrings, you've now spent over two thousand dollars on me. Honestly, I don't want you to buy me anything else." She waved her hands in front of her in a gesture that indicated she'd had enough.

"Please," he said, giving her his best impression of sad puppy-dog eyes. "I absolutely promise you're going to love this store."

She sighed as her shoulders slumped in defeat. A ghost of a smile touched her lips. "Fine," she said, "but only if you promise this is the last one."

"You got it, sweetheart." He chuckled before coming to a halt and extending his arm like a model. "Ta-da!"

Becca fought it, but a toothy grin spread slowly across her face as she looked into the window of a bookstore. "You know my weakness, and I think you're trying to take advantage of it."

"I told you I saved the best for last. Since books are your favorite thing in the whole world, I guessed this might your favorite store in the mall."

"You know me well."

"Better than anyone," he answered with a touch of self-satisfaction. "So what are you waiting for?" He grabbed a shopping basket from the rack near the entrance and placed it in her hands. "By the time you're done, I want to see that basket filled with all the latest romance novels."

As he propelled her toward the romance section, Becca giggled, and the sound was like music to his ears.

He picked up a book with a bare-chested, sword-wielding warrior on the cover. "Here, this one looks interesting," he said in jest while handing it to her. "Hello! I stand corrected. This one looks way more interesting." He waggled his eyebrows as he handed her a novel graced by a woman baring lots of cleavage.

"Ethan!" She grabbed the book and used it to smack him on the arm.

"Ow!" He put on a mock pitiful face while rubbing the assaulted appendage. "You know I'm just teasing, right?"

She nodded and smiled.

"Good. I'll leave you in peace while I go search out books about more *manly* pursuits."

It didn't take Ethan long to find what he was looking for. He picked up the latest sci-fi/fantasy and mystery/suspense novels by a couple of his favorite authors, and the new issue of *Business Weekly*. Then he headed for the non-fiction section, looking for some good books on pleasuring a woman.

He wasn't exactly a novice in the bedroom, but having always preferred relationships to casual sex, he wasn't vastly experienced either. After Becca's one and only disastrous sexual experience, he wanted their first time together to be perfect. She deserved that and so much more. He wanted nothing less than to take her body to the heights of sheer ecstasy. What a glorious sight that would be. His cock twitched merely thinking about it.

Ethan shook his head to clear the images of Becca in the throes of passion from his mind and perused the bookshelf headers. His height allowed him to see over the tops of the shelves, and before long, he spotted exactly what he was looking for, two aisles over.

Rounding the corner of the aisle in question, he stopped dead in his tracks at the sight of Becca standing there, an open book in her hands and a forgotten basket of romance novels at her feet. Not wanting to embarrass her, he didn't make his presence known and instead backed discreetly behind a cardboard display.

From his vantage point, he watched as Becca leafed through the book, stopping every once in a while to take a closer look. Whatever she was reading made her cheeks turn a becoming shade of pink. If he could get a look at the cover, it might give him more insights into her sexual fantasies.

Becca closed the book and placed it back on the shelf, then stood there looking at it as if undecided about something. She picked up her basket and turned to leave. After casting a wistful glance back over her shoulder and worrying her bottom lip, she quickly grabbed the book and secretively tucked it underneath the romances before finally walking away.

Ethan was too far away to see the title, but he could tell there were more copies of the book on the shelf. Desperately wanting to know what had caught her fancy, he ducked into the aisle she had vacated. When he reached the right spot and scanned the front of the book, his brows drew down into a frown. *Tickle His Pickle?* That certainly wasn't what he'd been expecting and was no help at all in giving him insight into the female mind.

Come to think of it, what was his sweet Becca even doing with a book like that? If she was serious enough about a guy to want to learn how to please him in bed, she must be in love. After her horrible first time, there was no doubt in his mind that she would never have sex with anyone if she wasn't. Which led him to the only conclusion he could come up with: she'd found a guy, fallen in love, and hadn't told him about it.

His heart plummeted to the floor.

He'd been so sure there was no other man in her life, and now it seemed like his arrogant assumption might leave him with a broken heart. This meticulously planned weekend could be all for nothing.

With a deep sigh, and his own idea of purchasing a sex book long forgotten, Ethan made his way to the checkout, paid for their purchases, and then proceeded to brood all the way back to the hotel.

Chapter 18

Throughout the limo ride to the hotel, Becca gazed out the window. Ethan was uncharacteristically quiet, but she didn't give it much thought. She was glad for the solitude, since it gave her time to think. Reflecting on the day so far, Becca was confident that Edna had been right about Ethan being in love with her. He'd bought her so many pretty things, she felt like Cinderella getting ready for the ball, and Ethan was her Fairy Godmother and Prince Charming all rolled into one. Even though she still felt a small pang of guilt for spending so much money, she was sure he wouldn't have done it if he couldn't afford it. And she couldn't deny that it made her feel like the most special girl in the world.

Heat rose in her cheeks as she recalled their foray into Victoria's Secret. She'd found the perfect outfit for seducing Ethan tonight. When she'd tried it on, it had made her feel pretty and–dare she even think it?–sexy. Not wanting Ethan to see what she'd picked out, she'd hurried to the cash register. Luckily, by the time he'd rushed over to pay, the cashier already had her purchase bagged. Now she couldn't wait to wear it for him and see his reaction.

Becca glanced at Ethan from the corner of her eye and saw him staring pensively out the window. She wondered briefly at his odd mood, but didn't dwell on it long before her attention was drawn to the shopping bag of books at her feet. The naughty book she'd purchased was tucked safely away in the bottom of the bag.

As she'd passed by the shelf, the goofy title had made her giggle. After glancing around covertly to make sure no one was watching her, she couldn't resist taking a peek. The humorous drawings made her chuckle, while some of the things she read made her blush to the tips of her toes. Before long, she'd been fantasizing about having Ethan in her bed tonight.

She almost hadn't bought the book, but Becca was glad now that she had. She wanted to learn how to please him in bed, and truth be told, many of the things she'd read about sounded like fun. If she could ever work up the nerve to practice some of the things she'd seen in the book on him, she felt certain he would appreciate them.

As the limo pulled up to the door of the hotel, butterflies fluttered in Becca's stomach. She was anxious to tell Ethan she loved him, but her old self-doubts resurfaced. The bellboy who'd carried her bags up the day before opened the door for them, and Ethan instructed him to carry all their shopping spoils up to the penthouse. As they rode the elevator to the top floor in silence, Becca remembered Edna's soothing voice encouraging her. If Edna believed in her, maybe it was time she had a little faith in herself.

As soon as Ethan opened the door of their suite, she rushed to her bedroom, flinging over her shoulder, "I'm going to change." She closed the door behind her, leaned back against it, took several deep breaths, and proceeded to give herself a pep talk.

All the way back to the hotel, Ethan had tried to come up with an explanation for Becca buying that book. He told himself she was simply curious. But would a woman buy a book like that out of mere curiosity? Especially a shy girl like Becca? Somehow he didn't think so. Which meant the only reason left that made any sense was that she had a man in her life and was planning to have sex with him...if she hadn't already.

His mood darkened, and he felt like ripping something–or someone–apart.

The friendly voice of the bellboy intruded on his reverie. "That's all of them, Mr. Montgomery."

Ethan drew out his wallet and tipped the guy, then thanked him and closed the door a little too firmly. The mirror on the wall beside it shuddered.

He scowled at his reflection. He was so sure he'd been picking up I-want-to-be-more-than-friends vibes from Becca since yesterday. The enthusiastic way she'd greeted him, the playful way she'd mentioned sharing her bed with him this morning... That one still had desire thrumming through his body. Maybe it was all in his imagination, his libido running wild from being so close to Becca all day.

With a frustrated growl, Ethan ran his fingers through his hair and paced back and forth in the foyer.

Then, in an instant, his restless pacing stopped and his eyes grew round as one more possibility he hadn't considered until now took shape in his mind. Holy shit! Was Becca planning to use what she learned from that book on him? Damn, if that thought didn't make his "pickle" stand up and take notice. He looked in the mirror and found a goofy grin plastered on his face.

He shook his head to clear his lustful thoughts. *Down, boy. Don't get ahead of yourself. You don't know that for sure yet. Just get a grip and think.* He had a beautiful romantic evening planned for Becca, during which he intended to declare his love and do a whole lot more, but he couldn't possibly go ahead with it if there was even the remotest possibility that he wasn't the intended recipient of her sexy fantasies. He'd look like a complete fool.

After a few minutes of contemplation, he decided there was only one logical course of action, and it was exactly what he had told Becca to do if she were ever in doubt about something important. Ask!

He made his way though the maze of boxes and bags lining the floor to Becca's bedroom door and knocked.

"Come in," she called out.

He eased the door open and stepped inside to find her sitting on the edge of the bed, her hands folded primly in her lap. She looked a little uneasy, but he decided to ignore it and plowed on ahead. "Becca, I need to talk to you about something."

"Oh." She seemed surprised. "OK, I–I need to talk to you too. Would it be all right if I go first?"

"Um...yeah, sure," he answered warily.

She patted the bed next to her, so he joined her. She turned her body to face him, slipping one knee up onto the mattress. Ethan noticed her hands trembling right before she clasped them together tightly. He wondered what had her so worked up.

"There's something I've been wanting to tell you for a very long time, and I'm not sure how to say it," she began breathlessly.

For the moment, his own concerns were forgotten. All he wanted to do was ease her mind of whatever was bothering her. He reached out to cover her hands with one of his and gave her a small smile. "Whatever it is, it's OK, Becca. We're best friends. I've told you before you can tell me anything."

Her gaze searched his for a long while, like she was looking for a sign. Finally she whispered, "Maybe I should show you instead."

He hoped his nod was encouraging. "Whatever makes you comfortable."

"I think it would be easier if you closed your eyes."

Now he was really starting to wonder what was going on, but wanting to put Becca completely at ease, he did as she asked. She slid a hand from beneath his, and the warmth of her palm pressed against his cheek. Her touch sent a trail of fire shooting straight to his groin, but that was nothing compared to the feelings that assailed him when she leaned forward and pressed her lips gently against his.

It was the sweetest kiss he'd ever experienced, but she ended the brief contact far too quickly, leaving his body screaming for more.

Then her breath fanned lightly over his lips as she whispered so softly he could barely hear her, "I love you."

His eyes flew open, and he gazed at her, stunned.

She blinked furiously. Her eyes glistened with unshed tears and a look of uncertainty mingled with hope. "Please say something, Ethan," she begged softly.

In that moment, he realized she was scared out of her mind that he wouldn't welcome her declaration. Unable to bear her worry a minute longer, he gathered her into his arms and lowered his head to claim her mouth with a tender kiss.

Oh God, he'd waited for this moment so long. Her lips were soft and sweet. His entire body hummed with desire, and as he sensed her passion rising too, he deepened the kiss. He slipped one hand behind her head and slid the other around her waist, anchoring her tightly against him. Her hands rose to circle his neck, and he gently slipped his tongue out to run it along the seam of her lips. When she rewarded him by her parting them slightly on a gasp, he plunged deep inside.

She tasted faintly of cinnamon and honey from the sopapillas they'd shared for dessert at lunch. Over and over, he slid his tongue along hers in a primitive mating dance, and when he began to pull back, she followed him, tentatively flicking the tip of her tongue against his lips. He instantly opened to welcome her in, then hungrily devoured her, trying to pour all the love in his heart into his kisses.

He wanted nothing more than to lay her back on the bed and release all the pent-up passion from the past year, but things were moving too quickly. With superhuman effort he brought the searing kiss to an end.

Struggling to calm his ragged breathing, he rested his forehead against Becca's for a moment before drawing back to study her face. Her hair was mussed, tears trickled silently down her cheeks, and her lips were swollen from his kisses. Even in her tousled state, she was still the most beautiful woman he had ever seen. And she stared back at him with a look of complete awe and adoration that was very nearly his undoing.

Ethan caressed her plump bottom lip with his thumb. "How's that for saying something?" he whispered.

Without speaking, Becca threw herself into his arms so hard he fell backward on the bed.

Her body stretched tantalizingly atop his. Her hands cupped his face, and she plied his lips with as much ardor as he had shown her moments before. He kissed her back, tasting the salty tang of her joyful tears.

After several minutes, he rolled them to the side and propped himself up on one forearm so he could gaze down at her.

"I take it you were happy with my answer?" he teased while caressing her cheek with the back of his fingers.

"Ethan, is this real, or am I dreaming? Because if I am, I don't want to wake up."

He took her hand in his and brought it to his mouth, placing a light kiss on her knuckles. "I promise it's all very real, sweetheart. I love you too. More than you can imagine. But maybe we should slow down a little. I think we have a lot to talk about."

He rose to a sitting position, bringing Becca with him. He ran a finger down her cheek and along her jaw, then trailed it down to the hollow of her throat and further, tracing a path along the top of the low neckline of her dress just above her breasts. She closed her eyes and leaned into his caress. He couldn't seem to stop touching her, and her fevered responses only added fuel to the fire that was about to set him ablaze.

Finally, he snatched his finger back and balled his hand into a fist, willing himself to stop, before clearing his throat. "Why don't you go wash your face and change into something a little more comfortable?

I'll meet you in the living room in fifteen minutes for your next surprise."

She nodded. "Only if you swear this isn't going to end. That it isn't all going to disappear in a puff of smoke. That I'm not going to wake up."

"I swear, Becca, honey, this is only the beginning," he replied earnestly before kissing her again.

This time, he kept it short and sweet, and when it ended, he forced himself to leave the room before he got ahead of himself again.

As the door clicked shut behind Ethan, Becca sat with her legs tucked beneath her, stunned. She grabbed a throw pillow from the bed, closed her eyes, and hugged it to her chest, trying to hold in the sensations of Ethan's body pressed against hers. She raised a hand to her lips, remembering the sweetness of his kisses. The peck he'd given her on the lips a few months ago hadn't prepared her for how skillful a kisser he actually was. She lost herself in the reverie. By the time she opened her eyes and glanced at the clock, ten minutes had passed.

Becca leapt off the bed. She was supposed to meet him in five minutes, and questions swirled through her mind. A quick look at herself in the bathroom mirror revealed a tear-streaked face and tangled hair. She groaned at her reflection before pulling her hair back with an elastic band and wetting a washcloth. She washed her face, then pressed the cool cloth over her eyes, hoping it would reduce the redness and puffiness. After drying her face with a soft towel, she pulled out the hair band and quickly ran a brush through the honey-colored strands. She briefly toyed with reapplying her makeup but decided to go *au naturel* instead. Ethan had already seen her many times before without it, so it didn't seem so important.

What Becca didn't know was what to wear. Had Ethan really meant to get comfortable, or was he using that phrase euphemistically, meaning she should change into something sexy? She stripped out of her dress and looked at herself again in the bedroom's full-length mirror. She'd purposely worn a pretty lace bra and panty set just in case. She could go out there in nothing but her underwear. That would certainly get his attention. Becca quickly discarded that thought as too forward, given that they had barely even revealed their feelings for each other.

Then her mind lit upon the perfect idea. She hurried over to where she had dropped her Victoria's Secret bag when she'd entered the room. Becca carefully unfolded the tissue paper and pulled out the silky white chemise and matching peignoir. They were much more elegant than her undergarments, while hopefully still conveying the message that she was his for the taking.

Becca removed her bra and slid the silken chemise over her head. The garment slithered down her body to just above her knees. She quickly donned the peignoir before taking another look at herself in the mirror. As she reached up to smooth a few stray hairs back into place, her hand trembled.

She swallowed hard. Her heart pounded like it was trying to leap out of her chest. She knew it was silly to be nervous–he was still the same Ethan, after all, the man she loved and trusted like no one else– but she couldn't seem to help herself. She'd waited for this moment for so long, and now that it was finally here, her mind failed her in knowing what to do. She went to the door and took a deep breath to calm her nerves before opening it and stepping into the living area.

The sight that met Becca's eyes made her gasp. A crackling fire burned in the hearth, casting a warm inviting glow over the sitting room. Its light was complemented by a half-dozen lit candles placed strategically around the room. The coffee table had been moved back against the wall to make space for a thick fur throw, which covered the floor in front of the fireplace. Several large throw pillows were piled at one end. Off to the side, a bottle of champagne was chilling in a bucket with two crystal flutes next to it.

Becca feasted on the scene before her. She couldn't have created a more romantic setting if she'd tried.

Her attention was suddenly diverted as Ethan strode from the kitchen carrying a plate of chocolate-covered strawberries. He still wore the same polo shirt, but he had changed into jeans, and his feet were bare. Immediately, Becca felt self-conscious of her choice of attire.

The moment Ethan caught sight of her, he stopped in his tracks. His mouth slightly agape, his gaze traveled the length of her body and back up before settling on her face.

"I–I'm sorry," Becca stammered. "I guess I'm a little under-dressed. I'll go change."

She turned toward her room, but Ethan quickly set the plate on the dining table and was at her side in an instant. He grabbed her wrist, preventing her from leaving, and pulled her back against his chest, wrapping his arms around her waist. The warmth from his body surrounded her as he leaned down to murmur in her ear, "Maybe it's me who's overdressed."

He chuckled before turning her to face him. The smile he wore lit up the room and warmed Becca all the way to her toes. As he held her gaze, Ethan lifted his hand to caress her cheek. "You don't need to change a thing. You're absolutely perfect the way you are." He lowered his head until his face touched hers and whispered, "You're so beautiful you take my breath away."

"Oh, Ethan." All coherent thought had left Becca's mind. For the life of her, she couldn't think of another thing to say.

Ethan kissed her temple, his touch sending a shiver down her spine. "Are you cold, sweetheart?"

The timbre of his voice rumbled against her cheek. Still unable to speak, Becca simply nodded.

Ethan stepped back and took her hand in his. "Come over by the fire."

He picked up the plate of strawberries and led her down into the sunken living room. After depositing the dish on the coffee table, he seated her on the fur rug.

He sat down facing her. Placing his hand on the other side of her legs, he leaned in close. His other hand trailed up and down her arm as he spoke. "I have a confession to make. The whole reason I brought you here is that I've been dying to tell you how much I love you for a long time."

"Really?"

He nodded.

"Why didn't you tell me?" she asked softly.

His hand continued its lazy exploration back up her arm. "I was afraid you didn't feel the same way, and it would ruin our friendship."

A little snort of laughter escaped her. "Me too. Edna kept telling me you loved me, but I didn't believe her."

"You should have," he murmured. "She's a wise woman."

Ethan tucked a stray wisp of hair behind her ear and then cupped the side of her face. The look in his eyes was one of complete adoration. "Oh, Becca." His Adam's apple bobbed as he swallowed hard. "I've been madly in love with you for so long it almost hurts to think about it."

Becca brought her hand up to cover his and turned her head to plant a kiss in the center of his palm. "How long?" she asked softly.

"I'm not sure. I think I fell in love with you the day we met, but I didn't fully realize it until that night you came to me. The way you trusted me to take care of you warmed my heart." He entwined his fingers with hers and nuzzled her cheek. "And waking up with you in my arms the next morning..." His voice trailed off on a sigh.

"I liked that too." Her mouth turned up at the corners as she recalled how safe she'd felt in his arms.

After planting a soft kiss on her temple, he pulled back just far enough to gaze into her eyes. "Do you realize that was one year ago tonight?"

Becca thought about it for a moment. "You're right. It was," she replied, rather surprised that he remembered the exact date. It had also been the day of her mom's funeral.

Becca experienced a brief moment of melancholy as she was reminded of her mother, but her joy over finally being with Ethan chased it away.

"Are you thinking about your mom?" Ethan asked gently.

Becca's head jerked up, and her eyes went wide with astonishment. "How did you know?"

"I thought I saw a little sadness in your eyes. You're a pretty easy person to read, you know."

"Am I really that transparent?"

"Mm-hmm." He smiled. "Well, sometimes anyway. I certainly didn't guess that you were in love with me, at least not until recently, and even then I had some doubts. Either you were really good at hiding it or I was too afraid to see it. But right now, everything you feel seems to be written on your face."

"OK then, what am I thinking right now?"

"Well, let's see." He looked contemplatively into her eyes. "You're thinking what an amazing, awesome guy I am, and how you can't wait to get me drunk, so you can take advantage of me."

Becca gasped in shock. She snatched up one of the pillows and started beating him over the head with it.

Ethan fell back onto the stack of remaining pillows, laughing. He grabbed the pillow she was using to pummel him, trying to take it away from her, but with her having a death-grip on it, he only succeeded in pulling her down on top of him.

Ethan instantly stopped laughing, and his eyes went dark with desire. With one hand, he grasped the back of her head and raised up until his lips met hers. His other arm wrapped tightly around her waist. His lips waged a sensual assault on hers while his tongue teased playfully, until all coherent thought left Becca's mind. When he finally pulled back, he was panting hard and his eyes were heavy-lidded.

"Why did you stop?" Becca asked softly, barely able to form the words around her own erratic breathing.

"Because if I don't stop now, I might not be able to."

"Oh." Becca's single-syllable reply sounded lame even to her own ears. She had no idea how to take Ethan's response. Feeling uncertain, she slid off his chest, although his strong arm around her waist kept her anchored to his side. Idly, she toyed with a button on his shirt. "Don't you want to..." She lowered her gaze as her voice trailed off in embarrassment.

"Becca, sweetheart, look at me," he commanded huskily.

Unable to resist, she lifted her head. He looked into her eyes lovingly as his hand gently covered hers. His eyes never leaving hers, he slowly slid her palm down his chest, to his abdomen, and even lower still until she cupped the bulge in the front of his pants. Becca's breath hitched at the intimate contact.

"Does that feel like a man who doesn't want you?" he asked, still gazing deeply into her eyes.

Her mind devoid of words, she merely shook her head in reply. Finally, her eyes flicked down to where her hand still rested on his erection. She'd never touched a man like this before.

Her curiosity aroused, she began to lightly caress him through the fabric of his jeans, and his flesh seemed to swell and become even harder than it was before. She wondered what it would be like to touch him, skin to skin, without the thick denim in the way.

As she raised her hand to the button of his jeans, he grabbed her hand. "Stop," he rasped.

Hurt washed over her at the harshness of the word, and she snatched her hand away.

Ethan lifted her chin to look her in the eye again. "Becca, honey," he said, his voice softening, "make no mistake. I love you, and I want you like I've never wanted any woman in my life. God, you have no idea how many times you've made me hard like this. But there's something I promised myself I'd do before I make love to you."

"What?" she asked, her brow wrinkled in confusion.

"Soon, sweetheart. I promise I'll get to that in a minute. It's another one of your surprises."

Finally relaxing a little, she gave him a small smile. "Ethan, I don't know how many more surprises you could possibly give me."

"I still have a few more up my sleeve." He grinned impishly. "How about some champagne first?"

She nodded. "I'd like that."

Ethan filled the champagne flutes from the chilled bottle in the ice bucket. He handed one to her and then reached for the plate of berries.

"Strawberry?" he offered with a quirked eyebrow.

"Please." She eagerly reached for one only to have Ethan pull the plate away. "What–"

He picked up a plump berry and raised it to her lips. "Allow me."

She bit into the sweet, chocolaty fruit. The pleasure bursting on her taste buds caused Becca to close her eyes and make a soft noise at the back of her throat. She opened her eyes again to see Ethan looking like he was being tortured–but in a good way.

"Do you have any idea how sexy you are right now?"

Becca demurely tucked her hair behind her ear. Ethan's compliments always had a way of making her feel shy. "Nobody's ever called me sexy before."

"Well, you are, and I plan on telling you that a lot more. So you better get used to it."

He offered her the rest of the strawberry. As she bit it off from the stem, a trickle of juice ran down her chin. She reached up to wipe it away, but Ethan grabbed her hand and pulled it away.

He leaned in so close she could feel his heated breath on her cheek.

"I wanted to do this last night when you had chocolate on your face," he whispered seductively.

His tongue lapped up the drop of juice and retraced its path back up to the corner of her mouth. Then his lips covered hers in a sensuous kiss. His tongue dipped inside as though searching for another taste of the sweet berry.

He pulled back a little and leaned his forehead against hers. "You're going to make me forget my promise," he chided with a smile.

"That was nice." She sighed. "You're a really good kisser."

"Thanks. So are you," he murmured while caressing her cheek with the back of his fingers.

"Really? I don't have a lot of experience, you know."

"You're a natural. And I fully intend to take care of that lack of experience."

"Do you now?" she asked coyly.

Ethan leaned in until his lips nearly touched hers. "That sounds like a challenge," he whispered in response before his mouth claimed hers once again.

His lips and tongue plundered hers with sensual abandon as he slowly laid her back onto the furry throw. He covered her body with his own, pressing her down into the softness of the pillows.

She wrapped her arms around his neck as he trailed kisses across her cheek to her ear. He gently nibbled on the lobe and the pulse point just beneath it. Her hands clasped his head, wanting to keep him there longer, and he obeyed her silent command, his lips and teeth continuing their tender ministrations before finally continuing their downward trek. His tongue dipped into the small hollow at the base of her throat.

Becca gasped as he placed tiny, feather-light kisses all along her collarbone. Her hands slid down to caress Ethan's chest. She hated that the fabric of his shirt was in the way, and began tugging it from the waistband of his jeans. When it was free, her hands slipped underneath to roam freely over the heated skin of his back, then around to his muscular chest and stomach.

Ethan groaned before lifting his head to look at her with eyes heavy-lidded with desire. His gaze traveled down to her breasts, which were heaving with her erratic breathing beneath the silky chemise.

He flicked one pebbled nipple through the fabric with the pad of his thumb, drawing a moan from her kiss-swollen lips. Ethan slipped the peignoir down one arm, raining kisses over her shoulder. He toyed with the strap of her gown before finally sliding it down as well. One finger glided along the upper swell of her breast above the falling chemise, sending tingling sensations throughout her body and moisture pooling between her legs. Then his lips replaced his fingertips as he kissed and licked a path across her chest while tugging her gown to her waist.

"You are so beautiful," he whispered, his voice husky with desire

as he gazed at her bare breasts. The combination of his heated stare
and the cool air washing over her naked skin made her nipples harden
even more.

Suddenly feeling shy, Becca resisted the urge to cover herself, and
she was glad that she had when his hands cupped her breasts and he
took one in his mouth. He alternated between suckling and swirling
the tip with his tongue before switching to the other side.

Becca's fingers tangled in his hair and her back arched as she
whimpered with need. Her legs moved restlessly. The soft hairs of the
furry rug beneath and the coarse fabric of Ethan's jeans above abraded
her already sensitive nerve endings, sending waves of pleasure through
her body.

Her fingers trailed around the top of his waistband to the button
at the front.

"Ethan, please make love to me," she begged shamelessly while
tugging at the stubborn closure.

Becca's fevered plea jolted Ethan out of his passion-drugged state.
He'd very nearly lost control, despite trying to keep his promise. His
breathing still erratic, he lifted his head to look into her eyes. The
yearning and desire he saw mirrored there almost made him toss his
promise out the window.

He closed his eyes and took a deep breath. "I can't," he ground
out through clenched teeth.

Her fingers stilled on his zipper. "Why?" she moaned in
frustration.

"Shh." He placed a finger to her lips. "Because I have something
to ask you first."

"What?"

Ethan could hardly stand the look of pained confusion on her face, but he knew that his next words would wipe it away. He turned onto his back, reclining against the pillows, then drew Becca into his arms, caressing her back while settling her head on his shoulder.

He reached into his jeans pocket and pulled out his grandmother's ring. The small heart-shaped diamond flanked by two tiny rubies glinted in the firelight.

Becca's head popped up as a small gasp escaped her lips.

"Becca, the day we met at the animal shelter, I thought you were the most beautiful woman I had ever laid eyes on. Even with a smudge of dirt on your face and soaking wet from Buddy pushing you into the tub. That hasn't changed one bit. If anything, you've only become more beautiful the longer I've known you, because I've gotten to know the person inside too. Your kind, giving, caring heart reinforces my belief in the goodness of humanity. Your passion for animals equals, if not exceeds, my own. The quiet strength you've shown through all the curveballs that life threw at you this past year is inspiring. You being a hopeless romantic who can't live without your romance novels is utterly endearing. Sweetheart, everything about you makes you perfect for me. I know this may seem fast, but I've spent a whole year thinking about it. Becca, I'm deeply, truly, passionately in love with you, and I want to spend the rest of my life with you. Will you do me the honor of becoming my wife?"

Almost the moment Ethan began his proposal, silent tears started coursing down Becca's face. "Yes," she replied tearfully before flinging her arms around him. She clung to his neck, sobbing.

Ethan held her tightly as he placed kisses in the silky hair that smelled faintly of her floral-scented shampoo. He kissed her temple and then her ear before teasingly whispering into it, "So can I put this ring on your finger now?"

Once again, her head shot up. "Oh God, yes!" Her voice still quavered as she offered him a trembling hand.

Ethan slid the ring on her finger and pressed his lips to the back of her hand, all the while smiling like a besotted idiot. He rolled Becca to her back and covered her with his body. One more time, his lips locked with hers, stirring the embers of desire. Her hands slipped under his shirt, heating his body again too. He pressed his erection to her mound and rubbed against her as his mouth left hers to nibble the tender flesh of her throat.

"Will you please make love to me now, Ethan?"

Ethan stilled his body and leaned his forehead against hers before answering. "I know it might sound old-fashioned," he answered, his voice hoarse with passion, "but I was thinking we should wait until we're married."

Her response was a tortured moan.

Ethan raised himself onto his forearms. "We've waited this long. What's one more day?"

Her face scrunched up in confusion. "One day?"

He gave her a huge grin. "Becca Anderson, will you marry me tomorrow?"

"Tomorrow?"

He shrugged. "Why not? We are in Vegas after all."

Becca's face lit up as though something had just occurred to her. "Did you have this planned all along? Is that why you asked me to come here?"

Ethan cleared his throat. "Guilty as charged," he answered without remorse.

"But how did you know I'd say yes?"

"I didn't. I decided to take a chance, and so far, it's really paid off." Still smiling, he continued, "So...you still haven't answered my question."

Her brows drew down contemplatively. "What question was that again?"

Ethan laughed and shook his head at her teasing. "You really like to torture a guy, don't you? I think that makes you a very naughty girl."

"Maybe I'm giving you a taste of your own medicine," she replied seductively as her hands resumed their exploration of his body. She lifted her pelvis to grind it against his still-firm cock. One hand slid inside the waistband of his jeans as she raised up to nip his bottom lip.

Ethan moaned. "Like I said, you're a very naughty girl."

She rewarded him with a giggle and one of her adorably innocent smiles. "So if I say yes, I have to wait until tomorrow. What happens if I say no?"

"Let's just say that if you say yes, I promise I'll make it worth the wait." Then he leaned down to murmur suggestively in her ear, "And in the meantime, I'd never leave a lady frustrated or unsatisfied."

A cute little whimper escaped her lips. "Deal."

With that, she reached up to grab the back of his head and pulled him down into a passionate kiss. Her tongue tentatively darted out to skim the seam of his mouth. He immediately opened up and tangled with hers.

The hand inside his pants was joined by her other one. They kneaded his buttocks, her long nails nipping at his taut flesh.

Ethan could scarcely believe his sweet Becca was being so passionate. The woman was full of surprises. He had a feeling she was going to be incredibly responsive, and he couldn't wait to see the look of pleasure on her face when he made her orgasm.

As Ethan continued his passionate assault of her mouth, she brought her leg up to hook it over his hip. He grabbed the back of her calf and skimmed his hand up past her knee to the softness of her thigh, then higher still to her firm bottom. He nibbled at her ear lobe, her neck, her shoulder, then dipped his head to place a tiny kiss on one hard pink nipple before capturing it in his mouth. He loved the taste of her and suckled greedily as her breath escaped in ragged gasps.

Ethan glanced up through his lashes to find Becca watching him. With one last deep pull, he drew back until her nipple escaped his lips with a slight pop. His gaze never leaving hers, he slid his hand over her belly and down to cup her mound.

A heady feeling of masculine satisfaction washed over him when he found her panties damp with her arousal. He rubbed his fingers back and forth between her legs while pressing his thumb to her sensitive nub.

Becca's body spasmed in reaction, and she made soft mewling sounds in the back of her throat. Pushing the fabric of her panties aside, Ethan circled her satiny, wet feminine flesh with one finger before carefully sliding it inside her slick hot passage. Becca arched her back and moaned deeply. Her fevered response and the way her inner walls contracted against his finger were electrifying, making him want to drive her to the brink of need and then take her over the edge.

Gently, Ethan slipped another finger inside to join the first. Her tight passage clenched around them as he slowly retreated and then thrust in again. His fingers continued their in-and-out rhythm while he massaged her clit with his thumb.

He dropped his head to take the pretty pink tip of one breast in his mouth. He could feel the tension mounting in her body as her needy whimpers reached a fevered pitch. One of her hands fisted in his hair and the other in the furry throw at her side.

Ethan lifted his head to whisper in her ear, "Come for me, sweetheart."

Seconds later she shattered apart in his arms, crying out his name. He continued to caress her sensitive flesh, milking every last spasm from her body until she went limp beneath him.

Becca's eyes were closed, and she wore a serene smile on her plump lips. Ethan held her close until her breathing slowed back to normal.

She sleepily opened her eyes and raised a hand to cup his cheek. "That was amazing," she said with a look of wonder on her face.

"It was my pleasure, m'lady."

She rewarded him with another sweet smile as her hand ventured down to grasp his still-hard cock. "But you haven't been pleasured yet."

The temptation to allow her to do just that was strong, but he tamped it down. For now, he wanted this to be all about her and nothing else. With a twinge of reluctance and a small sigh, he peeled her hand away from his erection and lifted it to his lips. "Don't worry about me. I'll be fine."

Already her eyes were drifting shut.

He leaned down to kiss her temple and murmur in her ear, "Go to sleep and dream of our wedding tomorrow."

Becca's eyes never opened, but she hummed softly as the corners of her lips turned up again. Within minutes, Ethan felt her relax into slumber.

He slid his arms from around her and arranged her comfortably against the pillows. He sat up, taking care not to wake her, and covered her with a blanket. For a moment he stared at her sleeping form and her lashes fanned over her porcelain cheeks.

He'd never tire of watching her sleep nor stop thinking she looked like an angel sent straight from heaven just for him.

Finally, he stood, rearranging his jeans to ease the ache in his groin. For one more night he would take a cold shower and get friendly with his own hand. Tomorrow, he'd make her his wife, his soulmate, and his lover...for life.

Chapter 19

Becca slowly awakened to bright fingers of sunlight streaming through the floor-to-ceiling windows in the adjacent dining area. The fire in the hearth had long since burned out, leaving a slight chill in the air.

She rolled onto her back and stretched languidly. A smile touched her lips as memories of the night before flooded her senses. Ethan had been so sweet and loving as he'd pleasured her body. If that was even a hint of the things that were to come tonight, she might not be able to move when he was through with her. She grinned at the thought.

When she raised her hand to rub the sleep from her eyes, the sun glinted off her engagement ring. She held her hand poised there a moment and stared at the beautiful ring. As she fingered the delicate band almost reverently, she could hardly believe that today was her wedding day. She'd come here merely wanting to share her feelings with Ethan, desperately hoping he would reciprocate them. Although she had dreamed of marrying him many times, she'd never entertained the notion that it would happen so quickly. And yet it all felt so right.

Thoughts of her upcoming nuptials made Becca realize that her groom was nowhere in sight. The last thing she remembered was Ethan telling her to go to sleep. She must have done exactly that. But where had he gone?

Thinking he was in another room, Becca called his name, but there was no response. Throwing back the blanket, she rose from her makeshift bed and began searching the suite. There was still no sign of him. The only room she hadn't looked in was the one which Ethan had told her not to enter because of the construction mess. Surely he wouldn't be in there?

In the interest of being thorough, she headed for the door anyway. As she grasped the handle and was about to turn it, the phone rang.

Releasing her hold on the knob, she retraced her steps across the living room to answer it.

"Morning, gorgeous." The masculine voice on the other end sent tingles down her spine.

"Ethan, where are you? I woke up and was looking for you."

"I couldn't very well see my bride-to-be on our wedding day, now could I? That would be bad luck."

"I guess you're right, but that doesn't answer my question."

"About where I am? After you fell asleep last night, I left to spend the night in another room here in the hotel."

"Oh, I see." Becca knew he was following tradition, but she couldn't help feeling a bit disappointed that he wasn't there when she woke up. "I missed you."

"I missed you too, sweetheart. So did you sleep well last night?" Ethan asked in a husky tone.

Remembering the intimacy they had shared last night made her suddenly feel a little shy again. She nervously tucked her hair behind her ear before answering. "Yeah, I did. How about you?"

"Actually, I'm a little sleep-deprived. My brother, Nathan, and my crazy best friend, Todd, kept me out until about three a.m. celebrating the end of my bachelorhood."

"Nathan and Todd are here? How did they... You little sneak! You really did have this planned all along, didn't you?"

He chuckled warmly. "Like I told you last night, sweetheart, guilty as charged."

"What if I hadn't said yes?"

"Then Nate and Todd would have gotten a free trip to Vegas, and I don't think they would've been complaining."

"So I take it you guys had a good time," she said wistfully.

"We had a great time, hon. But do I detect a note of jealously?"

"Maybe," she answered cryptically while twisting the belt of her robe around her finger.

"Well, don't be jealous."

"Why shouldn't I?" she replied in a huff. "You guys got to go out and paint the town while I slept."

"I didn't hear you complaining last night," Ethan replied suggestively.

"Maybe not, but I still don't think it's fair," she answered sulkily.

"Like I said, don't worry. I have it all taken care of."

"You have what taken care of?"

"In about one minute, your doorbell is going to ring. When it does, have fun. I'll see you in the chapel at seven. I can't wait to make you my wife."

"Ethan, I–" Becca was cut short by the chime of the doorbell.

"I love you, sweetheart."

"I love you too, Ethan."

"Now go answer the door." With that order, he hung up.

Becca padded to the entryway, still in her bare feet, wondering with every step what in the world Ethan had up his sleeve now. She clicked back the locks and swung the door wide only to have her mouth drop open in astonishment.

"Edna!" she practically squealed.

"Hello, dear."

Edna stepped inside. With a huge smile on her face, she opened her arms wide to give Becca in a tight hug.

"What are you doing here?" Becca asked.

"Well, I heard you're getting married, and I wouldn't have missed the wedding for the world."

"But how did you–"

Becca was interrupted by the sound of another feminine voice in the doorway.

"Bring everything in here ladies," the tall brunette called over her shoulder before turning to Becca. "Hi, Becca. How's the bride-to-be?" she asked as she embraced Becca warmly.

"Alex, I thought you were going back to Afghanistan."

"I was, but Ethan called about a week ago to tell me he was getting married. I wasn't about to miss my brother's wedding, so I decided to stick around for a few more days."

"A week ago? But he hadn't even asked me then."

Alex laughed. "Guess my brother made the biggest bet of his life, and it paid off."

Becca peered around Alex's statuesque frame to find the penthouse being invaded. There must have been at least a dozen women carrying in boxes and bags. Some were already unpacking the things they'd brought and setting them out anywhere they could find space. A young man was supervising the wheeling in of several clothing racks filled with garment bags.

"What on earth is all this?"

"Your wedding planning committee," Alex answered.

"My wha..." Becca's voice trailed off. She put a hand to her forehead and swallowed hard.

"Becca, sweetie. You look like you're about to faint. Come over here and sit down." Alex guided Becca to a chair at the dining room table that was now laden with all sorts of wedding accessories.

"I thought we were having a quick Vegas-style wedding. I–I don't think I can do this," Becca stated feebly.

"You're not having second thoughts about marrying Ethan, are you?" Alex asked.

"No. Absolutely not," Becca replied with more strength. "It's just all this..." She indicated with a wave of her hand around the room. "It's kind of overwhelming."

"That's why I'm here," Alex answered with a smile as she took a seat next to Becca. "I do have some experience with the whole wedding-planning thing, and Lord knows, I'm nothing if not efficient," she added with a laugh.

"Oh, that's right. I forgot you've been married before. I'm so sorry about how that all turned out."

"Yeah, well, that's water under the bridge," Alex said dismissively. "We're not going to ruin your special day by talking about my problems. Ethan asked me to take care of you, and that's what I'm going to do."

"So Ethan brought you guys here too? He mentioned that Nathan and Todd were here."

Alex nodded. "He flew us all up on the company jet last night. Mom and Dad and Gramps too. I hope you don't mind that he asked me to help with the wedding. He wanted you to feel like you were having a real one, and not a quickie Vegas wedding. I know we've barely begun to scratch the surface of getting to know one another, but I had a feeling from the moment I met you at the barbecue that you were the one for Ethan. Even if you were 'just friends.'" She punctuated her words with air quotes while giving Becca a conspiratorial smile. "Despite my current personal feelings on the topic of marriage, I'm really thrilled for you two. I think you make an awesome couple. Not to mention I finally get to have the sister I always wanted!" She practically shrieked with delight.

Alex's enthusiasm was infectious. Becca finally felt herself relaxing. "I guess I finally get to have a sister too. And a brother." She laughed and reached over to give Alex another hug. "And no, I don't mind in the least that Ethan asked you to help. I think I can use all the help I can get right now. I don't have a clue where to start."

"Well, what are we waiting for? Let's plan a wedding!"

Becca had almost forgotten the army of people still standing in the background waiting for instructions. Edna took off for the kitchen to fix her breakfast while Becca and Alex started looking at flowers, decorations, cakes, and menus. Since the wedding was going to be a small affair, with only a few guests attending, they didn't need to order much.

Alex hadn't lied about being efficient. With her practical experience and firm guidance, everything moved along smoothly. She definitely had a skill for knowing what needed to be done and making sure it happened.

After ushering most of the service people out the door to begin their preparations for the ceremony that evening, Alex rejoined Becca at the table.

Alex glanced at her watch. "Well, that didn't take long. It's only 10:30."

"Really?" Becca was astounded that they'd finished so quickly.

"Yup, all we have left is the gown. I had them bring a good selection. I hope you find something you like."

By then, all the gowns had been removed from their protective bags. Yards and yards of shimmering silk, frothy tulle, and delicate lace lined the living room, which now looked as if it had been turned into a bridal showroom all for her. Not for the first time this weekend, Becca felt like Cinderella living in her own fairy tale.

Still in her chemise and bare feet, she slowly circled the room, looking at each dress. She ruled out some gowns right away because they simply weren't her style. On her third pass through the sea of dresses, she finally selected three particularly elegant ones in different styles. Alex and Edna helped her carry them to her bedroom, where they assisted her with trying them on. They were all lovely and fit nicely, but she couldn't help feeling something was missing.

After taking off the third one, Becca flopped down on the bed. "I don't know, Alex. I like them all...but I don't love any of them. Does that make sense?"

"Sure it does." Alex sat next to her and rubbed her back soothingly. "It's your special day, and you want to look perfect. After all, you'll probably only be doing this once in your life."

"I hope so." Becca smiled. "What if I don't find The One?"

"Did you have something in particular in mind?"

"No, not really. I just feel like I'll know it when I see it."

"Well then, let's go back out and have another look."

"I don't know. I already went through them all three times. The ones I tried on were my favorites, and they still don't seem quite right."

"It can't hurt to take one more look, dear," Edna added. "Maybe you'll find something you missed before."

"And if you don't, no sweat," said Alex. "There's still plenty of time before the ceremony. We'll take you to a few boutiques."

Becca nodded and headed back to the living room. She looked at each gown very carefully this time. Alex held up a form-fitting sheath that was very classy-looking, but Becca was afraid she wouldn't be able to walk in it. She was already rather clumsy and didn't need to add to her handicap.

She shook her head ruefully at Alex, who put the dress back on the rack.

Next, Alex pulled out a little strapless number. "How about this one?"

Becca shook her head again. "I don't really have enough to fill the top, and I'd be forever worried that it was going to fall off," she said with a giggle.

"OK, how about this one?" Alex pulled out another one that had a very simple unembellished style.

Becca wrinkled her nose. "Too plain."

This continued until they had gone through about thirty different gowns and had exhausted all the possibilities.

"Well, that's all of them." Becca shrugged. "Maybe I should give the ones I tried on another chance."

Alex glanced at her watch. "I don't know, Becca. If those were your favorites, and they didn't do it for you, I think maybe we should save time and go for the boutique. After all, the gown is the most important part of the wedding for the bride, so you should be completely happy with your choice."

"Maybe you're right. I'll go get dressed."

Becca turned to leave the room. When she reached the entryway, she glanced up to see a garment bag draped over the Queen Anne chair next to the hall table. She walked over and picked it up. "What's this?"

The bridal coordinator, who was chatting with Alex, looked up. "Oh dear, did we forget one?"

She hurried over to take the bag from Becca and hang it on one of the racks. When the woman unzipped the bag and slid it off the gown, Becca gasped. It was almost identical to the one in the wedding dream she'd had the night before leaving for Vegas. It had the same sweetheart neckline, decorated with delicate lace and seed pearls, the same matching embellishment on the short train, the same fitted bust and gathered waist. In short, it was absolutely exquisite.

"Oh my God, this is it!" Becca exclaimed.

Alex's eyes lit up too. "Looks like we have a winner."

Becca tried on the dress. The seamstress measured and pinned to take in a tuck here and there, but it was nearly a perfect fit without any adjustments.

"All we have left are the accessories," Alex said.

Becca slipped back into the living room, where she perused all the little extras. She chose a gossamer veil held in place by a headband encrusted with faux jewels and a pair of low white satin pumps.

"Now for the underthings." Alex gently elbowed Becca and gave her a knowing smile.

Becca felt her face heating. She halfheartedly picked up a couple of items only to lay them back down again. She sighed. "Alex, what do guys like?"

"You mean lingerie?"

"Yeah. I don't have much experience with this sort of thing, but I know I want to look sexy for Ethan. Since you were married before, I thought you would know what I should wear to...you know...turn him on." Becca was sure her cheeks were beet red by now.

Alex smiled sympathetically. "Sweetie, judging by the way I've seen Ethan look at you, you could be wearing a burlap sack, and he'd be turned on."

Becca giggled at the thought of showing up at her wedding in a potato sack. "Not quite what I had in mind."

"OK, no burlap." Alex laughed as she made a slash on the imaginary list in her hand. "All right, let's get serious. I think you should keep it simple. First, this." Alex plucked a white satin and lace push-up bra from the pile of undergarments and held it up in front of Becca. "It'll give you some cleavage."

Becca grinned as she took the garment from Alex. "Cleavage is good, and it's pretty too."

"Unless you're going commando, you'll need some panties to match." Alex rummaged around and came up with a cheeky pair in white satin trimmed with wide stretch lace and a tiny bow in front. "How about these?"

Becca took them from Alex and turned them over in her hands. She nodded enthusiastically. "I like them."

"Next, you'll need these." Alex shook out a pair of silky white thigh-high stockings with elastic lace at the top.

Becca fingered the delicate, sheer fabric of the hose. "They're so soft and silky. I've only worn regular pantyhose. Never anything this nice before."

"And last but not least..." Alex twirled a garter, made of white lace with a blue ribbon woven through it, on her index finger before handing it to Becca.

"That's it?" Becca asked.

"That's it," Alex replied with a smile.

Becca hugged her soon-to-be sister-in-law. "Thank you so much, Alex. You've made this so easy. I never could have pulled together a wedding this nice in only a few hours."

"You're welcome." Alex checked her watch again. "Now go get dressed. We have lots more to do before the ceremony tonight."

Becca scurried off to do just that.

Edna stayed behind at the penthouse to handle some last-minute details while Alex whisked her off to the courthouse in Ethan's limo to sign the marriage license. They followed up with lunch at an upscale restaurant. Then Alex took her to a luxurious spa where, once again, Becca felt like a pampered princess. For the next two hours, she enjoyed a relaxing full-body massage, a facial, and a mani-pedi. After that, they visited the salon where she had her hair washed, dried and styled into a pretty French knot, and her makeup professionally applied.

"I feel like a movie star," Becca told Alex as the limo pulled away from the spa.

"Sounds like I can report back to Ethan that I've succeeded in my mission."

"Ethan? I thought this was all your doing."

"Oh, it was...mostly. He had a few suggestions, but being a guy, he didn't think of everything. I added to what he thought of to make a day of it. And he gets to foot the bill," Alex added with a saucy smile.

"Well, it's been an amazing day so far, and we haven't even gotten to the ceremony yet. It's only a couple of hours away." Becca took a deep breath and pressed a hand to her stomach. "I think I'm already starting to get butterflies."

Alex laid a hand on Becca's arm. "Don't be nervous, sweetie. Everything is going perfectly. When I saw Ethan this morning, he was over the moon. I don't think I've ever seen a man so happy and madly in love."

"I know he loves me, but it doesn't stop the jitters."

"That's completely understandable. I think every bride feels that way. But I have something that should distract you for a little while."

"What?"

"You'll see," Alex replied.

The limo pulled up in front of a theater. Becca followed Alex inside a dimly lit auditorium. Rather than the rows of seats she was expecting, the large room looked more like a nightclub. Becca spotted Edna and Ethan's mom at a cozy booth near the stage. Both ladies greeted Becca warmly as she approached their seats. Becca's eyes followed Alex, who hurried off to a dark corner where she appeared to be talking with someone in the shadows. Trying unsuccessfully to tamp down her curiosity, Becca took a seat next to the other ladies.

By the time Alex returned, Becca didn't think she could take the suspense any longer. "You're really not going to tell me what's going on?"

"Nope, you'll have to wait and see for yourself."

A moment later, a shirtless, bronze Adonis brought each of the ladies a glass of wine. Becca's jaw went slack as she took in the sight of him, all smooth, tanned skin and chiseled muscles. He gave Becca an extra big smile and teasing look before striding back to the bar.

"Better close your mouth, or you're going to catch flies," Alex quipped.

"Alex, is this what I think it is?"

Before Alex had a chance to answer, the lights darkened completely. Energetic music filled the room. Fog streamed onto the stage, which was now illuminated with colored lights. Seconds later, a parade of stunningly handsome men entered the stage, dancing to the brisk beat. All the men were dressed in different costumes. There was a cowboy, a fireman, a military guy. It was almost like the heroes of her romance novels had suddenly come to life right before her very eyes. It didn't take long before hats, shirts and other accessories began dropping to the floor as the lights glistened off their muscled chests.

Becca covered her mouth with one hand and felt herself blushing furiously. She'd never been to a male revue before. Her eyes feasted on the display of sexy male bodies in rapt fascination. In spite of her previous comments to Ethan about male strippers, she couldn't deny that they were quite attractive.

Oh, who was she kidding? They were all drop-dead gorgeous, and they were putting on a show just for her. How could she not feel like the most special woman in the world right now?

The hunky and now-shirtless cowboy descended the stage steps and stopped right in front of the ladies. He pulled his hat low over his eyes as his hips gyrated to the song "Save a Horse (Ride a Cowboy)." Next to Becca, Edna whooped and cat-called. When the stripper turned his back, giving them a nice view of a toned ass in his tight jeans, Edna reached out to give him a little swat.

Becca's eyes went wide, and her jaw dropped at the older woman's behavior. She knew Edna was a spitfire, but she'd never seen her like this before. Edna turned to give Becca a smug smile and a wink before returning her attention to the dancer.

All three of the other women were now chanting, "Take it off!" Watching them having so much fun, Becca soon forgot her embarrassment and joined them. As though he had been waiting for her to give him the order, the hunk obliged by tearing off his breakaway pants. He deftly flipped his cowboy hat onto Becca's head, so that he was now wearing nothing but a G-string and a smile. He gave her a wink before heading backstage.

For the next forty-five minutes, the stunningly handsome men performed in various states of undress for their audience of four. The ladies made up for their lack of numbers with sheer enthusiasm. By the time the performance was nearly over, Becca had completely forgotten all of her misgivings and was thoroughly entranced by the show.

Several of the men had come down to the floor to give the ladies some up-close and personal attention. At one point, Alex had leaned over to ask Becca who her favorite was. It was hard for her to choose amongst so much male perfection. She finally settled on a guy with dark hair, beautiful green eyes and a cute smile because he looked like her favorite vampire romance hero.

Not long after that, Alex got up and went to the bar. She spoke with the shirtless bartender for a minute but, strangely, returned without a drink. As another dancer moved into her line of vision, Becca all but forgot the oddity...until the finale.

As the show wound to a close, the dancer Becca had chosen as her favorite emerged from a curtain to the right of the stage, dressed in black leather pants and a black muscle shirt. He walked straight to Becca and held out his hand. Not knowing what he was going to do, Becca hesitated a moment before shyly placing her hand in his. He drew her up from her seat and toward the stage. Becca looked over her shoulder at Alex and mouthed, "Did you arrange this?"

Alex's only reply was a slow, mischievous grin spreading across her face.

The gorgeous man escorted Becca onto the stage and seated her in a chair in the middle. He carefully removed his comrade's cowboy hat from her head and replaced it with a little bridal veil and tiara. When the music began again, he danced in front of her in much the same way the other dancers had earlier on the floor, except that he began inching seductively toward her. He ripped his shirt down the front to reveal hard pectorals and washboard abs, then allowed it to slide off biceps that were nearly as big as her thighs.

Becca's mind turned to thoughts of Ethan. He wasn't quite as ripped the hunk in front of her, but he definitely filled out his t-shirts nicely.

The dancer leaned in close, giving her a huge smile that revealed...vampire fangs? Becca's hand flew to her mouth as she giggled in delight. Now she knew that Alex had set this up. He bent toward her neck, pretending to bite her. She closed her eyes and imagined that Ethan was nibbling her neck.

When she opened her eyes again, he had a tiny trickle of fake blood at the corner of his mouth and his legs straddled hers as his hips thrust forward. Becca's vision clouded as she fantasized that Ethan was doing this for her. Her mouth suddenly went dry, and the intimate place between her legs tingled with desire. Becca was so caught up in her daydream, she didn't even notice when the music ended.

The dancer offered his hand again, and this time when he took it, he placed a quick kiss on the back before helping her up. As he escorted her back to her seat on the floor, Becca's knees felt like Jell-O. If Ethan were here right now, she'd probably drag him off to a dark corner and jump his bones.

The hunky guy gave her one last grin, showing those fake fangs again before heading off to rejoin his fellow performers for the big finale. Becca fanned herself with her hand. The other women took one look at her flushed face and smiled knowingly, which only made her blush more.

Following the final number, all the guys came out to greet the ladies personally, and Becca thanked them for a memorable bachelorette party. It was something she definitely would never forget.

At the sight of the "vampire" who'd given her the sexy lap dance, Becca felt her cheeks flaming all over again, but she tamped down her embarrassment to go talk to him anyway.

"Hi, I'm Becca." She introduced herself and offered him her hand.

For a second, he seemed almost surprised before composing himself and taking her hand. "Ryan."

"Alex arranged for you to do the whole vampire act, didn't she?"

He gave her one his adorable smiles. Up close, without the harsh stage lights and the fangs, he looked almost boyish–definitely not any older than her. "Yeah, she did." He glanced over at her soon-to-be sister-in-law before turning his attention back to her. "Although we didn't know which one of us was going to get the honor until halfway through the show."

Strangely enough, he appeared almost shy about having been chosen, which seemed completely at odds with his on-stage persona.

"So that's why she went over to the bar and came back empty-handed," Becca mused. "Pret–ty sneaky."

Ryan laughed at her comment. "Actually, I think it was really nice of your friend to set this up for you." He gazed longingly at Alex again. Becca watched in fascination as he almost forcibly met her own eyes again. He cleared his throat. "I've never played a vampire before either. It was fun."

"Did she explain that to you?"

"Yeah, she said something about me looking like your favorite romance novel hero?" That modest smile of his was back, and darned if his eyes weren't straying toward Alex again.

Becca leaned in to whisper in his ear. "She's single."

His head whipped around. "What?"

"Alex. The woman you can't keep your eyes off of. She's single."

"God, I am so sorry. I should be–"

"Hey, it's fine, really. I enjoyed the show and all, but I don't need any special attention. I have a hunky groom waiting for me at the altar." Becca giggled briefly before resuming a more serious air. "I totally understand you admiring her. She's a beautiful woman."

"She certainly is," he replied wistfully, looking at Alex with those beautiful puppy-dog eyes.

"So what are you waiting for?" she prodded, tilting her head in Alex's direction. "Go ask her out."

"OK. Maybe I will," he said with a smile.

From her vantage point a few yards away, Becca watched as Ryan approached Alex. The couple talked for a few minutes. Although she couldn't hear what was being said, she gathered that Ryan had taken her advice, but apparently it was not well-received. Alex shook her head ruefully, and although he tried to hide it, the disappointment in Ryan's green eyes was obvious, at least to her.

Becca couldn't help feeling a little bummed out herself. She was so happy with Ethan, she had wanted to spread her joy by setting up a romantic rendezvous for Alex when she realized how much Ryan liked her. Maybe matchmaking wasn't her thing.

As they rode back to the hotel, Becca decided to broach the subject. "So...what were you and Ryan talking about?"

Alex glanced sideways at her. "You're on a first-name basis with the guy who gave you a lap dance? I might have to tell Ethan on you."

Becca swatted Alex's thigh with her handbag. "This from the woman who set the whole thing up? And for your information, while Ryan was giving me the lap dance, I was fantasizing that he *was* Ethan."

"Ugh, did you have to mention my brother and a stripper in the same sentence?" Alex shuddered. "Not that Ethan isn't attractive and all, but...ewww."

"You're being evasive."

When Alex still didn't answer, Becca repeated the question. "So what did he say to you?"

Alex sighed and all but rolled her eyes. "Something like he couldn't help noticing how beautiful I am, and would I like to go out for a drink."

"I'm guessing by the look on his face after you finished talking that you turned him down."

"Of course I did, Becca," Alex replied as though Becca should know better.

Becca tried again. "He seemed really nice."

"It's their job to act nice." Alex turned her head to look out the window.

"I know, but there was something about him that seemed different. Something in his eyes that seemed genuine."

"I know you haven't had much experience with guys like him—performers, I mean—but I have." Alex turned back to Becca. Her tone was softer, but there was fire in her eyes. "Let me give you a word of advice. They all seem nice at first. They draw you into their world.

They make you think that you're the most beautiful girl who ever lived until they find someone else who's even more gorgeous. And then they can't keep their pants zipped." Alex's voice cracked and she blinked furiously. "Next thing you know you're being kicked to the curb and taken to the cleaners in a divorce settlement." Alex shook her head vigorously. "No, the last thing I need is a boyfriend who's a stripper."

Becca laid her hand soothingly on Alex's arm. ""I'm so sorry. It sounds like your ex was pretty awful to you. If I'd known about your issues with performers, I never would have encouraged Ryan to ask you out."

"You did that?"

Becca nodded sheepishly. "I was only trying to return the favor. It was really sweet of you to set up a private party for us. I never could have gone to a show like that with a crowd. I was already embarrassed enough as it was, but the way you did it ended up being fun. Ryan seemed so sweet, and he couldn't take his eyes off you the whole time we were talking. I thought if you got to walk away from it with a cute guy and maybe find a little romance too, it would be my way of saying thank you for everything you did today." She shrugged. "I guess I kind of botched things up, didn't I? Can you forgive me?"

Alex shook her head. "There's nothing to forgive. It's the thought that counts, and it wasn't that big of a deal. I'll probably never see the guy again." Alex sighed and brushed the tears off her face as the limo pulled up to the hotel. "Enough about my unlucky love life. I swear I'm not going to shed any more tears today." She paused a moment before adding, "Well, at least not until you walk down that aisle."

Chapter 20

An hour later, Becca rode the elevator down to the hotel chapel. It hadn't taken her long to prepare for the ceremony. Since her hair and makeup had been done earlier, all she needed was a little touch-up. She had dressed quickly and taken a last look at herself in the mirror as Alex fastened her veil in place. Everything was perfect.

Now, as she waited to reach the ground floor, the butterflies that had settled in the pit of her stomach rose into her throat. All her dreams were finally coming true, and yet she'd never been so nervous in her life. As she and Alex exited the elevator and rounded the corner toward the chapel, Becca trembled in anticipation. She hadn't talked to Ethan since this morning, and she couldn't wait to see him again.

Alex helped her through the door. Becca remained in a small vestibule at the back of the chapel while Alex went to inform everyone that the bride had arrived. She took a few deep breaths in an attempt to calm her nerves.

It didn't work.

After what seemed like an eternity, but in reality was probably only a minute, Alex returned. She propped open the inner door and turned to Becca. "Ready?"

Becca already felt tears threatening to fall. Not trusting herself to speak, she merely nodded her assent.

The wedding march began to play, and Alex started her slow promenade down the aisle. When Becca stepped up to the doorway, awaiting her turn, she caught sight of her groom waiting at the altar. He smiled at her. The look of pure love and adoration in his eyes made it impossible for Becca to hold back the tears any longer. Her vision blurred, but her eyes never left his as she walked toward him. When she finally reached the altar, Becca handed her bouquet to Alex. Ethan took both her hands in his.

After that, everything proceeded in a haze. Becca repeated the words as the minister spoke them, promising to love, honor, and cherish Ethan until death parted them. Ethan did the same. They slipped rings on each other's finger, once again pledging their unending love. Before she knew it, the minister was pronouncing them husband and wife and giving Ethan permission to kiss his new bride.

Ethan folded back her veil and, just as he had done in her dream, drew her close, with one hand at her waist, the other tenderly cupping her face. His lips descended to hers, and this time–unlike in her dream–she knew that she had been well and truly kissed.

As his lips left her hers, a chorus of cheers erupted behind them. For the first time since she'd entered the chapel, Becca took notice of their small audience. Ethan's brother, Nathan, stood next to him as best man. His parents, grandfather, and best friend, Todd, and of course, Edna stood from their chairs to come greet the happy couple.

The ceremony was followed by a lovely reception dinner in a private dining room. The food was delicious, but Becca was so excited she could barely eat. When Ethan noticed her picking at her food, he leaned over to whisper in her ear. "You should try to eat more. You need to keep up your strength for tonight."

The love and adoration she'd seen in his eyes during the wedding were now joined by passion and lust. Becca smiled and ducked her head as her face heated to a blush.

"You're so pretty when you blush like that," he murmured as he nuzzled her cheek. "I can't wait to get you upstairs."

Becca's body hummed with desire. He wrapped his arm around her shoulder and kissed her temple. A gentle finger on her chin turned her to face him. As his lips were about to claim hers, their romantic interlude was interrupted by the wedding cake being brought in. With a deep sigh, he backed away.

Ethan rose from his chair and helped her up. With his arm circling her waist, he escorted her to the cake table. Becca took a moment to admire the beautiful white confection with real pink and white flowers draped down one side. It was a shame to have to cut it, Becca thought. It was practically a work of art.

Together, she and Ethan grasped the handle of the silver knife and sectioned off a slice of cake. Using the matching server, Becca lifted it onto a plate. Todd urged Ethan to smash the cake in her face. Ethan appeared to be dutifully ignoring his best friend, instead picking up a fork and carefully cutting a bite-sized piece. He then delicately lifted it to her mouth while Todd groaned in disappointment. Becca accepted the delicious morsel, and Ethan leaned down to brush his lips against hers. Becca did the same for Ethan, then they lifted their glasses of champagne. They linked arms, and each took a sip of the sweet libation. Once their arms were disentangled, Ethan gave her another kiss, this time deeper and longer.

With a hand on the small of her back, Ethan guided Becca back to their table, carrying the plate of cake in his other hand. Once she was seated again, he pulled her close and insisted on feeding her every last bite. As the final tidbit melted in her mouth, the small local band Ethan had hired began to play a slow love song.

Ethan laid the fork on the empty plate and offered his hand. "May I have this dance, Mrs. Montgomery?"

The sound of that name washed over her like a gentle breeze, bringing peace and contentment to her heart. She smiled. "Of course, Mr. Montgomery."

When they reached the dance floor, Becca placed her arms around Ethan's waist and laid her head on his chest. He wrapped her in his embrace and leaned his cheek against the top of her head. Their tight clinch made it nearly impossible to move more than a few inches at a time, so they merely swayed to the music. Snuggled close together like this, Becca felt blanketed in Ethan's love.

Soon Ethan's parents joined them on the floor, along with Edna and Ethan's grandfather, whom Becca noticed had been getting rather cozy throughout dinner. Now as they danced, they looked at each other like a couple of giddy teenagers experiencing their first crush. Becca smiled at the thought of her elderly friend possibly finding love again.

She glanced over at Alex, still seated at her table, and wished the same for her. She thought again of Ryan, and even though she barely knew the guy, Becca couldn't quite shake the strange feeling that he would be perfect for Alex if she could only open her heart to love again.

Some time later, as Becca enjoyed her fifth dance pressed against Ethan's body, she could no longer ignore the longing to be closer to him. She raised up on her tiptoes to whisper in his ear, "I'm dying to be alone with you."

He returned her sultry look. "Me too."

"Do you think it's too soon to leave?"

"Even if it is, I don't really care. How about after this song we toss the bouquet and garter and get out of here?"

Her face lit up with a smile as she nodded her agreement.

As promised, when the song ended, Ethan made the announcement for all the single ladies—who were really only Edna and Alex—to gather for the bouquet toss.

Becca turned her back to them, closed her eyes, and threw the flowers over her shoulder. She turned around to find that Edna had caught them. She was thrilled for her friend and went to hug her. After all, one was never too old for love.

Becca looked over at Alex. Although she had a smile on her face, it didn't quite reach her eyes. Becca thought she caught a glimmer of disappointment. She sensed that even though her new sister-in-law appeared strong and unflappable on the outside and claimed to be down on men, inside she was longing for love.

With a rueful smile she gave Alex a hug too, and words of encouragement. "Someday you'll find the right guy too, Alex, and he'll love you for who you are. I know it."

"Then you have more faith than I do, Becca."

As they parted, Becca shrugged. "I'm a hopeless romantic,

remember. I can have enough faith for both of us, and when it happens, I'm going to remind you of this moment."

Before Alex had a chance to say anything more, Ethan called Becca over to remove her garter. He pulled a chair out from one of the tables and seated her facing him, then knelt on the floor in front of her. Grasping her ankle, he removed her shoe and placed her foot on his thigh. His lustful eyes never left her as he slowly slid his hand up the back of her calf, over her knee and on to her thigh in search of the little elastic band. Her breath hitched, and she swallowed hard. He finally located the garter, and in an equally leisurely manner retraced the path that his hand had taken.

The man was driving her crazy with his languid pace. Becca closed her eyes and hoped that her own desire wasn't obvious to their guests.

When he reached her ankle, he gently lifted her foot to slide the garter off and carefully replaced her shoe.

After one last look at his bride, Ethan rose and called the single men forward. Just like Becca had done, he turned his back to them and tossed the garter over his shoulder. It was headed straight for Todd, but at the last minute he dove out of the way. The frilly piece of lace landed right in the hands of Ethan's brother, whose face registered shock.

Becca followed as Ethan went to shake hands with his friend. Ethan shook his head and laughed at Todd's antics. "That garter was headed right for you."

Todd lifted his hands, palms out, as though trying to ward off some dreaded evil. "And I want no part of it, thank you very much. I'm not ready to settle down. It's too much fun being single."

Ethan chuckled at his friend again before turning to clap his brother on the shoulder. "Looks like you're next, bro."

Nathan looked skeptical. "I don't know about that, Ethan. I think you need a girl for that, and in case you hadn't noticed, the only single ladies around here are our sister and a woman who's old enough to be our grandmother."

Becca put her arm around Ethan's waist before she piped up, "She's out there. I know it."

"If you say so, sis," Nathan replied.

"Hey, you should listen to my wife. She's a hopeless romantic, you know."

"Well, that makes one of us."

"Then I guess I'll have to have enough faith for you and Alex, that's all," Becca said. She smiled up lovingly at her husband. "Because I absolutely refuse to be the only one in this room who gets a happily-ever-after ending."

Ethan hugged his parents and grandfather, then gathered his new bride back into his arms. He leaned down close to her ear so no one else could hear. "Are you ready to go make some fireworks?"

That one question was all it took to make her body heat up all over again. She nodded. "Let's go."

Ethan turned to bid the guests farewell, telling them to stay as long as they wanted and enjoy the music, food, and champagne. He and Becca kept to a normal pace as they exited the room, but as soon as the door of the dining room closed behind them, they looked at each other, smiled, and took off running for the nearest elevator.

※ ※ ※ ※ ※

About half an hour after Ethan and Becca left the party, Alex said her farewells too. She left everyone with the impression that she was tired and heading for bed, but in reality, she simply wanted to be alone. She made her way to a bar on the other side of the hotel, where she hoped her family wouldn't find her.

After taking a seat at a small corner table, she ordered a strawberry daiquiri. While she waited for it to arrive, she scanned the room. A couple of older men sat at the bar nursing hard liquor, a group of four young women, probably on a girl's night out, tittered around a nearby table, and a cute couple nuzzled each other at the booth in the opposite corner. She turned away from the sight in disgust just as the waitress arrived with her drink.

Alex loved her brother and his new wife dearly and was truly happy for them, but their joy had only served to accentuate her own sense of loss. The divorce was still fresh in her mind. Granted, she hadn't loved Danny, her rock star ex, for a long time. Not since she'd caught him in bed with one of his back up singers. But putting her signature on that piece of paper made her feel like a failure.

She should have known that her marriage to Danny wouldn't last. Their mad dash to the altar when she'd found out she was pregnant should have been the first clue. Still, she had loved him and was determined to make it work for the sake of their child. Danny had made her believe that was what he wanted too, until there was no child to work for anymore. The miscarriage had left her devastated, and she was still recovering from that trauma when she discovered Danny's infidelity. No wonder she had run halfway around the world to Kabul to get away.

Once, Alex had been a hopeless romantic like Becca, but now she believed that happily-ever-afters were only meant for other people, not for her. She had been in exactly three relationships in her lifetime, all serious in her mind, all with men for whom she'd fallen hard and fast. All of them had craved the spotlight, and in the end, all of them had cheated on her or left her for another woman, leaving her crushed and demoralized. That was why she had turned Ryan down cold this afternoon.

Alex ran a finger thoughtfully around the rim of her glass before taking a sip. She couldn't deny the man was sexy as hell. Truth be told, she'd been a little jealous of Becca picking him as her favorite stripper. As she'd watched him giving her sister-in-law that sinfully decadent lap dance, she couldn't help wishing it was her up there with him. But when he'd actually asked her out for a drink, she couldn't bring herself to accept.

All she could think about was how he bared his body like that for hundreds of women every night. She was certain many of them pawed him and covertly passed him their phone numbers. How many of them had he slept with? No, Ryan would not make good boyfriend material. Would he? Becca seemed to think otherwise.

As Alex wrestled with that conundrum in her mind, she realized her glass was empty. She raised her head, looking for the waitress, only to have her eyes lock with the object of her daydreaming across the room. She swallowed hard as he headed straight for her.

When Ryan reached her table, he gave her a gorgeous, bone-melting smile that left her a bit breathless. "Hi, there."

Alex suddenly felt tongue-tied. "Hey."

"So we meet again."

She nodded.

Ryan indicated her empty glass. "Looks like you need a refill."

"Yeah." Alex tilted her head a little to see around Ryan's tall, muscular frame. "I'm not sure what happened to the waitress."

Ryan glanced over his shoulder, cursorily searching for the woman in question before turning back to Alex. "Look, I know you turned me down this afternoon, but since we've run into each other again, it seems like fate might have other plans for us. I don't know about you, but now that I've been handed a second chance to get to know you, I'd hate to pass it up. I'd always be wondering what might have happened if I didn't take another chance on you. So...can I buy you a drink?"

As Alex gazed into Ryan's striking green eyes, she was well and truly lost. No man had ever looked at her the way Ryan was right now, like he wanted to wrap her up in his arms and protect her, and at the same time, like she was the most desirable woman he'd ever laid eyes on. It was a heady combination that made the icy sheath around her heart melt just a little. It also made her forget that he was a performer, just like all the exes who'd betrayed her. It made her forget that hundreds of women lusted after him on a daily basis. It made her forget all the heartache and loneliness that had assailed her all evening. In that one moment, the desire to lose herself in those mesmerizing eyes trumped everything else.

Giving him the barest of smiles, she indicated the empty chair next to her. "Have a seat."

* * * * *

When Ethan and Becca reached the door of the penthouse suite, he opened it before swinging her up into his arms to carry her across the threshold. Once inside, he nudged the door shut with his foot and proceeded across the room.

"Ethan, the bedroom is that way." Becca pointed behind him. "Aren't we going the wrong way?"

"Nope," he answered. He stopped in the sunken living room, still holding her.

Becca gave him a bewildered look. "Last night, here in front of the fireplace was really magical, but I was kind of hoping for a real bed tonight."

"You shall have that and more, m'lady. But first, I need to give you your wedding gifts."

"Gifts? Ethan, you've already given me more than I ever could have dreamed of."

Ethan deposited her on the sofa. He reached into the inside pocket of his tuxedo jacket and pulled out a folded sheaf of papers that looked suspiciously like the repayment contract she'd signed a few months ago.

"Is that what I think it is?" she asked.

"If you think it's the repayment contract, then yes," he answered while unfolding the papers and smoothing them flat.

Becca frowned in confusion. "What–"

Before she could form the question, he ripped the documents down the middle, opened the fireplace doors, and threw them into the low-burning flames.

He sat down next to her. "You didn't think I was going to make my wife pay me back for her education, did you? In fact, when I drew up that contract, I was hoping I could convince you to marry me so you would never have to."

Now that she knew he'd planned to marry her all along, she regretted even more her outburst that had caused Ethan to take such actions. It had been the product of her fear–unfounded, as it turned out–that his intentions in giving her so many extravagant gifts were less than honorable. Slowly, she had come to realize that he was simply a generous man who would never take advantage of a vulnerable woman.

"I'm so sorry I didn't trust you when I found out. What happened to my mom was only part of why I behaved like that. Lindsay is the one who told me you were funding my sponsorship, and she made me think more than once that you were sleeping with her. I was just overwrought with emotions, not the least of which was jealousy."

"I have no idea how Lindsay found out about the sponsorship, but now that I know what she's capable of, it doesn't surprise me at all that she would do something like that to you. If I'd known how she was manipulating you–us–I would have put a stop to it months ago." Ethan drew her into his arms and gazed into her eyes, smiling. "But it didn't work. Our love won out. We're here, happily married." He nuzzled her cheek while murmuring in her ear, "And I don't know about you, but I'm ready to make you my wife in every way."

Becca hugged him tightly and smiled into his chest. "Make me yours, Ethan."

"In that case..." He pulled a handkerchief from his pocket and folded it into a wide band before placing it over her eyes and tying it behind her head.

"A blindfold?" she giggled. "Isn't that a little kinky?"

Even as she said it, Becca felt her face flush, but the mere thought of leaving it in place while Ethan explored her body made her breath quicken and her panties dampen.

Ethan's throaty laugh next to her ear sent shivers through her. He captured her lips in a deep, sensuous kiss that heated her entire being from the top of her head to the tips of her toes and left her breathless for more. When he pulled back, she felt disappointment at the loss of his touch.

"Wait here," he gently commanded. "And no peeking," he added playfully.

The sound of his pants rustling told her he had risen from the couch. She listened as he crossed the room, and she heard the sound of a door being opened and closed. Then she waited.

Her heart pounded as anticipation rose within her chest. A million scenarios ran through her mind as she wondered what he was up to this time. Knowing Ethan, it was sure to be something amazing. After what seemed like an eternity, the door clicked open again.

She sensed Ethan as he sat down beside her. "Miss me?" he asked as he wrapped his arm around her and planted a peck on her cheek.

She smiled. "Terribly."

She slid her arms around his neck as her lips sought his. He rewarded her with another scorching kiss that she didn't want to end.

All too soon, his lips left hers. "We better stop that," he said, "or we'll never make it to the bed."

He lifted her into his arms again, carried her into another room, and carefully placed her on her feet. From the direction they had gone, Becca sensed it was the room he had told her was under construction.

"I thought you told me this room was being remodeled."

"How do you know what room we're in?" he asked as he slipped his arms around her waist, pulling her back against his firm chest.

"Apparently, I have a good sense of direction even when I can't see. Did you lie to me, Ethan Montgomery?" she inquired with mock severity.

"Ah...maybe a little white lie. But I know when I take this blindfold off, you're going to forgive me."

"You sound pretty sure of yourself there, mister."

"Um-hmm..."

She felt one hand leave her waist and begin untying the loose knot in the blindfold, but he was taking his good sweet time.

"So are you ready for your other wedding present?" he asked.

By now she was breathless with anticipation. "Please..."

"Ooh, begging already, are we? I like it."

The deep timbre of his voice sent shivers down her spine.

"Just take the damn blindfold off already!"

She didn't mean to sound so testy, but she was practically bouncing with excitement.

"OK, I'll stop torturing you. Your wish is my command, Princess." With that, he finally slid the covering from her eyes.

Becca blinked as her eyes adjusted to the light and she took in the sight before her. To her left was a small fireplace, flanked by two wing-back chairs. A string of candles across the mantelpiece flickered cheerily. Softly lit by more candles on the bedside tables, a beautiful wrought iron bed sat to her right. Its headboard and foot board twisted in an intricate pattern of curlicue scroll-work. Sheer white curtains draped down from the canopy, tied back at the four posts with wide silken ribbons. The bed was made with white satin sheets and coverlet, already turned down for the night and sprinkled with red rose petals, their fragrant scent wafting across the room. The petals trailed down to the plush ivory carpet and across the floor to a set of glass French doors, left open to reveal a luxurious rose-tiled bathroom. The trail of rose petals ended at a huge bathtub already brimming with bubbles. Even more candles bathed the bathroom with their gentle light.

As what she was seeing finally registered, Becca raised a trembling hand to her lips, and tears coursed silently down her cheeks.

"You're not saying anything. Are you OK, sweetheart?"

At the sound of Ethan's kind voice behind her, a sob escaped Becca's lips.

Instantly, the strong arms encircling her turned her around to face him. As she cried uncontrollable tears of joy, he held her tightly.

"Shh...what's wrong, Becca?"

"Nothing." She reached up to touch his face and stared at this man before her with a sense of wonder. "You read my favorite book, and you actually listened when I told you about my favorite scene."

"Of course I did. Do you think a clueless guy like me could come up with all this on my own?"

Becca couldn't help but give him a watery laugh. Then she shook her head. "You're anything but clueless. You're amazing." She took another look around the room. "It looks exactly the way I always imagined it every time I read the book."

"I'm glad you like it."

"Like it? I love it!" Becca looked up into Ethan's eyes again. "You know, I didn't think this weekend could get any more wonderful, but this...this..." She fumbled around in her brain, searching for the right thing to say, but coherent thoughts seemed to elude her. After a long pause, she said, "I don't think you'll ever be able to top this one."

"Well, there is one more thing I'd like to give you that I hope will be even more amazing."

When his meaning sank in, Becca bit her lip and ducked her head, blushing. She'd dreamed of this moment for what seemed like forever, but now that it was finally here, she was a little apprehensive. What if it wasn't everything she'd fantasized about for so long?

Ethan lifted her chin with his fingertip. "Hey, I thought you wanted to get me alone so you could have your way with me. You're not getting shy on me, are you?"

She still had a hard time holding his gaze. "I don't have much experience at this, you know."

He caressed her cheek with the back of his fingers, then placed a butterfly-soft kiss on her lips that made her sigh. "Do you have any idea how long I've waited for this moment, Becca? I couldn't care less about your lack of experience. In fact, call me jealous and possessive, but I'm glad you aren't experienced."

Becca smiled at Ethan. She reached behind his neck to pull his head down for another kiss. She plied his lips with her own before boldly flicking his bottom lip with the tip of her tongue.

He instantly opened his mouth to capture it, drawing it inside to tangle with his own, and he slanted his head to thrust his own tongue more deeply into her mouth. His arms held her snugly against his body, and she could feel his growing erection against her lower belly. She clung more tightly to his neck and whimpered.

Ethan pulled back, leaving them both panting breathlessly. He nuzzled her cheek as he murmured close to her ear, "Tonight is all about you and your pleasure, m'lady. It will be my final gift to you this weekend."

Becca shivered with delight at his words. "Oh, Ethan, I'm all yours. Just tell me what you want me to do."

He trailed feather-light kisses across her face. "You don't have to do a thing." His lips continued to trace a path along her jaw. "Leave it all up to me." She tilted her head to the side as he nibbled further down her her neck. "Let me treat you like a queen for one night." Now his lips were on her collarbone and traveling lower still to the small swell of her breast at the top of her wedding dress.

A small sound escaped from the back of her throat. "Yes." She breathed the word on a sigh.

Ethan raised his head to kiss her lips once more before turning her around and slowly unzipping her wedding gown. His hands slid along her upper back to her shoulders, then down her arms, slowly slipping the dress from her body. When he reached her hands, he entwined his fingers with hers as the silken garment pooled at her feet. They stood there for a brief moment, hands enmeshed, before he kissed her shoulder and shifted back.

Still holding one of her hands, he helped her step out of the gown. His gaze traveled up and down her body, taking in the sexy undergarments she wore, then raised her arm to twirl her around like a dancer. When her back was to him again, he stopped for a moment, obviously admiring the hint of bare bottom peeking from beneath the cheeky panties.

Becca glanced over her shoulder. "Like what you see?" she asked coyly.

Ethan turned her the rest of the way before sweeping her against his chest again. His eyes darkened with desire. "God, Becca, if I had known you were wearing that under your wedding dress, I'd have had you up here the minute you said, 'I do.'"

Becca smiled sweetly. "Glad you like it."

"Like it? I love it!" he countered with a mischievous grin. "But you know what I'm going to love even more?"

Becca shook her head.

He cupped her bottom and pressed her against his hard length. "You completely naked," he answered, his voice raspy with need.

She looked up at him from under her lashes as she fingered the buttons on his shirt. "I would like that. But you know what I would like even more?"

It was his turn to shake his head.

With a jaunty grin, she slid her hand up his chest to toy with his bow tie. "You naked," she replied as she tugged on the end of the tie, making it fall free.

She started to work on his top button, but he caught her hands in his. He pulled them away and kissed the back of each one. "Allow me." He backed her up until her legs were touching the bed and gently pushed her down to sit on the edge. Placing his hands on the bed next to her hips, he leaned down to give her another steamy kiss. "I hear you had fun this afternoon at the male revue. How about a little private strip show, m'lady?"

Becca's breath caught in her throat. She nodded. "Please."

Ethan's lips connected with hers one last time before he straightened. Having removed his jacket earlier, he now unfastened his cuff links. She deftly caught them as he tossed them to her one at a time. His eyes locked with hers and never shied away as he slowly unbuttoned his shirt. When he reached the last button, he parted the garment to reveal his chest—broad and muscular, with a light dusting of dark hair. The shirt slid down his arms and fell to the floor. After turning around, he toed off his shoes and bent to remove his socks, giving her a tantalizing view of his rear.

Once he was upright, he turned and captured her gaze again as his hand went to his belt buckle. He unfastened it and the button of his pants, then unzipped them at an excruciatingly languid pace. Within moments, the pants joined his shirt on the carpet. He stepped out of them and kicked them aside.

He was now wearing nothing but a pair of black boxer briefs. Her eyes were drawn to the large bulge in the front attesting to his arousal. He saw where her gaze had traveled, and his hand went there too, stroking himself through the thin fabric.

A mischievous grin spread across his face. "Like what you see, m'lady?" he asked as his hand continued its lazy up and down motion.

"Oh yes," Becca croaked. Her hand ached to replace his, and her panties were fast becoming wet with her own desire.

Just when she thought he was going to torture her indefinitely, he moved his hand from his hard length to slip the underwear from his hips. His gorgeous cock sprang free, and for a moment, Becca forgot to breath. As he stepped from the briefs and came closer, her eyes never left his arousal.

Her mouth watered, wondering what it might taste like. "Oh my," she gasped weakly.

A chuckled rumbled through Ethan's chest, and when she looked up to meet his eyes again, he was watching her. "I guess I should take it as a compliment that the sight my naked body leaves a beautiful woman speechless."

Becca nodded vigorously. "Definitely!"

Ethan knelt at her feet. He grasped one ankle and removed her shoe. "Your turn now, gorgeous," he murmured seductively.

"Um-hmm." Still robbed of coherent speech, it was all she could manage.

He slid his hands up her leg to the top of her thigh-high nylons. "Know what I was wanting to do the whole time I was taking that garter off?"

She shook her head.

"This." He touched his lips to the bare flesh of her thigh at the top of the stocking. As his hands languorously rolled it down, his mouth kissed, licked, and nibbled its way down her leg inch by inch as her skin was bared to his touch. Every caress of his hands, every flick of his tongue was like an electric shock that sent waves of pleasure straight to her core. It was the most delightful kind of torture. By the time he slid the nylon from her foot and placed a final kiss on her toes, she was panting.

Becca leaned back on her hands as he reached for the other leg and repeated the sweet torment. Her eyes fell shut as she savored each sensation his hands and lips evoked from her body and strangled sounds escaped from her throat. This time, when he reached her toes, she was whimpering and moaning with need.

His hands went to her knees. Gently parting them, he slipped his body in between. She forced open eyelids heavy with desire.

The look he gave her was filled with tenderness and love, underlaid with a hint of something darker. "God, I love all those little noises you make. You're so beautiful when you're aroused. I can't wait to watch you come again."

Becca smiled at him and raised her hand to caress his face. His hand covered hers, and he turned his head to plant a kiss in the center of her palm. Then he reached out to trail a fingertip over the swell of her breast. He stopped at the front clasp of her strapless bra, toying with it a moment before unfastening it. As it fell to the bed and she was bared to his gaze, her arousal and the slight coolness in the air hardened her nipples. Even though Ethan had already seen her breasts when he pleasured her last night, she couldn't help feeling a little self-conscious about their small size. She ducked her head and resisted the urge to cover herself.

Ethan lifted her chin. "You aren't getting shy on me, are you?"

"I–it's just..."

"What, sweetheart?" Ethan ran his thumb over her bottom lip in a way that almost made her forget her uncertainty.

Becca shrugged. "They're small," she finally finished, glancing down at her chest.

Ethan's gaze lowered to her breasts. His brow creased in thought as though he were pondering a difficult problem. "Hmm...are they? I hadn't noticed."

He leaned his head back and forth, carefully considering each one. Becca felt her face heating under his intense scrutiny. Seeming to notice her discomfort, he slipped a hand behind her head and drew her down to meet his lips. It was a tender kiss full of love and the promise of passion that made Becca relax almost instantly.

Ethan pulled back and smiled. "I think this might require a more thorough examination to disprove your theory." He trailed both index fingers around her collarbone and down to the twin mounds.

With deliberately slowness, he circled each one. "Nice, plump, round. So far, so good."

Becca's heartbeat was already picking up speed again at his touch. The concentric circles he drew with his fingertips gradually became smaller and smaller until he brushed the sensitive tips, making her gasp. "Pretty pink nipples. Check."

He lightly grasped her ribcage, just beneath her breasts, and moved upward until his hands were cupping her. He looked into her eyes and gave her the hint of a lopsided grin. "They fit my hands perfectly."

He began to knead her flesh tenderly. She raised her hands to cover his and leaned into his palms. She couldn't seem to get enough of him touching her. Becca closed her eyes momentarily, reveling in the sensations he was evoking from her body.

"I see that you're enjoying that," he said, smiling, "but I have one more test to perform before I can say whether I agree with your assessment."

Ethan removed his hands from her. The absence of his touch immediately left her feeling bereft, but he wrapped his arms around her and pulled her close until his face was buried in the valley between her breasts. He embraced her tightly, breathing in her scent before placing a kiss there. Then her lifted his head and flicked one pebbled nipple with his tongue before taking it fully into his mouth. He ran his hands up and down her back, and around to her sides, as he suckled greedily.

Becca's hands tangled in Ethan's hair, trying to show him she wanted more. She rested her cheek on the top of his head, breathing heavily.

When he released her, she whimpered briefly until his hot mouth descended on the other side, giving it the same attention. Her head fell back as delicious tension built throughout her body. Soft mewling sounds escaped her throat.

"Oh, Ethan," she moaned. "Please..." She begged, wanting his hands, his lips everywhere at once.

"It's OK, sweetheart," he murmured while trailing kisses down her belly. "I'm going to take care of you." He dipped his tongue into her navel, drawing another whimper from her.

"Lean back on your forearms," he ordered.

She instantly complied as he moved away from her. He lifted her hips to remove her now-soaked panties, then repositioned himself between her legs, with her knees over his shoulders. His heated gaze on her most intimate place sent a frisson of excitement straight to her core.

"God, you're so beautiful." The words spilled from his lips almost reverently before he lowered his head to place a gentle kiss on her mound. He looked up at her as though asking permission to continue before his tongue snaked out to claim her. He licked a slow lazy path from the bottom of her slit, up through her feminine folds. When he reached the top, he flicked her clit with the tip of his tongue, sending an electrifying jolt through her whole body.

Becca's head fell back and her eyes closed as she savored the sensations. Her hands fisted in the duvet as he repeated the motion several more times. Each pass of his tongue over the little nub drew her muscles more taut until she thought she couldn't stand the sweet torture another minute.

Then he dipped his tongue inside her, and she cried out. He

withdrew his tongue to travel that slow path again before settling his lips over her clit. As he licked, flicked and suckled it, he slipped a finger inside her. Her inner muscled clenched as he leisurely withdrew it, then thrust it back inside. Soon it was joined by a second finger, and together they lazily caressed her inner passage as his lips continued their gentle pull on her sensitive nub.

Becca willed her eyes to open, and she looked down her naked body. Ethan's head between her legs as he pleasured her was the most erotic thing she'd ever seen. Even her sexy romance novels couldn't have prepared her for the intense emotions that coursed through her body at the sight. If that wasn't enough, he was gazing up at her with passion-darkened eyes as his lips, tongue, and fingers continued to work their magic.

Then he thrust his fingers deep, hitting her G-spot at the same time his lips sucked hard on her clit. Becca's eyes flew wide, and she cried out in ecstasy as her body spasmed over and over again.

Ethan's lips and hands didn't leave her until he'd milked the last wave of passion from her. Her breath still came in gasps, but her body went limp with bliss. Her arms no long able to support her, Becca dropped back onto the bed, and her eyes drifted shut.

She felt Ethan rise from his kneeling position to slide his naked body over hers and plant a kiss of her still-parted lips. Somehow she found the strength to lift her arms and wrapped them around his neck to deepen the kiss. He tasted of her, with a hint of champagne left over from the reception. His hard length pressed against the apex of her thighs. After a searing orgasm like she'd just experienced, Becca wouldn't have thought she could possibly want more for a while, but he was already bringing her body back to life.

She opened her eyes to see love and passion mirrored in Ethan's gaze. He slid to his side and raised his hand to tenderly caress her hair, her cheeks, her lips. "Watching you come apart like that was the most erotic, the most beautiful, the most amazing thing I've ever seen. God, I love you." He leaned down to press his lips to hers again. "I want to make that happen again while I'm inside you," he whispered against her mouth.

His words brought a smile to her lips. "What are you waiting for?"

Becca's blatant invitation was very nearly Ethan's undoing. He closed his eyes for a moment, willing his body under control. He had put a lot of effort into making this night unforgettable and special, everything her first time should have been, but wasn't. Even though his cock was practically screaming for him to take her, he refused to deviate from his plan. With great effort, he took a deep breath and opened his eyes.

She had turned on her side to face him. The look she gave him was one of pure love and adoration, and his heart leapt at the sight.

He trailed his fingers up and down her arm in a tender caress. "What's your hurry?" he asked softly. "We have a lifetime of lovemaking ahead of us. Let's savor the moment. After all, you are queen for the night, and I have lots more pampering to give you first."

Becca gave him a sweet smile. "Ethan, I know I've already said this before, but you're going to spoil me."

He leaned over to kiss her shoulder. "That's my evil plan," he said with a smile.

Ethan sat up and grasped Becca's hand to pull her up beside him.

When he stood and scooped her up in his arms, she let out a little squeal of delight. "Where are you taking me now?"

"I'm going to give you a bath, because you're a very dirty girl," he replied with as much seriousness as he could manage.

Becca responded to his double entendre by rolling her eyes and swatting his shoulder. "I am not dirty."

"Oh, so you don't want me to bathe you?"

Becca opened her mouth as though to contradict him, only to snap it shut again. She gave him a look of consternation as she seemed to consider her options. Apparently finding none that suited, she looked up at him through demurely lowered lashes. "Maybe I'm just a little dirty."

No longer able to keep a straight face, he laughed as he padded across the thick carpet toward the bathroom. He sat her down on the tiled edge of the big jacuzzi tub for two. Testing the water and finding it a bit cool, he drained some out and refreshed the bath with hot water, adding more bubble bath. Becca waited patiently, watching him work.

When he was satisfied with the water temperature, he lifted her back into his arms and stepped over the side into the tub. Carefully, he lowered them both down into the foamy water. Spreading his legs, he settled Becca between them and drew her back against his chest. She curled into him like a cat, laying her head against his shoulder.

Holding her snugly in his embrace, Ethan relaxed against the back of the tub. The candles he'd lit earlier reflected in the mirrors, enveloping them in a warm glow. Grabbing the remote he'd left by the tub, he turned on the MP3 player on the bathroom vanity. Soothing ocean sounds emanated from the speakers. Together, they soaked in the warm water while listening to the peaceful ebb and flow of the surf. Cherishing the feel of the woman he loved in his arms, Ethan lost track of time.

He had no idea how many minutes had passed before Becca broke the silence. "Mmmmm," she purred. "This is so nice." She turned sideways and lifted her head to look at him. "Thank you for all this."

She brought her body around to fully face him. On her knees, she placed her hands on his chest and leaned in to press her lips against his. When her tongue tentatively touched his bottom lip, he opened his mouth to allow her entrance. She dipped inside with shallow, gentle strokes that belied how innocent she still was. He tangled his own tongue with hers, but allowed her to set the pace.

She finally pulled back with a smile. "That was nice too."

"If you thank me like that every time I give you a bath, I might have to do it every day."

She lowered her gaze, but not before he caught a hint of passion mirrored there. "I want to do more than that," she replied with a sensual undertone.

Her hands slid over his chest; her fingertips circled his nipples. Ethan took a deep breath as she explored a bit lower to the taut muscles of his abdomen. As they'd relaxed together, his erection had abated somewhat, but now it came roaring back to life.

Her hands disappeared beneath the bubbles. He gasped as one finger circled the head of his penis and slid down the underside. When she cupped his balls in one hand and wrapped her other around his shaft, he knew he wasn't going to last much longer unless he put a stop to it now.

He grasped her wrists and reluctantly pulled her hands away with a groan. "Becca, my self-control is good, but not that good."

She stuck her bottom lip out in a cute little pout. "But if I'm the Queen, doesn't that mean I get to do what I want?"

He chuckled at how adorable she looked. "Right now, it means you get all the pleasure, and I'm not done pleasuring you yet."

"Since you're doing such a good job, I guess I can't argue with that," she replied, as he turned her back around. Once her back was to him again, she teasingly pressed the crease of her bottom against his hard length.

"Becca," he ground out in a scolding tone.

She relaxed back into her previous position. "Fine, but as soon as you're done with me, I'm going to make you king, so I can return the favor." She twisted her head to give him a mischievous look from the corner of her eye.

"I don't think I'm ever going to be done with you, but I like the sound of that." He wrapped his arms tightly around her and placed a kiss on her temple. He let his hands glide over her abdomen, slowly working his way up until his palms covered her breasts, then whispered in her ear, "And by the way, *these...*" He paused to give the mounds a gentle squeeze. "...are absolutely perfect in every way."

"Oh, Ethan." Becca turned her head and reached over her shoulder to grasp his neck, pulling him into another kiss.

Having her lips on his again was driving him mad with desire.

When she ended the kiss, she added, "You always know how to make me feel good about myself."

"I'm glad. But let's get you bathed before you turn into a prune and I explode from wanting you."

He reached for a washcloth, dipped it into the soapy water and ran it over her entire body. As he washed her, he was reminded of a year ago when she'd come to him, her spirit all but shattered by the stressful events of the day, and he'd drawn her a bubble bath. Seeing her in his tub, looking like an angel fallen from heaven, was the moment he'd realized how deeply he loved her. He chuckled softly at the memory of how horny that had made him.

"What?" she asked.

He continued sliding the cloth over her body. "I was just remembering something."

Becca turned her head to look at him from the corner of her eye. "Tell me."

"Remember last year when you took a bath at my house?"

She turned her back to him again, and he thought he detected a slump in her shoulders. "You mean the worst night of my life?" she asked ruefully.

The hand holding the cloth stilled. He placed a soft kiss on her shoulder. "I'm sorry. I didn't mean to stir up bad memories for you. It's just that...that was probably the best night of my life."

Even from the side he could see her forehead scrunch up in confusion. "Why?"

"Because it's the night I realized how much I loved you."

She seemed to ponder that for a moment before a slight smile touched her lips, and she snuggled back against him. "Actually, now that I think about it, it was the worst night of my life, but I guess it was also the best."

"Really?"

She nodded. "It's when I started falling in love with you."

"You did?"

"Um-hmm. I don't think I would have been OK with anything more, but there were a couple of times that night I really wanted you to kiss me."

Ethan smiled. He hugged her tightly and kissed her cheek. "I had no idea. And here I thought I would scare you if I tried."

"You wanted that too?"

He huffed out a laugh. "That, and a whole lot more." He trailed his lips down the curve of her neck.

She arched into him as a sound of delight escaped her throat. "How much more?" she asked breathlessly.

"I wanted to climb into the tub with you and do all the things I'm doing to you now." His lips nibbled her damp shoulder. "I wanted to show you how a man should treat a woman and pleasure you until you couldn't stand it anymore." One hand curled around her breast while the other dipped below the water to caress her sensitive nub. "Like this."

He slid a finger through her slick feminine folds before slipping it inside to stroke her inner passage. When he discovered that she was already aroused, he added a second finger and, with the heel of his hand pressed against her clit, rhythmically thrust in and out. Gradually, he increased the speed as his mouth plundered every part of her it could reach–her earlobe, her cheek, her neck–while his hand kneaded her breasts and flicked her hardened nipples.

He was rewarded with a series of breathless pants and moans. He knew she was approaching her climax when her inner walls clenched tight around his fingers. Her hands grasped his thighs until her nails dug into his flesh. She arched her back and cried out as she found her release. He held her and continued to stroke her until the spasms finally subsided and she relaxed against him with a moan of exhausted bliss.

Becca slumped bonelessly against Ethan's chest. Her gorgeous husband certainly knew how to drive her wild, and even after two intense orgasms, she still wanted more. She wanted to feel him inside her, his body pressing down on her own, the friction of his naked skin against hers.

"Oh, Becca," Ethan all but growled in her ear. "God, I can't take it anymore. I have to be inside you." It was as though he had read her thoughts.

She nodded in agreement. "Like I said before, 'What are you waiting for?'"

That was apparently all the encouragement he needed. He sprang from the tub, heedlessly dripping water on the tiled floor, then lifted her out to join him. Grabbing a soft fluffy towel, he began to dry her off. He knelt to reach her feet and legs, slowly working his way up until the towel gently rasped against her most intimate place. The sensation made her hot and ready for him all over again. After placing a light kiss on her swollen mound, he rose to his feet and quickly toweled himself off.

Carelessly tossing the towel to the floor, he reached for her, pulling her close. He leaned his forehead against hers as his hands settled on her hips and his erection pressed against her lower abdomen. She lifted her arms to encircle his neck.

His hands slid down to cup her bottom, then he lifted her high on his chest.

"Wrap you legs around me, sweetheart."

Becca did as he commanded, locking her ankles at the small of his back. The tip of his penis brushed her opening. She gasped at the intimate contact, then leaned down to kiss him.

The touch of her lips on his seemed to stoke his passion. With her securely held in his arms, he strode back to the bedroom. Never letting go of her, he climbed onto the bed and laid her back against the pillows. As he gently probed her feminine folds with the velvety tip of his shaft, his mouth devoured hers in reckless abandon. He reached behind his neck to pull her arms down to rest on either side of her head and entwined his fingers with hers. Finally, he lifted his head to look at her with passion-dark eyes. He held her gaze as he gradually eased his hard length into her slick passage, inch by inch, until he was fully inside her.

She felt a bit stretched, but there was no pain like there had been before. She sighed at the delicious sensation of being filled by him. An exquisite sense of completeness washed over her.

With deliberate slowness, Ethan withdrew until only a fraction of his length remained inside her. He paused briefly before seating himself fully again with a forceful thrust.

She gasped. Her eyes fluttered shut as his mouth claimed hers once more. His tongue dipped inside, mimicking the strokes of his lower body at their intimate joining. He released her hands to brace himself on his forearms.

She explored his chest with questing fingertips before slipping her arms around his waist. The soft hairs of his chest tickled her engorged nipples, and she arched her back to press herself more fully against him. All the while, the rhythmic thrusting of his tongue and cock raised the delectable tension in her body higher and higher. She grasped his buttocks, digging her nails into his taut flesh, drawing him more deeply inside her. Becca moved restlessly, meeting him stroke for stroke until electrifying points of light seemed to explode throughout her body. She screamed his name as her release overtook her.

Above her, Ethan groaned deeply. His head dropped to her shoulder as his body shuddered with his own orgasm. She caressed his back until his body relaxed and he collapsed on top of her.

Becca wrapped her arms and legs tightly around him, relishing the weight of him pressing her into the mattress. The scent of the rose petals crushed beneath their hot bodies permeated the air. She breathed deeply of their sweet fragrance and delighted in the feel of the satin sheets at her back. Becca didn't think she could possibly be any happier than she was at that moment.

After a long while, Ethan finally rolled to his side. He raised himself on one elbow and lifted his other hand to caress her cheek lovingly, then leaned down to place a soft kiss on her mouth. He lay down with his head pillowed on his folded arm, watching her with a look of awestruck bliss.

"I knew it was going to be amazing, but that went way beyond even my wildest fantasies."

Becca turned to her side to face him. She pulled his hand to her lips and smiled. "Glad I could rock your world, tiger." She giggled before taking a more serious tone. "'Cause you sure rocked mine."

He returned her smile. "It was my pleasure." He paused for a moment before adding with a chuckle, "and yours."

Ethan turned to his back and drew her into his arms. With her head resting on his shoulder, they snuggled close, silently caressing one another and sharing tender kisses.

Before long Becca's eyes began to feel heavy. She yawned sleepily.

Ethan kissed her forehead and murmured, "Go to sleep, sweetheart."

With the warmth of his touch still fresh on her skin, she drifted off into peaceful slumber.

Ethan lay there for a long while, simply holding Becca and watching her sleep. Her soft breath feathered over his chest. She looked utterly serene in repose, and he thought he caught a hint of a smile curving her rosy lips. He would never tire of seeing his beautiful wife like this.

He marveled then at how surreal it felt to call Becca his wife. He hoped he wouldn't awaken tomorrow morning to find this was all just a dream.

Carefully, so as not to rouse Becca, Ethan slid his arm from beneath her head and settled her against the pillow. She stirred briefly but didn't awaken. He rose from the bed and padded about the room, snuffing out all the candles. He did the same in the bathroom and drained the tub before returning to their room, which was now lit only by the dying embers in the fireplace.

As he approached the bed, he smiled. Becca had turned over so her back was toward him, but the silhouette of her pert little bottom was still visible, peeking from beneath the sheet. His cock stirred at the sight, but he mentally reprimanded it, reminding himself that after three earth-shattering orgasms, she needed rest. Instead, he straightened the covers, pulling the duvet up to her shoulder before sliding into bed behind her. Wrapping an arm around her her waist, he spooned snugly against her back.

In her sleep, Becca pressed her bottom into his half-hard length. He gritted his teeth in frustration, but couldn't help lifting his hand to cup one soft breast. He tried to ignore his body's insistent call to take her again and instead tried to clear his mind. Eventually, his efforts were rewarded when he fell into a sound sleep. His dreams took him to a place where all his sexual fantasies were fulfilled by the one woman he would love for the rest of his life.

He had no idea how long he'd been sleeping, but the dream world and the real world gradually blurred together. The feel of long, slender feminine fingers caressing his cock teased him toward consciousness. From far away, he thought he heard someone moan. Was that him? Soon the gentle fingers were replaced by a hot, wet mouth. This time he knew the groan belonged to him.

He cracked an eyelid to see the duskiness of the night sky being chased away by dawn's light through the French doors leading to the balcony. Turning his head, he looked down his naked body. The sight of his wife's sweet mouth wrapped around his erection quickened his heartbeat and made him all but whimper. God, he couldn't think of a better way to be woken up.

As a strangled sound escaped his lips, Becca looked up at him. A mischievous glint lit her eyes, and he could feel her mouth curving around him in the semblance of a smile. Slowly and deliberately, her gaze never leaving his, she slid her hot tongue up his hard length before releasing him.

She slithered up his body until she was straddling his hips and her upper body pressed into his chest. Placing her hands on either side of his face, she claimed his lips in a passionate kiss.

When she finally raised her head, she gave him a wide grin. "I got to be queen for the night. Now it's your turn to be king for a day."

He sighed with anticipation. "Sweetheart, I'm all yours."

Ethan was pretty sure he had a goofy grin on his face as his lovely wife proceeded to make all his dream-world fantasies come true in the light of day.

Epilogue

Three Years Later

It was late spring in Phoenix, but the temperature had already risen to a toasty ninety degrees. Ethan was glad to be under the shade of a large tent-like canopy equipped with a mister, which made his long wait in the heat more bearable. He'd insisted on having front-row seats for Becca's graduation ceremony and had been patiently waiting for nearly an hour, saving the entire row for their family. The seats had been slowly filling up, and the tent now buzzed with activity as the time neared for the festivities to start. His parents, Nathan, and Alexis had already arrived.

Ethan glanced nervously at this watch. It was only ten minutes to start time, and the others still weren't here. He looked back over his shoulder, scanning the crowd before turning back to his sister. "I wonder where they are."

"Don't worry, Ethan," Alex replied. "They'll be here. They were getting everything ready to go when I left the house. They shouldn't be far behind."

"Hey, speak of the devil," Nathan added as he got to his feet and waved.

Grandpa Harry returned the greeting. With his arm around Edna, the newest Mrs. Montgomery, he nimbly navigated his way through the crowd in the main aisle.

The little girl in Edna's arms started bouncing up and down until her great-grandma had to lower her to the ground. Once on her feet, the toddler bolted down the aisle and flung herself into Ethan's arms. "Daddeee," she squealed.

Ethan swung his daughter up onto his lap and gave her a bear hug. "Hey, pumpkin. How's my girl?"

She clung to his neck and giggled with delight. "Good," she answered in her little pixie voice. "Where Mommy?"

"Look right there," he said, pointing to the stage. "Do you see her up there in her cap and gown?"

His little girl nodded vigorously, her golden brown pigtails bobbing. "Hi, Mommy," she called, waving a pudgy little hand.

Becca's face lit up with a smile when she caught sight of them. She wiggled her fingers in a discreet wave, then blew a kiss in their direction.

Ethan pretended to catch it. He planted a kiss of his own on their daughter's head just before she squirmed down to greet her Aunt Alexis, who cooed, "Hey, Caro, sweetie, do you have a hug for me too?"

Ethan watched as his beautiful little girl charmed her way down the row, doling out hugs and kisses to her doting aunt, uncle and grandparents. Little Caroline was named after Becca's mother, and looked so much like Becca, it was uncanny. Ethan was already trying to figure out how to keep the boys away when she became a teenager. At only two years old, the toddler was a bundle of energy and already as smart as a whip.

Caro had been born nearly nine months to the day after their honeymoon. Thankfully, Becca had been on spring break, so the weekend had stretched into a full week of sheer bliss. Remembering it filled Ethan with a sense of euphoria. Becca had said she was up for starting a family anytime, so they hadn't used protection. Still, he hadn't expected it to happen quite that fast, but considering that they had spent most of that week in bed–and in the jacuzzi, and on the floor in front of the fireplace–he couldn't honestly say he was surprised. When the pregnancy test stick had turned pink one month later, he was ecstatic, but that was soon followed by worry over whether it was too soon to add a child to the mix. Thankfully, Caro had been an easy baby, and their little trio, plus Buddy and Miss Kitty, had adjusted to family life beautifully. In fact, things were going so well, they had decided to have another baby.

Ethan roused from his reverie as the graduation ceremony began. Anticipation filled him as he waited for the moment that Becca had been working toward for so long. He was so glad she had returned to school. It really seemed to boost her confidence, and it gave her a sense of accomplishment, not to mention she had a real gift with animals.

When Becca's name was finally announced and she crossed the platform to receive her diploma, his heart swelled with pride. He knew she was going to make a great doctor, and he couldn't wait to give her the graduation gift that he and Alex had been working on for the last few months.

When the ceremony ended and Becca joined them, Ethan wrapped his arms around her waist. Lifting her feet off the ground, he swung her around before planting a kiss on her delectable lips.

"So how does it feel, Dr. Montgomery?"

She laughed giddily. "Oh, Ethan, it feels wonderful." She curled a hand around his neck and brought his forehead down to rest on hers. "But I couldn't have done it without you by my side."

"That's where I always plan to be, sweetheart."

Just then, Ethan felt a little kick coming from the swell of Becca's belly, pressed against his.

She gasped. "Did you feel that?"

"I did. Maybe I should swing you around a couple more times. I think he liked the ride."

"He?" Becca rolled her eyes at him and giggled.

"It would be nice to have a boy next, but you know I'm fine with another girl, especially if she looks like her mommy and sister."

"Aw, Ethan, you're so sweet."

She ducked her head shyly, and he kissed her temple.

Nathan joined them, carrying Caro in his arms. "Hey, you two love birds. I don't know about you, but I'm ready for the party."

They all agreed and headed for Ethan's parents' house.

When they arrived, Becca was shocked to find a huge gathering there, which included many of the people she had met at her first pool party here three years ago. She recalled that most of them had expressed an interest in her idea for a free animal clinic and shelter, and she couldn't help wondering if they might still be open to making a donation to help make her long-time dream finally become reality. With Ethan by her side, she excitedly mingled with the crowd.

After a while, Ethan parted company with her to speak with a business associate. Left alone, Becca wandered in the direction of the bar to get a cold drink. As she waited for the bartender to pour her a glass of iced tea, a sticky-sweet voice she hadn't heard in ages came from behind her. "Well, look at you, Becky. I leave town for a couple of years and come back to find you've taken on the shape of a beached whale."

Becca's jaw tightened. "Lindsay," she ground out before slowly turning around to face the other woman, her back straight and her head high. She let out a huff of laughter. "I see you haven't changed a bit."

"No, but you certainly have." Lindsay smirked as she looked pointedly at a Becca's swollen belly. "I can't imagine Ethan finds that attractive. In your condition, I bet his needs aren't being attended to very well either. Maybe he'd like some more attentive, shapely female company."

Becca took a deep breath to steel herself against the horrible woman's jibes, then looked her straight in the eye while answering. "You know, Lindsay, just because your marriage to that European count didn't work out, it doesn't mean you can waltz back to Phoenix and try to steal *my* husband. Ethan *chose* me. He *loves* me, and our children. Nothing you say or do will make him leave us for you."

"We'll see about that," Lindsay replied with a smug pout of her bright red lips.

Alex sidled up next to Becca and placed a hand on her shoulder. "Is she bothering you, sweetie?"

"It's all right, Alex. I'll handle it," Becca replied softly. Her sister-in-law's presence bolstered Becca's confidence even further, and she met Lindsay's steely gaze with one of her own. "I may have allowed you to cow me in the past, Lindsay, but I'm not afraid of you anymore. I'm completely secure in Ethan's love for me, and I know beyond a shadow of doubt that there's nothing you can do to turn his head. He doesn't love you, and he never did. Three years ago, you manipulated me into thinking that Ethan didn't care about me. Every word out your mouth was a lie, but it still didn't break us apart. Give it up."

Throughout Becca's speech, Lindsay's face gradually turned to ice.

Having said her piece, Becca turned to leave, but then she recalled the words Lindsay had uttered in this very spot. She knew it wasn't a nice thing to do, but Lindsay obviously didn't understand or respect nice. Slowly, Becca turned back to the other woman and, in a calm even tone, twisted those words back on her nemesis. "Actually, Lindsay, I didn't give you full credit. There was one thing you did tell the truth about."

Lindsay gave her a questioning look, but said nothing.

"Ethan is damn good in bed. Too bad you'll never know."

Lindsay's face registered shock. She opened her mouth as if to say something, but couldn't seem to think of a snide comeback. She snapped it shut again, spun on her heels, and stalked out of the party in a huff.

Beside Becca, Alex gasped. "I can't believe you said that. Way to go, girl!"

Becca struggled not to smile as a huge sense of relief and satisfaction washed over her. She'd finally gotten the upper hand, leaving that blonde bitch speechless. With any luck, Lindsay would think twice about trying to tangle with her again or steal her man.

* * * * *

Hours later, after the party wound down, the family went inside. They all took seats in the living room, and Ethan drew his lovely wife into his lap. He pulled her close, caressing her pregnant belly, and whispered in her ear, "I have something I want to give you."

"Ethan!" she squeaked as her face turned a rosy pink.

His eyes went wide. The comment had been completely innocent, but obviously, she thought he meant something else.

"Hey, what are you doing to your wife over there, bro?" Nathan razzed from across the room.

Ethan held up his hands in surrender. "Not a thing, I swear."

"What *did* you mean?" Becca asked in a hushed tone.

He leaned forward to murmur in a low voice no one else could hear. "Not what you meant. Apparently, my sweet little wife has a very naughty mind."

The color in her cheeks rose even higher. "Oh."

"Don't worry," he whispered. "I'll be happy to oblige whatever thoughts were running through that pretty little head of yours when we get home tonight."

He could tell she was still embarrassed, but she rewarded him with a beautiful smile.

Louder, so that everyone could hear, he said, "I was just getting ready to tell Becca about her graduation gift."

Alex took that as her cue. She pulled a large manila envelope from her tote bag and gave it to Ethan.

Murmurs of congratulations ran through the assembled guests as he handed it to Becca.

"Becca," he began, "you've worked really hard to reach this moment, and we all think you deserve to be rewarded by having your dream come true. Ever since she came back from Afghanistan for good, Alex has been helping me put this surprise together, and this gift is from all of us. Congratulations, sweetheart!"

Could he really mean what she thought he did? Unshed tears stung Becca's eyes. With trembling fingers, she opened the envelope and pulled out the thick sheaf of papers inside. As she sifted through the sheets, the tears trickled down her cheeks. There was a property deed, legal papers setting up a non-profit organization, and pictures of the inside and outside of a beautifully designed animal clinic and shelter, complete with state-of-the-art equipment.

"Is this really what I think it is?" Becca asked, stunned.

"It is, sweetheart. I've been working on this for months. We're always looking for worthy causes to support. When I told the family about my idea to start the Montgomery Foundation for Animal Welfare to help you realize your dream, everyone thought it was a wonderful idea. We pooled our resources together and collected donations from all the people here today to make it happen. The foundation will fund the Loving Hearts Free Animal Clinic and Shelter, and you and Alex will run the whole show."

Tears threatened to fall again at Ethan's lavish gift. He always knew how to give the best surprises and never seemed to tire of spoiling her.

She flung her arms around his neck and hugged him tight. "Thank you, Ethan. You're the best husband in the world."

After a long while, she released him. "You know, I didn't think you could possibly surprise me any more than you did three years ago in Vegas. If you're going to make a habit out of this..." She shook her head in wonder at the amazing man she'd married.

"You'd better get used to it, sweetheart. Because I'm never going to stop surprising you. It's just too darn much fun."

He laughed, then gave Becca a passionate kiss filled with the promise of more surprises awaiting her once they were alone.

ABOUT THE AUTHOR

Julianna is a hopeless romantic and believer in fairy tales. Even as a little girl, her fondest dream was to find a Prince Charming who would sweep her off her feet. She's happy to report she's been married to him for twenty years. Although she's been an avid reader since she was two years old, she never envisioned herself as a writer until five years ago. Now she feels like she's finally found her life's passion. The muses keep the ideas flowing faster than she can put them on the page. She hopes that her readers will love her characters and stories every bit as much as she's loved creating them.

Julianna currently lives in hot, sunny Phoenix, Arizona with her husband, their two teenage children (one boy, one girl), a Husky/Great Pyrenees mix dog, and three cats. In addition to writing, she enjoys reading, hanging out on GoodReads, surfing the web, watching TV or movies, book shopping, and feeding her insatiable thirst for knowledge.

Julianna loves to hear from her readers. You can contact her at http://www.juliannadouglas.com/.

JULIANNA'S CHARITIES

Julianna strongly believes in giving back to the community, and that is why a percentage of the proceeds from the sale of each of her books will be donated to charity. Your purchase of *His Heart's Desire* benefits Best Friends Animal Society, the largest no-kill animal shelter in the US. Best Friends is committed to making the euthanizing of healthy, adoptable animals a thing of the past. For more information on pet adoption or to make a donation to Best Friends, please visit Julianna's website at http://www.juliannadouglas.com/ or Best Friends Animal Society at http://www.bestfriends.org/.

Made in the USA
Charleston, SC
07 June 2014